DANGEROUS HABITS

LEAH NASH MYSTERIES BOOK 1

SUSAN HUNTER

SEVERN RIVER PUBLISHING

DANGEROUS HABITS

Copyright © 2014 by Susan Hunter.

All rights reserved.

Severn River Publishing
www.SevernRiverBooks.com

ISBN: 978-1-64875-453-1 (Paperback)

ALSO BY SUSAN HUNTER

Leah Nash Mysteries

Dangerous Habits

Dangerous Mistakes

Dangerous Places

Dangerous Secrets

Dangerous Flaws

Dangerous Ground

Dangerous Pursuits

Dangerous Waters

Dangerous Deception

Dangerous Choices

To find out more about Susan Hunter and her books, visit

severnriverbooks.com/authors/susan-hunter

For Irene, who always believed.
For Gary, who always loves.

1

I've seen a lot of really ugly things happen in my 10 years as a reporter. Good people suffer, bad people thrive, and it all seems pretty random to me. A friend of mine keeps telling me I have it wrong. Life is a tapestry woven with the threads of all that is good and bad in each of us. But in this world, we're limited to viewing it from the underside, full of knots and tangles and hanging threads that seem to have no connection or purpose. It's only after we reach the next world that we can see how everything fits together in an amazing, beautiful picture.

Maybe. But what I know for sure is that when I started to pull on one of those tangled threads last spring, a lot of lives unraveled, and I almost lost my own. It was pretty hard to see a Grand Design in that unholy mess.

My name is Leah Nash. I'm a good reporter and an even better smartass who, as it turns out, isn't all that smart. That's why, instead of driving around sunny Miami chasing leads, I was slip-sliding down a riverbank in Himmel, Wisconsin, on a particularly nasty early April day last year. My assignment—and I had no choice but to accept it—find some wild art to fill a gaping hole in the front page layout of the *Himmel Times Weekly*.

Wind and sleet riled the normally placid Himmel River into foaming whitecaps. Miles upstream the force of the current had uprooted a dead oak and carried it on a collision course with the dam supplying hydroelectric power to the town of Himmel. Now, city crews in two boats were trying to harpoon the tree with hooks and ropes before it wreaked havoc at the dam. I was hoping to get some action shots before deadline.

When I reached the bottom of the steep incline, I saw that a massive winch had been set up to haul the tree in. As I shifted my camera bag from my shoulder, a fresh gust of wind sent an icy trickle of water down my neck.

"I'm gonna kill Miguel." Miguel Santos is the other staff writer at the *Times* and a much better photographer than me. It was his turn to follow up on the scanner chatter that had alerted us to the renegade tree photo op, but he'd begged off with a dead car battery. So, I was the one shivering and reaching for the telephoto lens.

"Whatsa matter, Leah, Ricky Martin afraid the rain will mess up his coiffure?" Darmody asked, pronouncing it cough-your and then guffawing.

"Quiet, would you, Darmody?" I said, though I was more distracted than annoyed. The boats were already halfway to the tree by the time I got the lenses switched. Dale Darmody, the Himmel Police Department's oldest, but not smartest, cop was still droning on.

"That tree must be 80 feet long. And lookee all that stuff hangin' from the branches. Musta picked up a load of crap goin' downriver." His chapped red nose wiggled as he talked. Little tufts of gray hair sprang from it and from his ears. His watery blue eyes blinked in the wind.

"Darmody! Make yourself useful and help Bailey with the winch." The order came from Darmody's boss, David Cooper, now striding toward us.

"Right, LT," said Darmody, scurrying off.

"Hey, Coop. What good's a promotion to lieutenant if it doesn't keep you warm and dry behind a desk? What are you doing here?"

"Crowd control," he said, clapping his hands together to warm them and glancing up at the high bank above us.

"Right." The nasty weather meant only a fraction of the usual gawkers were on hand, and all were neatly contained behind yellow police tape. But the faithful few who kept watch were about to be rewarded.

A sudden shout from the water signaled the tree had been hooked, and we both turned our attention to the river. As the winch roared to life, I focused the camera and started shooting pictures but soon realized I needed a better angle. I glanced around for a higher vantage point then spotted a half-dead birch jutting from the bank a few yards downstream. I sprinted behind the winch and shinnied up to a Y-juncture in the tree. It wasn't a very sturdy perch, but I only needed it for a minute.

I looked through the lens and zoomed in. As I did, the winch groaned against the weight of the tree and gave a banshee wail. The men in the boats pushed hard at the trunk with long poles topped by metal hooks. The tree began bobbing up and down and rolling side to side, slowly at first, then picking up speed. The pressure from the poles, the pull of the winch, the force of the current, and its own growing momentum caused the tree to rock faster and faster. It began to buck, one side dipping low in the water as the other raised higher with each rolling motion.

"Look out! Look out! She's going over!"

Poles dropped and motors roared as the boats pulled away from the wake of the giant tree. With a lurch, the part of the oak that had been underwater shot upward. Branches that had been submerged lifted toward the sky. Hanging from one of them was what looked like a flapping sail. But as the tree bounced up and down more slowly, the horrifying truth became clear.

"Somebody's caught; someone's on that tree!" came a shout from the onlookers.

Tangled in the web of branches was a body bobbing up and down in awful rhythm as the winch groaned slowly on and the oak neared the shore. The crews moved back in quickly to steady the tree and free the body. By the time they pulled it into one of the boats, someone had already radioed for EMTs. The other crew and the guys on the bank continued to maneuver the tree to shore, but our eyes were on the boat speeding in with the unknown victim.

I scrambled down from the birch and waited in silence with everyone else as two men carried the body to a grassy spot a few feet from where we stood and laid it gently on the ground.

Rivulets of dirty river water ran down a narrow face above a once white collar now muddy and askew. Wide open eyes didn't blink as sleet fell on their sightless stare. The veil that had once covered curly black hair was gone, and the gray color of the long robe had gone black with water and river grime. For a minute, no one said anything. Then an anonymous voice broke the silence.

"Holy shit! It's a goddamn nun."

Two EMTs came up behind me with a stretcher. "Ma'am, you'll have to get out of the way." Nodding, I took a step backward. Stumbled. A hand under my elbow kept me from falling.

"Leah? You OK?"

I grabbed the arm and looked up. "Coop. I know her. She—" I stopped and looked again at the battered body, the blank eyes and slack mouth, and remembered the last time I saw her. I looked away.

"Leah?" Coop repeated. "Who is she?"

"Sister Mattea Riordan. She's a nun at DeMoss Academy. How could this happen? She was fine the last time I saw her." An irrational wave of anger rose in me. What? Like the mere fact of seeing her alive a week or so ago made it impossible she was dead now? I gave my head an impatient shake, sending droplets of water flying off my hair and into Coop's face.

"Sorry. I'm all right. Really. I need to grab the rescue guys before they get away." I looked at my watch. "What will you have for me before deadline?"

He shook his head. "Nothing official before you go to press, I'm sure. Probably not even confirmation that she's dead."

I gave him an incredulous look.

"I know, I know." He held up his hands to ward off my scorn. "But a body pulled from cold water isn't dead until a doctor says she's warm and dead. Then we have to contact her order, her next of kin; there'll be an autopsy, and, well, you know the drill."

"Coop, are you serious? A dead nun floats into town on a tree and the *Times* has nothing but 'no comment' from the police?"

"Yeah. I'm serious. Nothing official. I mean it. And don't try any 'highly placed sources in the police department' bull either. The last time I gave you a heads up, the chief nearly took my head off. I got nothing for you, Leah."

"I already know who she is. Remember? I just told you."

"True, but you're not going to print the name of an accident victim before the family gets notification, are you?"

I pounced. "So, you're saying this is an accident?"

"Am I talking to Leah Nash or Lois Lane?"

"I just want to know what you think. Not officially, just as a regular person. You are still a regular person sometimes aren't you Lieutenant Cooper?"

He took off his HPD ball cap and ran his hand through short dark hair, a sure sign that he was irritated. I was a little irritated myself. After two months back in town, I still had a hard time accepting the ways of the local police department. Everything was on a need-to-know basis, and the chief's point of view was that the paper never needed to know anything. I could rarely even get anything attributable to an anonymous source, because the department was so small it was easy for the chief to pinpoint a leak.

"Off the record, right now I can't see anything but accident, but that's not official. We still have to investigate. Look, when I have some answers I'll make sure you have them too. Is that good enough?"

"I guess it'll have to be."

2

I got what I could at the scene, then headed back to the office. The unexpected death of someone I knew and liked had left me unsettled. It wasn't that Sister Mattea's absence would leave a hole in my life. We barely knew each other. But her death did feel like a tear in the fabric of the universe that I vaguely believe holds us all together.

Funny, smart, not much older than me, she was someone I'd planned to get to know when I had time. But we don't hold time in our grasp. Time holds us and often as not lets go when we least expect it.

The rain beat steadily as it had for days. My normal route back to the paper was blocked by flooded intersections, forcing me to go the long way round. The resulting drive was a small-scale sociological survey of Himmel that added to my depression. On Worthington Boulevard, upscale homes rested safe and secure behind high hedges and wrought iron fencing, seemingly unaffected by the weather or the changed fortunes of my hometown.

Further on the southeast, things were definitely different in the once well-manicured subdivisions, where middle class managers, young professionals, and factory workers with plenty of overtime bought their homes. Now, many of the houses were fronted by frayed, raggedy lawns with weather-beaten For Sale signs swinging in the wind. Driveways were empty and curtains were closed.

A few blocks later I turned onto a street in Himmel's poorest neighbor-hood. There, slapped together rentals still bowed under the burden of sagging roofs. Ancient asphalt siding still curled and peeled on the houses. Scrappy lawns were still littered with broken bicycles and rusty lawn tools. The major difference from years past was the number of vehicles crowded into the rutted gravel driveways and parked on front yards, a sign of extended families huddling together, one paycheck away from financial disaster.

A turn north through town took me past empty storefronts that once housed the hardware store, the shoe store, Straube's Men's Wear. They were all going businesses when I was a kid, but our small town was living on borrowed time even then. A couple of big box stores moved in with lots of choice and low, low prices. We didn't realize what the bargains would actu-ally cost. Specialty stores began closing their doors, unable to compete with one-stop shopping.

By the time the first of Himmel's several manufacturing plants closed, the town was already in trouble. Jobs left, then families left, then one morning we woke up and Himmel was a struggling community of 15,000, not a bustling town of 20,000. The citizens who remained were frustrated and not quite sure who to blame.

"Much like me," I said out loud, as I pulled into the newspaper parking lot and turned off my car. But that wasn't really true. I knew exactly why my fortunes had changed. The fault, dear Brutus, lies not in my stars but in myself, that I am a stubborn smartass. But I had neither the time nor the inclination for self-reflection just then. I had photos and final edits to do if we were going to make our Thursday night deadline. I grabbed my stuff and slipped through the side door of the building.

Max Schrieber, owner and publisher of the *Times Weekly* was nowhere to be found, and Miguel was still among the missing. I filed cutlines for the photos, wrote up a brief on the officially unidentified female found in the river, and went out to the front desk to check for messages. We have a lot of walk-in traffic at the *Times* as well as a fair number of callers who would rather leave word with a live person at the reception desk than record a voice mail. Though that can only be because they don't know Courtnee Fensterman, our receptionist.

Courtnee's slightly buggy blue eyes peered out from under a feathering of light blonde bangs as she gave me a wad of pink message slips from the spike on the corner of her desk. Then she patted my hand.

"Wow, Leah. That is so weird. It's like you're one of those middles. You know, getting messages from dead people."

"What are you talking about, Courtnee?"

"The Sister. The dead Sister. Sister Mattea, the one in the river."

"How—" I cut myself off. There was no point asking how she found out about the death, let alone how she knew the identity of the body. The *Himmel Times* can't compete with the Himmel grapevine.

"My cousin Mikey was at the hospital with my Aunt Frances, she had another spell. He saw them bring Sister Mattea in, and he told my mom, and she called me. But anyway, like I said, Leah, you're like a middle or something. Kind of."

"You mean a medium?" I asked, mystified but game.

"I'm pretty sure it's called a middle, Leah," she said kindly. "I mean, because they're in the middle of like two worlds, right? The living and the dead."

"OK, I'm a middle. But what are you talking about? Messages from the dead?"

"Well, the Sister. She's dead. And she gave you a message. Only wait, maybe that's not right. She wasn't dead when she was here, so that probably doesn't count. Right?"

"Sister Mattea? When was she here? What kind of message? Where is it?"

A blank stare from Courtnee told me my rapid-fire questions had caused a temporary interruption in brain service.

"Well..." her light blonde eyebrows pulled together in a frown of concentration, and she bit her lower lip. Taking a deep breath, I tamped down my impatience and altered my approach. I became the Courtnee Whisperer.

"Courtnee, Sister Mattea stopped by and left a message for me, right?" I said in a low, measured tone. I all but started stroking her withers.

She visibly relaxed and nodded.

"Well, she had this book she wanted to give you. But then you weren't here so she was going to leave it. She asked me for a Post-it, so she could write you a note. Then she asked me to give it to you. But then I thought, no, I'll put it in a manila envelope so the book and the note will stay together."

She paused for a lump of sugar.

"That was a great idea, Courtnee. Now, can you think where you put the envelope?"

"I put it on your desk, silly. What else would I do with it?"

What indeed. "Actually, no, Courtnee, you didn't. I didn't have an envelope left on my desk any day this week. Do you think maybe the phone rang before you could take it to my desk, and maybe you set it down somewhere and forgot about it?"

She turned slowly around her cubicle and patted papers on her desk like a horse pawing the ground. After shifting a few issues of the *Himmel Times*, lifting a couple of flyers and picking up a stray box from Amazon.com, she gave a small whinny of happiness. Then she faced me, holding a large manila envelope in her hand.

"Here you go!"

My name was neatly written across the front in Courtnee's carefully rounded handwriting. I grabbed the envelope wordlessly and headed back to my desk.

"You're welcome!" she said in a reproachful tone as I closed the door behind me.

The newsroom was still empty. I sat down and tore open the sealed flap, reached in and pulled out the contents, a paperback edition of *Echo Park* by Michael Connelly, with a sticky note attached to the cover.

Leah—sorry I missed you. I need to talk with you about something as soon as possible. It's quite important, and I'd rather do it in person. Please give me a call to let me know when we can meet—M

P.S. Here's the book I told you about.

I went back to the front desk.

"Courtnee, what day did Sister Mattea stop by?" She looked up from opening her box of Milk Duds and took a couple before answering.

"This week or last week?" she asked, her voice a little muffled by the need to talk around the sticky caramel.

"She was here last week?"

"Mmmph," she said nodding, then swallowing her candy.

"She was looking at the bound volumes, and I made some copies for her."

"What was she looking for?"

She shrugged. "I don't know. Some old stories about the school the Sisters run for criminal kids, you know, Dumbass Academy?"

"It's DeMoss Academy," I said coldly. "She didn't say anything about me or wanting to see me?"

"It's not all about you, Leah, you know," she said. "We had a really good talk about my cousin Andrew. He just got busted for weed, and now my Uncle Don thinks he's a drug addict. Sister Mattea was really nice. She said Uncle Don might be over-reacting, but at least he cares. Most of the kids at Dum—DeMoss Academy, their parents are just a waste of space, my dad says." Clearly Courtnee had forgotten that my sister Lacey had spent time at DeMoss, but there was no point in pointing that out.

"She said not everybody is cut out to be a mom or dad. And then I told her about Max. How he's a great dad to Alex, even though he's like so old. And crabby. It's kinda cute, him and Ellie. But it's probably good she already had her own baby when they got married, because I mean like, could Max even, well, you know, have sex? I mean you'd always be thinking is he having a heart attack? What if he, like, dies right on top of me! Then I thought, whoops, maybe I shouldn't be talking about that to a nun—"

"You think, Courtnee?" I shuddered at the thought of Sister Mattea subjected to Courtnee's oversharing about Max's love life. Though it was a nice story. Max and his first wife Joyce never had children, and he was so lonely after she died. Then he met Ellie on a trip to Ohio. It was a love-at-first-sight romance. At age 50, he became a newlywed with a toddler and a whole new, happier life. A lot of people had a lot to say about the 20-year age difference, but it didn't seem to matter to them.

"I don't really need a line by line of your chat, Courtnee, just the essentials. So, Sister Mattea left, and she didn't say anything about wanting to see me. Then she came back on Monday, and she wanted to see me, but I wasn't here, so she left the book and the note for me. Is that right?"

"Well, I have to think, Leah. I don't keep everything, like, right at the top of my head." She tilted said head to the right and squeezed her big blue eyes to narrow slits.

"Courtnee?"

She batted her hand at me, lest I further disturb her concentration, then began speaking, her eyes half-closed like a psychic in a trance.

"It wasn't Monday, because the day she came in we were real busy. Mrs. Barry was yelling at me because I mixed up the numbers on her classified and everybody that called got a phone sex message. It wasn't my fault. My mom says I have undiagnosed dyslexia and—"

"Right, Courtnee. This was what, Tuesday?"

"I'm trying to tell you." Her eyes flew open in exasperation. "I was telling Sister Mattea you weren't here, and she asked could she leave you this book and a note and blah, blah, blah. Then Mrs. Barry busted in and started yelling. I handed Sister Mattea a Post-it, and out of the corner of my eye I saw Max coming in, and I didn't want Mrs. Barry telling him all about my mistake. So, I sorta pushed Sister Mattea off on him, and Brad came in to fill the Coke machine.

"Then the phone rang, and I accidentally knocked my water over onto my keyboard, and Brad jumps over the counter—he's really sweet—and he helps me." She paused for me to celebrate Brad's heroic action, but the look on my face got her back on track.

"Well, then Mrs. Barry starts again, so I gave her a refund and a free ad for next week to get her to leave. Then both lines start ringing, and, like I've told Max before, I can't do everything. And I look over to see if he'll help, but he's walking out the door again without even helping me, and Sister Mattea hands me the book, and she leaves, and then after she's gone, I notice—"

"Courtnee! What. Day. Was. It. That's all I want to know."

"Well. Pardon me for trying to give some context." She pouted for a few seconds as I stared at her and briefly wondered where she'd picked up that phrase. Then she continued in an injured tone, as though waiting for me to beg forgiveness. That would not be happening.

"I told you. It was Tuesday. Brad always fills the Coke machine on Tuesdays. Why does it matter when she came in anyway?"

"Because, Courtnee, she asked me to call her, and two days went by and I didn't. And now she's dead, and I never will."

"Well, it doesn't matter then, right? Like you said, she's dead."

"Find your silence, Courtnee. Please."

I stepped back into the newsroom, closed the door, and sighed. Courtnee had a point. Sister Mattea was dead and whatever was on her mind didn't matter anymore. Still, her note bothered me. Why did she want me to call?

I'd met her briefly when I first got back to town. Then I ran into her again at the bookstore a few weeks ago. She was buying a Michael Connelly paperback, and I kidded her that Connelly didn't seem like typical nun fare. She laughed and said she loved the way he wrote about LA. Then she offered to lend me one of her favorites. But time went by, and I assumed she'd forgotten, like people do.

I picked up *Echo Park* and started leafing through it. Something fluttered from between the pages to the floor. I grabbed it, unfolded it, smoothed it straight. It was a two-sided copy of a page from the *Himmel Times*. A photo in the lower left caught my eye—Max, Ellie and Alex grinning above a cutline naming them St. Stephen's Family of the Year.

Above that was a story about water line replacement on Main Street, a grip and grin check-passing photo of some Rotary Club donation, an ad for Bendel's Ford. Typical page two copy. I flipped it over and read the front page headline. The air rushed out of my lungs as though I'd been punched in the gut.

Missing Teen's Death Ruled Accident
By Mike Sutfin, Times Staff Writer

Himmel, WI – The death of Himmel teenager Lacey Nash has been ruled accidental, according to Grantland County District Attorney Cliff Timmins, speaking at a press conference on Wednesday. Nash, 17, disappeared last November from DeMoss Academy, a residential facility for troubled youth run by the Daughters of St. Catherine of Alexandria. Her body was discovered two weeks ago in a ravine on the 300-acre estate owned by the nuns.

"The autopsy indicated cause of death was a head injury sustained in a fall. The sheriff's department has re-interviewed witnesses, and its findings, coupled with the autopsy results, have led us to conclude the death was accidental," said Timmins in a prepared statement. There will be no inquest.

Nash had been a resident of DeMoss Academy for approximately 6 months at the time of her disappearance. She was reported missing the morning of November second by a representative of the school. At the time authorities believed that Nash, a student with a history as a runaway, had left on her own. An undisclosed sum of money was also reported missing at the time.

Timmins declined further comment, but turned the press conference over to Sheriff Lester Dillingham.

"Now, I want to make this clear. In no way did we not do a professional, thorough investigation of Lacey Nash's disappearance. At the time, we had every reason to believe she had run off like she did other times," Dillingham said. However, a witness, who had previously not made a full statement, came forward after the body was discovered.

The witness, whom Dillingham refused to identify citing her status as a minor, told investigators that she and Nash had both attended a party at the abandoned Lancaster farm adjacent to the nuns' property. The site is popular with underage drinkers, Dillingham said.

"We can't be everywhere. We patrol that area as much as we can, but kids do gather there to drink; it's a fact. Our witness said Lacey became highly intoxicated and belligerent and said that she was leaving that night and never coming back."

Nash left the party, and the witness assumed that she had made good on her threats. She didn't come forward at the time out of fear that she would get herself in trouble, and she believed that Nash had run away, Dillingham said.

"It's a sad story, but you get a kid with some booze and drugs inside her —it'd be easy to get disoriented in those woods at night. Then she trips, falls down the gully, hits her head on a rock, and that's all she wrote."

The sheriff confirmed that an empty liquor bottle was found near the body. An unlabeled bottle containing several hydrocodone tablets, better known by the trademarked name Vicodin, was found in Nash's purse. However, the autopsy report does not indicate Nash was intoxicated.

"Well, I don't want to be crude, but a body exposed to the elements for better than six months, you've got your accelerated decomposition to deal with. And out in the woods, you've got your animal factor. Let's just say there wasn't much left for testing and leave it there."

Sister Julianna Bennett, director of DeMoss Academy, issued a formal statement. "We are saddened at the loss of Lacey, and our hearts go out to her family. She remains in our thoughts and in our prayers." Representatives of the order refused any further comment.

The funeral for Lacey Nash will be held May 5 at St. Stephen's. (See Nash obituary, p. 10)

After I finished, I took a deep breath that ended on a ragged note. Why did Sister Mattea have this clip about my sister Lacey tucked in the book she gave me? Was that what she wanted to talk to me about in person? Did she want to tell me something about her, or how she died?

When Lacey disappeared, she and I were barely speaking. But it wasn't always that way. Lacey wasn't even a year old when Annie, our middle sister, died. I was 10. Not long after that, Dad left. He just couldn't deal with the sadness, Mom said. But my mother pulled it together, and we survived. Her parenting style was closer to Roseanne Connor with an English degree than to Carol Brady, but it worked for us.

Lacey used to dissolve in giggles that gave her the hiccups, when Mom would belt out "I Am Woman" and point to us to come in on the chorus. Mom said we were the three Nash women, and we could take on the world. Only it turned out after Lacey turned 14, we couldn't.

I had just taken a job at the *Green Bay Press-Gazette*, after spending the first year out of college working at the *Himmel Times*. It was only a few hours away, but a small daily that's short on staff doesn't leave a new reporter much free time. Lacey and I emailed and talked a lot on the phone, but she was as busy with school and her activities as I was with mine. The next year when I took a position at the *Grand Rapids Press,* a mid-size daily in Michigan, Lacey and I had an even harder time connecting.

By then I was caught up in my first serious relationship. So caught up that it took a while before I realized, that when I did call, Lacey didn't always call me back. When I asked her about it, she brushed me off. But then things got worse. Lacey started lying about where she'd been, staying out past her curfew, skipping school, hanging out with kids she never used to like.

It was as though someone had taken our Lacey and dropped a demon child in her place. Her behavior escalated for almost three years—drinking, smoking weed, doing other drugs. She stole, she ran away, she blew off the counseling sessions Mom set up for her. And lying. She was always, always lying.

When I questioned her, she was evasive. When I talked to her, she was sullen. When I yelled at her, she was defiant. Nothing I did could reach her. She caused Mom a hundred sleepless nights and me a hundred furious days. It just kept getting worse. I dreaded answering the phone or opening my email, because there was always some fresh crisis that I couldn't seem to fix. When she was 17, she stole my credit card, took my mother's car, and headed for parts unknown with her boyfriend. That was it. I was done. I had to be. Trying to save her was killing me.

She was headed for juvenile detention, but my mother's parish priest, Father Lindstrom, intervened. He got her into DeMoss Academy, a residential school for hard case kids run by an order of nuns outside of Himmel. I didn't care where she went as long as it was out of the house.

No more screaming fights, no more nights driving around looking for her, no more missing cash, no more futile attempts to comfort Mom, no more feeling like I couldn't breathe. I hated my sister and what she had done to our lives. Or, maybe more truthfully, I hated that she made me realize we're never safe. Nothing lasts. No matter what dues you think you've paid, they're never enough to keep the next bad thing from happening.

I drove, and Mom sat tight-lipped but dry-eyed all the way to DeMoss. Lacey lounged in the back with her ear buds in, listening to her music and staring straight ahead. I wasn't mad, I wasn't sad, I wasn't anything. I just didn't care anymore. All I wanted was to get it done.

There was only one minute when I felt anything at all. After we finished the intake and met the staff, Lacey was her usual self: defiant, angry, sullen. She endured Mom's goodbye hug and ignored my "See you."

I watched her go down the hall with her counselor. She looked so small. She held her body stiff with her shoulders squared and her chin high. She walked the same way the first day of kindergarten, trying not to show how scared she was. Just before they reached the end of the corridor, she half-turned and our eyes met. The lost look I saw there hit me so hard it took my breath away.

Later, after her body was found, I saw her in my dreams for months— the way she used to be. Running toward me with soft black hair flying, dark blue eyes shining, laughing, holding out a flower or a pretty stone or a butterfly she caught.

But as she got closer, the flower turned into a phone and she was crying into it, "Lee-Lee, Lee-Lee." I reached down to pick her up, but she slipped right through my arms. And she kept running. And crying and crying and crying. I would wake up in a cold sweat and know that I was only fooling myself. I never stopped caring about Lacey. In my unguarded dreams, it all came flooding back—the guilt, the anguish, the sorrow, the love.

That's why I had to know what Sister Mattea was trying to tell me with that newspaper clip.

3

"Refill?"

"Definitely." I was sitting in McClain's Bar & Grill waiting for Max and Miguel to join me for our usual Thursday night post-deadline drink. I'd already downed one Jameson.

"Better bring me a hamburger with that, too, please, Sherry."

"Are you waiting for Coop?" the waitress asked, casually tucking a strand of curly brown hair behind her ear.

"No, but Miguel and Max are supposed to be here shortly. Will they do?" Though I knew they wouldn't. Sherry made it pretty obvious that she had a thing for Coop. We had gone to high school together. She was a cheerleader and I wasn't. She still had rosy cheeks and round brown eyes, and she looked good in the bar's requisite clingy t-shirt and tight black pants—despite two kids and a divorce. I became conscious of my baggy sweater and jeans and my hair jammed up under a red Badgers baseball cap.

"Do you mind if I ask you something?" she said, then asked without waiting for my assent. "Why are you in town, really? I know you're filling in for Callie Preston while she's on maternity leave, and I know your mom's here and all, but you've been back for what, a year? You always said you were getting the hell out of Himmel and never looking back. I heard you were some big shot reporter at a paper in Florida. But here you are, Leah. Back. How come?"

Ouch. That was surprisingly malicious. And bonus points for the repeated use of "back" to emphasize the direction my life had taken. There was more going on than I had credited behind those big brown eyes. I looked at Sherry with new respect. Dislike, but respect.

"Two months, Sherry, not a year. I've been filling in for two, and I promised Max I'd stick it out for six." Then I decided to yank her chain a little. "And, besides, it's been great seeing Coop again. No matter how long it's been, we always just pick up right where we left off," I said, with what I hoped was the right touch of innuendo. I wasn't sure though. I don't do subtle very well.

The truth was that Coop and I had a low-maintenance relationship that suited me perfectly—long periods of limited contact, but no recriminations, no apologies, just slipping back into an easy friendship based on shared history but no romance. OK, there was a beer-fueled hook-up once during college that neither of us ever talked about again, but that hardly constituted a romance.

"Now, if I could have that refill and my burger?" Her color rose, but she just grabbed the empty glass and walked away.

My triumph in the mean girls skirmish didn't count for much though, because Sherry was dead-on about my career. *A problem ignored is a problem solved*, is engraved on the Nash family crest, but this one stubbornly refused to go away. Over a year ago I'd had a blowup with my editor. My threat to quit was unexpectedly accepted, and suddenly I had no job.

I searched for months, but with papers folding and cutting back and an extremely negative reference from my last employer, I had no luck. My patchwork of freelance and stringer work wasn't enough to pay the rent, and I was up against the wall when Max Schreiber, the man who got me started in journalism, called. I suspect my mother put him on to me, but he never said. He just asked if I was available to do him a favor and fill in for his senior reporter while she was out on maternity leave. So, there I was, back in Himmel at the job I'd left for bigger and better things 10 years earlier.

I didn't plan to stay, but I was pinning my hopes on a long shot. During my long exile from regular employment, I'd outlined a nonfiction crime story about a murder I'd covered several years earlier. I'd finally found an agent willing to take me on when Max called. So far, he hadn't had any luck placing my book, but hope springs eternal. Especially when it's all you have to hold on to.

All I ever really wanted to do from the time I was 13 was to be a reporter on a big daily newspaper. I made it, too, until my temper finally got me into real trouble. If I couldn't find a way to write about something more than county fair board meetings and school talent shows, I—well—I didn't know what I was going to do.

"*Chica*! Hellooo, are you in there? Why isn't your phone on? Did you lose it again? Is your battery dead?" A graceful hand waving in front of me broke my reverie. I looked up into the face of the *Himmel Times* junior staff writer, Miguel Santos. Six feet tall, shiny black hair, dark brown eyes, long thick eyelashes, a wide full mouth, and skin the color of a chai latte. Miguel is also witty and charming and almost ten years younger than me. And gay. There is that, too.

"Sorry. I forgot to charge it last night and—"

"Yes, yes, I know your sad story. You need to go retro and get a beeper for back up," he said, pulling out a chair and neatly folding his lean body into it. He was wearing a bright yellow cotton sweater under a brown leather jacket and looked like my favorite candy—chocolate with a lemon cream center. I must be getting hungry.

"Coop called right after you left. They released the identification of the nun and confirmation of death. I just had time to squeeze it in your story before Max said we had to go to press."

"Nothing else? Like how she got in the river?"

He shook his head. "The autopsy is tomorrow. Coop said no official word yet. Good thing you were on the scene, or we wouldn't have anything.

Oh, and the pictures—*muy bien, chica*. Almost as good as mine," he said, and winked. That's how good looking he is—he can carry off a wink.

Sherry returned with my Jameson and burger.

"A Kir Peche for me, *mi bonita*," Miguel said.

She rolled her eyes. McClain's is a dark paneled lair of scarred wooden tables, duct-taped vinyl booths, and the after smell of a million cigarettes. It runs more to Leinenkugel and JD than to Miguel's exotic cocktail orders, which are a source of wonder and amusement to the staff.

"You know this is just a working class bar. If you want fancy drinks, they have them over at the Holiday Inn."

"Ah, but they don't have you, my Sherry," he said, taking her hand in both of his and flashing a smile with his perfect teeth. She pulled away, laughing, and went to confound the bartender with Miguel's cocktail order. He turned back to me.

"*Chica*, when you gonna let me take you to see my *Tía* Lydia at her salon? Those lips, those eyes, that hair!" He reached over and tugged off my ball cap, causing my reddish brown hair, badly in need of a trim, to fall in a shaggy curtain round my face and shoulders.

"A little liner, some mascara. What Aunt Lydia could do. It's a shame. No, it's a crime. I know you got it goin' on, but not everybody has my eye. No wonder you're sleeping alone."

"Shut up," I said, laughing and yanking my cap out of his hand. I grabbed a handful of hair and shoved it back under my Badgers hat. "And who says I'm sleeping alone?"

"Your *mamá*."

That was probably true.

"My mother talks too much."

"She cares about you, *chica*, that's all. You have the beautiful hazel eyes, the million dollar smile. But you don't do anything with them. You got no game, Leah."

"OK, OK. Enough." He was hitting a little too close to the bone to be comfortable.

"So, where were you all day today? I'm not sure I believe that 'my car was in the shop' story. Very convenient when the wind chill was about 90 below out on the river today. And Max was missing in action too. He—"

"Bad mouthing the boss again, kid?" A chair scraped noisily across the floor and groaned as the owner, editor, and publisher of the *Himmel Times* dropped heavily onto it. Max flagged Sherry down and ordered his favorite, a Manhattan made with cherry juice, before I answered.

"I was just saying it seemed more like the Nash News today than the *Himmel Times*. Miguel took up residence at Parkhurst's garage most of the afternoon, and I had to cover the Milk Producers Association meeting for you this noon. That was a lot of fun, I can tell you. Hey, what happened to your pants? And your shoes?" I asked, noticing the streaks of mud on his khakis, the dried dirt on his loafers. "You look like you've been playing in mud puddles."

"Yeah?" He pushed his glasses up on his forehead, then rubbed his temples for a minute. Max has an unruly mop of grayish brown hair and brown eyes that droop at the corners. He looks a little like a weary Basset Hound wearing a short-sleeved white dress shirt and an ugly paisley tie. But when he smiles, he has a certain charm. Though he hadn't been very charming of late. The last week or so he groused at everything.

"I never even made it to the office this morning. Got a flat on the way in, and then I fell on my can in the mud trying to get the lug nuts off. Finally got the spare on, went back home to change, and the basement was flooded. Ellie was at some committee meeting, so I was on the phone trying to get a plumber for an hour. I hadda wait around for him to show, and wait while he routed out the line. What a mess.

"It was past two by the time I got out of there. I almost missed my interview with the president at the technical college, and I forgot to change my clothes. Don't give me any more grief. I had enough today." As he waved his arm for emphasis, I caught a gust of a powerful but pleasant, almost grassy scent.

"Well, at least you smell outdoor fresh. I like your cologne."

"From Alex," he said momentarily distracted. "He made it himself from some recipe he found online. Gave it to me and Ellie for our anniversary. Said it's "gender neutral." What kind of 10-year-old says things like that?" He shook his head, but the pride in his voice was unmistakable. "I know you can smell it a mile away, but I'm glad today, because whatever I fell in changing my tire, the smell was like—"

"OK, OK. You win. You had a worse day than everyone."

"Except for that dead nun in the river," Sherry injected as she set the drinks down, then moved on to the next table.

That shut us up for a minute. Max took a gulp of his Manhattan, Miguel sipped his cocktail, and I took another bite of my burger. Then I said, "You know, something odd happened with Sister Mattea."

"What do you mean odd?"

"She left me a message, but I didn't get it 'til after she died. Thanks to ditzy Courtnee." I told them the story and added, "I'm pretty sure she wanted to tell me something about Lacey. Maybe she found something of Lacey's, or maybe there was something new about how she died."

"You already know how she died, Leah. What could Sister Mattea have to add five years later?"

"I don't know, and now I can't ask her. But, come on, she left me a book and inside the book was a photocopy of the front page of the *Times*. The lead story, the only story that has any connection to both me and Sister Mattea, is a report on Lacey's autopsy. The one where Timmins says her death was accidental."

"You don't think it was, *chica*?" Miguel asked, intrigued.

"Well, I have to ask."

"No, Leah. You don't. How's Carol gonna feel if you go digging all that up again?"

"Mom will be fine. She'll want to know if there's anything new."

"There isn't anything new. You may not like it, but you know it."

"Max, Courtnee said you talked to Sister Mattea on Tuesday. Did she say anything, give any hint at all why she wanted to see me?"

"Just small talk. How busy we were, what a nice day it was, were we gonna cover the fundraiser for DeMoss. That's all." He paused a minute and tried to reason with me again. "That was a rough time for you and Carol those last years with Lacey. She was a mixed-up kid. She made a lotta bad choices, and she paid the price. You all did. But you can't go back. Let it go."

"Sister Mattea had a message for me. I just need to find out what it was." I could feel my chin setting and hear my voice getting louder.

"Leah's right, Max, what does it hurt to ask?" Miguel said.

Max ignored him.

"How? How you gonna find out, Leah? What are you gonna find out the police didn't already? Where you gonna even start?"

"I'll start at the nuns' place. That's where Lacey was when she died. What are you so crabby about? I'm not asking you to do anything. I just thought I might get a little support from my friends."

"Christ almighty, what makes you so stubborn? If I don't support you, I don't know who does. What are you trying to prove, Leah, and to who? It's not your fault that Lacey's dead. Let it go."

I slumped back in my chair, stung. Miguel looked nervously back and forth between us.

"So, I was telling Leah—the pictures on the river today, *fantásticos*. One of them, there's a break in the clouds. A little light comes through—everything glows: the water, the river, the tree, the yellow slickers on the police. Like a Thomas Kinkade picture. Only beautiful."

"Hey, I like Thomas Kinkade." Sherry arrived at that moment. "*I* think his pictures are beautiful."

Miguel gave her a pitying look and shrugged his shoulders.

"My mother gave me one of his paintings for my birthday. He's very famous. They're collector's items." She gave a little flounce and walked away without checking on refills.

I finished off my Jameson, put some money on the table for drinks and dinner. "I gotta go. G'night."

Max nodded but didn't say anything. He was pissed. That's OK. So was I.

"Hey, *chica*. Great pictures. See you tomorrow."

"Leah? Is that you?" a sleepy voice called from the far end of the house as the latch on the front door clicked. I had closed it as carefully as I could, but my mother can hear a snowflake fall at 50 yards.

"Yes, Mom," I said, watching her walk down the hallway toward me, tying the belt on her blue chenille robe. Her black hair is shot through with silver, and she wears it short and spiky. Her eyes, slightly out-of-focus without her contacts, are the same midnight-blue color as Lacey's. In fact, in that light she looked so like my sister that I started talking to rush past the sudden lurch in the pit of my stomach.

"Sorry. I tried not to wake you. Max and Miguel and I had a few at McClain's."

"Don't call me to bust you out of a drunk driving charge."

"Mom, a couple of drinks after work, that's all. Plus, I ate dinner too. I'm good. Besides," I said to divert attention, "we had a pretty big, pretty sad story today."

"You mean the nun who was found dead this afternoon in the river?"

Why did we even bother to publish a paper?

"Who told you? Never mind. Doesn't matter. Yeah. It's Sister Mattea Riordan." I hesitated, thinking about Max's warning, but plunged ahead. "A weird thing. She left a note for me at the paper a couple of days ago. But I didn't get it until today."

"Was she a friend? What was the note?"

"I've run into her a few times since I've been back, but no. We weren't really friends, more like friendly. But she went out of her way to see me, and her note asked me to call. Said she had something she wanted to talk to me about in person. And that's not all." I explained about finding the old *Times* story on Lacey in the book Sister Mattea left, and waited for my mother to tell me to leave it alone.

She had padded into the kitchen and was turning the burner on under the tea kettle, setting out cups and reaching for chamomile tea. Then she stopped, took the Jameson out of the cupboard and poured me some over ice. Then one for herself. We both pulled up stools and sat down at the bar separating the kitchen from the living room. Finally, she said, "What are you going to do?"

"Max thinks I should let it go. He thought you'd be upset if I started asking questions."

She waved off Max's concern with a lift of her hand. "Of course it upsets me, but that doesn't mean we should just ignore it. It sounds like Sister

Mattea wanted to tell you something about Lacey. Why else would she give you the clip and ask to talk to you in person?"

My mother is awesome. "Exactly. I was thinking about starting with the Catherines. Do you think Sister Julianna is still in charge at DeMoss?"

"I know she is. The bishop said Mass at St. Stephen's last Sunday and she was there. We took up a special collection for DeMoss. Leah, what do you think it is? Maybe Lacey told her something, gave her a message for us?" She shook her head. "No, that can't be it, Sister Mattea would have told us right away. Maybe she found something of Lacey's and wanted to give it back, or—"

"That's just it. It could be anything. Or nothing. Maybe she just wanted to say that Lacey didn't really hate me after all."

"Leah! Don't say that. Your sister didn't hate you."

"Really? She gave a pretty good imitation of it."

We were both quiet for a minute, each following our own train of thought.

"You know it wasn't your fault. None of it. I was the adult in charge. I was her mother and a piss poor one as it turned out."

"I'm gonna have to cut you off. Quit crying in your whiskey. And quit fishing for compliments. You were a great mom. You still are." I couldn't imagine trying to raise a smart-aleck, stubborn kid like me, or the pain of watching Lacey turn from sweet kid into monster child, but my mom just kept on doing what she did —loving us and believing in us and always, always being there for us.

"All right, Leah. All right. I'm going to bed." She drank the last of her Jameson. "You should think about it too."

"I will." It's not true that you can't go home again. You can as long as you're willing to regress from 32 to 13.

But I didn't go to bed. I took my drink and moved to the rocking chair in the living room. I found what Miguel calls my "sad bastard" playlist, because it's composed mostly of singer-songwriters in a melancholy mood. I turned the volume down low.

I went over to the mantel and took down a framed photo of me and Lacey going down a giant waterslide in the Wisconsin Dells when she was about seven. Her face was a mix of terror and delight. I closed my eyes, and

I could feel her sturdy little body leaning back against me as we barreled down the slide laughing and shouting.

I carried the picture over to the corner chair with me and held it in my lap, slowly rocking, listening to Big Star and Bon Iver and Lucinda Williams until I finally fell asleep.

4

"So, she just fell into the river? That's the conclusion of Himmel PD's crack investigation team?"

"You're in a pleasant mood," Coop said. We were sitting in his office at the Himmel Police Department on the Saturday after Sister Mattea died.

"Sorry. I haven't been sleeping very well. So, what's the story?"

"She drowned, according to the autopsy. There was water in her lungs. Body had bruises and contusions—she must have bounced off the rocks and bushes sticking out of the bluff, and then hit the water. Even if she was a strong swimmer, her habit would have pulled her down and the current is powerful right now."

"But how did she even wind up in the river in the first place?"

"Sister Julianna said Sister Mattea always took an early morning walk on the trail that runs along the river from the edge of their grounds toward the county park. Every day, same time, no matter what the weather she never missed. A couple of people saw her set out from the convent that morning, same as always.

"We checked the trail after the body was recovered. It was a mess. Any tracks that might have been there were washed away. That whole area should've been cordoned off all week. The ground is unstable."

"So, what do you think happened?"

"I think she stopped at the Point, went to the edge to take a look at the river rushing by there. She watched for a minute, then turned, pushed off, and a chunk of ground broke loose under her foot. She tried to catch her balance, got hold of a branch. It bent, held for a minute, but then she went over the edge. She kicked out with her feet, tried to get a toehold, but the limb broke. There were gouges in the dirt just below the overhang."

An image flashed into my mind of Sister Mattea, panicked, clutching onto a flimsy limb, feet flailing as she tried to get a foothold. Then the sharp crack of the branch and the tumble down the steep side. I shuddered and pushed it away.

"How long was she in the water?"

"She left for her walk around 6:45, probably got to the Point by 7 at the latest. Given the current and the way the river flows, that fits with her getting down to the dam in six hours or so."

I needed caffeine. The bookshelf behind me held a selection of mugs and the coffee-maker. As I poured a cup and dug around for a spoon to stir in some sugar, I glanced at the titles on the shelf above. Lots of cop manuals and procedurals, a thick notebook marked City Ordinances and assorted books on managing and supervising. Slightly unexpected, but not out of character, were a couple of mysteries by James Lee Burke. What threw me off was a small paperback called *Buddha's Little Instruction Book* and a hard-back copy of *The Collected Poems of Robert Frost*. I caught Coop's eye, then gestured toward the books.

"David Cooper, man of mystery. What's up with these?"

He shrugged. "I have eclectic tastes."

I had been kidding with the 'man of mystery' line, but it was true in a way. We moved in and out of each other's lives easily, using the foundation of our 20-year friendship, but we weren't kids anymore. We each had things that we hadn't shared.

I sat back down and took a sip of thick and bitter coffee, and wished I'd added another pound of sugar to my cup. "What about Sister Mattea's family? Have you talked to them?"

"Parents are both dead. She had a brother in California. I talked to him yesterday. He's making arrangements with the Catherines. The body was released to the nuns this morning."

I forgot myself and took another sip of coffee, then used the subsequent coughing fit to decide whether to mention the newspaper clipping and the note from Sister Mattea. Coop beat me to it.

"So, aren't you going to tell me about your message from beyond the grave?"

"Sounds like you already heard about it."

"Yeah, I ran into Miguel yesterday morning."

"So, I suppose now you're going to tell me it's stupid, let it alone, it doesn't matter now, blah, blah, blah."

"Nope," he said, shaking his head and reaching into his desk drawer. He pulled out a manila file folder and tossed it across to me.

"What's this?"

"A copy of the files on Lacey's case from the sheriff's department. I went over and got them after I talked to Miguel. I knew you'd want to see them."

I stared at him. "So, you don't think I'm crazy? You do think Sister Mattea was going to tell me something about Lacey?"

"Well, those are two different questions. Sure, I think you're crazy." He raised an eyebrow and gave me a half-smile. "But, yeah, maybe Sister Mattea wanted to tell you something. I'd want to know if I were you."

"Did you look at the file?"

"I haven't had time. I tried to talk to Charlie Ross, the investigator on Lacey's case, but he wasn't around when I picked this up."

"Doesn't matter. I remember him. He makes Darmody look like Sherlock Holmes. Coop, does it seem weird to you that Lacey died in a fall and then five years later Sister Mattea dies in a fall, and they're both accidents, and they both happened at or near the Catherines' place when no one else was around?"

He was quiet for a minute considering his response.

"No, Leah, it doesn't. It's like asking if I think the drunk driving accident on High Street five years ago is linked to the fatality last year when the traffic light malfunctioned. Two totally different things."

I started to answer, but he wasn't finished.

"I'm just gonna say this straight. Your sister had a history of drug and alcohol abuse. She was found with hydrocodone in her purse and an empty bottle of booze near her body. She was on the road to that accident a long time before it happened, and she was driving herself. Sister Mattea was different."

"Oh, because Lacey was a drug addict slut, and Sister Mattea was a saint?" I snapped out the words without thinking. Where does that atavistic urge to defend the family honor come from? I knew Coop was right, but it was like I can say whatever I want about my sister, but don't you try it mister—even if it's true.

He started over in the calm voice I hate, especially when I need calming.

"Leah, what I'm saying is that the circumstances surrounding Sister Mattea's death—the weather, the soft ground, the high wind—those circumstances came together in a way that made for a freak accident. Take any one of them away and it might not have happened. But Lacey's case is different."

He could see the anger rising in me. "Get as mad at me as you need to, I can take it. But like I said, Lacey's case is different. Her high risk behavior—drugs, bad decisions, worse friends, finally, that party in the woods—take any one of those factors away and she's still on a collision course with an unhappy ending. I think Sister Mattea's death was just plain bad luck. Lacey's death was predictable for the last three years of her life. I'm sorry. I don't think they're the same at all."

"Well, if Lacey was just a waste and her death was her own fault, why did you bother to get me the files?" I knew I was being unreasonable, directing at Coop the anger I felt at myself for not taking care of Lacey, but I couldn't seem to stop.

"Quit putting words in my mouth. I never said and I never will say Lacey was a waste. Like I told you, I got the files because I knew you'd want to see them, and because maybe Sister Mattea did want to tell you something that might help you and your mom feel a little more at peace with things. Maybe if you look at the records now that time's gone by, something will strike you that helps you figure out what that might have been. I didn't get them for you because I think there's some *DaVinci Code* plot linking the two deaths." I should have laughed off his slight sarcasm, but I didn't.

"You're such a patronizing jerk sometimes I—"

My cell rang. I stopped, looked at the caller ID. Miguel.

"I should take this."

"Sure, feel free to stop ragging on me anytime."

"Miguel? What's up?"

"Leah—Alex is hurt. He's in the hospital. Max is freaking out."

"What? What happened? When?"

"He fell out of a tree, and he's in the ER. That's all I know."

"OK, OK. Are you at the hospital?"

"Yes, I drove Max over. We were at the paper when Ellie called. I don't know what's going on." The usual teasing note in his voice was gone, and he sounded sober and scared.

"OK. It's all right. I'm on my way."

I turned to Coop. "Alex is in the hospital. I'm going over there."

Alex cracked me up. He was only 10, but he'd already announced he was going to be a forensic architect. Seriously, how many 10-year-olds even know what an architect is, let alone one who specializes in determining how and why buildings fail? Last time I talked to him, he showed me the plans he and his best friend, Lincoln Methner, had drawn up for their tree house—excuse me, tree condo. Max built the platform for them, but the boys had big expansion plans. Their version looked more appealing than my last apartment.

I pulled into the parking lot, ran to the ER and headed for the desk, but Miguel intercepted me.

"How's Alex? What's going on?"

"I guess he tied a rope to a branch so he could swing down from his tree house like Spiderman. The rope broke and he fell. Then his friend ran in and told Ellie Alex wasn't breathing. She called 911, then Max. He was so freaked out, I drove him here. It feels like they've been in there a long time."

At that moment, the doors from the ER swung out, and Max's wife Ellie came through. She had the bright blue eyes, long curly red hair, and impossibly perfect body of an animated Disney heroine. Normally, I kind of hate her. To my surprise, as soon as she spotted us, she ran straight toward me and flung herself into my arms, tears streaming down her face. People don't usually turn to me for comforting hugs, but I tried to step up. I noticed in a distracted way that she exuded the same grassy fragrance Max had. Alex's signature scent.

"It's OK. He's going to be fine," I murmured, though what did I know?

She hiccupped as her sobs subsided and then pulled back from me. Miguel, who had been hovering anxiously on the sidelines, brought her a wad of tissues big enough to sop up the Mississippi.

"I know, I know. Alex is fine. That is, he'll be fine. It's just. Oh—" Her eyes welled up again, and she blew her nose.

"That's good, that's good," Miguel said, gently leading her over to the couch and adroitly sitting them both down. I pulled up a chair across from them.

"What did the doctor say?"

She took a deep breath, held it in for a minute and got her thoughts together.

"He has a concussion, but the doctor thinks he'll be fine. He had the wind knocked out of him, and he was a little woozy, and that scared him—and me. But he's alert, and his memory seems fine. I'm sorry to be such a hysteric. I was just so scared when Lincoln came running in and said Alex couldn't breathe. Then, I saw him lying on the ground, gasping for air, and I thought, 'Oh, God, what if he broke his back or—'"

"*Pobrecita*, poor baby," Miguel said, patting her hand.

"But the doctor said he's going to be OK?"

"Yes. They're keeping him overnight just for observation. We were lucky. So, so lucky. If anything happened to Alex, I just couldn't go on. I just couldn't," she repeated. From the look on her face, I believed it.

She made a shaky attempt at a smile. "You'd never know I was a nurse in a past life, would you? The way I fell apart."

"Cut yourself some slack, Ellie, it's your kid. You're allowed to fall apart a little. Hey, you got him here, he's fine, and it's all good. Can we stop in and say hi, just for a minute?"

"Let me go and see if he's settled in."

In a few minutes, we were hovering in the doorway of Alex's hospital room. I peeked inside. He was sitting up in bed, a small bandage on his forehead, talking excitedly. His brown eyes grew large as he used his hands to make a point. A piece of dark brown hair fell forward, and he pushed it out of the way.

On either side of him, Max and Ellie stood gazing at their only son with such intense, naked love that I had to look away. But then Alex spotted us and shouted hello.

"I didn't really fall, Leah," he asserted.

"Oh? You gave a pretty good imitation of it, I hear."

"Well, yes, I fell, but the rope broke, so it really doesn't count. I mean, it's not because I didn't do the jump right. How could I know the rope was going to break?"

"How about you were told not to put one up at all?" Ellie made an attempt at sternness, though the fact that she was gently pushing his hair back from his forehead took a lot of the oomph out of it.

"I know. I'm sorry, Mom. We just thought—I just thought—it would be so cool, and Dad told me how when he was my age he used to swing out over the Himmel River and drop in and so I—"

"Hey, I can get in enough trouble with your mother without you helping me," Max said. "You're supposed to be smarter than me." He gave Alex a fierce look that didn't faze the kid a bit.

"Leah, I got an MRI and a CT scan. I have a first degree concussion. That's the minor kind. Good thing I had my lucky dog tags, right?"

"Lucky tags?" Miguel asked.

"Yeah, didn't you ever see them, Miguel?" He reached over and pulled a set of silver tags on a chain from his bedside table and motioned Miguel to come closer.

"Cool, huh? They were my dad's. I mean my first dad. Ian. He died before I was born."

Ian McCallister
  493 Waterford Way
  Los Angeles, CA

Blood Type O negative
Religion Presbyterian

"See, my dad was O negative. I'm B positive. The nurse told me I should always 'be positive.' Get it? B positive and 'be positive.' That's a pun."

For a second I flashed back to Lacey. She loved puns, too, when she was a kid, and as she got older she loved wordplay and puzzles of all kinds. She was so smart. And so lost. I gave myself an internal shake and turned my attention back to Alex.

"Mom gave me these tags to wear so I'd know my birth dad was always looking out for me."

I glanced at Max to see if he was bothered by Alex's obvious attachment to the tags, but he just rubbed his son's head and said, "Buddy, I'm glad Ian was watching out for you, but those things aren't magic you know. You have to make smart choices. And swinging out of a tree isn't a smart choice."

"I know, Dad. But still, they *are* my talisman. That means lucky charm," he added, lest Miguel and I not understand.

"You're lucky, that's for sure. I hear you have to stay tonight though, yes?" Miguel asked.

"Yeah. The nurse said they have to observe me tonight, so I have to stay. Mom thinks she has to stay, too, but she doesn't. I can be here by myself," he said, enough anxiety creeping into his voice to make it clear he hoped she would insist.

"Of course, you could stay yourself, no doubt about it," Ellie said. "But let me put my nurse's training to use a little. I could use some practice just to keep my hand in. You can be my guinea pig."

"Did you know a long time ago, like the 1700s, scientists used to almost always use guinea pigs for experiments, instead of rats or mice like they do now? That's why people started saying 'guinea pig' when they were going to try out something new. And, besides, it sounds better than saying, 'You can be my rat,' " Alex informed us.

"Little man, nothing wrong with your brain. How you come up with that stuff?" Miguel asked, giving Alex a light tap on the shoulder.

"It's a gift."

"And, on that note, I think we'll take off." I moved closer to Max and gave him a sideways shoulder squeeze—neither of us would have been comfortable with a full-on hug, but I wanted him to know that any tension between us was over—at least as far as I was concerned.

"Don't worry about anything at the paper. Miguel and I can handle it. And Courtnee, of course we have Courtnee to count on, too."

Max smiled. "Hey, before you go, why don't you take Ellie down to the cafeteria for some dinner? I'll keep Alex company, and then we can get things squared away for the night."

"Max, I don't need—" Ellie started to protest.

"Yeah, you do. Besides, me and Alex are gonna catch the last inning of the Brewers game."

"OK." She threw up her hands in surrender.

Miguel had excused himself because he had a date, so it was just me and Ellie at the small round table. She picked at a chef salad, and I dug into a surprisingly good cheeseburger.

"Ellie, are you all right? Seriously?"

"Yes, I'm fine, Leah. I know Alex will be OK. It's actually Max I'm concerned about."

"You mean because he's so worried about Alex?"

"No, not that. Has he talked to you at all about the paper? Never mind, you don't need to answer. I'm sure he hasn't. He's barely talked to me."

"You mean the finances? He hasn't said anything, no, but I can see ad revenues keep falling. When I left the paper, we had three sections of the *Times* every week. Since I've been back, we're lucky to have enough advertising to support two. And Max hasn't been himself lately. He's been pretty cranky."

"I know. He's even been a little short with me, which isn't like him at all. It would hurt him so much to lose that paper, the paper his grandfather started."

Her words gave me a sick feeling. "I knew it wasn't good, but I didn't realize things had gone that far."

"He has a meeting with Miller Caldwell next week, trying to get some kind of business loan from the bank. But he's worried about it. Max thinks Miller isn't going to be supportive, and there's another board member who thinks it's a bad investment."

"Who's that?"

"His name is Reid Palmer. He's a retired lawyer or investor, something like that."

"What's he got against the paper?"

"I don't know. Max said he met Miller for lunch last week, and they ran into Reid, so he joined them. Max was sort of testing the waters about the loan, but Reid wasn't very encouraging. Talked about online newspapers and how every change brings some casualties. Max didn't think it went very well."

"Max is a really smart guy, and he's got a lot of friends in this town. This Reid Palmer guy won't be the deciding factor."

"He could be. He has a lot of influence, not just with Miller but with other people on the bank board. And he's a big contributor to Miller's campaign for the senate." She hesitated, as if deciding whether to say something, then went ahead. "Max told me you're planning to dig around at DeMoss Academy, question the nuns and things. Reid Palmer is on the board there, too."

"And so?"

She sighed in exasperation. "So, think about it from Max's point of view. We don't need the paper stirring things up, maybe upsetting the nuns—the board, Reid Palmer."

"I don't want to stir things up, Ellie," I said, a little puzzled at the direction our friendly conversation had taken.

"But you *will* stir things up if you go out to DeMoss, asking the Catherines questions about your sister, implying they didn't take proper care of her, and they were keeping something from you. That's not going to go over very well. What if they complain? What if Reid Palmer gets upset and pressures the bank not to loan Max the money? Have you thought about that?"

"No. Why would I? Why would he get mad at Max or the paper?"

"Oh, don't act so naïve. You don't think the Catholic Church might be just a little sensitive these days to a reporter nosing around?"

"I'm not going as a reporter. I'm going there as Lacey's sister. I won't pretend I'm representing the paper. I'll make it clear the only thing I'm representing is my family. I can't see why you and Max are so worked up about it. I think you're a little over the top on this one."

"My family is the most important thing in the world to me. I would do anything to keep Max from being hurt. And it will kill Max if he has to close that paper. So, I really don't care if you think I'm 'over the top.' If Max thinks it's a bad idea, I think you should respect that. Surely you owe him that much."

"I understand."

"Then you'll drop this?"

"I'm sorry. I wouldn't hurt Max for the world, but my family is just as important to me as yours is to you. And I need to find out what Sister Mattea wanted to tell me."

The look on her face made it pretty clear it was just as well I hadn't brought any of my Leah Nash Fan Club membership forms with me.

5

My mother took off early Sunday morning to go antiquing with Paul Karr, so I was alone with the file that Coop had given me. Paul had been our family dentist forever. Then, after he and his wife Marilyn divorced a few years ago, he and my mother started seeing each other. He's a nice guy; they seem to enjoy each other's company, and that's as far as I want to go in thinking about my mother's romantic life.

With the house to myself, I sat at the bar and spread out the material. I looked over the crime scene photos, then put them in a pile turned upside down. They weren't something I wanted to keep seeing. I settled in to go over the written summaries, most of which had enough misplaced modifiers and missing punctuation to make reading very slow going. Like most cops I've encountered, the sheriff's department personnel were men of action, not words.

There were references to Lacey's drug and alcohol use, her history of running away, the long string of minor and major infractions that ultimately led up to her placement at DeMoss. Charlie Ross, the lead investigator, had interviewed the school staff, my mother, me, Lacey's old boyfriend, her roommate; but it was as clear now as it was to me then, that he was convinced Lacey had simply run away. And, I had to admit, I thought the same thing at the time.

As I read the reports filed after her body was found six months later, I grudgingly gave Ross a little credit. He had stepped up his game a bit. He re-interviewed witnesses and expanded the file to include a lot of the people who had been at the annual fund raiser held at the school that night. I knew many of the names: Miller Caldwell, his wife Georgia, Paul Karr and his then-wife Marilyn, Father Lindstrom, the priest at St. Stephen's, Ellie's bogeyman Reid Palmer, plus dozens of others, including most of the staff and many of the nuns.

And, of course, he had talked to the woman who found the body, Vesta Brenneman. Vesta is a local eccentric who lives in a tumbledown shack at the edge of town and spends most of her time pedaling around the county on an ancient Schwinn bicycle. Her little dog Barnacle sits in the bent metal basket attached to its handlebars. She found Lacey's body on one of her rambles in early spring. A groundskeeper heard her screaming in the woods.

When he got there, she was at the bottom of the ravine, her dog going nuts, and Lacey's body just feet away. But Vesta couldn't tell them much, just kept repeating Bible quotes. The investigators at the scene surmised that Barnacle had gotten loose, and she'd gone after him, finding Lacey's body in the process.

The follow-up reports were peppered with references to Lacey's drug use, her past misdeeds, even the general character of the kids at DeMoss Academy. The contents of her purse were listed: the unmarked bottle of pills that turned out to be hydrocodone, a cell phone with no contacts or texts or anything useful on it, her wallet with only her ID and a few bucks, her MP3 player, a little sketchpad with some random drawings. Lacey liked to sketch and was almost as good at drawing as she was at singing.

Then I found what I was looking for. The revised statement from the last-minute mystery witness, Lacey's roommate Delite Wilson. She reversed her earlier insistence that she had not seen Lacey that night and knew nothing about her disappearance. The second time around, she admitted that she and Lacey had snuck out to a party at the old Lancaster farm next to the Catherines' property.

She said that Lacey was really upset and kept repeating she was going to get away from DumbAss Academy as soon as she could. At the party she got pretty wasted, pretty fast. When she wanted to leave, Delite wasn't ready to go. Lacey got mad and took off on her own back toward the school.

"That's the last I seen her. I figured she just did what she kept saying she was gonna do—took off. I couldn't afford any more trouble. This is my last stop before juvie. But now I know she's dead, well, like I had to come forward. Her family should know what happened. For closure, like."

Delite named a college student who was working off community service hours tutoring at DeMoss as the source of her invitation to the party. When questioned, he denied inviting her, then confessed that he didn't remember for sure; he'd told a lot of people about the party. He didn't remember seeing Lacey there, but the party was pretty big and he didn't know a lot of the kids who turned up. He offered up a few names, but police drew a blank there, too.

Most said they didn't know Lacey; they didn't recognize her picture either. A couple said maybe they talked to a girl who looked like her, but they couldn't be certain. Not surprising. You put a bunch of drunk teenagers together and you're not going to get much in the way of recall, especially six months later. Ross's conclusion was that Lacey went to the party with Delite, got drunk, tried to walk home, slipped, fell, and died of head wounds and exposure.

But there was something in the file that didn't quite fit. I skimmed the medical examiner's report. Then I re-read the crime scene description, and then riffled back through the original report on Lacey's disappearance. I stopped mid-paper shuffle as the doorbell chimed "I Will Survive."

"*Tu mamá* is so cool." Miguel stepped inside, but not before hitting the buzzer once more to fill the front hall with the '70s anthem. Some days it was Gloria Gaynor, some days it was Motown or Carole King. After my mother installed a digital doorbell that used tunes from her MP3 player, there'd been no stopping her. Mom has always marched to a different drummer.

"At least she's not here to bust out her disco moves."

"C'mon. You know you love it. Hey, what are you doing, *chica*? I thought we were going to see *Mama Mia* at Himmel Tech. Abba? It doesn't get better. What is all this stuff?" He pulled up a stool and picked up one of the crime scene photos, then quickly put it back.

"It's the police report on Lacey. Coop got it from the sheriff's department for me. I'm just trying to see if there's anything...I don't know...odd I guess."

"Is there anything about your nun in there, Sister Mattea?"

"Not really."

"So, maybe Max is right. There's nothing to investigate?"

"Probably. Except there is one thing that's bothering me a little. It's not what's there, it's what isn't there. The night Lacey disappeared, so did $1,500 from the administrative offices at DeMoss Academy—money from a raffle that should have been deposited but got left in an unlocked drawer instead. Everyone assumed Lacey stole the money to fund her runaway adventure."

"So?"

"So, if Lacey took the money, where did it go? There's no mention of it in the crime scene report, nothing about it in any of the follow up interviews after her body was found."

"Maybe whoever found her body took the money."

I shook my head. "Vesta found her. I'm not sure she even knows what money is. Besides, Lacey's purse was under her body. There's no way Vesta would have poked around to find it."

"Maybe the deputy took it. Or maybe some *pendejo* found your sister and took the money and never reported the body?"

"That's pretty cold."

"It's a cold world, *chica*. That's why I got my friends to keep me warm."

"There's another possibility. Maybe Lacey didn't take the money. Maybe that's what Sister Mattea wanted to tell me. That there was one crappy thing my sister didn't do. Like steal from nuns. One thing that wasn't her fault, that she shouldn't be blamed for."

He nodded. "You could be right, *chica*. The money was gone, Lacey was gone, but there were a bunch of other mixed-up kids living there. Maybe one of them took the money, and when Lacey disappeared, they let her take the blame."

"I think it's worth checking out. It might be that whoever took it saw the light or found the Lord and confessed to Sister Mattea. Maybe they told her something else, something good about Lacey. And too bad if Max and Ellie think I'm obsessed for asking."

"Hey, I'm with you, *chica*. Lacey, she's your sister. She matters."

On Monday, I talked to Sister Julianna to get some information for a fuller story on Sister Mattea's death, but I didn't mention anything about the note she'd left. I felt virtuous. Separation of the job and the personal—isn't that what I told Ellie? Who said I wasn't professional? And sensitive? Then we got so busy that I didn't have time until the paper came out on Friday to follow up on my personal quest. Publication day always gives you a little breathing space at a weekly. No matter what happens, you still have six more days to get things together for the next edition. That afternoon I headed to the Catherines' place about 10 miles from town.

The Daughters of St. Catherine of Alexandria order is actually head-quartered in upstate New York where it runs a small Catholic college. A branch of the group wound up in Himmel in the late 1920s, after a bene-factor gave the order 300 acres and a spare mansion. Her instructions were to set up a school for the faith formation of young women. The Catherines chose not to dwell on the source of the donor's wealth, which was mostly amassed through illegal whisky runs from Canada during Prohibition.

The colonizing group that went west to Wisconsin did a pretty good business with a boarding school serving the daughters of the rich and Catholic for a number of years. But after Vatican II, the Catholic Church's major rebooting of 2,000 years of tradition, their fortunes declined. Most religious orders lost numbers, and recruits were hard to come by. Boarding schools for young ladies also began to fall out of fashion, and the one-two punch forced the closure of the school.

The order replaced its long habits with more modern garb and sent its nuns to work in social agencies, schools and hospitals in the area, but membership continued to decline. After flailing about trying to find their niche in the world, the Catherines decided to return to a more traditional approach. The order abandoned pantsuits and social justice for traditional habits and semi-cloistered living. That move proved very appealing to some. Finances improved, the college in Brampton, New York, achieved greater stability, and the number of new entrants to the order itself began to rise.

Fortunes changed so dramatically that the Wisconsin site was not only maintained, but the school was reopened with a new mission thanks to an infusion of money from the alumna for whom the institution was named. DeMoss Academy was established as a residential facility for troubled youth of both sexes and various income levels. Over the years it gained a reputation for achieving results with some hardcore kids. Just not Lacey.

The school grounds were beginning to show signs of spring as I turned through the entrance gates and onto the winding drive leading to the main part of the campus. Trees and bushes were sprouting buds and yellow daffodils poked up in flowerbeds. The paved road led me by the original mansion, which served as the convent, and past the main classroom facility for the 200 or so students in residence. Then a jog to the left took me past a chapel, a couple of dorms, and a counseling center, according to the signs. It looked like a prosperous New England prep school. Or, at least what I thought one looked like based on repeated viewings of *Dead Poets Society*.

The main artery, St. Catherine's Way, ended at the central administration building, which housed the director and various staff. I walked through the door of the one-story T-shaped building and flashed a confident smile at the elderly nun sitting behind an enormous wooden desk in the center of the reception area.

6

"I don't have an appointment, but I wondered if Sister Julianna might be able to spare just a few minutes for me? It really won't take long, Sister Margaret," I said, glancing quickly at the nameplate in the corner of her desk.

"She's in a meeting right now, but if you can wait a few minutes, she might be able to see you. She does have a little free time. That doesn't happen very often. Are you a family member of one of our students?"

"Not a current student. My sister was Lacey Nash. I'm Leah Nash."

"Oh, Lacey. Oh, yes." Was that good or bad? Given Lacey's track record, odds were on the "not good" side. I offered a neutral response.

"You remember her?"

"Of course. She was a lovely child and such a beautiful voice. She could sing like an angel. Are you a singer too, Miss Nash?" She settled back a little in her chair and perched her hands lightly on the desk, tilting her head slightly, her dark eyes as bright and blinking behind wire-rimmed glasses as a robin's.

"Call me Leah, please. No, I'm afraid Lacey got all the musical talent in our family."

"What was it you wanted to see Sister Julianna about, dear?"

"It sounds a little weird, I know, after all this time, but I'd like to talk to her about Lacey."

"Not weird at all. When someone so young dies, it's very hard to let go. Death is something we're built to resist, even though it opens the door to all that we've been living for. I'm sure you know we just lost one of our own far too young. Sister Mattea," she said, her eyes dimming a little with tears.

"I'm so sorry for your loss. I knew Sister Mattea a little. I've been wondering if she knew Lacey—though she never mentioned it to me."

"Oh, I doubt she did, dear. Sister Mattea was working on her MBA when your sister arrived. She wasn't working with our students at all."

"I didn't know she had a business degree."

"Whip smart she was. I was so happy when she was named Sister Julianna's assistant director. Sister Julianna works far too hard, does everything here, academics, student discipline, finances. Sister Mattea was so enthusiastic, so eager to lift some of that burden. She did so much in the two short months before she died. She would have been Sister Julianna's successor someday, no doubt about it."

"I didn't realize she had such an important job at DeMoss."

"Oh, yes. And so many plans she had. Right away she got working on a surprise for Sister Julianna. She got her brother to donate some big wheelie dealie software to revolutionize—that's what she said, 'revolutionize'—our accounting system. To hear her tell it, the new program would do reports, fraud audits, inventory control, time sheets, payroll, and then shine your shoes for Sunday Mass. She was so excited to do that for Sister Julianna. She was such a dear girl, a wonderful person. And a real firecracker, too."

She laughed and repeated, "Oh, a real firecracker. It seems so unfair. Ours is not to question God's ways, but I confess I have raised an objection over this one." She was quiet for a minute and so was I. Then I brought the conversation back to Lacey.

"Sister, I feel the same way about Lacey. She was so young. It seems unfair that she didn't really get a chance to turn her life around. I'm just trying to understand. What do you remember about the day she disappeared?"

"I recall that Friday very well. Very well. It was the same day Mary disappeared."

"Another student took off when Lacey did?" I asked in surprise.

Inexplicably, Sister Margaret chuckled. "No, no. I meant Mary, the Virgin Mary. The statue I kept on my desk."

"I'm not sure I – ?"

"I'm being a little silly, I know. But I loved that statue. It belonged to my dear father. Large and clumsily made, but in its own way, rather beautiful. For all it was a bit battered with the years. Had a long white scratch at the base. I was going to have it fixed, then I thought no, it's just like Papa. Because aging gave him character and it gave my Mary statue character, too.

"Anyway, she was there when I left for the day, I'm sure, because it was a very difficult day and I gave her a little pat on the hand like I did sometimes, just for a bit of comfort when things had been especially trying. The next afternoon when I came in, I noticed right away she was gone."

I wanted to get her off the Virgin Mary track and back to Lacey, but then I thought maybe the best way to get her to tell me what I wanted was to listen to what she wanted to talk about first. So I nodded.

"There was a lot of hubbub that day. Sister Julianna thought one of the cleaning staff or a visitor must have broken it and thrown it away. But I don't see how it could have broken, really. It was heavy enough to stop a door. It was marble, you see. I had one of the younger nuns look through the trash bins, but it wasn't there. No, I suspect one of the students took it for a prank, and with all the commotion, forgot about it. Strange that young people feel things so deeply, but they're so often careless about the feelings of others, isn't it?"

I nodded again, then made an effort to get the conversation back where I wanted it to go. "So, you were saying things were very intense the day Lacey disappeared?"

"Oh yes, that was a wild and wooly day. We had intake for three new students and one of them was very unhappy to be here, and there was a little ruckus. Actually, he turned out to be one of our best students. He just graduated last year and—"

"And so there were lots of things going on. Did you see Lacey that day?"

"Yes, I did. She came in to see Sister Julianna, and she sat right over there waiting. She had her little sketchpad with her. I remember that because she drew a little picture of me and gave it to me. Not the most flattering I must say, but the young are fearless truth-tellers, aren't they?" She gave a rueful grin, and I had to smile back even though I was anxious for her to get on with the story.

"Anyway, it was such a busy day Sister was running behind. We had the annual fundraiser that night and that is always a command performance. All hands on deck. Everyone was running around like crazy getting ready, and all staff had to be there. And then as I said, there was all the ruckus with the student and such a to-do, and Sister Julianna needed copies made for the Board packets. And I can tell you that old copier was just one step above a mimeograph machine. And she was getting quite impatient and—"

I felt a flutter of sympathy for Sister Julianna.

"Yes, well, it sounds like a lot of commotion that day. But you said Lacey was here. Do you know why?"

Sister Margaret seemed a little flustered as she tried to bring herself back from the meandering story I'd interrupted.

"Ah, well, I think Sister Julianna wanted Lacey to sing at St. Catherine of Alexandria's feast day. Our order is named after her, you know, and we always have a big celebration on her saint's day. But then what with all the commotion and things, Sister Julianna didn't get to see her at all. I think your sister was a little upset, and she slipped away. If I had known it was the last time I'd see her, well I—" she paused as though trying to think of exactly what she would have done.

"Well, I don't know, but you like to think you could have done something, said something that would have made a difference, don't you? I tell you, I usually count every day a blessing—at my age you have to. But that day—well, that was one of the worst days I've had since I started working here as receptionist and that's been almost 15 years."

The door to the director's office opened then with a sharp click. A slender middle-aged man with close-cropped dark hair emerged and walked toward the desk. He wore an expensive looking gray suit, a shirt so white it seemed to glow, and a navy tie patterned with tiny gold *fleur-de-lis*.

"Sister Margaret," he said, with a nod and a quizzical look at me. He smelled of some expensive and very subtle men's cologne that made me want to lean in for another whiff.

"Mr. Palmer!" she said with obvious pleasure. "I didn't know that was you with Sister Julianna. How are you today?"

"Well, Sister Margaret. Extremely well." His voice was tinged with a slight Southern drawl. He wasn't much taller than me, and as he turned my way I saw that his eyes were an unusual silvery blue. The contrast with his dark brows and dark lashes was disconcerting. "And you are?"

"Oh, my manners. Mr. Palmer, this is Leah Nash. Leah, this is our Board Chairman, Mr. Reid Palmer. Leah is the sister of one of our former students, Lacey Nash. She was also a friend of Sister Mattea's."

"Ah. Pleasure, Miss Nash," he said, taking my hand in a light but firm grasp, then quickly letting go.

"Leah is here to get some closure. You remember the story of poor Lacey, I'm sure. Sister Mattea's death brought back the memories for Leah," Sister Margaret happily volunteered for me before I could speak.

"Yes, well—" I said, trying to stem the information flow, but Palmer jumped in himself.

"Closure. Ah. A worthy goal, but one that I have found most difficult to achieve. I wish you success in your quest, Miss Nash." His speech was oddly formal, but appealing. I quashed the sentiment as I remembered that this was the man who stood between Max and his dreams. But he did smell really, really good.

"Thank you." We looked at each in silence and then he said—perhaps to stave off another tidal wave of chatter from Sister Margaret— "I must be going. Wonderful to see you, Sister Margaret. Delighted to meet you, Miss Nash." With a nod of his head, he was gone.

"Such a kind man. He's a very good friend to DeMoss Academy. Very good. Of course, his grandmother gave the money that reopened the school. I don't know what Sister Julianna would do without his advice. Well, I do know. We were that close to closing the one time, just before he came on the Board." She held up thumb and forefinger with an infinitesimal gap to demonstrate just how near to the financial edge the school had been.

"Really? I thought your order had loads of money."

"Not us. That's the motherhouse in Brampton," she said with an unexpected note of tartness in her voice. "We're responsible for our own funding to keep the school open. It was touch and go there for a while. Then Mr. Palmer stepped in and set things right. And they've been right ever since."

Riding to the rescue didn't sound much like the action of a rampant capitalist ready to grind Max's business under his heel. "Mr. Palmer is a pretty good guy then?"

"The best. As I say, everything has been right as rain since Mr. Palmer took over on the Board. Now, that's not a criticism of Sister Julianna, she just has so much on her plate. She travels so much you know, always presenting papers and making speeches all over the country at conferences and such. She's very high up in her profession. Just last month she—"

"I'm sorry, Sister Margaret, but do you think Sister Julianna might have time to see me now?" I interrupted as gently as I could, afraid that I'd miss the narrow window of opportunity to talk to the director.

"Oh, yes, of course. Let me just pop in and ask her." She sprang lightly from her chair and hopped with quick little steps to the office, tapped on the door and went in. Within seconds she came out smiling.

"Go right in. Sister can give you a few minutes."

7

I had met Sister Julianna at Lacey's funeral, and saw her again briefly when I attended the rosary for Sister Mattea. She was about my height, 5' 7" or so, and her perfect posture made her seem even taller. Her jaw was square, her nose short and straight. Her eyes, the color of cognac, were warm as she smiled and stood up to greet me. But when the smile left, the warmth was replaced by something in her gaze that made it clear she'd have no problem keeping a school of tough kids in line.

She took my hand in both of hers and gave it a light squeeze with long cool fingers before releasing it and gesturing toward a chair opposite her desk.

"Please, sit down. I want to thank you again for the lovely obituary you wrote for Sister Mattea."

"You're welcome. Thank you for seeing me without an appointment."

"What can I do for you, Leah?"

"This might sound odd," I began, feeling less certain of my mission under her intent gaze. "But I've been thinking a lot about my sister lately, and it's because of Sister Mattea. I have to ask, was there a connection between them?"

She looked surprised. "Not that I know of. I'm not even sure they knew each other. Sister Mattea was finishing her studies, traveling back and forth to school. She wasn't assigned to any direct student contact at the time Lacey was here. Why?"

"She left a message for me before she died. I think she was trying to tell me something about Lacey's death."

"A message? What kind of message?"

I explained about the note and the clipping in the book. She listened attentively, then drew a breath and sighed.

"Leah, I'm so sorry that Sister Mattea's death has stirred up painful memories for you, but whatever she may have wanted to ask or tell you, I'm sure it wasn't about your sister. How could it be?"

"I know it seems unlikely. But there is the thing with the money."

"Money?"

"The $1,500. You told the investigator, Detective Ross, that the day Lacey disappeared, $1,500 went missing from the school. But if Lacey took the money, where was it when her body was found? Couldn't Sister Mattea have found out something about that—that Lacey didn't take it, maybe she was just a scapegoat for one of the other kids? Or, maybe there was something else that she had learned, maybe she found something of Lacey's, or one of the other students confided something to her—"

She raised a hand. "Leah, I'm afraid there isn't any mystery, but I'm not sure it will help to tell you what I know."

"But it will, Sister. I really need to hear it."

"All right, Leah, if that's what you want." She sounded reluctant but resigned.

"Early the morning of the day Lacey disappeared, Father Hegl reported to me that he had found her lurking around the dispensary. It looked to him like she was trying to get into the locked prescription drug cabinet. She denied it. She told him she was just looking for the nurse, but he felt she wasn't telling the truth. I called her into the office immediately."

She stopped for a minute as though gathering her thoughts, then looked directly at me again.

"I was very stressed that day. It was the annual fund raiser as well as the Board meeting. There was a great deal to be done. I've gone over the events in my mind several times. I do believe I handled it as well as possible given everything that was going on."

"What? What did you do?"

"I was very direct. I told Lacey about Father's suspicions and that she would be required to undergo regular drug screening and increased counseling sessions. She became very angry and stormed out of the office. On a normal day, I would have gone after her immediately, but there were so many issues that morning."

"Wait. So, you did actually see her, speak to her?"

"Yes, of course."

"But Sister Margaret said Lacey was waiting for you and that she left without seeing you. She said you wanted to talk to Lacey about singing for St. Catherine's feast day."

She hesitated as though searching for the right words. "Sister Margaret is very important to us here, but as she's gotten older, she's become less— discreet. I may have implied to her that the meeting was about Lacey singing for us. Your sister did have a remarkable voice. But that wasn't the topic we discussed. Sister's recall isn't always reliable, and in the five years since Lacey's disappearance, she's obviously confused her memories. It was a very chaotic day."

"I see. So, you told Lacey you were on to her, and she got belligerent and left."

"Yes. I think it's only logical to believe that Lacey took the money. It was in an unlocked cupboard behind Sister Margaret's desk. Another example, I'm afraid, of Sister's memory problems. It should have been deposited in the bank, not left to tempt the students.

"As for why it wasn't found with her body—she was at a drinking party and in a highly intoxicated state. She could have given the money to someone or bragged about having it and someone at the party took it from her. Does it matter now? Frankly, the money was the least of our concerns, and I would think of yours as well."

"I'm not 'concerned' about the money. I just think it's odd that Lacey would have lost $1,500 without leaving the grounds."

"Perhaps she connected with her supplier."

"You say that like you know she had one."

"We know that there were no drugs missing from the clinic, yet there was hydrocodone found in her purse. And we don't know how long she'd been pursuing her prescription drug habit."

"If that's true, she must have been getting them from someone here."

"Our staff are screened and the students are monitored. But we can't prevent every breach. We're not a maximum-security prison, Leah. You'll see no armed guards or barbed wire fences here."

"You didn't answer my question. Do you know who her supplier was?"

She leaned forward and brought her fingertips together, pressing them against her mouth and the tip of her nose, her elbows resting on her desk. She looked at me as though weighing carefully what she was going to say.

"After Lacey's body was discovered, our head maintenance man, Leon Greer, came to me and admitted that he had hired a temporary grounds employee without vetting him to help with fall clean up."

"And?"

"He was fired a few days after Lacey left when Leon found him smoking marijuana on the grounds. Sometime later he heard that the man had been arrested on a drug charge. When Lacey's death became known, and the paper reported her drug use, Mr. Greer became concerned that this Cole person may have been her supplier."

"Cole? Not Cole Granger? Lacey's boyfriend?"

"Yes. I believe that was his name."

"He's the one who got her using in the first place. What were you thinking?"

"I didn't even know he had worked here until Leon informed me. And I certainly didn't know anything about his history with drugs."

"Did you tell the police?"

"Of course I did. I called Detective Ross. He investigated and later assured me that Mr. Granger had denied being her supplier, and that his time the night Lacey disappeared was accounted for."

"Sister Julianna, Charlie Ross couldn't investigate his way out of a roundabout."

"Leah," she said in a patient voice, "You're playing a guessing game in which there are no answers. I've worked with troubled children and their families for many years, and I've seen this sort of thing before. The desperate need to find a reason, the refusal to accept that not everyone can be saved. I understand why you came but believe me when I tell you that refusing to face facts won't change them."

"Why didn't you call at the time and tell my mother and me that Lacey was suspected of trying to steal drugs? That seems like a pretty big thing to ignore."

"I didn't ignore it, Leah. I would have informed your mother, of course, but Lacey disappeared the day Father Hegl came to me. I would never have called without gathering the facts. Then, when she ran away, or we thought she had, there seemed no point in further upsetting you or your mother. Without drug testing, I had no proof. It was a suspicion, but there were no drugs missing. In hindsight, I can see that may have been an ill-advised kindness."

"Sometimes kindness is just a cover for what's convenient. Maybe it wouldn't be so good for word to get out that prescription drugs were getting passed around, and donated money was getting stolen by kids that are supposedly rehabilitated." OK, so that wasn't exactly fair, but her refusal to even consider that Lacey wasn't the culprit was making me mad.

She stood up then, saying, "I really am sorry for your pain, Leah, and I understand it. We've just lost a sister, too. But I can't agree with your theory that Lacey was wrongly accused. I don't see what more I can say. I'll continue to keep you and your mother in my prayers." She walked over and opened the door. Clearly, this interview was over.

I stood up. "Sister, Cole Granger is a known drug dealer. If Lacey was back on drugs, he was the logical supplier. And if you're wrong and Lacey wasn't using again and didn't take the money, I'd really like to know that. I'd think you would, too. Thanks for your time." With that, I walked through the door, nodded to Sister Margaret, and left the building.

I yanked open my car door and dropped down onto the seat. I hate being condescended to and, in my book, Sister Julianna was the patron saint of patronization. I pulled out my cell and punched Coop's speed dial number.

"Is Cole Granger still in town?"

"Yeah. He got a job at Jorgenson's Tire. Been there awhile, ever since he got out of jail. Why?"

"I'll tell you later. Gotta go. Thanks."

All right, that would be my next stop. Right after I had a chat with Father Hegl. I rolled down the window and asked a passing staff member where I could find him. Per instructions I took the first turn to the left, and a short way down the graveled side road, I spotted a small bungalow. As I pulled in the driveway, a man in sweatshirt and jeans rounded the corner of the house carrying a rake.

"Father Hegl?" I asked, leaning out the car window.

"That's right," he said, walking toward me and smiling. "How can I help you?"

"I wonder if I could talk to you for a few minutes," I said, getting out. "I'm Leah Nash. Lacey Nash was my sister."

He looked puzzled and something else—uncomfortable, maybe?

"Really, it won't take long."

He hesitated still.

"Please? It's important to me."

"All right. Come on in." He leaned his rake against the side of the house, and led me through the front door and into a large living room. The first thing I noticed—it would be hard not to—was a floor-to-ceiling shelf on the west wall, filled not with books but with the largest collection of kitschy religious statues I'd ever seen.

"Wow."

"A little overwhelming, isn't it?" He flashed a disarming grin. "It started as a joke gift from my sister when I entered the seminary. She gave me that little dashboard Jesus up there in the corner. Then, over the years, people kept adding to it. Now, it's a kind of competition among friends and family to see who can gift me the most garish saint."

There must have been dozens of plaster, plastic, wooden, marble, painted, carved, cast statues. Most that I could see were hideous.

"Who's winning? The contest, I mean. There's some seriously wrong stuff up there."

"It's ongoing. And I guess it could be worse. She could have started me a Beanie Baby collection."

I liked the way the corners of his mouth turned up when he smiled and his blue-green eyes crinkled at the corners. He had light brown hair that fell casually onto his forehead and gave him that boyish appearance a lot of women like. He looked a few years older than me, maybe late 30s. He pointed me toward a worn leather chair, sat down himself in its counterpart, and waited for me to begin.

"Father, I was speaking to Sister Julianna, about my sister Lacey's death—"

"Sister Julianna sent you here?"

"Not directly." I explained to him about my failure to connect with Sister Mattea before she died, and the cryptic message I was trying to decipher, and my puzzlement over the missing $1,500. I may have implied that Sister Julianna was as intrigued by the mystery as I was.

"Sister Julianna seems convinced that Lacey was using drugs again, based in part on your story about finding Lacey trying to break into the dispensary drug cabinet."

"It's not a story, Leah. It's what I saw. And I was very sorry to see it. Your sister had a lot of promise. A beautiful voice, one of the best I've ever coached. I tried to get her to join our choir. We perform nationally, you know. But I'm afraid she wasn't ready to give up the things that brought her here."

I started to follow-up with a question about Cole, but his cell phone began to ring.

Digging it out of his pocket, he glanced at the number and said, "Sorry, I need to take this," and stepped into an adjoining room.

I seized the opportunity to snap a picture of the wall of saints and texted it to Miguel. He would love it. Then I glanced around the room while I waited and noticed another unusual decorating touch—for a priest anyway. A lighted display case on the wall behind his desk contained a selection of handguns. I walked over to peer in closer, then jumped when I heard a voice in my ear.

"Are you a collector?"

Startled, I took a step back to reclaim some of my personal space. "No. I'm kind of surprised you are. Handguns and priests don't go together very well, do they?"

He smiled. "I agree. The collection was my dad's. He was a handgun enthusiast. I'm not, but we spent some quality time together at the shooting range, and he left the collection to me when he died a few years ago."

"Isn't that a little dangerous to have around with all these troubled kids?"

He shrugged. "Students aren't allowed in staff housing. I doubt if anyone even knows the collection is here. Besides, it's locked—and wired with an alarm. If anyone tried to break in, security would know right away. Now, where were we?" He moved back to his chair and indicated I should resume my seat as well.

"I wanted to ask you about Cole Granger. Did you ever see Lacey with him?"

"Cole Granger?"

"The temporary groundskeeper, the one who got fired for smoking weed on the job?"

"That's right. I forgot about him. As a matter of fact, I did see him once with your sister."

"When was this?"

"A few days before she disappeared."

"Did you report it?"

"No. Why would I?"

"Because he's a known drug dealer. Because he was Lacey's ex-boyfriend. Because maybe, if she was using, he was supplying her."

"I'm sorry, but I didn't know any of that. So no, it didn't occur to me to link Lacey's drug use with Cole Granger."

"Suspected."

"What? Oh, all right. Her suspected drug use."

"What were they doing—Lacey and Cole?"

"Just standing on the sidewalk talking."

"You didn't hear what they were saying, can't remember how they looked? Was Lacey agitated, or was Cole threatening in any way?"

"Leah, I'm sorry. I don't think so, but I don't really remember much about it. It was just a few seconds and I went on. I only remember it because Cole left a rake laying across the walk, and I tripped and almost broke my neck."

"All right," I said, down but not defeated. "What about Sister Mattea, can you tell me anything about her? Can you think of anything, anything at all that she might have wanted to tell me about Lacey or the way she died?"

He shifted in his seat a little, clasping his hands together and leaning slightly forward.

"Leah, I'm very sorry that your sister is dead. But Lacey died because she wasn't able to overcome her demons. We offered her help, just as you and your mother must have offered help before she wound up here. But no one, not you, not me, not Sister Julianna, or any of the staff here can force someone to be saved if they don't want to be. Do you really think Sister Mattea had some knowledge that would magically make you and your mother feel better? You can't rewrite history." His words were a little harsh though his voice was not.

"You don't get it. I'm not trying to rewrite her history. I'm trying to understand it. I think Sister Mattea had a piece of that, and I'm going to keep asking questions until I get the answers I need. The fact that nobody else gets that doesn't change my mind at all."

"Obsession isn't healthy, Leah."

"I'm not obsessed."

"Five years after your sister's death and you're still looking for answers? Be careful."

What was he getting at? Be careful of obsessing? I didn't need his advice.

"Meaning?"

"Meaning your sister's life is over. Yours isn't. God always answers our prayers, but sometimes the answer is no."

"What's that, the Catholic version of a fortune cookie?"

To my surprise he smiled and shook his head, raising his hands in a gesture of surrender. And there was that crinkle around his eyes again. This time I didn't find it so appealing. Why was everyone talking to me like quick-fix therapists from some reality TV show?

8

The faded black and white sign for Jorgenson's rested on top of a pea-green cinderblock building that wasn't flaking so much as molting. A rusty purple Camaro, with "Bad to the Bone" stenciled on the side over a skull and crossbones, was the only car in the lot. I parked and went inside, but there was no one behind the scratched and dented Formica counter.

An out-of-date State Bank of Himmel calendar on the wall announced that it was December 2009. I opened the door on the left and was immediately hit with mixed smells of rubber, oil, and gasoline. Rows of tires lined one wall. The concrete floor was sticky with accumulated layers of grease and dirt. On the far side of the garage, a pair of legs on a rolling cart protruded from beneath a green van.

"Hello? Have you got a minute?" I called.

There was no answer, but after a few seconds the cart came rolling out from under the van. A man in greasy jeans and dirty t-shirt stood and swaggered toward me.

"You need your tires rotated, sweetheart? You oughta make an appointment, but I might be able to fit you in." He gave me a look that I guessed was supposed to be sexy. It wasn't.

"Forget about it. It's me. Leah. Lacey's sister?"

We hadn't exactly been friends, so I wasn't surprised that he didn't recognize me. But I wouldn't forget him. Thin, petulant mouth, yellow-flecked green eyes, slicked-back mud-colored hair, thick-chested, muscular body. A dragon tattoo started under his sleeve and ran all the way down his hairy forearm.

He did a double-take, and his demeanor went from flirtatious to surly.

"Huh. Whadya want?"

"I want to know if you were supplying Lacey with drugs after she went to DeMoss Academy."

"What're you talkin' about?"

"Let's cut the crap, Cole. I know you worked there. I know you saw Lacey there. I know you got fired for smoking weed on the job. And I know you spent time in jail on drug charges. What I want to know is, did you sell to Lacey while she was at DeMoss?"

"I ain't got time for this."

"I'm aware that you and my sister were in a relationship."

"In a relationship?" He snorted. "Me and your sister wasn't in a relationship. We was hook-up buddies more like." He watched to see my reaction. What had Lacey ever, ever seen in this guy?

"I know you and Lacey had sex; you're not shocking me. I'm pretty sure that's all you had. But she spent a lot of time with you before she went to DeMoss, and I know you saw her there. It's a simple question. Did you sell her drugs?"

"No. And I never hooked up with your sister at her junior jail. And I ain't no drug lord either. Would I be workin' here, if I was? Or at that lousy job they fired me from at the nuns?"

"You might. Nice potential customer base there. And if you weren't selling how'd you wind up in jail?"

"Somebody had it in for me, that's all."

"Right." I tried changing tactics. "Look, Cole, I'm trying to find out what happened the day Lacey died. I'm not here to bust your balls, or get you in trouble. I just want to find out the whole truth about my sister." I explained briefly about Sister Mattea's message.

"Mattea. She the one used to walk out to the Point every day?"

I nodded.

"She was all right. Least she'd say hello like you was a human being."
He seemed to be softening a little.

"Cole, you told the police you didn't see Lacey the day she disappeared.
I think maybe you did."

"Yeah? Why's that?"

"If she was running away, she'd need someone to help her at least get
into town so she could catch a bus, or to the highway so she could hitch a
ride. Who could she call, but you? And you were talking to her just a few
days before she left. Did she ask you to help her?"

He looked at me, seemed to be weighing something in his mind, then
shrugged.

"All right. Yeah. I seen her. But I ain't tellin' the cops that because I don't
know nothin' about what happened to your sister. She told me she was
bustin' out of there. Said could I give her and a friend a ride, and we could
have a little party before she left town. Lacey always was a party girl. So, I
said yeah."

My heart started racing but I tried to look calm. I didn't want to spook
him. "So, what happened?"

"I meet her like we planned at that big rock, Simon's Rock they call it,
off the Baylor Road entrance around 10:30. I ask her where's her friend, and
then this snot-nosed little kid, he comes creepin' out from behind the rock.
I didn't want no part of some whiny brat. I said no way. She tried to sweet
talk me. When that didn't work, she pitched a fit. I grabs her arm, just to
calm her down like, but then she hauls off and kicks me in the nuts. Then
she and the kid took off. Your sister was batshit crazy."

"What kid? What was Lacey doing with a kid? Who was it?"

"How should I know? I didn't want to get mixed up in anything then,
and I sure as hell don't want to now."

"Did she go to a party that night with her roommate?"

"Like I said, I don't know what happened to your sister. Alls I know is I
had nothin' to do with it. She took off, and I went over to my girlfriend
Amber's. I told the police that's where I was, and she did, too. Except for the
part about seein' Lacey."

"Nothing to do with it? Don't you realize that if you had given Lacey a
ride like she asked, she might still be alive? Or, if you at least had told the

police—they could've found that kid. Maybe he had something important to tell them.

"My mother and I put up flyers at bus stops, and haunted teen runaway centers and jumped every time the phone rang for six months, trying to get word on what happened to Lacey. Until we got the call that my little sister was dead! If you had helped her, maybe she wouldn't be!" My voice was loud and ragged, and my nails bit into the palms of my hands.

He stepped in so close I took an involuntary step back. His face was contorted with anger and he spat out the words. "You always did think you're better'n me and your shit don't stink. Well it does lady, and there's a pile of it in the middle of your nicey nice little family."

"What do you mean?"

"I mean Lacey's problem wasn't drugs. And it wasn't me. It was whoever made her his little baby doll. You had to know. You just didn't want that kind of mess in the middle of your perfect little life."

What was he talking about? That I wasn't there for Lacey? I already knew that. I didn't need this jerk to tell me. "What are you saying?"

"I'm saying somebody raped your little sister and kept on doin' it, and you didn't do nothin' about it."

"You're lying." My brain refused to process what he was saying, but my stomach had dropped like I'd stepped off a cliff.

"You ask yourself, why would that nice little girl from nice little family USA start hangin' out with the likes of me and my friends? Why'd she start smokin' weed and poppin' pills? Why did little princess turn into such a mad little bitch. Somebody turned her into one. I ain't lyin.' "

"Stop it. You are. You're lying. Lacey would've told me something like that. She would've told me. It's not true."

"Would she now? Seems like she didn't though. Maybe you was too busy with your big, important career. Cause you're so important ain't you, Leah? And you're so much smarter'n the rest of us, ain't you?"

"You're lying," I repeated in a flat voice. I pressed my lips and swallowed hard against a wave of nausea. Could it be true? Had Lacey been sexually abused? Was that why she was so angry, so self-destructive? But why wouldn't she tell me? It didn't make sense. But why would Cole even say it? Why would he lie?

I realized that he was still talking. This time, though, there was a smirk on his face and pseudo sympathy in his voice.

"It sure would be upsettin' to me. Thinkin' I let my little sissy down like you did. The guilt must be killin' you. I'd help if I could, but I can't tell you much except it happened. See, Lacey talked a lot. She was one of those drunks that just can't shut up. But me, I'm not what you'd call a real good listener. But I bet your Sister Mattea was. Maybe that's the big secret she wanted to tell you."

"Shut up. Shut the hell up." My head had begun to pound and a warm flush spread through my body. I needed to go.

He leaned in close again, and I felt his hot, fetid breath on my face. He grabbed my wrist and in a rasping whisper said, "Alls I know is, if it was me, I wouldn't be wasting time botherin' a poor, workin' man like myself. I'd be askin' to find out who messed with my little sis. Cause maybe that's the one who really knows what happened the day she died. And don't be tryin' to drag me into it. I said all I'm gonna say, and I ain't sayin' nothin' to the police."

He flung my wrist down so forcefully it cracked. Then he said in a normal voice, as though we'd been doing normal business, "Tell your boss we been holdin' his spare here for two months. He needs to pick it up. He gets a flat, he'll be shit outa luck. Besides, we ain't a storage locker."

9

I must have stopped at traffic lights, and yielded for pedestrians, and driven the speed limit, and parked my car, and passed for a normal person on the drive from Jorgenson's to McClain's, because I didn't get pulled over, but I had no awareness of the trip.

Coop was waiting when I got there. I guess I looked as bad as I felt, because within seconds of spotting me walk through the door, he led me to a booth, ordered me a drink, and sat down across from me. "What's wrong?" His eyebrows were drawn together in a concerned frown.

"I'm all right. Stop looking at me like you expect me to keel over."

"Take a drink," he said as the waiter put down a Jameson on the rocks. "Then tell me what's going on. Something is up." His dark gray eyes searched my face.

"I think Lacey was sexually abused when she was 14."

There. Saying it out loud should make it go away, right? I mean, it was crazy. If I said the words, I'd hear how ridiculous they were. But they weren't.

"All right. OK, take it easy. Why would you think that?" His voice was carefully neutral, but he couldn't conceal the shock in his expression.

I told him what Cole had said. He rubbed the side of his jaw with his thumb and waited for me to go on.

"I know Cole lies as easy as breathing, but think about it, Coop. Why this lie, why this time? What's the purpose? It's not getting him out of anything, in fact, it's getting him in deeper. He could've just kept denying that he saw Lacey at all. What he said, I just have a gut feeling it's true."

I waved away Sherry who had come to take our order, apparently having ousted the waiter when she realized Coop was sitting there. But Coop overruled me and asked for two burger baskets and water for both of us. Sherry tried a little flirting, but got nowhere. For once I didn't have the stomach for even a small victory smirk.

"What do you think?"

"I think you're putting a lot on the word of a punk."

"But it's not just him," I said, eager to make my point. "It's not just what he said. Look at the rest of it, Coop. I did a story on sexual abuse of adolescents a couple years ago. The sexual acting out, the drug use, the withdrawal from family, those are all symptoms. Lacey was a textbook case.

"She didn't morph into a demon child. Somebody made her that way. I just don't understand why she never told us, or at least me." Except, maybe I did. I had been really wrapped up in my own life then. Involved in my first serious relationship, anxious to prove myself at work, to get ahead. I didn't have as much time for my family as I should have. Maybe I didn't want to hear anything that would disrupt my happy new world.

"Slow down, Leah. For the moment let's say you're right. There are lots of reasons for a teenage girl not to talk about sexual abuse. Shame, guilt, fear. Her abuser can convince her it's her fault. Tell her that no one will believe her, maybe even threaten her or her family."

"I should have seen. I should have known. She should've been able to trust me."

"It's not a matter of trust. Are you listening to me? Kids that age, they've got so much going on, they don't think straight. She may have been trying to protect you. Or your mom."

"I should have figured it out."

"Leah, c'mon. You don't even know that it happened." He was right, I didn't *know*, but somehow it felt true.

"I know it might not make sense to you, but I have a feeling—all right, maybe it's more like a fear—I don't think Cole is lying."

He tried another tack. "OK, even if it did happen. You can't do anything about it. Lacey is gone and without her, how could you prove anything? Timmins isn't about to prosecute on behalf of a dead sexual abuse victim."

"No. But he'd have to if she were a murder victim." Where did that come from? I didn't even know I was thinking it until I said it, but Coop's immediate negative response didn't dissuade me.

"Whoa. Whoa, whoa, whoa. How did we get from suspected sexual abuse to murder?"

"Did you read the investigation report?" I reached across the table and grabbed his arm, trying to shake him into the growing sense of certainty I felt.

"I looked at it. It wasn't as thorough as it should have been—"

"Not as thorough? You must've just skimmed through it if you didn't see the gigantic holes. Look, Lacey disappears on the night of the big DeMoss fundraiser. Half the town was out there, coming and going all night. No nuns, no staff, no students, no visitors, nobody noticed Lacey where she shouldn't be? OK, give that it was a big night. Maybe most people wouldn't realize anything was wrong even if they saw her.

"But Ross does a half-assed investigation and doesn't even ask the right questions, because he's sure slutty little Lacey Nash just took off on her own. And pretty much everybody, including me, thinks he's probably right. Then, when her body is found, oh-oh that doesn't look so good. How to explain it? Oh, well, suddenly her roommate decides to come clean and confesses that Lacey went to a party with her and got wasted. Then, Ross and the medical examiner and Timmins all agree, she fell down the ravine in a drunken stupor and died of head injuries and exposure. Everything all tied up nice and neat.

"Until Cole finally tells me the truth. She met up with him that night. She wasn't going to any party. She was taking off, but for where? And she had a kid with her. What happened to him? Why didn't he come forward? And where's the money? She stole $1,500. She didn't leave the grounds, but it's gone? And her phone. What about her phone?"

"What about her phone?"

"It didn't register until now. She wasn't even supposed to have a phone. Students aren't allowed."

"She wouldn't be the first kid to get hold of a contraband pay-as-you-go phone."

"Sure, I know. But why wasn't there anything on it? The police file said there were no emails, no texts. No record of calls. Really? No emails? No texts? What teenage girl isn't texting? Where was her music, her pictures, or at least a few contacts?" I felt like I was channeling Sherlock Holmes, because I hadn't even thought of those anomalies until that very minute.

"If Lacey had a phone, why would she bother with Cole to get her out of there? Why wouldn't she call your mom and ask for help?"

"Because she'd be afraid Mom wouldn't believe her. That she'd call the school and they'd stop her. Maybe it had something to do with the kid she had with her. I don't know. But I know she did make a call. And it should have shown up on her phone. She called me. Only I didn't pick up. I didn't recognize the number. She left a voicemail." I let the words hang there, stark and ugly. I'd never said them out loud. To anyone.

Coop waited, not saying anything.

"I was covering a big accident, lots of casualties and chaos. We worked all evening and into the night. I just flopped into bed when we finished, didn't check my voicemail until the next morning. The connection was bad and kept breaking up. Lacey was talking so low, and she didn't make any sense. It was kind of a drunk whisper. I thought—" I stopped for a minute, took a big drink of Jameson. Coop still didn't say anything.

I finished in a rush.

"I thought she drunk dialed me. She just said Lee-Lee and then something like 'It's legal.' It didn't make any sense. I just felt so mad at her, Coop. I thought she had thrown out her last chance at DeMoss—that she was right back at it. And I couldn't jump back in with her. I deleted the message and didn't even try to call her back.

"When Mom told me she was missing, and it looked like she'd run away, I didn't say anything about the call. I didn't want Mom to think I could've stopped her, and I didn't bother to answer my phone. It didn't seem to matter. It was just like all the other times, and she'd surface after a few days or weeks."

Only, of course, it wasn't. I knew I should have picked up or at least called her back. That's why when her body was found, I felt so guilty, I was physically ill. Maybe, if I'd called her back, I could've saved her.

"You should have told Ross."

"You think I don't know that? You—"

He went on as though I hadn't spoken.

"I think you've got way more guilt than facts lined up here, Leah. It's clouding your judgment. The things that don't add up? Yeah, they do. Lacey took $1,500 and somebody at the party took it from her when she was drunk. Or, I'll even give you that maybe she didn't take it at all. Some other kid did and got lucky when Lacey disappeared the same day and the blame fell on her.

"But the other stuff—this mystery kid and the sexual abuse—that's all from Cole, nobody else. And he's a con man who already told you he won't stand by his story. Lacey's rebellion, her drug use, her anger—well, sorry to tell you but that can be part of being a kid. And the phone call? You had reason to think she was drunk dialing—and Leah, do you get this? You still have reason to think that. Lacey backslid, got drunk, called you—same old, same old. That makes a lot more sense than this theory you're floating."

He paused for a moment to see if he was making an impact. My crossed arms and the set of my jaw told him he wasn't.

He leaned forward and put his head between his hands in frustration for a second. The jagged scar running the length of his left index finger made a pale zigzag against his skin. When he looked up, he spoke in a much less understanding tone.

"What are you doing here, Leah? You're going to make yourself and everyone else crazy going over and over this stuff. I get it. You feel like you weren't there for Lacey. But you were.

"You were there every day of that kid's life, and you and your mom gave everything you had to help her. But sometimes, some kids can't be helped. It's just the way it is. And making up some crazy idea about sexual abuse and cover ups and murder, for God's sake, that's not going to help anything. And no one is going to get behind you on this. Not the sheriff, not the D.A.—"

"Not even you? What about you, Coop? Will you get behind me?"

"Ahh, don't do that. Don't make this about our friendship. It's not personal. I'm trying to help you here," he said. The thing is, I knew that he was. But he was wrong.

"Oh. I get it. You think I'm a delusional idiot. But nothing personal."

"That's not what I meant, and it's not what I think."

"Let me ask you this. If your sister died, and you thought there was something suspicious about it, would you stop asking questions?"

"No, I wouldn't. But I wouldn't create suspicions either, just because I couldn't deal with my own guilt."

We stopped talking then. I picked at my burger and fries, and Coop demolished his. Finally, I dug in my wallet for my share of the bill, then put it on the table.

"See you."

He nodded, and I left.

Instead of heading home I found myself driving toward the south end of town. When I pulled into the parking lot of Riverview Park, it was almost dark, and the grounds were deserted.

The grass was shaggy and sparse, overcome by dandelions and brown patches and the shrinking Himmel municipal budget. I got out of my car and walked to a weathered wooden picnic table. The flaking brown paint bore scratched random messages: of devotion "AK loves JB," self-promotion "Kiley 2010," and judgment "John Z is an asshat."

I sat down and looked at the sun-faded plastic "safe" playground equipment that had replaced the multi-level jungle gyms and hand-over-hands of my youth. I got my first broken bone at the park trying to beat Coop's time on the hand-over-hands.

In the dimming light, I could see the railroad trestle crossing the river at the north end of the park's boundaries, and beyond that JT's Party Store, home of Sour Patch Kids, Charleston Chews, and Slush Puppies, as well as more adult treats. I stared into space thinking about Lacey and what I'd done wrong. How I could have tried harder, been more patient, listened better, just have been a better sister.

Why didn't Coop understand? I wanted him to back me on this, help me figure it out, find the truth. But maybe he was right. Maybe Cole was just jerking me around. Once a con man always a con man. But why would he do that? What was in it for him? No. He was telling the truth. I just knew it. But I'd feel more sure if Coop could see things the same way.

My thoughts went round in useless circles, until finally the repeated wailing of a train in the distance penetrated my consciousness and took my mind in another direction. To another spring evening when Coop and I were both 12 and he got that zigzag scar on his finger. We'd gone to the park after dinner and time got away from us. It was almost dark and we were supposed to be home before the street lights came on.

"C'mon, hurry up. I'm gonna get grounded if I'm late again," he said as I stopped to tie my shoe. I was wearing a cool pair of Adidas that my mother had picked up for half-price. The only flaw was that they were almost a full size too big. I tried to remedy the situation by tying the laces extra tight and double-knotting them. They weren't coming off, that was for sure—though I was starting to lose circulation in my toes.

"Chill. We can go the back way, across the trestle and save 10 minutes." The trestle spanned a narrow spot on the Himmel River, just outside the park boundaries. It wasn't very high or very long—maybe 18 feet above the water and 60 yards or so across. It only took about 10 seconds to scamper across, and there was rarely any train traffic. Nonetheless, my mother had forbidden me to take the shortcut. Then again, she had forbidden me to miss curfew, too.

"OK."

We took off at a run across the park. When we were almost at the trestle, we heard the long, plaintive wail of a train whistle.

"Crap, the train's coming. We're gonna have to go the regular way," Coop said, turning to go back toward Main Street.

"No!" I grabbed his arm and pulled him back. "We won't get home in time. That train's miles away, we can make it, c'mon."

"No, I'd rather get grounded than creamed by a train."

"I'm going this way. You do what you want. I'm not getting grounded!" I said, impulsively, daring him to be as brave as me. Or as stupid.

I ran onto the trestle. I could see the train way down the track ahead, but I wasn't worried about it. What bothered me more was the simple act of crossing the narrow bridge. I'd always been a little scared of it—there were no guard rails, just open air on either side, and when you looked down, you could see the river below through the spaces between the ties. Other times, I'd kept my eyes straight ahead, looking at Coop moving confidently in front of me and just imitated his stride. This time, I was on my own.

But buoyed by the notion that I was going to best Coop at something and beat him home, with my mother none the wiser, I felt agile as a mountain goat. I moved with quick hops over the wooden ties, skipping over scattered broken glass and sharp pieces of rusty metal.

The train wailed again much louder this time, but when I looked up it was still a non-threatening distance down the track, and I had almost reached the far side. I looked over my shoulder for a second to give a victory fist pump to Coop, still watching me from the spot where I had chosen the road less traveled. I flashed a triumphant grin.

But as I turned around again and took the last step, instead of landing lightly at the edge of the bridge, I sprawled forward, my arms flung out in front of me, my cheeks scraping the rough wood of the splintered railroad ties. I could feel the vibration of the train through the track and a corresponding shudder of fear ran through me. I scrambled up but only got as far as one knee.

My left foot was caught and refused to break free. My foot in its too-big shoe was firmly wedged between two railroad ties. I reached back and grabbed my ankle with both hands and gave a tremendous yank. My foot, and the shoe, stayed put. I dimly heard Coop yell, "Leah, Leah, the train!"

I looked up. The engine that had been so far from me was coming at warp speed. My fingers fumbled as I frantically tried to untie my knotted laces. Tears streamed down my face.

"Leah!" Coop was beside me. I felt the trestle shake as the train rumbled closer.

"Get out of here!" I shouted above the din of the train's whistle.

He shoved my hands out of the way and sawed at the laces of my shoe with a piece of rusty metal.

"Hurry, hurry, hurry, hurry!" I repeated in a frantic mantra, though he couldn't hear me. I put my hands to my ears to shut out the sound and squeezed my eyes tight against the terror, but my entire body was filled with the noise and throbbing of the oncoming engine. I couldn't tell where the pounding of my heart ended and the shaking of the trestle began.

"I'm sorry, Coop, I'm sorry, I'm sorry."

He kept sawing, then gave a fierce tug and the lace broke. My shoe loosened, and with a tremendous yank, I pulled my foot free. At the same moment, I felt a hard shove in my chest. Then I was floating in open space. A half-second later the hot breath of the diesel engine as it roared past hit me with the force of a blow, and I fell.

When I hit the water, it was with body jolting force. I plunged to the bottom of the muddy Himmel. I came up coughing, sputtering, and missing a shoe but otherwise fine. Wiping my eyes, I saw Coop clambering up the bank. I swam the few yards to join him. He was shivering and his finger was bleeding pretty badly.

"You all right?"

"You are such a dickhead," he said.

I had to agree.

What with the police coming, and half the gawkers in town converging on us, and stitches, and tetanus shots, and a chewing out from Officer Darmody, who was first on the scene, any hope of keeping our parents from finding out died.

Coop was grounded—though he was featured as a hero in the *Himmel Times*. I was under house arrest for a month with my Aunt Nancy keeping watch over me and Lacey, because as my mother said, "I can no longer trust your judgment, Leah Marie."

Coop had my back then, like he always did. And now, just because he didn't agree with me about Lacey's death, it didn't mean he wasn't on my side. Maybe it meant he was right. To be honest, this wouldn't be the first time I crossed the line from reasonable doubt to unstoppable obsession. I just can't give up when something doesn't make sense. That's what makes me a good reporter. It's also what lands me in trouble more than I like.

But this time I wasn't pursuing a story, trying to get an exclusive. This time it was about my little sister and what happened to her and why. The anger and resentment I'd felt toward her for so long was gone. Coop was wrong.

It wasn't guilt that was driving me, though I had that in spades. It was a burning need to resurrect Lacey the way she had been, and perhaps, underneath all the rage and rebellion, the way she'd remained. I wanted to see her again, I wanted my mother to see her again, the way she really was. And

I wanted whoever took that away from her, and took her away from us, to pay.

10

When I got home, my mother was loading the dishwasher.

"How was your run?" I asked. She tried to get in a couple of miles after work most days, and she was still wearing her running gear.

"I was on my way out the door, but I wound up not going. The blood drive called their list of O negative donors and asked us to come in because they didn't meet their quota or something. Ellie Schreiber was donating right next to me."

"Yeah?"

"She seemed really worried, Leah."

"About Alex?"

"No, no, he's fine. She's concerned about Max. She said he's worrying himself sick trying to keep the paper going."

"Yeah, I know. It's rough on him." I knew where this was heading and tried to distract her. "Too bad you had to miss your run. Your time has really improved. Of course, you'd probably pick up an extra 10 minutes if you dumped that lanyard you wear. It kind of makes you look like a preppie coach from 1980."

She lifted it off the little nail by the kitchen door and waved it in front of me, then pointed with her finger ticking off the items.

"I refuse to be shamed for being prepared. My front door key, my car key, my mini Swiss Army knife. I can get into my house, start my car, open a wine bottle, tighten a screw, defend myself or file my nails. Quit trying to distract me," she said, hanging it back up and walking over to lean on the bar where I had pulled up a stool.

"Ellie said Max got a call from Sister Julianna. She was concerned that the paper was questioning the school's role in Lacey's death."

"Yeah? Well, that's not what happened today. Ellie should mind her own business."

"I think she thinks it is her business. She's anxious. She's afraid you're making things harder for Max. She's worried about his health, too. Max is under a lot of stress. His father died of a heart attack at exactly his age. Did you know that?"

"Oh, come on. Ellie's trying to play the health card? And if she's really concerned, maybe she should make him cut down on his double burger baskets. Max will outlive all of us. And I'm just as concerned about Lacey as she is about Max. I found out some things today, and they're not very good." I struggled with how to tell her what I knew and what I suspected it meant. There wasn't any easy way to say it.

"What sort of things?"

I explained my questions about the missing money, and told her what Sister Julianna and Father Hegl had said about Cole and the drugs. I didn't say anything about the phone. I wasn't ready to face the look in her eyes if she knew I could've helped Lacey that night and hadn't.

"Leah, everything is so black and white with you, isn't it? First, Lacey is a monster child you can't wait to drop off at DeMoss. Now, she's an inno-cent scapegoat? You know how much I loved Lacey, but I've had to face the fact that it wasn't enough. Don't forget, there was hydrocodone in her purse. She was drunk the night she fell. I've known since her body was found that she must have been using again."

"I'm not saying she was innocent. I'm saying something happened to her, something really terrible, and we didn't see it. So, there was no way we could help her." I searched for a way to soften the blow, to keep her from feeling the sharp, searing guilt I'd felt when Cole told me. But there wasn't any way to make it less awful to hear than it was.

"What are you talking about?"

I dropped the bombshell and told her what Cole had said. She pulled out a stool and sank onto it.

"I don't believe it. I would have known. I couldn't not know something like that."

I put my hand on her arm. "I'm sorry, Mom."

She shook it off. Her expression had gone from stunned to angry. "It isn't true. It is not true."

"I think it is, Mom."

"No. Stop talking like that."

"I thought you wanted to know what really happened to Lacey."

"I know what happened to Lacey, and you do too. She wasn't sexually abused. She would have told me."

"Mom, you have to see it makes sense."

"No. It doesn't. This isn't some front page story you're trying to get. This is real. This is our family, and you are wrong. I won't listen, do you understand?" She stood up without another word and left the kitchen. In a second, I heard the door to her room close with a violent thud.

Well. That's what you call a first-rate day. A sleazeball drug dealer informs me my sister was sexually abused and hints she was maybe murdered, my best friend thinks I'm an obsessed conspiracy nut, and my mother is so angry, she can't stay in the same room with me.

The next morning, when I wandered into the kitchen, I found a note. "I bought you some Pop Tarts yesterday. Coffee is made. LOL." Which my mother persisted in thinking meant "lots of love" instead of "laugh out loud."

I tried to respond in kind. Food is the way we apologize, celebrate, comfort, and commiserate. Nothing says Nash family love like a heaping helping of something to eat. I took off early from work that day and hurried home to make the one thing I have in my cooking repertoire. Coincidentally, it happens to be my mother's favorite meal: Grandma Neeka's meatloaf and twice-baked potatoes. Her car pulled in the driveway just as I pulled the meatloaf out of the oven.

The kitchen was still pretty much a disaster. I'm not sure how it happens, but whenever I cook, things turn chaotic. Every cupboard door was open, there were pans on the stove, spills on the counter, measuring spoons and aluminum foil on the stove, and pans soaking in the sink. But I hoped the tantalizing scents of dinner would blind her to the post-Katrina conditions in her kitchen.

"It smells great," she said, walking through the door. "What are you doing home already? And cooking?"

"I have a ton of comp time, and I was just hungry for some meat loaf." I moved around the kitchen shutting doors and sweeping errant utensils and cups into the sink.

"That's nice."

"How was work?"

"Busy. Karen's in the middle of a complicated probate case, and our secretary quit with no notice." My mother was a paralegal for a one-woman law practice, and her boss, Karen McDaid, was also her closest friend.

"Mom, about what I said last night—"

She interrupted me before I could finish. "No. Stop. I shouldn't have just walked out on you. We should have talked." She put her purse on the bar and cleared a space in the sink so she could wash her hands. Looking over her shoulder as she lathered up, she continued.

"Leah, I was in therapy for a year trying to figure out how I could make such a mess of two great kids. I finally got to a place where I could forgive myself for not being a perfect—or even a very good—mother. When you hit me with the idea that Lacey had been sexually abused, and I was too dense to see it, I—well, it took my breath away. I wasn't angry at you, not really, but it was just so hard to hear."

She wiped her hands and walked over to where I was standing. "I've been thinking all day, and I don't want to believe you're right. But I do want to know the truth. And there's a little part of me that says maybe, maybe. Lacey's behavior was so different, so self-destructive. There has to be a reason. Doesn't there?"

"I think so."

She helped me set the table and get the food on. When we were seated, she asked me, "What does Coop say about what you're thinking?"

"He thinks I'm crazy, like you do, and there's no point anyway, because Lacey is dead. And even if I found evidence, they wouldn't prosecute, and what can I expect to find after all these years, and don't be so stupid."

"Don't exaggerate. I didn't say you were crazy, and I'm sure Coop didn't either. Isn't he right, though? After all this time, what can you hope to find? And even if you do turn up something that supports Cole's story, they won't prosecute with Lacey gone."

"That's true." I paused a beat, then said, "Mom, there are so many off-kilter things about Lacey's death. It really bothers me. The missing money, her phone with no contacts or anything else on it, the convenient story her roommate suddenly came up with, everything Cole said. Sister Mattea's note with the newspaper clipping. Something is seriously not right with this whole thing."

"It seems like you're taking it for granted that what Cole said is true. Why do you believe him?"

"Because there's no advantage to him in making up that story. In fact, it puts him in line for more trouble if it's true. I know he's a liar. I just think this time he's telling the truth. I'm going to find out one way or another."

"How?"

"I'm going to start at the beginning. Eight years ago, when things started to go to hell. The summer she was 14."

"But who are you going to talk to? You can't think anyone we know, any of our friends could have molested Lacey."

"Most abusers are someone the victim knows, not some guy in a van with candy." I was already running and rejecting possibilities in my head, but the next words I spoke I hadn't intended to say out loud.

"What about Paul Karr?"

She looked stunned. I tried to backpedal. I didn't really think it was Paul —at least I had no reason to think he was more likely than any of the other men Lacey was around a lot.

"I'm not saying he did anything. I'm just thinking of adults she knew who had the opportunity."

"Not Paul."

I understood her reaction. I liked Paul too, though probably not nearly as much as she did.

"Nobody can be off-limits. Not even people we like a whole lot. The police didn't even try to find the pieces the first time around. I'm going to pick up every last one of them, and see what kind of picture I get." I leaned across the table and covered her hand with mine. I'd taken the conversation this far, I might as well go the whole way.

"Remember what Cole said? That whoever 'messed' with Lacey might be the one who really knows what happened the night she died? I don't think Lacey's death was an accident, Mom. You're right. The DA will never do anything about an eight-year-old sexual abuse case with a dead victim. But if I find enough evidence, he'll have to reopen it. This time as a murder investigation."

The word "murder" hung oddly in the air in our bright white and navy kitchen with the cheery yellow accents—as out of place as *The Scream* hanging on a wall of kindergarten drawings. But there it was.

Then the doorbell rang.

11

"It's Paul!"

We both jumped like guilty things surprised. Mom opened the front door just as Paul hit the buzzer again. He grabbed her hand and started an impromptu swing dance to the opening strains of *In the Mood*. I'm not much of a one for spontaneous dancing, and the sight of two late-middle-aged people engaging would be disconcerting under normal circumstances. In the current situation, it was all kinds of wrong. Paul caught my eye mid-twirl and his grin faded. He stopped, then looked at my mother and raised an eyebrow.

"Carol? What's going on?"

"Nothing," she said with an attempt at a smile that didn't get beyond a grim baring of her teeth. He looked back and forth between us, puzzled.

"What's going on?" he repeated.

"Come on in, Paul," I said.

He sat on the couch, then leaned forward with his long-fingered hands clasped in front of him. His sandy-colored eyebrows were drawn together in a frown that looked odd on his normally cheerful face.

"Carol?" he asked again.

"Paul, would you like a drink?"

"Do I need one?"

"I do," she said. I waited while she made two strong bourbons on the rocks and handed him one.

"Paul, you know that one of the nuns from DeMoss died last week."

"Sure, yes. Everyone knows. Someone's head should roll for not putting a barricade up at the Point. Never should have happened. Was she a friend of yours, Leah?"

"I knew her. The thing is, Paul, she left a message for me a few days before she died. A message about Lacey."

"Lacey?" His dark brown eyes registered curiosity but nothing more that I could see.

"Yes. I think she was trying to tell me that Lacey's death wasn't an accident." I explained about the clipping and some of the inconsistencies in the police report. "I've found out a few more things, too."

"I don't understand."

My mother, who had been tapping her foot up and down and fidgeting in her chair, could contain herself no longer. "Oh, for God's sake, Leah, just say it." Then she proceeded to say it for me. "Leah thinks Lacey was sexually abused, and that's why she started getting into so much trouble. And she thinks Lacey was killed by her abuser, because she was going to identify him."

If it weren't so serious, it would have been funny to watch the slow motion changes on his round open face as the words sunk in. His jaw dropped, and his eyebrows lifted on his high forehead. "You can't be serious! The police investigated—twice!"

"They did a bad job. I should have seen it at the time." I gave my increasingly familiar summary of what I believed had happened.

"If your friend the nun knew about this, why didn't she just tell you?"

"I don't know what she knew, Paul. Maybe she just had a suspicion, maybe she remembered something, maybe someone told her something. But she died before she could tell me."

"So now Leah is planning to investigate it herself," my mother said, in the same tone she might have used announcing that I was planning to become a pole dancer.

"How?"

"By talking to people. Somebody could be holding on to a piece of information they don't even know they have, or that they don't understand the significance of."

He shook his head, ran his hand through his curly hair and then turned to my mother.

"But if she were abused, wouldn't she have told you, Carol? Surely Lacey would have said something?"

"I don't know. Maybe not. Maybe she didn't feel like she could come to me. I don't know."

"That's ridiculous. Of course she'd come to you. You were her mother."

"Kids don't always find it easy to talk to their parents. Sometimes they confide in other adults they trust," I said. Now things were going to get really awkward. I mean, there's no easy way to question your mother's beau about your sister's sexual abuse. It wasn't that Paul topped my list of suspects by any means, but despite my mother's understandable distress, I had to start somewhere. I had to ask.

"Lacey didn't say anything to you, did she, Paul? She worked with you in your yard a lot that summer you put in your rose gardens. You spent a lot of time with her."

"Yes, but we didn't have that kind of relationship. She'd never confide something like that to me."

"She never said anything about a teacher at school, or a friend's father or anything that seemed maybe just a little odd, something out of the ordinary?"

"No, never."

"What about after she went to DeMoss? Did you ever see her? You used to volunteer with the mentor program there. Did you ever run into her? Did she seem any different?"

"No. I never saw her."

"That last night, the night of the fundraiser. You told the police you left early with Miller Caldwell, because he had a toothache. You went to your office. Did you go by the main drive? It would have been shorter to take Baylor Road."

"Miller drove. He took us down the main drive. It was a toothache, not life and death. We didn't need to save three minutes going the back way. Why?" His voice sounded puzzled.

"You didn't see anything, any parked cars where they shouldn't be, any students walking toward the park trail?"

"No."

"What time did you leave?"

"I don't know, maybe 6:30, 6:45."

"So, did you go back when you were through with Miller?"

"I didn't. Miller did. His tooth was fine. Sometimes that happens, just a sudden jolt, but there's really nothing wrong. Those fancy dinners were Marilyn's thing, not mine. Once I escaped, I stayed at the office and did some work. Marilyn wasn't happy."

"How did you get home?"

"My car was at the office. But when I went to leave, it wouldn't start. I wound up walking five miles home. She was just pulling in when I got there, and she couldn't have been happier to see me coatless and freezing. I damn near caught pneumonia. Why does it matter?"

And here we go. Paul is not a stupid man, and he clearly got the implications of my questions. He was mad. I couldn't blame him. But, as is my gift and my curse, I pressed on.

"What time did you get home?"

"I don't know, somewhere around 11:30, I think." His voice had hardened. "What is this, Leah? Do you seriously think I sexually abused Lacey? That I would ever do anything to harm your sister? What's the matter with you?"

"I don't think anything, Paul, I'm just trying to gather as much information as I can. You're not the only person I'm going to talk to."

He had placed his drink on the table and was standing. I stood too.

"Strangely enough, it doesn't comfort me to know that I'm only one possibility on your list of suspects. I did not molest your sister. I did not kill her to protect my dirty little secret. For the record, I don't believe anyone did. I think you're chasing after a bad guy who doesn't exist. But you should be careful. Because if it turns out to be true and you ask the wrong person the right questions, you could find yourself in a very bad situation. Carol, I'll call you later."

Then he turned and walked out without another word.

I was afraid to look at my mother.

"Could that have gone any worse? You really hurt Paul. Do you intend to interrogate every adult male who knew Lacey that summer? Miller Caldwell? Father Hegl? Max? Dr. Steffenhagen? Don't let the fact he's been in a wheelchair for 15 years stop you."

"I won't."

"You can't randomly accuse people we know, people who have been our friends for years, people who would never—"

"I didn't accuse Paul. Why don't you ask yourself why he was so uptight?"

"Why wouldn't he be? He comes to what he thinks is a friend's house and instead he walks into the lion's den. He is not going to forget this. Neither is anyone else you talk to. This is going to hurt people, change lives. Our lives, if you go ahead."

"Mom, our lives are already changed. They've been different for the last five years. The only way I know how to go ahead is to go forward with this. I have to know."

We both sat quiet for a minute, then I said, "What did you mean just then when you asked was I going to talk to Father Hegl? Why him? "

"Because he was Lacey's director on *The Wizard of Oz*, that summer she turned 14."

"He never said that he knew Lacey before she went to DeMoss."

"Well, he did. The first year he was here they asked him to step in when the regular director got sick. It was just after he arrived at DeMoss. He probably forgot."

"Hmm." I was following another train of thought. "Remember how Lacey was babysitting for the Caldwells all the time that summer? She was either at rehearsal or at their house. Saving money for her Spanish Club trip to Spain. And then, boom, she stopped. No reason, just didn't want to anymore."

She sighed and stood up, taking her glass to the kitchen and putting it in the sink before she said, "Could you please stop, just for tonight? You do realize that you waltzed in here this evening and told me that my youngest daughter wasn't only sexually abused, she was possibly murdered. And, oh yes, maybe by a man I really like. Someone who's been a friend for 30 years.

Or by one of our other friends. Once you get an idea nothing else matters. You're ready to mow down everyone with a machete to prove you're right."

"Mom, I—"

"I really can't talk about this anymore tonight. I'm going to bed."

"I'm sorry. Really. I just don't know how else to do this."

She nodded, then turned and walked down the hall. It wasn't until after I heard her turn off her light that I remembered something she'd said earlier. "I was in therapy for a year trying to figure out how I could make such a mess of two great kids."

Make a mess of two great kids—what did she mean by that? I wasn't a mess. Was I?

12

The interview with Paul had turned really ugly, really fast. And my mother and I were at odds again. Was I obsessing instead of investigating? I wandered around picking up the glasses, loading the dishwasher, and wondering if I'd have any friends—or a mother—left by the time I was done. I looked at the clock. 11:15.

On impulse, I grabbed my wallet and keys and headed out the door. In a few minutes, I was pulling up in front of a small brown brick bungalow. Through the curtains I could see the gleam of lamplight in the living room. I knocked on the arched wooden front door. I heard footsteps coming and the door swung in, revealing a short little man with fluffy white hair and a surprised but welcoming expression on his face.

"Leah! How nice. Come in, come in."

"Hi, Father Lindstrom. I'm sorry it's kind of late, but I know you're a night owl."

"Yes, yes I still am. In fact, I'm just having a cup of tea," he said. "Can I interest you in one?"

"Sure, that would be great."

Father Gregory Lindstrom was the parish priest during most of Lacey's troubled years. He's been a good friend to our family. I really like him, even though I haven't been a practicing Catholic since I was 12.

He led me into the kitchen, and as he fussed around putting the kettle on to boil I asked, "How's retirement? Everything you hoped for?"

He half turned as he set the gas flame to the right height and gave me a rueful smile.

"I'm afraid I've found that my expectations and the reality are quite different. When I was serving as a parish priest, I was anxious for the time when I could spend my days fly fishing, researching, reading and thanking God for the privilege. But after a few months, I found myself praying to Him for some real work to do.

"It seems I value leisure only when it's measured out in small doses. So, when the bishop called and asked me to return to St. Stephen's while Father Sanderson is undergoing cancer treatments, I was only too happy."

The kettle whistled, and he prepared the tea, handing mine to me in a cup bearing the image of Mr. Spock. As he sat down at the table with his own mug, I saw it bore the phrase *The Truth Is Out There*. He noticed my glance. "Father Sanderson is a diehard *Star Trek* fan. I've always been an *X-Files* man myself."

We sipped for a few minutes in companionable silence, and then Father Lindstrom spoke. "Leah, I'm delighted to see you, of course. But a visit at this hour is unusual. Is there something on your mind?"

I was finding it unexpectedly hard to get started. I began by dancing around the topic.

"Did you know Sister Mattea Riordan, the nun who died recently?"

"I had spoken to her once or twice but, no, I can't say that I knew her. Was she a friend of yours?"

"More of an acquaintance. It's quite an operation they have out there. The Catherines. DeMoss, I mean. Why do they wear those old-fashioned habits, do you think? Most of the nuns I know—well, actually I only know two other nuns—but both of them dress pretty regular, you know, pants and blouses and things."

He gave me a look that said he knew the clothing preferences of religious orders had nothing to do with what was on my mind, but he gave my inane question the same thoughtful attention he gave to every conversation.

"There are quite a few orders that either never gave up or have returned to traditional habits. It's a form of identification as a community, and it signifies a new way of life, like taking a new name when you take your vows, as I believe the Catherines do. A habit is a sign of commitment and perhaps a sort of protection."

"Protection? From what?"

"We all wear habits, Leah, physical or emotional, as a way to protect our secret selves. I have a habit of dispassionate observation to preserve the illusion that my soul is untouched by the messier pangs of human emotion." He paused and took a sip of his tea.

"You have a habit of cynical wit to mask the pain of a loss-filled life. The physical habits the Catherines wear may be important to them as a way to help protect their integrity as a community of faith. But they are far less interesting and certainly far less dangerous than the emotional habits we all use to cover ourselves. Don't you agree?"

And, we're done. A look-see at my psyche was definitely not where I wanted to go then. Or ever. But Father Lindstrom's incisive observation did have the benefit of plunging me right into the subject I'd come to discuss.

I set down my cup and opened the floodgates, telling him everything that had happened since Sister Mattea's body was found. He didn't say anything, just let me unload my suspicions, my guilt and my theories.

"So, everyone thinks I'm overreacting. Mom is really mad, because I questioned Paul Karr tonight, and Ellie thinks I'm going to give Max a heart attack, or make him lose the paper, or both, and Coop just thinks I'm on the wrong track and too stubborn to admit it. And what if I am? What if all of them are right, and I'm all wrong?" I wound down. I half-expected him to tell me something about letting go and forgiving myself and letting God take care of things and blah, blah, blah. But I should have known better.

"What about you, Leah? What does your experience, your instinct, your heart tell you?" He had taken off his black plastic rimmed glasses and was carefully polishing the lenses.

"That Lacey's death wasn't an accident. That she was crying for help for years but I didn't hear her. That now I do, I can't ignore it. I have to find the truth. I have to know the answers."

"Well, then. Does it really matter what others are telling you? Keep your heart with all vigilance, for from it flows the springs of life."

"You know I'm not much into the Bible stuff. That is the Bible, right?"

"Yes. Proverbs 4:23. Follow your heart, Leah, but be careful. It can lead you toward the darkness as well as toward the light." His eyes behind his thick lenses were steady and serious.

A little shiver ran through me and a sudden suspicion arose. "You know something, don't you, Father?"

He shook his head. "About Lacey's death? No."

"What then?"

He took a last sip from his mug of tea. "Finding the truth isn't always the same as finding the answers, Leah. It requires great discernment to know which is most important."

"I don't understand."

"When you need to understand, you will." He stifled a small yawn, and though I was far from satisfied with his answer, I felt guilty when I looked at my watch and saw it was nearly 12:30.

"I'm sorry for keeping you up, Father. I'd better get going. Thanks for, well, thanks for being here."

"My door is always open, Leah."

Finding the truth about Lacey was always on my mind, but work that week didn't give me much chance to do anything about it. In addition to the regular paper, we were putting out a special section: *Summer Fun in Grant-land County,* allegedly a celebration of the wonders of Wisconsin—our piece of it, anyway. In reality, it was an attempt to generate additional ad revenue. Max and the sales guys had been beating the bushes for business from the local pontoon factory, the festival and fair committees, restaurants, canoe rentals, and any other business remotely linked to summer activities.

That meant writing a ton of puff pieces designed to please the advertisers who purchased space in the section. It went against every journalistic bone in my body—and it used to Max's, too. It was a sign of how desperate he was for revenue. Other times I might have mouthed off, but things were not that great between us at the moment, so I shut up, hunkered down, and cranked out the copy.

On Saturday morning, I was at the office writing a piece describing the joys of kayaking down the Himmel River, with quotes from expert kayaker Punk Onstott. Punk, not coincidentally, was the owner of Onstott Hardware & Sporting Goods selling a full range of quality kayaks and accessories. I paused for a minute and leaned back in my chair for a good stretch, then jumped when I saw a figure looming in the doorway. "You scared me! What are you doing here, Miguel?"

He looked perfect, even on a weekend morning, wearing dark wash skinny jeans, a navy striped shirt, a close-fitting gray vest and a pair of Converse sneakers. He sat down on the corner of my desk.

"I could ask you the same, *chica*. If I knew you were here, I would've brought you a chai latte. Of course, if you showed up to meet me and Coop at the Elite, like you were supposed to, you could've got your own."

"Oh, I'm sorry, I forgot! I just—"

"Hey, I'm cool. Coop's the one who was not so happy. What's with you two?"

"He thinks I should leave Lacey's death alone. That I'm not being objective, I have too much guilt to see things clearly."

"Well, do you?"

I shook my head. "Of course, I feel guilty. I am guilty. I did about a thousand and one things wrong, and if I hadn't maybe Lacey would be alive. But that doesn't mean that everything I've found out doesn't count."

"*Dígame*. And don't leave anything out."

I'd done my best to avoid Miguel since my meeting with Cole. I didn't want Max getting mad at him for getting caught up in my Lacey drama. I should have known that wouldn't work for long. I told him my current working theory. Miguel was a much more receptive audience than anyone else had been to date.

"So, if I accept that Cole is telling the truth, which at the moment I do, then I have to find out who abused Lacey, because there's a damn good chance that he had something to do with her death. So far I've talked to Paul Karr—"

"Your *mamá's* boyfriend?" His eyes widened.

"He's not her boyfriend."

"No?"

"Well, she's a little old for a 'boyfriend,' don't you think?"

He laughed. "*Chica*, just because you got no social, don't try to step all over your *mamá's*. She's a pretty lady. She should have some fun. So should you, but you, you are so *obstinada*! But I'm not giving up."

"Yeah, well, whatever. I want her to have fun. And I know that Paul's always seemed like a good guy, but..."

"So why did you accuse *mamá's* boyfriend?"

"You sound like my mother," I snapped. "I didn't accuse him. I just asked some questions; that's what reporters do. Don't you want to be one of those when you grow up?"

He looked surprised. And hurt.

"I'm sorry. That was nasty. I should be snapping at myself. I'm so frustrated. I feel like I'm going nowhere. Maybe I'm too close to this. Maybe I shouldn't do it."

"*Chica*! Don't talk crazy. You have to try. You always have to try for your family."

I knew he understood in a way that Coop couldn't. When he was 16, Miguel's older cousin was collateral damage in a robbery gone wrong in Milwaukee. Miguel was a witness, and got a beatdown to keep him from testifying, but he did it anyway. Afterward, his mother sent him to Himmel to live with his Aunt Lydia and Uncle Craig.

"You can do it. I can help you. I'm a professional reporter, *mi querida*. It says so right here on my notebook." He held up the narrow flip-top pad most journalists use to take notes. The brand we used at the *Times* had the words *Professional Reporter's Notebook* on the front cover. I laughed.

"You're right, Jimmy Olsen, it does."

"So, who do you think besides Paul Karr?"

"Miller Caldwell."

"The bank guy? The one who's running for senator? You think he abused Lacey?"

"He could have. He had plenty of opportunity. Lacey took care of the Caldwell kids all the time. She even went on trips with them once in a while."

He still looked skeptical.

"But Miller Caldwell—he gives big money, I'm talking serious *dinero*, to that foundation for abused kids."

"I know. He's also on the board at DeMoss Academy. But think about it. Maybe he protests too much. Maybe he does so much good to make up for doing so much bad."

"I don't know, *chica*, I think—"

"Look, I'm not saying he's the one. But you asked. Then there's Father Hegl."

"The priest at DeMoss? Why?"

"He knew Lacey before she went there, and he never said a word to me. He had plenty of opportunities to be alone with her when he was directing *The Wizard of Oz*. And he's a charmer if you like the type. He'd be able to manipulate a teenage girl, and smart enough to figure out what would keep her quiet after."

"OK, well, let me help. I'll take the *padre*, see what I can find out about his back story."

"No, seriously, I can't let you do that. I'm likely to make a lot of people mad, including Max, and I don't want you tangled up in that."

"Too late, *chica*. I already wrote it down in my notebook. Now, it's official. I gotta follow the lead."

I hadn't talked to Marilyn Karr since Lacey's funeral, and then it had been a stilted thank-you-for-coming conversation. She had looked very *Vogue* in a black dress, her carefully highlighted auburn hair pulled back in a French twist, her expert make-up unmarred by tears of sympathy. She didn't reach out to hug me the way most people did, just held out her hand for me to take, then withdrew it and gave me a slight nod.

I had never gotten over the habit of calling her Mrs. Karr, and around her I always felt as though I should be apologizing in advance for social errors she could see in my future.

But for this conversation we needed to be on equal footing. I wanted to check Paul's story. If his car really wasn't working, and Marilyn really did get home around 11:30 just as he was getting there too, that would mean he hadn't been back at the Catherines' running into Lacey after Cole dumped her. I practiced calling her Marilyn in my head until the name came easily before I punched in her number.

"Marilyn? Hi. It's Leah, Leah Nash."

"Leah?" she sounded surprised as well she might. The last time I had called her was never.

"Yes. Hey, I'm sorry to bother you on a Saturday afternoon, but do you have just a minute to talk?"

"I am rather busy—"

"This will just take a minute."

"Well," she hesitated, but curiosity got the better of her. "Yes, I suppose so, Leah."

"Great." A brief but awkward silence fell as I tried to summon up the appropriate tone for the questions I was going to ask.

"Great," I repeated.

"Yes," she said with some impatience. "I really would appreciate it if you got to the point?"

"Right. Sorry. Marilyn, do you remember the night of the DeMoss fundraising dinner, the night my sister Lacey disappeared?"

"Your sister? Leah, I don't understand—"

"You do remember that she disappeared the night of the dinner, right?"

"Yes, yes, I suppose so. It's been so long—"

"You were at the dinner with Paul, and he left early with Miller Caldwell."

"Yes," she said, obviously puzzled. "What has that got to do with anything?"

"Was Paul just getting home when you got back from the dinner around 11:30? Was he walking because he had car trouble?"

She didn't answer immediately, and in the pause that followed I heard what sounded like wine glugging into a glass and then a long swallow. Possibly Marilyn enjoyed a late afternoon cocktail hour. "Why don't you ask your mother about Paul's whereabouts that night?"

"My mother?"

Another swallowing sound. "I know Carol Nash is seeing Paul. Probably was seeing him for years before our divorce."

"That's not true. My mother wouldn't do that."

"Oh really? Well, all I know is Paul left me at the dinner with some ridiculous excuse about taking care of Miller's tooth. And he never came back. It was humiliating. I'd like to forget everything about that night. I wasn't even seated at the bishop's table. Sister Julianna was. And Reid Palmer was. But not me. No, not the person who served as fundraising chair for three years. No. I was seated next to Sister Margaret and one of the DeMoss scholarship winners. It was unbelievable!"

She said it as though she'd been relegated to sit in the fireplace ashes next to Cinderella. I tried to get her back on track with Paul's movements that night, but she was determined to air her grievances.

"You must have been glad when the night ended. When you got home—"

"It was an interminable evening. Sister Margaret could not stop bleating about her mundane duties, and that scholarship child talked of nothing but her pathetic 'future.' And then Reid deliberately undermined me.

"He said he 'forgot' the large-scale drawing of the new rec center I wanted to use in my after-dinner speech. He said he'd go to the administration building to get it right away, but he didn't come back until my speech was over. In fact it was after eleven and the dinner was over before he showed back up. Everyone was leaving.

"Oh, he was *so* apologetic, said he had trouble locating it. He poured on that phony Southern charm. But I wasn't fooled. I was a threat to his dictatorship on the board, so he ruined the recognition I should have gotten that night.

"I resigned the next morning. And I take great pleasure in knowing they still haven't raised the funds to complete that center."

"I'm glad you found the silver lining. I'm sorry the evening was so disappointing."

"I never think about it. I've moved on." Another long swallow.

"I don't want to keep you, Marilyn, but I did just want to clarify that after the dinner, Paul arrived home about the same time you did, around 11:30."

"He wasn't home when I got there. I have no idea when he got in, but his car was in the driveway when I got up the next morning. I don't have any more time for this now. Or ever. If I were you, I'd ask your mother where she was that night. Goodbye, Leah."

And we're done. Or at least Marilyn was.

Paul's tone was frosty when I called to check Marilyn's version of the story.

"I'm sorry to bother you, Paul. I just had a conversation with your wife—your ex-wife—that has me confused."

"I think you're confused about a lot of things, Leah."

"Marilyn said you weren't there when she got home, and she didn't see you again until the morning. And your car was in the driveway when she got up."

"Of course it was. I called the garage, and they jumped it and drove it back for me."

"You didn't say that before."

"You seem to be under the impression that I owe you some kind of minute-by-minute accounting of my life. I don't. Marilyn is either misremembering—an unfortunate side effect of her drinking—or she's lying."

"Why would she do that?"

"She enjoys wreaking havoc. Maybe she has that in common with you."

"Paul, I know this is awk—"

"It's more than awkward Leah, it's insulting. Don't call again."

13

When I got home, I didn't bother to tell my mother what I'd been up to, and she didn't ask. We had been tiptoeing around each other for days, neither wanting to get into it again. So, she pretended that I had heeded her advice and dropped things, and I pretended that she had decided to let me do what I had to do. We Nashes are skilled in the art of denial.

However, as soon as I walked in, she pounced on me with a box of groceries and some old clothes and said, "Good! You're home. Could you deliver these to Vesta Brenneman? I have to go back to the office. Karen's out of town and needs some information from the files ASAP."

"What is it?"

"Just some summer clothes from St. Vinnie's and a few groceries and treats."

"You know Vesta hates it when people go to her house. The last time I delivered something, she threw crabapples at me. She's crazy."

"What are you, 12? She's not crazy. And you're not kind. She's old and she's eccentric. It's not a crime."

"Eccentric? Mom, she stares right through you when you talk to you, or she starts shouting Bible verses. She rides around on her bicycle all day, scares little kids—and some big ones, too. She looks—and smells like—she hasn't taken a bath in months. Is it really 'kind' to let her fend for herself? Maybe she needs social services help, not random charity."

"She's living as she wants to. What's wrong with that? And if we can help her do it with just a little effort, shame on us if we don't. If you go now, she won't be home. She'll still be out riding. You can leave the things by her door."

"OK, OK. I'll fill in for you, Mother Teresa, but remember, I'm just the understudy. Don't plan on me taking over your starring role. Give me the stupid box."

She grinned because she got her way. She usually does. "Kid, you're walking out there an understudy, but you're coming back a saint!"

I laughed because I have the same stupid sense of humor she does, and because it felt nice not to be quietly tense with each other as we had been for the past week or so.

She handed me the box, gave me a shove, and sent me out the door.

Vesta lives in the only house on the last block of Birch Street before the metropolis of Himmel gives way to country roads. It's not much of a street, cracked asphalt instead of concrete, and there isn't a birch tree in sight, just a few scraggly box elders. My heart sank as I turned in her driveway and saw her faded red Schwinn leaning next to the front door. She was out on the front step before I got the box off the back seat, her little mixed-breed terrier tagging at her heels.

She wore a shabby gray cardigan over a flowered print house dress of the kind someone's grandma might wear on *The Waltons*. Underneath was a pair of tan men's work pants rolled up to her ankles, and on her feet were black high top tennis shoes with no laces. Her stringy gray hair was pulled back in a long ponytail, but wisps trailed across cheeks that were as brown and wrinkled as old ginger root. She stared at me, arms folded across her bony chest.

"Hey, Vesta. Remember me? I'm Leah Nash. Carol's daughter. Just dropping off a few things Mom was hoping you could take off her hands."

"You got any tin foil?"

"Why, yes, yes I do. As luck would have it, here's a nice roll of it."

Her eyes lit up the way mine would if you offered me a box of chocolates. She came down off the step and rooted around in the box. I struggled to balance it on my knee to give her easier access as she dug through the contents. Apparently satisfied, she said, "In there," pointing to the front door, then motioned for me to follow her. I'd never been invited in before.

It was dark and crowded inside, but relatively neat. A metal bed with springs was set in the corner, covered by a pink chenille bedspread. A wooden rocking chair was next to it and beside that was a basket full-to-overflowing with balls of aluminum foil of various sizes. A table made out of an old door and two saw horses were in the middle of the room, bowed under the weight of glass jars filled with rocks and gravel. Beside them was a large family-style Bible. Plastic bags filled with feathers lined the window ledge above her kitchen sink. She had a mini fridge and an ancient apartment-sized electric stove in the corner.

I let out a gasp when I turned to the left and saw a chest of drawers piled high with dozens of babies, then quickly recognized them as naked plastic dolls.

"My collections. You got collections?"

"No, not really."

She nodded as though it were to be expected.

"Well, can I set this here?" I nodded toward the table and she nodded back. "There, that's that then."

"Charity never faileth: but whether there be prophecies, they shall fail; whether there be tongues, they shall cease; whether there be knowledge, it shall vanish away."

"Absolutely. Well, I'd better get going. See you, Vesta."

"My Dorrie is dead."

I wasn't sure if Dorrie was a daughter or a sister or a friend—or a figment of Vesta's imagination.

"Dorrie?"

"My Dorrie," she said a trifle impatiently, as though she'd explained all this to me before. "My sister. Your sister is dead."

"Yes." I wanted to get out of that hot, musty room, away from the uncomfortable presence of this suddenly intense, more than slightly crazy lady, but my mother's words, "if we can help her with just a little effort, shame on us if we don't," inconveniently came to mind.

"I'm sorry about your sister. When did she die?"

"*You were there. In the twilight, in the evening, at the time of night and darkness.*"

"No, Vesta, I wasn't there. Do you mean you were with your sister when she died?"

"*Her feet go down to death; her steps lead straight to the grave.*"

Oh boy. Had I just encouraged her into a full-blown psychotic break?

"Vesta, are you all right? What's wrong?"

"*And I looked, and behold a pale horse: and his name that sat on him was Death, and Hell followed with him.*"

Her eyes were unfocused, and she started making little humming noises.

"Vesta!" I said as sharply as I could. She looked at me in surprise.

"Don't take my collections."

She pushed at me with unexpected strength.

"It's OK. I'm leaving. Just dropped the box off from Carol Nash," I repeated trying to reorient her in reality. "But I'm going now."

I backed out lest she bash me in the back of the head with a jar of rocks and then beat me to death with a dead doll baby. I got in my car and shoved it into reverse, while she stood on her front step and watched me. An involuntary shudder ran down my spine as I sped down the street. That was spooky.

And that was the last time I was running this particular errand for my mother. I took the corner onto River Street just a hair too fast, and the squeal of my tires reminded me I needed to get air in them. There was a gas station just a few blocks away, but within several yards of my *Fast & Furious* turn, I saw a blue light flashing in my rearview mirror.

Great. I pulled over and watched as the cop got out and came toward me. Darmody. Even greater.

I rolled down the window, and he leaned in. "Where's the fire?"

"Nowhere. My tires are just a little low, so they squealed when I rounded the corner."

"Uh-huh. I clocked you at 45 in a 25."

"Come on, Darmody. I was just doing a good deed. Took some food and stuff to Vesta."

"You want to watch it out there. She's kinda unpredictable. Where you been lately?"

"Oh, pretty busy at the paper." I tried to be pleasant in the hopes he wouldn't write me up, but I wasn't anxious to pass the time of day with Darmody.

"Yeah? I heard you and the lieutenant got into it at McClain's the other night. Sherry said that—"

"Yeah? Well Sherry doesn't know what she's talking about."

"I get it. You got a little cat fight going there, Leah?"

"Darmody, I think you need a refresher course from HR on sexual harassment. Are you going to give me a ticket or what?"

"Nah. I'll let you off with a warning. Don't use a hair dryer in the bath-tub." He then laughed so hard he started snorting and had to wipe the tears from his eyes. I shook my head.

"Thanks."

Seeing Darmody reminded me how much I missed Coop. But I wasn't ready to talk to him about Lacey again. Not until I had enough to tell him so that he couldn't blow me off.

....

To my surprise, I'd had no trouble booking an appointment with Sister Julianna when I called, though Sister Margaret warned me the director was on a tight schedule. I'd have to be there before eight o'clock, so she could make her flight to a conference. Early mornings are no problem for me, but when I arrived at 7:30 Sister Margaret wasn't at her desk, and the door to Sister Julianna's office was closed. I walked to the reception desk and called, "Hello? Sister Margaret?"

There was a thudding sound from the direction of the small room that housed the copy machine behind the reception desk. A second later a little nun came scurrying out, a guilty look on her face.

"You caught me! I was just closing the window in the copy room before Sister Julianna gets in."

"You're not allowed to open the windows? Sister Julianna runs a tight ship."

"It's not a problem during the day, of course, but when the security system is on at night, we shouldn't," she said, in a voice that sounded like a small child repeating a parent's reprimand.

Then she grinned. "But it's just a small window, and I open it just a smidge. It makes such a nice little bit of fresh air here in my corner in the morning. I just turn that zone off on the alarm system and no one is the wiser."

"Your secret is safe with me."

She sat down and wiggled around on her chair for a minute like a bird getting comfortable in its nest, then looked at me with her bright eyes. "So nice to see you again. Sister should be here in just a few minutes. Did you get a chance to talk to Father Hegl about Lacey?"

"I did, thanks. And I've talked to a few other people as well. It sounds odd, I know, but I really don't think I knew my little sister as well as I thought I did."

"Well, we all have our secret selves."

I wondered what dark depths might be hidden beneath Sister Margaret's cheery persona. "Sister, do you remember Lacey's roommate?"

"Oh, yes. Delite Wilson. She was a tough cookie, that one."

"Did she finish out at DeMoss?"

"Yes, but it was touch and go, I don't mind telling you. Sister Julianna didn't want to give up on her though, especially after she came forward and told the truth about going drinking with Lacey that night. Sister thought it showed some evidence of conscience. I wasn't convinced."

"Why was that?"

"Well, it sounds unkind to say, but I'm afraid Delite didn't have much spiritual integrity."

"You mean like faith?"

"No, not exactly. I've seen many children come and go, and the ones who make it have what I think of as spiritual integrity. You know, a core of basic decency. I pride myself on being able to spot it. Sister Julianna may be the expert, but I know what I know."

"What happened to Delite?"

"If I remember correctly, she moved to Appleton to live with a sister after she graduated. I hope I was wrong about her, but I'm usually not," she said, with more regret than complacency in her voice.

"I'd really like to talk to her. Do you think you could get me her sister's name and address?"

"Well...," She hesitated.

"Please? It's just that she was the last one to see Lacey."

"We're not supposed to give out student information, but I suppose in this case...well, it's not really student information, is it? It's just her *sister's* address." She struggled with her conscience for a second, then said, "All right dear, I'll see what I can find."

"And, I wonder, could you give me Father Hegl's phone number? He was really helpful, and I'd like to talk to him again."

"Oh, I know that one by heart. 292-5731."

The light on her phone blinked, and she picked it up. "Yes, Sister. She's here. I'll send her right in."

She saw my puzzled expression. We'd both been standing in the middle of the room, and Sister Julianna had definitely not passed us on her way to her office.

"Sister has a door with direct access to the outside in her office. There's a nice little courtyard there just off the side drive."

Sister Julianna smiled as I walked in and moved around the corner of her desk, her hand extended. I shook it and said, "Thanks for seeing me, Sister, I understand you have travel plans this morning."

"That's quite all right. I know you weren't very happy with our last conversation, Leah. I'm hoping to hear that you've found some peace of mind." She surprised me by sitting down in one of the chairs in front of her desk and motioning me to the other, instead of moving back to her power seat.

"Really? I thought that you called my boss to complain that I was harassing you."

"I did call," she said, showing no sign of embarrassment. "But not because I felt we were being harassed. I was worried about your state of mind. And I suppose when you tried to link Lacey's disappearance with Sister Mattea's death, I was a little concerned that you were trying to sensationalize things for the paper."

"Sister, if I wasn't clear before, let me be now. I'm not representing the *Times* in any capacity here. I'm asking questions as Lacey's sister, not as a reporter."

"That's what your editor said. I'm sorry if I caused you any problems there. It's just an upsetting time for everyone. Are you feeling more at ease now that you've had time to reflect on things?"

"Actually, I've got more questions now than I did before."

"Oh?"

I plunged right in.

"I think that Lacey was sexually abused before she came to DeMoss. I want to know if there's anything in her records or counseling files that would confirm that."

She flinched, but she answered calmly. "That's very serious. If we had had any knowledge of sexual abuse, it would have been reported to the police. It's both a legal and moral obligation. Are you sure about this?"

"Pretty sure. Lacey showed all the typical signs of sexual abuse in adolescence—the behavior changes, the anger, the sexual acting out, drug use. It all fits."

She relaxed a little and put her hand on my arm. "Leah, you must know those behaviors are common in troubled adolescents. Sexual abuse is far from the only cause."

"I understand that. But Lacey confided in someone at the time. Just not in me. I blame myself for that."

"And you blame DeMoss as well?"

"No. But I'm hoping DeMoss can help. Are there any case notes or a counseling file I could look at? Maybe I'd see something there that wasn't apparent to the counselor at the time, or maybe—"

She was shaking her head before I even finished. "Our counselors are professionals, trained to help children in crisis. It's highly unlikely that you'd find anything in a file that they had overlooked. In any case, we purge the records of minors five years after treatment ends. There are no counseling files to look at."

"What about talking to her counselor?"

"Our professional staff comes and goes—it's not a very well-paid job, I'm afraid. They usually leave for more lucrative practices once they get some experience. I don't believe we have anyone here now who was on staff then. And I really can't recall who Lacey's counselor was. We have over 200 students and that was almost six years ago."

"So, you're saying there's no one in the whole school who can tell me anything about what Lacey might have been thinking while she was here?"

"I'm sorry. I really am."

"I'm going to find out who sexually abused her."

"To what end, Leah? And how can you even hope to know for sure that she was abused after all these years and without her corroboration?"

"Sister, do you know who the young boy Lacey was seen with that last night might have been?" If she was startled by my abrupt shift she didn't show it.

"This is the first I've heard of a young boy. You think another student was with Lacey? I doubt that. I would have known about it at the time."

"But you didn't know about Lacey. I think there were a lot of things that none of us knew. Someone got away with sexually abusing her. I'm beginning to think they may have gotten away with killing her as well. And I have to wonder if that isn't what Sister Mattea wanted to tell me."

"You can't be serious." Her mouth had dropped slightly open in astonishment.

"Oh, but I am."

There was a light tap on the door, and Sister Margaret stepped in. "I'm so sorry to disturb you, but Sister Esther is waiting in the side drive. You'll miss your plane to the conference if you don't leave right now. Here are the reports you wanted to take. Your luggage is in the car." She thrust a brown leather briefcase into Sister Julianna's hand and gestured toward the door that led to the side drive. Uncharacteristically, Sister Julianna dithered. "Ah, Leah, just—Sister Margaret—please—"

I took the opportunity to slip through the main door. "No problem, Sister Julianna. I think we covered everything. Don't miss your flight on my account."

In a few seconds, Sister Margaret came hop-stepping into the reception area where I waited by her desk. "I'm sorry I had to interrupt. But Sister Julianna has no sense of time. As it is she's cutting it fine to make her plane. I don't envy her. I couldn't stand all that flying around the country giving speeches. But, like she says, the board does like the recognition it brings DeMoss. Oh, I did get the name and address of Delite's sister for you." She tore a sheet from a pink notepad and handed it to me.

"That's great, thank you. Just one more thing, Sister Margaret. Do you remember if Lacey was friendly with a blonde kid, a boy somewhere around 9 or 10?"

"Oh yes. That would be Danny Howard. Beautiful child, small for his age though. He was actually 12, I think. She stepped in when one of the bigger boys was bullying him one day. He was devoted to her. Just devastated when she disappeared. He became very withdrawn and uncooperative. In fact, he was outplaced not long afterwards."

"Outplaced?"

"Yes, sometimes the children who aren't doing well in the group environment here are sent for one-to-one intensive family care. Some of the students do better in that setting."

"And Danny, did he do well?"

Her chipper expression faded.

"No. I'm afraid he didn't. Eventually, he ran away. He was never found."

I thanked her and turned to leave, clutching Delite's phone number in my hand. I had almost reached the door when she called me back.

"Leah, wait! I'd forget my head if it weren't screwed on." She waggled back and forth in a gesture of self-exasperation that sent her veil fluttering.

"What is it, Sister Margaret?"

"You should talk to Mr. Palmer. He had Lacey in his office the day she disappeared. Maybe she said something to him that would help you."

"Isn't disciplining students a little below the Board Chairman's pay grade?"

"Oh, he wasn't disciplining her. He was rescuing her. Remember, I told you one of our new intakes kicked up quite a ruckus that day? Sometimes that happens and with this boy there was a lot of shouting and some language, I can tell you. The things I've heard would make my father blush, and he had quite a salty tongue.

"I had to call security. Lacey was sitting in that corner chair over there waiting to see Sister Julianna, and Mr. Palmer had come out to see what the commotion was. He spotted Lacey and right away he went over and took her to his office to get her out of the fray. It was a good 20 minutes or more before things calmed down. So, when I remembered, I thought maybe you'd like to speak with him."

14

As I walked to my car, a gust of wind caught hold of Delite's address while I was trying to tuck it in my purse. After a few undignified stoop-and-runs across the concrete, I nabbed it with my foot and bent down to pick it up. When I stood and turned around, Reid Palmer was directly behind me.

"Wow. *The Secret* really does work," I said.

"I'm sorry?"

"I was just wishing I could talk to you, and here you are."

"I saw you on your paper chase and came to offer my assistance. It's an unexpected pleasure to see you again so soon. Not thinking of joining the order, are you?" It was a lame joke and the delivery suffered from his oddly formal diction, but still, he was trying to be pleasant.

I smiled. "No, I'm pretty sure I'm not Catherines material, Mr. Palmer. I just had an appointment with Sister Julianna." I dropped the note in my purse.

"About your sister again?"

I nodded.

"Was she able to help you?"

"Not really. But I wonder if you might be able to. Sister Margaret just told me that you spent a little time with Lacey the day she disappeared."

He frowned in thought for a second, then his brow cleared.

"Yes, of course. That was the day one of our new students precipitated an incident in the reception area. I do remember now. I brought your sister into my office until things calmed down." His slight drawl was very comforting to listen to. He smiled.

"Would you like to come to my office for a cup of coffee, Leah? If I may call you Leah? And you must call me Reid. I have a special French roast I think you'd like."

"Sure, that would be nice." As we walked I asked him, "Why do you have an office in the administration center? I thought you were a lawyer or investor or something like that."

He smiled. "Something like that is quite right. I am a lawyer, but it's been years since I practiced. I have been fortunate in my life to have the means to indulge myself by doing things I enjoy. One of those things is helping DeMoss and the students here."

Sister Margaret looked up as we walked back in, but she was on the phone and just nodded.

His office was large and well proportioned. It included built-in bookshelves holding equal parts books and things that looked a little too classy to be called knickknacks. I sat down at a small round table while he went to a credenza behind his glass-topped desk. He poured water from a carafe into a high-tech coffee maker. While he searched out his French roast, I got up to look closer at a pencil sketch matted in gray and resting on a miniature silver easel on his bookshelf.

The drawing featured a kneeling boy offering water to an eagle. The artist had used hatching, shading and shadows to give depth and life to the sketch. The child's body looked smooth and supple, and the eagle feathers were so detailed the bird looked three-dimensional.

"Do you like it?"

"Yes. Who's the artist?"

"Thank you." It took me a second to get the implication. "You?"

He nodded. "I do a little sketching. Purely for stress relief."

"It's amazing. It looks...Greek?"

"Very good. It's actually a drawing of a sculpture in the Thorvaldsen Museum in Copenhagen. It depicts a scene from Greek mythology. The boy Ganymede offering water to Zeus, who has appeared to him in the form of an eagle. I made the sketch some time ago on a trip to Denmark. I have a copy of the sculpture in the gardens at my summer home."

"Did you make that too?"

"No," he said as he handed me coffee in a gold-rimmed china cup with saucer. "I'm afraid my artistic talents end with a little pencil scratching on paper. I commissioned a sculptor to make the piece for my garden. You can see it if you look closely in that picture," he said, pointing to a large photograph on the wall opposite his desk. "That's Highview. My summer home. I host an outing there every year for DeMoss students and staff. Perhaps you'd like to come this year."

A beautiful garden ablaze with summer blooms was in the foreground of the photo, and to the left, part of the sculpture was visible. In the background, a white two-story Greek revival mansion sat atop a hill. It looked like something out of *Gone With the Wind*.

"That's your *summer* home?"

He smiled.

"It is. A trifle ostentatious, I know, but my great-grandfather was a Southerner to his core. He grew up in Florida, but his wife, my great-grandmother DeMoss, was from Wisconsin. He fell in love with the north woods and built Highview for her as a summer place to showcase his Southern heritage. My grandfather was born there in 1910."

"So, it passes from one generation to the next?"

"It has, but unfortunately I'm the last of the direct line. My wife died several years ago. We never had children. Perhaps that's why I put so much energy into the school here."

"Didn't your grandmother start DeMoss?"

"Helped to fund it is more accurate. Yes, she spent summers in Wisconsin and went to boarding school here when the Catherines ran an academy for young ladies. She was very fond of the order. When they decided to reopen the school with its current emphasis on helping troubled children, she set up a trust to support it."

"Very generous."

"Giving back is a tradition in our family. What about you Leah, and your family? You wanted to ask me something about your sister?" He sat down and began drinking his coffee as I put my cup down.

"What did you and Lacey talk about after you brought her to your office that day? Was she upset? Did she tell you anything?"

"She didn't. I tried to engage her a little. I like to talk to the students and find out something about them when I have the opportunity, but your sister was... uncommunicative. She answered all my questions with yes and no and didn't volunteer anything. I could see she didn't want to talk to me. So, I just brought her a Coke and left her here while I tried to help settle things out front."

"Did she seem upset? Anxious? Afraid?"

"Upset? Yes, I'd say so, but that was understandable. The scene out front was unsettling. But afraid? No. I wouldn't have left her if I'd thought that. Why would she be?"

I debated how much I wanted to say. But no doubt Sister Julianna would tell him everything I'd told her anyway, so I might as well. "It's not very pretty. I'm afraid that my sister Lacey was sexually abused, and her death was a direct result of that."

"You think someone at DeMoss molested your sister?" He looked shocked, and I almost felt bad for upsetting his Southern gentility with my bluntness.

"I didn't say at DeMoss. Actually, I think it was before that."

"But even if that were true, how would that have led to her death?" He paused then answered his own question. "You mean because she responded to the abuse with her drinking and reckless behavior?"

There it was again. The underlying implication that Lacey had only herself to blame for a tragic but predictable end.

"No. I mean because someone killed her. Probably the person who abused her."

"Ah. To keep her from revealing the secret?" Well, bonus round to Reid Palmer the first person whose immediate reaction wasn't, "You're crazy, Leah."

"Exactly."

"Interesting theory, but what evidence do you have that your sister was abused?"

I told him what I'd told Sister Julianna, but I couldn't guess what he was thinking. His colorless eyes made him hard to read. For some reason, it felt really important that I convince him I was on the right track.

I found myself going into detail about Sister Mattea's note and outlining for him the inconsistencies in the police report: the fact that Lacey had confided in someone else about the abuse, and finally, that she had been seen with a young boy, a student at the school, the night she disappeared.

"I agree with the original police assessment—she was running away. But everyone was wrong about why. She wasn't just trying to get away from DeMoss rules and restrictions, she was trying to save herself. I think she was afraid she was in danger. And I think Sister Mattea learned something about that—I don't know how. She died before she could tell me."

He had sat perfectly still while I spoke, his eyes fixed on my face and an unreadable expression on his own. When I finished, he took a sip of coffee, placed the cup down to his left, then leaned back in his chair, his arms casually crossed. I waited.

"You're certain the source who told you about Lacey and about the child is reliable? More reliable than the young woman who was her roommate and related the story of their illicit drinking party?"

"Reasonably sure. My source isn't exactly above reproach, but has no reason to lie, and telling me was unplanned, I think."

"But what reason would your sister's roommate have to lie?"

"Maybe she was smart enough to know that Sister Julianna was a sucker for a sinner who'd seen the light. It could be that she saw an opportunity when Lacey's body was discovered. There wasn't anyone to dispute her story. And it worked. She wasn't transferred."

"Possible, I suppose."

Encouraged, I pressed. "The little boy is the kicker. I mean, why would Lacey have a little kid with her if she was going out to get wasted? She wouldn't."

"That's a valid question. Do you know who the child was?"

"Yes. Danny Howard. Trouble is, I understand he was shipped out for bad behavior not long after Lacey left, and he ran away from there. Sister Margaret said the school wasn't able to find him, and no one knows where he is now."

"Yes. Quite possibly he's living on the streets. It happens more often than people realize. That's why DeMoss is so vital. Unfortunately, we can't save everyone. This Danny must have been a particularly hard case." His pale eyes seemed to darken a little—with sadness? "What about your sister's abuser? Do you have any idea who that might be?"

"A few." He waited, but I'd done enough sharing.

"Well. I'm sure anything DeMoss could do to help, we'd be happy to."

"You might want to check with Sister Julianna on that. I don't think she's so keen on it."

"I'm sure she's just concerned that the reputation of the school not be compromised. That doesn't mean she wouldn't want to know the truth as you find it."

"Maybe." It was hard to keep the doubt out of my voice. "Reid, are you certain that Lacey spoke with Sister Julianna that day?"

"When things calmed down, I took her from my office to Sister Julianna's myself, so I'm fairly certain."

"It's just that Sister Margaret thought that Lacey left without speaking to her."

"As I said, there was a great deal of commotion that afternoon. I suspect she's just misremembering. Is it important?"

"No, no. I'm sure you're right."

I felt a twinge of disloyalty toward the little nun who had been so helpful. I stood to go, and he rose as well. Then he said something that made me take a step back.

"Leah, if you think your sister was killed, and you believe Sister Mattea had some knowledge of that, do you also think Sister Mattea was killed?"

"It crossed my mind. But so far, I'm the only one who even thinks Lacey's death is suspicious. Everyone would think I'd really lost it, if I started questioning Sister Mattea's death, too," I said, thinking of Coop's deflating skepticism when I tentatively brought it up with him.

"You don't strike me as someone who seeks approval before taking action, Leah."

"Are you saying you think I should be linking the two deaths?"

"No. Definitely not. I was just wondering if that's where your thoughts were heading. On the one hand, the story you present is quite fantastical."

He smiled, perhaps to take the sting out of his words.

"On the other, the inconsistencies you point out are puzzling. I've always been fond of puzzles."

"Be straight with me, Reid. You think I'm on to something. You think Lacey's death is suspicious, don't you? And you agree Sister Mattea knew something about it?"

"I don't know if you are 'on to something,' or not, Leah. I do believe you have a curious mind, in the best sense of the word. But as my grandmother was fond of saying, 'Curiosity killed the cat.' Not very original. Still, there's a good deal of wisdom in the old sayings. Do consider that, if you're right about your sister, pursuing this could put you in danger as well."

He stepped aside so I could leave, saying in clear dismissal, "Please keep me informed of your progress. Perhaps I can help at some point."

15

When I walked in the front door of the *Times,* Courtnee was redoing her makeup. I don't mean opening her compact and dabbing some powder on her nose. I mean sitting in front of the makeup mirror she keeps in her bottom drawer, reapplying shadow, eyeliner, and mascara. From the look of the supplies in front of her, that was only the beginning.

As soon as she saw me, she jumped up. Not because she felt guilty about turning her cubicle into a Mary Kay consulting room, but because she had something to impart. I could tell by the light in her baby blue eyes.

"Max wants to see you as soon as you get in. I think he's mad," she said in a conspiratorial whisper, leaning over the counter as I checked the spike for messages.

Gossip is the real coin of the realm in Courtnee's world, and she clearly felt like she was about to make a killing on the market.

"What's he mad about?"

"He got a phone call from someone, and after a while came out looking for you, and then he said to tell him as soon as you got back."

"Who called?"

"I was on another line, wasn't I? I think he said Rick Panther or something like that, but I had to get back to my mom, so I didn't really listen that well. Aren't you going to go and see Max?"

"Yes, don't worry about it." I grabbed the box of baklava—Max's favorite—that I'd picked up on impulse on my way back from the Catherines and headed down the hall.

Max's office looks like Miss Havisham's house without the decaying wedding cake. Open bags of snacks on the desk, stacks of newspapers on the floor, M&Ms (plain, not peanut) in every available container, manila file folders piled high at crazy angles, bowling trophies on dusty bookshelves, Kiwanis Club plaques on the wall, and a clock that shows the time in six different time zones. All incorrect.

"What's up?" I asked, moving a pile of papers off the chair in front of his desk.

He had been tilted back in his seat, his favorite death-defying balancing act. Now he leaned forward, bringing the front casters down with a thud.

"What the hell are you doing?"

"Bringing you baklava?" I smiled and held out the box, but without much hope that it would placate him. It didn't. He set it down on top of a pile of old newspapers.

"Leah, it's not funny. I asked you. No, I told you. Stay away from the Catherines. Leave your crazy theory about Sister Mattea and Lacey alone. There's no story there. Why can't you just once do what I tell you? I'm not gonna let you cost me this paper." A little vein on the side of his forehead had popped out and throbbed for emphasis.

"But, Max—"

He continued as though I hadn't interrupted. "I talked to Reid Palmer a little while ago."

Of course. Rick Panther. "Oh?"

"You know anything about that?"

"No. Well, that is, I saw him this morning, and we had coffee, but I don't know why he'd call."

"Because you're poking around bugging the Catherines, and that's bugging him!"

"Is that what he said?"

"He *said* that he wanted to talk with me about my refinancing plan. He *said* that there are a lot of things to consider. And then he said he saw you this morning at the Catherines.'"

"Max, what's wrong with that?"

"Read between the lines, Leah. Guys like Palmer don't come out and say things. They hint, they imply, and you better understand, because they're not spelling it out for you. He's telling me I might have a chance to get the money, but there are 'a lot of things to consider.' Like whether we do a story that makes it look like DeMoss was responsible for Lacey's death."

"Max, you're losing it. I talked to him, and I talked to Sister Julianna this morning, and they both know that this has nothing to do with the paper, that I'm pursuing my own theory. And besides he was sympathetic to me, he didn't seem threatened. I told him I didn't blame DeMoss. I—"

He ignored me, and his face got redder as his voice got louder. "I'm warning you, Leah, and I am serious as a heart attack, you'd better damn well stay away from the Catherines, stay away from DeMoss Academy, and stay away from Reid Palmer. Otherwise, you're gonna have plenty of time to work on that true crime book of yours."

I sat back in my chair and stared at him without speaking. I'd seen him angry before, plenty of times, and more than a few of those times it was at me. But never like this. In the face of my silence, he calmed down a little.

"I'm sorry. I know you think I'm going off the deep end. But I can't let anything get between me and the loan I need. Not even you. If I do, the paper is going to close. For the first time in more than 75 years, there won't be a *Himmel Times*. This has to be it. Period. End of discussion."

―――――――――

Courtnee was lurking in the hallway, and I nearly knocked her over as I beat a hasty retreat.

"Wow. Max really got after you for bothering the nuns, didn't he? I thought he was gonna fire you!"

"Max isn't going to fire me," I said, with more confidence than I felt, because there was no way I was going to stop trying to find the truth about Lacey, and no way that truth didn't somehow involve the Catherines. I dropped the camera bag and my purse on my desk and realized that Courtnee had followed me into the newsroom.

"Don't you need to be out front?"

"I'm on break. What are you wearing to Miguel's *Cinco de Mayo* party on Saturday?"

"I don't know."

"You know how I have this little dress with red and white stripes and blue stars that, like, I wear for the 4th of July? I thought I'd do, like, that. Only for Mexico, with this really cute red skirt and a yellow top. Like, my outfit will be the same color as their flag for their Independence Day."

"Mexico's flag is green, white, and red, Courtnee. Spain's flag is red and yellow."

She stared at me for a minute. "But my outfit is red and yellow. Are you sure?"

"Yep. And Cinco de Mayo isn't Independence Day for Mexico—that's September 16. The 5th of May is the date the Mexican Army won the Battle of Puebla."

"You always know everything, don't you? Well, I think it's stupid that they have a different day for the 4th of July than we do. I mean all Independence Days should be the same no matter what country you're in. Like, how can they just pick any day they want? It doesn't make sense. I mean, Independence Day is Independence Day, like Christmas is Christmas, right? It'd be like we go, Christmas is December 25th, but Mexico goes, our Christmas is the 3rd of March."

Now it was my turn to stare.

At that moment Miguel came through the door wearing a stack of sombreros on his head and carrying two large bags from Pat's Party Palace. He put the bags on the table and the sombreros on his desk. Then he grabbed one of the hats, put it on Courtnee, and danced her across the newsroom, singing a salsa version of "Careless Whispers," finishing with a swooping dip that sent her into a fit of giggles.

"Miguel, Leah told me my yellow and red outfit is the wrong colors for Mexico."

"Courtnee, you will be *muy bonita* no matter what you wear."

She gave me an I-told-you-so look, as though I had banned her ensemble and Miguel had issued a pardon. "Courtnee, I don't care what you wear. I don't even care what *I* wear."

"Well," she sniffed, looking over my khakis, white t-shirt and black blazer. "That's pretty obvious."

Which was a pretty good comeback for Courtnee. Miguel is on Team Courtnee when it comes to my clothes.

"She's a little bit right, *chica*. Look at you today. You look like an Amish lawyer." He shook his head in mock despair. I started to protest, but before I could, he went on. "Never mind. Both of you, wear whatever you like. You will be beautiful. Is your boyfriend, Trent, coming, Courtnee?"

"Trent? I thought his name was Brad."

"I broke up with Brad. We looked too much alike."

"What?"

"My grandma said couples who look too much alike never last. Like Brad Pitt and Jennifer Aniston. Or Ellie and her first husband."

"Ellie's first husband died, Courtnee."

"Well, but they're not together, are they? And she told me once people used to tease them about looking like twins. And Brad and I both have blonde hair and blue eyes and we're both hot, so I'm just sayin.' "

"You're just 'sayin' nothing that makes any kind of sense and—"

I was interrupted by an uncertain-sounding voice calling from the reception area. "Hey? Is anyone there? I'd like to place a classified ad? Hello?"

The phones had been ringing nonstop while Courtnee took her break and dispensed culture lessons with fashion accents. But now the in-person request rescued her from my coming rant, so she happily returned to her rightful place at the front desk.

When she was gone, Miguel said, "You know, *chica*, Courtnee is right. It wouldn't hurt to add a little color, maybe a nice green to bring out your eyes? I promise you, it's gonna be so worth it. Lots of hot guys coming to my party. Coop is gonna be there," he said, hopping up and coming to rest on the corner of his desk.

"And so? Right now, we're barely speaking to each other."

He lifted his shoulders in a shrug.

"OK. But if you don't want him...I wonder if he's heteroflexible?"

I couldn't help it. I tried not to let it, but a laugh snorted out.

"Knock it off," I said. "I've got serious stuff going on here. Max just about fired me 10 minutes ago."

I gave him a brief recounting of my Catherines adventures, and he agreed that Max was overreacting. Then I told him about my conversation with Marilyn Karr.

"Do you think she's telling the truth?"

"I don't know. Paul says she just wants to stir things up."

"Well, I got something else for you to think about."

He pulled a notebook out of the inside pocket of his denim jacket and flipped it open.

"Father Hegl used to be the priest at San Carlos parish in Florida. Then one day—poof he's gone. Didn't say *adios* to anyone and didn't stay in touch."

"Caught with an altar boy?"

He shook his head. "I don't think so. The church secretary, she was very helpful."

"Of course she was." I have yet to meet the woman Miguel couldn't charm.

"She said that Father Hegl was very close to the Perez family. *Especialmente* to their beautiful teenage daughter Olivia. He was her voice coach. She died in a car accident just before the *padre* left."

"When was that, Miguel?"

"May 2004. I checked. That's when Father Hegl showed up in Himmel."

"Yeah. That's the summer Lacey was 14. Were Hegl and this Olivia having an affair?"

"Rosa, the church secretary, didn't want to say, but yes, I think so. Olivia was just 18, but already she was married. Sad, so young. Her family didn't like the husband, Vince Morgan. He was wild, and he was white. Not good. And worse, he was not Catholic. But the *chicas* sometimes they like the bad boys, yes?"

"Or the bad priests? Hegl, another beautiful young girl and another death. What about the accident, was Olivia alone?"

"The police report says yes. She was over the limit and drove off the shoulder. The car rolled. She got thrown out. Massive head injuries. Died in the ambulance on the way to the hospital. She had a younger sister, Carla.

I'll call her. Sometimes the sisters, they know things the *mamá* and *papá* don't, right?"

"You did great, Miguel, thanks. But let me call Carla. I might be able to make a connection because of Lacey."

He looked disappointed. No one likes a lead taken away.

"No worries." He smiled, but I knew I'd hurt his feelings.

Sometimes I can't believe what a jerk I can be. Most of the time I can though. Miguel busted his butt to get background on Hegl, and then I snatched his lead right out from under him. Max threw me a job lifeline, and I tied it to a personal investigation that could sink him. Coop disagreed with me, and I cut him off at the knees. I hit my mother with the news that Lacey was abused and possibly murdered, and I suggest that Paul might be involved. Then I wonder why she's not on the same page with me.

It's true. I can be bossy, overbearing, arrogant, know-it-all, stubborn, single-minded (I really should write that down for my online dating profile). But it's not because I don't think other people are competent or smart. I do. I really do. It's just that no matter how hard I try, I can't believe that anyone else is really going to care as much as I do, or get it done the exact way I think it should be done. So, I have to rely on myself.

The catch is, despite my confident exterior, I don't really believe that I'm going to do it right either. And if you make the mistake of thinking I can do it, then how dumb are you? Which just proves I can't trust your judgment, and I better do everything myself. I shook off my circular self-reflection and pulled out the number Sister Margaret had given me and tried Father Hegl's cell phone.

"Yes?"

"Father Hegl? This is Leah Nash."

Silence, then a business-like but not unfriendly greeting. "Yes. Hello. How can I help you?"

"I just had a quick question for you, Father. I wonder if you remember seeing anything unusual the night of the fundraiser. That was the night

Lacey disappeared. I've been reading the police report, but I can't seem to find an interview with you."

"That's because I wasn't interviewed. I wasn't there the night of the fundraiser."

"But I thought everyone at the school, all the staff, had to go. A command performance, I think Sister Margaret called it."

"Yes. Normally, that's the case, but I had an unexpected call from an old friend who needed my help on an urgent personal matter. Sister Julianna gave me permission to miss the dinner."

"Oh, I see. So, you weren't there at all?"

"I got back quite late, long after everyone had left. So, I couldn't have seen anything that would help you, Leah. I'm sorry. Are you having any luck elsewhere?"

"Father, why didn't you tell me you knew Lacey before she came to DeMoss?"

"Didn't I? I'm sure I mentioned it."

"No. You didn't."

"It must have just slipped my mind. Well, if there's nothing else—"

"Just one more thing. Your friend, was it someone you knew in Florida?"

Silence. Then "I, uh, I really can't say. As I said, it was personal. And confidential. I have to go now, Leah. Goodbye."

Well, something was making Father Hegl nervous. Was it getting caught lying about knowing Lacey? Was it the Florida reference? Or was it to do with his mystery friend? Or were they somehow all connected?

16

Early the next morning I stood shivering in the early morning cool on the doorstep of Miller and Georgia Caldwell's tasteful brick colonial. Dressed in jeans, a UW T-shirt and my favorite Keens, I hoped my downscale ensemble would emphasize that I was not working; I was not representing the *Himmel Times*; and nothing I did or said could be held against me in a court of Max. I wasn't even the one who set up this little *tête-à-tête* with Miller. He had called me the night before.

I know Miller in the way I know most high-profile people in Himmel, because of my job. We don't exactly travel in the same social circles, although he and his wife both go to St. Stephen's like my mother. When he called and asked me to come by, he said it wasn't for a story, but he'd rather talk to me in person. Since I had some non-story chatting I wanted to do with him, too, I accepted.

I rang the bell and waited for a maid or housekeeper to answer, but it was Miller who stood there when the door swung open. At well over six feet tall, his muscular frame filled the doorway. His carefully cut brown hair was touched with gray; his eyes were a shade of blue so bright, they might have owed their hue to colored contacts. The smile he gave me was the broad grin required of every candidate. I was surprised when he shook my hand to find that his was calloused, more like a farmer's than a politician's.

"Thank you for coming, Leah."

"Sure, no problem." He led me through the large entrance hall to his study. Rows of books in ceiling-high glass-fronted cabinets lined one wall. An ornate mahogany desk dominated the far end of the room and, in the other end, two wing-back chairs upholstered in a rich looking burgundy fabric flanked a sofa with striped silk cushions. An Oriental rug of intricate pattern covered the oak floor. The room looked like a photo spread for *We're Old Money* magazine.

Miller sat down on the edge of the sofa. I took the chair nearest him. I accepted a cup of coffee and waited as he poured one of his own. He added sugar. Stirred it. Offered me biscotti, and when I refused, put the platter back down without taking one himself. I maintained a politely curious expression as I waited for him to speak.

He finally did.

"I understand you've talked several times with Sister Julianna and Reid Palmer about your sister's accident."

I didn't respond. It's a technique Max taught me a long time ago. If you just let the silence hang there, most people can't stand it. They have to fill the gap.

"I was very fond of Lacey. We all were."

Again, I didn't say anything, but this time I nodded.

"We were so upset when she," he hesitated, picked up his coffee and put it back down without taking a drink. "When she lost her way."

"That's a pretty delicate way to put it."

"May I ask why you're going back over things, so long after Lacey's death?" His fingers played with the gold band of the wristwatch on his left wrist.

"I've learned something that casts a different light on Lacey's death— and on the last few years of her life. I'm just following up on it."

"You mean the note from Sister Mattea?"

"You're well-informed. Yes. That and some other information. I'm pretty certain now that Lacey was sexually abused. I'm going to find out who did it."

"Leah, that's appalling." His face registered concern.

"You don't seem that surprised. I suppose Sister Julianna or Reid Palmer already told you. Isn't that what lawyers do, ask questions you already know the answers to? Did they also tell you I believe it happened the summer before she went into ninth grade? Lacey spent a lot of time with your family back then. Did she ever talk about anyone, a teacher, a coach, anyone who had a lot of contact with her?"

"Surely you or your mother were in a better position than me to notice anything like that."

"Yeah, that's true. But for a while there it seemed like she was here more than she was at home. That's what Mom said anyway. One time, didn't she even spend the night with you?"

"I'm not sure I understand."

"I'm just trying to think if I'm remembering that right. You and Lacey got stranded on your way to your cottage up north when the car broke down. You had to stay overnight, just the two of you at a motel, right?"

"Are you insinuating—"

"Miller, why did you ask me here? Why do you care if I'm talking to people about my sister?"

"Lacey was like a daughter to me, an older sister to Charlotte and Sebastian. When I talked to Sister Julianna, she said you seemed over-wrought. She was concerned about you, and that you might inadvertently cause some damage to the school. That's why she turned to me, because I'm on the board."

"That's funny, because when I spoke to Reid Palmer, who is also on the board, he didn't seem worried about my questions."

"Reid is inclined to take a detached view of things. I'm not sure he realizes how much doubts and rumors could affect the reputation of DeMoss, or of the Catherines for that matter."

"And so you offered to step in and what? Soothe the troubled waters, shut down the inconvenient questions?"

"Leah, please. I was just trying to ease Sister Julianna's mind, just trying to do a kindness. Nothing more. What are we here for if not to make life less difficult for each other?"

"Very inspiring. But you shouldn't worry. I don't think Lacey's sexual abuse will reflect on DeMoss. She wasn't there when it happened. Though that's not to say her abuser didn't track her down there. In fact, I think he must have. Because I think that's why she died. Did you ever run into Lacey there?"

"No. I didn't see her again after she stopped caring for the children. I heard about her ... troubles ... of course, in a small town like this, you do. But I never spoke to her again."

"I see. So, the night she disappeared, the night of the big fundraiser for DeMoss, did you go back after you left with Paul Karr?"

"Back? Yes, I think so. I can't be sure. That was five years and at least 50 charity fundraisers ago."

"Did you see anything when you were driving back in, or even later when you left for the night?"

"What sort of thing?"

"Maybe a little boy wandering the grounds? A car leaving from the side entrance? A girl, maybe Lacey, standing near the Baylor Road entrance?"

"Leah, what's the point of this? I was interviewed by the Sheriff's Department at the time, and whatever I said then was fresher than what I could hope to remember now. Do you really think anyone will be able to tell you anything useful at this late date? Is it worth reminding people all over again about Lacey's problems, worrying good people who are trying to help other children like Lacey, risking the school's reputation and its funding for an unprovable theory? Do you think your sister would want that?"

"My sister would want justice. I don't believe she got it. Why are you so interested in stopping me?"

"I'm not trying to stop you, Leah. I'm just trying to get you to think through what is really in the best interest of you, of Lacey's memory, and I admit, of DeMoss Academy."

"And you, Miller? What's in your best interest?"

"Dad? Dad! Telephone. It's grandma." A girl's voice sounded from somewhere upstairs.

"I have to take this call, my father's not been well. I think we're finished here. Can you see yourself out?"

"Yeah, sure. Thanks, Miller."

He nodded and walked out of the room and down the hall. As I left, a pretty girl in running gear came clattering down the stairs.

"Oh! Hi," she said. "I didn't know Dad was with anyone."

"That's OK, we were finished. Could you possibly be Charlotte?" I asked, as I noted her big brown eyes and remembered the solemn little girl Lacey used to bring to the house sometimes.

"That's me," she said, sweeping silky blonde hair into a ponytail and securing it. "Who are you?"

"Leah Nash. Lacey's sister."

"Oh sure, I remember you now."

"It's been awhile. The last time I saw you, I think Lacey brought you over to see her cat Zoey. You couldn't have been more than—"

"Ten. I was 10. That was just before Lacey stopped coming. Sebastian and I felt really bad. We loved her."

We had walked through the door and were standing on the flagstone path leading to the drive where my car was parked.

"Did she ever tell you why she stopped babysitting?"

She shook her head. "No. We used to see her at least twice a week—Mom and Dad are pretty social. I thought she liked us. Then one day Dad said Lacey told him she wouldn't be coming anymore. She was too busy. I called her and asked if she could visit us some time, but she just said no, she didn't think so.

"I was really bummed. And Sebastian cried that he wanted his 'Wacey' every time a new sitter came. He was only five. For a long time, we thought we did something wrong and she didn't like us anymore. But when I got older, I figured it out."

"What did you figure out, Charlotte?"

"Mom fired her because we all liked her so much—me, Sebastian, even Dad. Mom doesn't like it when she's not the center of the universe."

"But Lacey wasn't fired, she quit. That's what she told us—my mother and me."

She shrugged.

"Well, then she quit because Mom was such a bitch to her. Mom told us Lacey wasn't our friend, she was only nice because she was paid to be, and we should get over it. I'm sorry about what happened to Lacey, Leah. She was always great to us, and that's how I remember her, no matter what people said."

A car pulled into the drive just then and a very beautiful woman, the image of Charlotte in 20 years, got out. Georgia looked surprised—and not in a good way.

"Leah, what are you doing here? Charlotte, I really need you to go back inside and change into something more suitable."

Her daughter's tight-fitting tank top and shorts were more revealing than I'd choose, but with her lithe body and long legs, Charlotte looked good, and she was dressed pretty much like other girls her age.

She had begun inserting her earbuds as Georgia approached, and now said, "Sorry, Mother, can't hear you. I've got to run. Literally." She gave me a small wave and took off with a steady stride, her ponytail bouncing behind her.

Georgia trained her icy gaze back on me and repeated her question. "What are you doing here?" She pressed her carefully outlined lips into a thin pink line as she waited for my answer.

"Miller asked me to stop by. He wanted to talk about Lacey."

"I don't believe it."

"Why would I lie?"

"Why do reporters do anything? To dig up dirt. To make trouble. To ride on the coattails of people who are better and smarter than they are. But I'm sure my husband did not initiate a conversation about your delinquent, dead sister."

"Why did you dislike her so much?"

"Dislike a predatory, oversexed teenager who couldn't leave my husband alone? What's not to like?"

"That's not true, Georgia. Lacey was a kid. She was 14 years old when she babysat for you."

"Lolita was 12, right?"

"You really are a horrible person, aren't you?"

"You don't know the half of it. And trust me, you don't want to know."

The carefully cultivated mask of wealth and privilege fell away for a minute. Underneath I could see the viciously ambitious girl from the poor side of Himmel. Not Georgia then. No, she was plain old Crystal Bailey before she clawed her way up the social ladder and snagged the son of the wealthiest family in Himmel along the way.

"Your sister was a little bitch who tried to worm her way into my family and turn my own children and my husband against me. I knew her game. I'm telling you, you'd better not make any trouble for us. I didn't get here by playing nice. Miller is going to win his state senate race and that's only the beginning. I won't allow you to tie him to that little slut and her drunken death."

"Do you even know how pathetic you sound? Lacey was in ninth grade! She was into Justin Timberlake, not some guy old enough to be her father, like Miller. You know what, Georgia? If I were you I wouldn't invest too much in my campaign wardrobe. Because it could be that when I get the answers I'm looking for, Miller might be fighting for his life, not for a state senate seat. You may find that your future is not very bright at all."

I had nothing to base it on. I was just trying to give back a little of the trash talk she had thrown at me.

I was too slow on the uptake to see it coming. She stepped back to give herself room then shoved so hard she knocked me on my butt. As I sat staring up at her in surprise, she turned and marched to her front door, high heels clicking on the pavement.

17

I'd been calling and leaving messages at the number Sister Margaret gave me for Delite Wilson's sister, Brandee Holloway, for a few days, but she wasn't picking up, and she wasn't answering my voicemail. When I got home from the Caldwells to change for work, I gave it another try. After three rings, someone answered, but it sounded more like an adolescent boy than an adult woman.

"Yeah?"

"Hello. May I please speak to Brandee Holloway?"

He didn't answer, but there was a slight clunk as the phone was tossed down, and I could hear him yell.

"Ma! Phone!"

"Who is it?"

"I dunno. Sounds kinda like the counselor from my school."

"Whadya been doin'? I told you I ain't got time to go runnin' to your damn school every day. And I told you, don't answer my phone!" There was the sound of a *whap!* And a sharp cry of "Oww!"

Then, "Who is this?"

I talked fast, trying to get my question in before she hung up on me.

"Hi, Brandee, this is Leah Nash. I left a couple of messages. I'm trying to reach your sister Delite. Does she still live with you?"

"No. Whadya want her for?"

"She was my sister Lacey's roommate at DeMoss Academy. I don't know if you know this, but Lacey died in an accident there, and I'm trying to talk to some of the people who knew her then."

"What for?"

"Lacey and I weren't close when she went to DeMoss, but I miss her a lot. I just feel if I could talk to people who knew her then, I might feel closer to her, might understand her better. You know how it is with sisters." I'd decided to play the we're-all-sisters card, but now that didn't seem like such a great idea.

"I know how it is with my husband-stealing, lazy, lying half-sister, if that's what you mean. I threw Delite out two months after she got here from Loserville. Right after I caught her screwin' my old man. Him, he's a piece of shit. But my own flesh and blood? I tossed her little bitch ass right out, and I ain't talked to her since."

"Uh, I'm sorry to hear that. Do you know where she went?"

"Last I heard she was workin' at a casino in Michigan up to Mixley. I gotta go. I don't know nothin' about Delite. Don't call me anymore."

Before she clicked off, I could hear her yelling at her kid again. "Don't you goddamn pick up my phone you little fucktard! I don't have time for your—" and she was gone.

My mother walked into the kitchen dressed for work as I hung up.

"Leah? What are you doing home? I thought I heard you leave over an hour ago," she said, tilting her head as she fastened a silver hoop earring.

"You look good, Mom." She did, dressed in a bright green blazer and knee-length skirt—she still has great legs. I thought of Brandee and her harangue at her unknown son, and I walked over and gave her a hug.

"What's that for?"

"Because you've never called me a little fucktard."

"At least not when you could hear me."

"Funny."

"But what are you doing back home at 8:30? I did hear you leave once already, didn't I?"

"Yeah, I had an early coffee date."

"Hmm. Dressed like that I guess it's safe to assume it wasn't with one of the royal family."

"Actually, it was. Himmel's, anyway. Miller Caldwell asked me for a coffee at his house this morning."

"Miller called you?" The look of astonishment on her face changed to suspicion. "Why? Leah, you didn't accuse him of hurting Lacey, did you?"

"I asked him a few questions. Look, Mom, like I said, he's the one who called me. He heard I was asking about Lacey and wondered why. Sister Julianna put him up to it."

"Leah, you haven't said anything about that for the past few days. I was hoping you'd dropped it."

"I haven't said anything, because I don't want to fight with you. I know you're angry, and I'm sorry if I messed things up for you with Paul I—"

"Leah, it's not just that—have you thought at all about what Paul said? This could be a lose-lose situation. If you're wrong, you can hurt a lot of innocent people. Like Paul. If you're right, ask the wrong person, and it could be dangerous. I'm worried about you."

"Well, maybe if someone tried to kill me, I'd finally convince you and Coop and Max that I'm on to something."

"That's a terrible thing to say, Leah."

She was right, but I never stand stronger than when I'm wrong.

"Look, let's not talk about it anymore, OK? We're not going to agree, and neither of us is going to change her mind. Besides, you'll be late for work."

"We're not through with this conversation, Leah. You don't need to be sarcastic with me and treat me like I'm some kind of overprotective nitwit. Karen is worried too. And she mentioned something I hadn't even thought of—possible libel or slander suits. You think you've got career and money problems now—you ain't seen nothin' yet if Georgia Caldwell decides to take a swing at you."

Now didn't seem the time to confess that indeed Georgia already had.

"Mom. I don't think you're a nitwit, and Karen isn't either."

Karen had been like a second, less-guilt-wielding mother to us growing up. She tried to help Lacey almost as much as Mom and I did, but Lacey cut her off just like she did us. I knew it hurt her, but she never said a bad word about my sister. She stayed a good friend to us when some others didn't.

"But just think about this, Mom. You're afraid I'm not being objective, that I'm seeing connections that aren't there, because I feel guilty. Isn't it possible that you're refusing to see things that *are* there for the same reason? I'll be late tonight. There's something I have to do after work."

Instead of heading to McClain's for our usual post-production drink and dinner, I jumped in my car after we put the paper to bed, ready to head out for a four-hour drive to Shining Waters Resort Casino in Mixley, Michigan. According to the staff person I spoke to, Delite Wilson was working a 9 p.m. to 3 a.m. shift. That was my best chance of catching up with her. A rap on my window made me look up from buckling my seatbelt.

"*Chica,* where are you going?" Miguel's expression was similar to that of a golden retriever hoping for a trip to the park.

"To the casino in Mixley. I've got a line on Delite."

"That's at least an eight-hour round trip. You won't get back here until morning!"

"That's OK. I don't have any assignments until afternoon. If I get too tired driving back, I'll just pull into a rest area and catch a nap."

He ran quickly around the car and jumped in the passenger seat before I could say anything. "I'm coming with you. We can split the driving."

I turned to face him and started to protest but he waved me off. "No. You need me. You don't see Frodo without Sam, Buffy without Willow, Abercrombie without Fitch."

"No. Seriously. Thanks, but no. You've already done enough." He continued as though I hadn't said anything.

"Lilo without Stitch, Holmes without Watson, Jerry without George—"

"OK, OK, OK. Enough. Buckle up and let's go."

I reached over to plug in my iPhone for some music, but Miguel grabbed it away. "No-no. I am so not listening to Adele for four hours. I'm in charge of the tunes for this road trip. Hey, don't you believe in security, *chica*? Your phone should be password protected."

"I know. But it's too much trouble. I don't like to keep putting the pass code in every time it's idle for a few minutes."

"Oh, *dios mío*. It's worse than I thought. *Journey*? Seriously?" he said as he scrolled through my song list.

"You know my secret, now I have to kill you. Besides, you're the one with Susan Boyle on his playlist."

"I'm not ashamed. The voice of an angel. Ohh, OK, here we go, let's go retro."

Soon the Bee Gees started pouring out of the speakers, and by the time we pulled out of town, we were both singing and car dancing to *Stayin' Alive*. Almost four hours later when the lights of the casino lit up the night sky, we weren't quite as lively. It was about 11 when we pulled into the parking lot.

If you've never been to a casino in rural Michigan, let me hasten to assure you it is not Monte Carlo. Or Las Vegas. Or even Atlantic City. There is no glamour and precious little excitement, unless it excites you to watch people who look like they haven't a dime to spare, wheezing their way around game tables and slot machines on electric carts. There's an air of noisy desperation about the whole scene that I find extremely depressing. Miguel, I discovered, did not share my feelings. Bouncing out of the car, he almost danced his way through the big double doors and immediately pulled me over to the dice table.

"C'mon, *chica*, let's roll the dice. I feel lucky tonight."

"Roll away, buddy. I've got work to do. Life's a big enough gamble for me, thanks. Besides, I haven't the faintest idea how to play craps. It looks way too math-y to me."

"No, no, *chica*. It's so easy. You've never played?" His eyes lit up. "Then you'll be super lucky. Here, just roll the dice, please?"

"No. Seriously. You go ahead and make new friends. I'm going to look around for Delite."

The room was dark and the air redolent with smoke despite the air purifying system. I wasn't sure I'd recognize her. I'd only seen her once before, when DeMoss brought a contingent of kids to Lacey's funeral. I remembered her as a pale ash blonde with flat blue eyes and a discontented mouth. I scanned the gaming tables. Outside of the dice table only three were open; a raucous three-card poker game staffed by a skinny young guy with glasses, a let-it-ride game with a balding dealer and two hard-bitten women playing, and an empty blackjack table with a female dealer. Something about her cocky stance made me think I'd found her. As I got closer, I could see that her nametag read Delite. Jackpot.

Her hair wasn't ash blonde anymore, instead it was a streaky yellow-orange color not found in nature. Her eyes were the same though, hard and dull.

"Delite. Hi. I'm Leah Nash. Lacey's sister."

"Yeah, so? You wanna play or what?"

"Yeah, sure." I placed a bet and then said, "Actually I wanted to talk to you. To ask you about Lacey. Lacey Nash," I added, as she showed no sign of recognizing the name.

"What about her?" She shuffled the deck and dealt me a card and turned over her own.

"You and Lacey were roommates. You must have talked a lot. Did she ever tell you that she was worried, or afraid?"

"No," she said, giving me another card.

"Did she seem unhappy?"

"Everybody was unhappy. We was at Dumbass Academy, wasn't we?" She looked at her second card. Ace. I busted.

"She never said anything to you about before she came to DeMoss? About what happened to her when she was younger? Did she ever say anything about being sexually abused?" Her face kept the same disinterested stare.

She shrugged. "She mighta said somethin' about some big shot makin' her screw or something. Too bad, so sad, we all got somethin'."

"Lacey said she was abused? Think, did she say who?"

"I don't know. It's not like I really cared, I got my own problems. You gonna play another hand or not?"

"Yeah, yeah, sure," I said, putting another $5 on the table. "Did she say why she didn't tell the police?"

She dealt me a card and turned her own over.

"Delite?"

"Look, I don't know why she didn't tell. I don't know if she was gonna. I don't know anything. Except your sister stole my phone. And that was f'n' hard to get, too. Had to have it sneaked in, cost me a lot in trade. And I had some pretty special pictures on there, if you know what I mean." I signaled for another card.

"Are you saying it was your phone the police found with her body?"

She shrugged and laid down cards for both of us.

"I'm sayin' I had a phone and then I didn't. I'm sayin' I shared a room with your sister. I'm sayin' if she had one on her, and mine was missin,' which it was, she took it."

"Do you know if Lacey was using drugs again?" I signaled and she dealt me another card before answering. I busted again.

"I got hold of some Vicodin one time, offered to sell her some, but she didn't want any."

"They found drugs in her purse when they found her body."

"Don't know anything about that."

"Did you ever see Lacey and Father Hegl?"

She shook her head. "She couldn't stand him. He was always buggin' her to be in his stupid choir. Your sister could sing," she added with a grudging note of admiration.

"Why did you lie and say you didn't see Lacey the night she disappeared, then come forward after her body was found and claim she was at a party with you?"

"Like I told the cops, I didn't want to get in more trouble. One more screw-up and I was going to juvie."

"Weren't you afraid of that when you finally did confess?"

Her face had a sly expression, and she answered as if tutored by Dr. Phil. "I wanted to give your family, like, closure, right? I couldn't cover for her anymore. It was dysfunctional. For me. Mentally, like. I didn't want to be doing codependent behavior anymore."

"But Lacey wasn't with you, was she? You made that up."

Her eyes hardened as she said, "Look, I'm workin' here. If you're not gonna play, you better move on."

Two men, one wearing a Brewer's T-shirt that rode up on his belly and left a hairy gap above the top of his droopy jeans, and the other sporting a Green Bay Packers sweatshirt, lumbered up to the table and put down a stack of chips.

"No. I'm done, thanks. But if you do think of anything," I reached in my purse and found a business card. "That's my cell phone, you can reach me anytime."

"Hey, honey, you got one of those for me?" said hairy belly.

"No."

Delite hesitated for a second, then scooped the card off the table and put it in her pocket.

"See you."

She didn't answer.

18

I was ready to go, but I saw that Miguel was the center of a group of players urging him on at the craps table. He'd come all the way up there with me. I couldn't make him walk out on his run. Instead, I wandered over to a video poker machine near the cashier's window. I put $5 in a nickel machine and settled down to play some draw poker, but all I did was stare at the screen thinking about what Delite had said.

I still didn't believe her story, but I no longer thought she had offered a fake confession to demonstrate she was a reformed sinner who should be allowed to stay. No. That sly look on her face, those psychobabble words she used, "closure" "codependent"—someone was feeding the rationale to her.

But who and why? She said Lacey was abused by a "big shot." What would a big shot be to Delite? A doctor? A lawyer? A dentist? Miller Caldwell was a lawyer. Did he connect with Delite, get her to lie when Lacey's body was found to wrap things up quickly, keep the police from doing an actual investigation, instead of the pro forma walk-through Ross had led? Or, there was Hegl. Would a priest be a big shot to Delite?

Miguel walked up just then with a big grin, waving three $100 bills.

On the ride home I told him about Delite and speculated a little more about Miller Caldwell, but I was hit by a sudden wave of sleepiness and begged off further chatting. Miguel drove all the way back. I was a little coma-sleep groggy when I woke up as we pulled into the parking lot at the *Times*. But by the time I pulled in my driveway, I had started to perk up a bit. I opened the front door quietly, but knew that my mother and I would have to do our usual call and response.

"Leah?"

"Yes, Mom."

"You're awfully late."

"Sorry, I know. I'm fine. Go back to sleep."

"Goodnight, sweetheart."

"G'night."

It was 4 a.m. but no way could I go back to sleep. Instead I got my phone and switched over from Miguel's playlist to stream a mix of old-school folk/rock—Joni Mitchell, Joan Baez, The Band—singers my mother had conditioned me to like growing up. I turned it down low, so I wouldn't wake her. I made some tea and sat down in the rocker to think. After a few minutes, I got up and set my laptop on the kitchen table, and typed in www.delaneysmemorialgarden.com.

When the site came up, I clicked on *For Always*. From the list there I chose "Lacey Nash," and then there she was in a smiling school picture, wearing the silver locket I gave her for her 13th birthday. Delaney's Funeral Home, for a fee, provides permanent memorial web pages with photos, condolences, memories, and comments for its "clients." Mom and I never talked about setting one up for Lacey, but she must have wanted something she could go back to. I'd only visited it once.

I reread the obituary that Max had written for her.

I had tried to write it myself, but the anger and sorrow got so tangled up in me that I couldn't make it work. I wanted people to remember the good about her, but it felt like a lie to ignore all the terrible things she'd done. I couldn't strike the balance between tribute and truth. Max did a beautiful job.

Lacey Nash, 17, daughter of Carol (Collins) Nash and the late Thomas Nash, died November 2, 2007. Cremation has taken place and the funeral Mass for Lacey is scheduled for 11 a.m. Tuesday at St. Stephen's Church with the Reverend Gregory Lindstrom officiating.

Lacey was born in Himmel, Wisconsin, where she spent her entire life. She loved singing. She was also a talented artist, often sketching pictures of her family, friends, and pets.

As a member of the Himmel Community Players, Lacey found an outlet for her vocal talent. She was chosen for a role in the Sound of Music at age 10. She performed with the local theater group for several years and was always a crowd pleaser. Her last appearance was as Dorothy in The Wizard of Oz.

Lacey was also active in swimming and church choir, and she enjoyed helping others. At age 12 she organized a carnival for Muscular Dystrophy in her back-yard that raised more than $1,000. After a heavy snow, she often rounded up neighborhood kids to help her shovel the driveways of elderly neighbors.

As a youngster, Lacey's favorite author was Dr. Seuss, and her favorite book was Horton Hears a Who. As a middle schooler, she loved Madeleine L'Engle and she read A Wrinkle in Time multiple times. She also loved the movie The Parent Trap and is believed to hold the world's record for number of viewings.

But this bright, talented, kindhearted girl entered a very difficult period as a teenager. She spent her last years troubled and isolated, and that was a great sorrow to the people who loved her.

May she be remembered for the happy and loving spirit inside her and granted compassion for the tragic ending of her too-brief life.

Lacey is survived by her mother Carol Nash of Himmel, her sister Leah Nash of Grand Rapids, Michigan, her aunt Nancy Taylor of Wadley, Michigan and several cousins. She was preceded in death by her sister Annie and her father Thomas.

I scrolled down through the comments. Lots from old classmates, stuff about school and favorite class trips, and I'll-never-forget-the-time stories. They were fun to read, because they reminded me of a time when Lacey was like any other kid.

There were some nice tributes from teachers and old neighbors, and as I moved on through I noticed over the years people periodically posted things, though far less often, of course, than when the page first went up. Most were signed by name but a few weren't.

And then as I read through them, I realized there was one that had recurred each year since Lacey died. The same quote, no signature.

"Thank you for making life less difficult." Earlier I would have skimmed right over it. But this time the phrase set off an echo in my mind, and I heard Miller Caldwell say as we sat sipping coffee in his sumptuous home, "What are we here for if not to make life less difficult for each other?"

First thing in the morning, I stopped by Delaney Funeral Home and talked to Mary Beth. She co-owns the business with her husband Roger.

"Mary Beth, is there any way to tell who posts anonymous comments on a memorial website?"

She looked startled, though with her carefully drawn in and unnaturally high arched eyebrows, Mary Beth always appeared somewhat surprised.

"I don't know, Leah. I suppose maybe. I wouldn't have the faintest idea how to do it. And don't even think about Roger. He still doesn't really get what the online site is. Our oldest boy talked him into it. Why?"

"There's a comment on Lacey's site that I'd like to track down. Thank the person, you know. They've posted it every year, so I know Lacey must have been special to them. Could I talk to whoever set up the page for you? There's probably something that could be done through the host site to track messages."

"Well, I don't know. Really, the page kind of belongs to the person who paid for it, and I wouldn't feel right without talking to him." She started twirling a strand of copper colored hair that had escaped from the old-fashioned bun on the back of her head. Her eyes blinked rapidly.

"Him? Don't you mean her, don't you mean my mother?"

Mary Beth's discomfort increased. "I promised it would be anonymous. I thought it was such a nice gesture. A lot of our families would like to do it but, well, it's no secret funerals are expensive, and so many people just don't have the extra money. Not that we're overcharging, mind you.

"There's a lot involved with keeping the online memorial garden up. I just thought it was such a nice thing, to set up the perpetual site for a family in need. Not that your family is in need, I didn't mean, that is—" If she could have blinked me away, it was obvious she would have.

"Ahh, of course. I should have realized right away. How nice of Miller," I said, taking a guess that I knew Mary Beth would confirm.

She looked relieved. "Exactly. That's what I thought, and to pay in advance. We charge the yearly fee you know, and really $200 is a good rate, I think, but he asked how much it would cost to keep it up indefinitely. We do offer the perpetual package for $5,000. He wrote me a check for the full amount right on the spot. Such a good man."

I nodded. "Did he say why he did it, Mary Beth? Just a random act of kindness or what?"

Now that her secret was in the open through almost no fault of her own, she could indulge her natural inclination to chat.

"That's what I wondered when he came in. 'Miller,' I said, 'that's really nice of you, but can I ask why?' And he said that he and his family were so fond of Lacey and wanted to be sure her memory stayed alive. But he didn't want you and your mother to feel uncomfortable or obligated or anything. That's why he swore me to secrecy. You just don't see that kind of thing often enough, do you? I mean, just doing good for the sake of doing good. You're not upset are you, Leah? You wouldn't even know about it, if you hadn't come in here and tricked me. Now, don't tell him I told you."

"Sorry, Mary Beth, I can't promise that."

I went into the office for meetings with two school board candidates and got their views on test scores, and school improvement, and the importance of an upcoming referendum vote. And when they left, I wrote up the story, but my mind wasn't on any of it. By then it was nearly noon, and I decided to take a run over to the cop shop. The bare bones activity log is online, but I wanted an excuse to run into Coop, and see if we could end the weirdness that had sprung up between us.

I pushed through the double doors and into the scruffy reception area. The Himmel Police Department is on the first floor of the city hall and looks like it hasn't been redecorated since 1975. The avocado green and beige tile floor is cracked and chipped. On one side of a scarred, wooden counter is a row of orange plastic chairs bolted together, apparently to prevent someone from absconding with valuable late-20th-century arti-facts. On the other side is a large metal desk where Melanie sits. Coop's office is down the hall.

"Hey, Melanie. How's it going?"

She looked up from her computer screen and didn't answer. Instead, she frowned at me and shoved reading glasses onto the top of her curly, gray hair, then laboriously lifted her heavy body off her chair. She walked slowly over to the counter with a side-to-side gait. Reaching underneath it, she pulled out the logbook and shoved it toward me, then went back to her desk. Still without speaking. Sometimes she was friendly, other times not. This was apparently a "not" day.

"Hey, I see Harold Dane had his house TP'd again. Wouldn't it be easier for him just to quit yelling at kids to get off his lawn?"

She looked up, but just shrugged.

"I'm thinking about doing a story on vandalism, maybe how neighbor-hoods can get together to help prevent it, that kind of thing." It sounded lame, and Melanie didn't bother to respond.

"So, is Coop around? I thought I might get some ideas from him."

She picked up her phone and punched in his extension. "Leah's here."

I prepared to stumble through my story all over again. But when Coop came through the door, he smiled and said, "Hey. Hi. C'mon back." He lifted up the pass-through in the counter so I could follow him. Relief rushed through me as I realized how easy it was going to be to get back to our old familiar footing.

I dropped down in the chair opposite his desk and shook my head when he offered me coffee. He sat in his chair and leaned back a little.

"Haven't seen much of you lately. Nice special section you guys did on the summer recreation stuff."

"Thanks. *Grantland's Summer Wonderland* isn't exactly the high-water mark for Himmel journalism, but it generated some ad revenue for Max."

He nodded. I nodded. This was the most stilted conversation I'd ever had with Coop. We waggled our heads at each other like bobbleheads for another few seconds, and then I took the plunge.

"Look, I haven't called you back because I didn't want to hear you tell me how ridiculous I am, and how I'm wasting my time, and how my ideas are stupid, and I should just let things go."

"I don't recall saying you're ridiculous. Or stupid."

"You might not have said it in so many words, but admit it, you think tracking down the truth about Lacey is a waste of time."

"Leah, c'mon. I don't want to fight with you again. But I'm not going to lie to you either. So yeah, I still have serious reservations about what you're doing. I'm hearing things, and it worries me."

"What things?"

"Like you're stirring things up, harassing people even. I saw Mary Beth at the Elite today and she was all shook up because you pressured her into giving out confidential information. Max is scared to death you're pissing the bank board off, and Georgia Caldwell is telling people you're trying to sabotage Miller's campaign. You're setting yourself—or the paper—up for serious trouble. Maybe a libel suit."

This wasn't going the way I planned at all. "Slander. It's only libel if it's printed."

"This isn't funny, Leah."

"Coop, listen, just for a minute. I know when I talked to you before I wasn't connecting the dots. I didn't even know where the dots were. But I do now, I've found out a lot more."

I told him about Hegl hiding the fact that he knew Lacey before she went to DeMoss, about his abrupt departure from Florida after another young girl died; about Miller paying for Lacey's perpetual memorial and posting to it every year; how I was sure Delite had lied about going to the party with Lacey, how she confirmed—sort of—that Lacey was sexually abused; and that I knew the name of the kid who'd been with Lacey. I finished in a rush, as though by spilling it out fast I could speed by his skepticism and bring him over to my side again. Where he had always been before.

Only it wasn't working.

"Leah, I wish you could see yourself, hear yourself. You look like you haven't slept in days. You drove eight hours round trip to the UP for a 10-minute conversation with Lacey's old roommate? You just said yourself she wasn't changing her story about the night Lacey died. She didn't admit to lying; you're basing that on the look in her eye?" His tone was mocking.

"And she didn't give you a name for this alleged sexual abuser, did she? As far as the young kid with Lacey, you still have no proof that Cole even saw her, let alone that she had a kid with her. All you know is the name of a boy who was a friend of hers. And what were you doing dragging Miguel along with you? If you don't care about your job, you should at least give a thought to his."

I recoiled as though he'd hit me. He'd been leaning forward with his hands resting on the desk. Now he lifted them up in obvious frustration.

"Leah, you're so fixated on—I don't know, making up for not saving Lacey?—that you can't think logically. You're tearing through this town hurting people, whether you mean to or not. It's reckless, and it's cruel. Look what you're doing to Max, to Paul Karr, to Miller and his family. You and your mom are at odds too. If I thought you were right, I'd be behind you a hundred percent. But I think you're wrong, and somebody's going to get hurt. I don't want it to be you."

I felt tears stinging my eyes and blinked hard to keep them from falling. I was so angry my voice shook.

"Just stop it. I came here to try and make things right between us. But you won't even listen. I don't know if somebody got to you or what—obviously, you've been talking about me to half the town. I may not have it all right, but I know in my gut I'm damn close. Don't worry. This is the last time I'll bother you with my obsession." I stood up and headed for the door.

"Leah! Stop. I'm just trying to help you see—"

"Don't bother. I can see just fine."

Darmody was in the front talking to Melanie.

"Hey, Leah, where's the fire? Should I call 911?" His laugh filled my ears as I pushed through the double doors and ran to my car. I pulled the door open and tumbled into the front seat. For a full minute, I pounded my fist on the dashboard, waiting for the sick feeling in my stomach to subside. Finally, it did.

19

All right, fine. I couldn't count on Coop, but he was right. I shouldn't be dragging Miguel into this. I had an idea of what I wanted to look into next, but first I had to do some "day job" work.

I stopped by the fire hall to take a picture of the chief with the department's new truck, then went to the County Extension office to talk to the agricultural agent, Jerry Grosskopf, about the potato-crop outlook. It was good. Unless the weather didn't hold. Then it was bad. I could feel another cutting edge story in the works. It was 4 p.m. when I finished and called in to tell Courtnee I wouldn't be back.

"Must be nice to be a reporter. You can, like, just come in when you want and you don't even have to stay until 5."

"That's right, Courtnee, reporters have it easy. I mean after all, it's so much fun to go to a county commissioner meeting that doesn't end until 10 p.m., then come back to the office, write up the story, and then get called out to a fire that lasts until 4 a.m. Then go home to sleep for two hours so you can be on time at the Rotary Pancake breakfast. All said, it's really a cushy job."

"Whatever. I just know I have to be here, like, from 8 a.m. until 5 p.m. It would be nice if I had some flexibility."

"I'll see you tomorrow."

Despite Courtnee's efforts, I didn't feel guilty at all. It was a rare week at the *Times* when we didn't put in 50-60 hours, and weekends didn't really exist. Neither did evenings off, if it was your turn to take home the scanner and monitor police and fire calls.

When I got home my mother was still at work. She didn't have a "cushy" job like me either. I sat down at the kitchen table and scrolled through my phone for the number of Sister Mattea's brother. I had met Scott when I stopped by the rosary for Sister Mattea, and I got his business card. I always save contact information, because as a reporter, you just never know. Scott worked in San Francisco, so it would be around 2 p.m. there. I tapped in his number, and on the second ring, a woman answered.

"Riordan Software Development, Miss Adams speaking. How may I direct your call?"

"Hi, Miss Adams, this is Leah Nash. May I speak to Scott Riordan please?"

"I'm sorry, Miss Nash, Mr. Riordan is away from the office. Can someone else help you?"

"Not really. Actually, this is a personal call. I need to speak to Scott."

"I see," she said, in a voice that conveyed she did not approve of this personal intrusion during business hours. "I'm afraid that's not possible. As I said, Mr. Riordan is away. Perhaps you'd like to try his cell phone?"

"That would be great. Can you give me his cell phone number?"

"Oh no, I couldn't do that. We're not allowed to give out personal cell phone numbers. When you said personal business, I naturally assumed you were a personal acquaintance and would have Mr. Riordan's non-work number."

"Right." Self-important flunky, I thought but realized it was a good time to use my filter. "Well, can you tell me if he'll be in later?"

"Oh, I hardly think so. Mr. Riordan is in China on a business trip. He has an open-ended return date."

"Could you give him a message?"

"That's my job," she said noncommittally.

I spelled my name, gave my number, and asked that Scott call me on a matter related to his sister. I'd been hoping to get some insights into Sister

Mattea—anything that would help me find the elusive link between her and Lacey. That plan would have to wait.

I had better luck following up with Miguel's information on Father Hegl. If I hadn't been a reporter, I definitely would have been a librarian. I love the research. I love trying first one tactic then another, searching out unexpected connections, going at the problem from all angles. Once I'm on the Internet trail, I can't let go.

I opened my computer and typed "Sean Hegl" into Google. Multiple pages popped up, but the first listing that caught my eye was the obituary for Noreen Holcomb Ramsey of Naples, Florida, whose survivors included a son, the Most Rev. Joseph Ramsey of Braxton, Florida, a daughter, Rita Ramsey Hegl of Jacksonville, Florida, a granddaughter, Claudia Hegl Patterson, and a grandson, the Rev. Sean Hegl. Neither grandchild's address was given. But Hegl's uncle was a "most reverend," which translated to bishop in Catholic speak.

Next, I bounced around between several aggregating sites that compile public information and can provide you with a person's age, address, phone number, relatives, and sometimes even roommate names.

Hegl didn't have a Facebook page that I could find, which was too bad because you can find a lot of stuff there. It's amazing how many people don't restrict access to their photos or their list of friends. Between the two of those and professional sites like LinkedIn, you can collect a lot of intel.

But I did pretty well even without Facebook. I found Sean Hegl, age 38, with possible relations Rita Hegl and Noreen Patterson, and several addresses in Florida, though nothing in Wisconsin. The first address was the same as that listed for Rita Ramsey Hegl, so that was probably the family home. The second one I checked turned out to be a Catholic seminary in Boca Raton. The third was what I was looking for—when I typed the address into Google, I got a nice little map with an arrow pointing to San Carlos Catholic Church.

I went to the church website which listed all of the pastors and the years they served under the "Our History" tab. The welcome page identified San Carlos as part of the Leesville Diocese and its bishop was the Most Reverend Joseph Ramsey. Well, well, well, Father Hegl had worked for his uncle.

I could call the diocesan office, but my gut told me it wasn't a good idea for Uncle Bishop to know someone was tracking his nephew.

I switched gears for the moment and looked for a number for Carla Pérez, the sister of Hegl's teenage "protégé" Olivia Pérez Morgan. No luck. I found some info on Carla—the school she graduated from, a couple of jobs she'd had, but no phone number. That's one of the current obstacles to tracking people online—the lack of a decent cell phone directory to take the place of the old-fashioned phone book.

But, fortunately, the elder Pérezes, Carlos and Laura, had not cut the cord, and they still had a landline. I called their number as I mentally readied my story. The phone was answered by a woman with a soft, pleasant voice.

"Mrs. Pérez?"

"Yes?" she said, in the tone of someone ready to give a thanks but no thanks as soon as I identified myself as a telemarketer. I started talking fast, a slight uptick in the end of each sentence.

"My name is Andrea Lawson, I'm on the All Class Reunion Committee at St. Francis High School? We're trying to get a database of everyone's email and phone numbers? It's driving me a little crazy?"

Pause for a slightly airheady giggle.

"Could I get Carla's cell phone number from you?" I put all I had into sounding like a cheerful, school spirit-filled alumna.

"Oh, that sounds like a good way for all of you to keep in touch. I'm sure Carla will want to be included. What was your name again?"

"Andrea Lawson?"

"Were you a friend of Carla's in school?"

"More of an acquaintance? How's she doing?"

"Very well. She's in the RN program at the community college, and she'll graduate next year. What about you Andrea, what are you doing?"

"I just got a new job in Orlando? I start next week at Sea World as a dolphin trainer?" When I'm making up a back story I won't need again, I like to fill in with jobs I think would be really cool, and for which I am not remotely qualified or suited.

"Oh, that sounds so interesting. Well, I'm sure Carla will be glad to hear from you. Hold on just a second. I have to scroll through the menu here. I have her on speed dial, so I can never remember her number."

She was quiet for a second and there were several beeps, and then she came back on the line with Carla's cell phone number.

"Thanks so much for your help, Mrs. Pérez? You have a great evening now?"

"You're welcome, Andrea, you too."

For my conversation with Carla, I opted for the truth, partly because I couldn't use the same lie, but mostly because it would be easier and cleaner.

"Hello?"

"Carla? Hi. My name is Leah Nash, I'm from Himmel, Wisconsin, and if you have just a few minutes, I'd like to ask you some questions about Father Sean Hegl."

The line went so quiet, I checked to see if we were still connected.

"Hello? Hello? Are you there, Carla?"

"Yeah. Yeah, I'm still here."

"Carla, this might sound weird, but please hear me out. My younger sister Lacey died five years ago. She was 17. I know your sister Olivia died when she was very young as well. And I know that she was connected to Father Hegl. I'd like to hear anything you can tell me about Father Hegl and your sister."

I heard a sharp intake of breath, then, "Why?"

"Because I think there's more to the story of how my sister died. I'm trying to find out if Father Hegl had any link to it. And I'm wondering if you think he had any connection to Olivia's death. She died in a car accident, right?"

"Yeah. They said she was drinking and driving too fast. She hit the shoulder and rolled her car. She got thrown out, hit her head. She wasn't wearing a seat belt."

She paused, and I waited, trying not to signal how badly I wanted the information I knew she was about to give.

"She was meeting him that night. Father Hegl. She took her car, because he didn't want to take the chance that someone would recognize his where it shouldn't be. But he always drove. He liked to be in charge, Livy said. She thought it was romantic."

"Always? She was in a relationship with Hegl?"

"Yes, for months. I knew it; her husband Vince suspected there was someone, but my parents were clueless. They always were with Olivia. She was my father's little princess."

"Was the affair serious?"

"Olivia thought it was, but she thought Lifetime movies were real. I mean, even a 15-year-old like me could tell he wasn't that into her. She was always talking about how they were going to get married and move to New York. You know, daydream stuff."

"What happened the night your sister died?"

"Olivia said she was going to tell Hegl she wanted to go public—you know, tell her husband Vince and Hegl tell his bishop, and then they'd be together forever. She never thought things through."

"So, that night..."

"Olivia did her hair, make-up, put on this sexy new dress, gave me a cover story to give to Vince in case he called to check on her."

"But the police report said she was alone in the car."

"Maybe. Maybe Hegl just let her drive off drunk after he dumped her, but I don't think so. I think he was right behind the wheel driving drunk himself. Tell me this—what was she doing on that dark country road in the middle of nowhere in the middle of the night? Alone?"

"Who found her?"

"An anonymous 911 call reported the accident. She might not have been found for days otherwise. It was way out in the country."

"The 911 call was anonymous? How do you know?"

"A deputy told my parents the call came from a pay phone at a gas station on the main road a mile away. He said one of the local weed growers probably spotted the car but didn't want to risk getting busted.

"What I want to know is, why did Hegl leave town right after the accident? He didn't even go to her funeral. And why did Olivia's husband Vince all-of-the-sudden have enough money to buy a boat and move to the Keys?

That *perezoso* deadbeat couldn't get enough money together to buy a fishing pole, let alone a fishing boat."

"Carla, did you tell anyone you suspected Hegl might have been involved?"

"I was 15 years old, nobody cared what I said. I told the cop who came to the house to tell us Olivia was dead, but he didn't listen. My mother was hysterical, and my father slapped me when I said Olivia was going to meet Father Hegl that night. They're old-fashioned, and they couldn't think a priest or their little princess would do anything like that. My parents were grieving, but they were embarrassed, too, ashamed about Livy drinking. They thought it was their fault. They told me to pray and quit talking about it."

"But, Carla, the crime scene reconstruction that must have been done, it would have shown if anyone else was in the car."

"Would it?" she asked in a tone that told me, if I were there, I'd see a sardonic sneer on her face. "Could they really tell? The sheriff's department isn't exactly *CSI Miami*. And they started out thinking they knew what happened. Drunk girl, drunk accident, dead drunk girl. End of story."

"So, you think someone helped Hegl cover-up the fact that he was involved with Olivia, and maybe even that he was driving the car that night?"

"That's right. And somebody must have been a little worried about my 'hysteria,' because Father Herrera, my mother's cousin, who works in the diocese office, came to visit. When my mother left to make coffee, he talked to me. Told me that it was a sin to spread rumors. Said that I would only hurt my sister's memory and my parents. Said making up stories wasn't the way to get attention.

"He told me Father Hegl couldn't have been with her, because he was at dinner with the bishop and a very important donor the night Olivia died. The bishop told Father Herrera so himself. After that, I knew it wasn't any use, so I did shut up. It made my parents happy, and it made my life easier."

"But you've never been convinced."

"No. My sister was a naïve kid with too many *telenovela* plots running in her head. She always fell for the good-looking guy—whether he was riding a motorcycle like Vince, or wearing a priest collar like Hegl. She could spin a fairy tale for any situation. With her as the heroine. Only this time, she was the victim. What I can't forget is that she was still alive when the EMTs got there. It was just too late. She didn't have to die."

"But you don't have any proof?"

"If I did, maybe the cops would've done something. But maybe not even then. This is like little Vatican here. The priests are like saints to people like my mom and dad. It was just easier for everyone if drunk Olivia had a terrible accident and crazy Carla—who doesn't even go to Mass!—just lied for attention."

"Did your priest happen to mention the name of the bishop's friend, the donor he and Hegl supposedly had dinner with that night?"

"I don't remember, I'm sorry."

"That's OK."

"It's been so long. Why are you calling now?"

"Because of my sister. Her story is a lot like Olivia's. It's possible Hegl was involved, but no one wants to hear it."

"So, what are you going to do?"

"I'm not sure."

So now, although Miller was still the odds on favorite, Hegl had just moved up a length.

20

On Saturday, the last thing I wanted to do was go to the *Cinco de Mayo* party, where, according to Coop, half the guests thought I was unbalanced, and the other half thought I was a malicious character assassin. But I had promised Miguel I'd be there, so I had to show up at least for a little while.

The May night was unseasonably warm. Cars lined both sides of the street, and I could hear laughter and music when I parked and turned off my engine a few houses away. The party had spilled into the backyard where the fence was strung with white lights and a large *piñata* hung from the branch of an oak tree. I rang the front bell. The door was opened by a guy around my age that I hadn't seen before.

"Hi, come on in. I'm Ben Kalek. You're Leah, right?" he said in the kind of husky voice I find quite appealing. He smiled and revealed well aligned and very white teeth. His blonde hair was short and a little messy, and his eyes reminded me of the periwinkle blue in a box of crayons. Miguel's latest conquest?

"How did you know?"

"Miguel's talked about you. You look just the way he described you."

"So you were expecting an Amish lawyer?"

"I'm sorry, I didn't catch that?" he said, tilting his head down toward me.

"Nothing. Never mind. So, how do you know Miguel?" I asked as we stood in the front hall.

"We met at the gym a while ago."

"Ah," I nodded. "So, you haven't been together long?" I fished, wondering why Miguel hadn't told me about his crush. He usually can't contain himself when he meets someone new, which is about every other week.

"What?" Ben said, looking confused. "No, no I'm not gay—"

"Not that there's anything wrong with that," we both said at the same time and laughed.

"No, we just hang out sometimes. A bunch of us play pick-up basketball on the weekends."

Hmm. I didn't get why he was playing host/doorman for Miguel. But he was very pleasant to look at. Nice enough that I wished I'd worn something besides jeans and a white oxford shirt with rolled up sleeves. But I had gotten a haircut that day, so there was that.

"How about a drink? Miguel mixed up a big batch of margaritas, and they're pretty good."

"Sure, thanks."

"Be right back."

I wandered into the living room and sat down on a folding chair near the fireplace. As I did, Miguel spotted me and came dancing over. He leaned in and gave me a big hug.

"*Chica*! I saw you talking to Ben. Nice, yes?" he nodded his head up and down.

"Yeah, he seems pretty nice."

"Pretty nice? I special-ordered him for you."

"What?"

"You need a little spice in your life. Ben, he's perfect for a little spring fling." He grinned broadly and lifted his eyebrows up and down in mock lechery.

"You didn't! Miguel, I hate set-ups and I don't have time for one now. I can't—"

Instead of listening, he reached over and undid a button on my shirt, shaking his head. "This a party, *chica*, not a deposition. You gotta work it a little. C'mon. I can't do everything. Ben's hot and hetero. Get in the game."

Before I could answer, someone yelled to him from across the room that the *empanadas* were running out. He patted me on the shoulder and said, "I'll be back. Now get out there and make the magic happen."

I was mortified. Who knew what he had told Ben—take pity on my desperate, lonely friend? I headed through the patio doors and out to the backyard in hopes of avoiding him. I made a beeline for a punchbowl set up on the picnic table, filled a plastic cup to the rim, and took a big gulp. Whoa! That was one strong margarita. I found an empty chair in a corner of the yard and sat down to nurse my drink and watch the revelers.

Several couples were salsa dancing with varying levels of skill, and I recognized Courtnee's flag of Spain colors swirling around. She and her boyfriend Trent were actually pretty good dancers. The stars were out, the music was lively, and the embarrassment over Miguel's matchmaking began to fade as I downed my margarita. I started to feel a pleasant glow that ended abruptly as my benevolent gaze picked up Ellie steaming across the yard toward me.

"Leah, is it true you confronted Miller Caldwell at his home and accused him of being involved in Lacey's death?" she demanded without preamble. A fresh grassy smell wafted off her.

"Miller asked me to stop by for coffee. He invited me. I didn't call him. We talked about Lacey. I didn't accuse him of anything. I just asked a few questions."

She shook her head, making flame-colored hair swirl around her shoulders and land in charming chaos above her close fitting purple tank top. I had the urge to tell her she looked like the Little Mermaid and smelled like a field of clover, but fortunately my prefrontal cortex hadn't yet surrendered to the tequila.

"I've asked you, begged you, and Max has ordered you to stop this stupid attempt to rewrite your family history. It's bad enough to fool yourself, but your selfishness is hurting my family. I won't have it." She was actually shaking her finger at me.

"You know, I'm getting a little tired of you telling me how to live my life.

How is me finding out how my sister died hurting your family, Ellie? I mean, seriously. I make sure everyone I talk to knows this is my deal, not Max's."

"I wouldn't care what you're doing, Leah, if it didn't affect Max. I don't know why he's so fond of you, because you sure don't seem very fond of him. All you care about is what you want to do, what you think is important, and to hell with everyone else. But I care that my husband is juggling creditors, and cutting his pay in half, and dodging old friends, because he owes them money. I care that he has to take Ambien every night to get to sleep. I care that you're a major part of the stress he's feeling.

"And no matter what you tell the nuns, or Miller, or anyone else connected with DeMoss, nobody likes feeling they're under investigation. Least of all the Catholic Church. And that kind of people take care of their friends, and they don't leave fingerprints. They won't have to refuse Max's loan to punish him. If they delay acting on it long enough, Max will go under. And I hope you can live with that, knowing it's partly your fault, after all he's done for you."

I didn't know that about Max. I didn't realize he'd cut his own salary.

"Look, Ellie, I'm sorry. I really am. But Max's problems with the paper started long before I got back. You know that. I'm finally getting somewhere with this, and I can't stop now. Things are starting to make sense. I'm even beginning to see how Sister Mattea fits into the picture." OK, so I was exaggerating, but in the face of Ellie's anger I guess I was trying to justify myself.

She looked at me nonplussed.

"You are unbelievable! Now we'll have every Catholic in town cancelling his subscription to the paper because you're trying to dig up dirt on a nun!" Then she turned on her heel and strode away. Ellie's rant shook me up. It made me sick to think of Max's situation. Maybe there was a little truth in Ellie's fears. If someone like Reid Palmer or Miller Caldwell thought I was going to hurt something they cared about—in Palmer's case the DeMoss family legacy, in Miller's his political future—they might put pressure wherever they thought it would help. No matter what I said about Max not being part of it.

I became aware that someone was watching me.

"I've been looking for you. You're not trying to avoid me, are you?" Ben asked, but in the teasing tone of someone who knew he never had to worry about being ditched. He held a plastic cup toward me. I accepted and took a big gulp. One and a half margaritas in, I was a little less uptight about Miguel's matchmaking efforts.

"Hey. Thanks. I just saw someone I know, and we got talking."

"Ah." He nodded as he pulled up a lawn chair and sat down beside me. "It's a beautiful night, isn't it?"

"Yeah, it sure is." We were both silent for a minute, then both started talking at once.

"So Miguel says—"

"So where are you—"

"No, you go," I said.

"All right. Miguel said you're a big-time journalist. What are you doing back in Himmel?"

"He's exaggerating, as usual. I'm back to take care of some family stuff. You know," I said evasively and took another sip. His hand accidentally brushed against my arm as he leaned over to reach for the chips sitting on the table next to us. He really was good looking. Or did I just think so because I was in the middle of a long dry spell, tempered now by a wet margarita haze?

"Yeah, I hear you. So, you're from here then?"

"Born and raised. How about you?"

"I live in Chicago, but I used to spend summers here with my grandmother. She died a couple of months ago. I'm staying at her house, trying to fix it up to sell."

"I'm sorry."

"Yeah. Well, she had Alzheimer's. It was pretty hard to have her go like that. She was a special person."

"I'm sorry," I said again. I changed the subject.

"So what do you do, Ben? When you're not fixing up houses?"

"I'm an IT security consultant."

"No way."

"Way. Why not?"

OK, I wasn't so far gone that I was going to tell him he looked too hot to be a computer geek. But I was close. "You just seem too, too, uh—social. You seem too social."

"C'mon. You don't seriously think all IT people are awkward social misfits?"

"Um, kind of."

"You're a very biased person, Leah. I'm surprised. I thought journalists were supposed to be all about getting the facts, no judgments, just the facts."

"I think you're thinking of Joe Friday."

He looked blank.

" 'Dragnet.' 'Just the facts, ma'am.' 1987 Tom Hanks/Dan Aykroyd movie? Old-timey TV show? Really bad remake with Ed O'Neill 2003?" Oh boy. He looked dreamy, but he was dropping in my esteem. I put a lot of store by old movie and TV references.

"Sorry."

"I forgive you." He really was very pretty. "So how long will you be here?"

"Couple more months, I think. Until the house is in shape to put on the market. Right now the interior needs a lot of work."

"I hope you're handy."

"I've been told I am," he said with a grin. I was glad it was dark as I realized I'd walked right into that double entendre and felt a flush rise on my cheeks. And remembered Miguel's comment about picking Ben out special for me. I was going to make an excuse to circulate, but he said, "Would you like another drink?"

Suddenly, that seemed like a really good idea. Why couldn't I just once, just let things happen? I wasn't judgmental. I wasn't obsessed. I knew how to have a good time. I could get in the game.

"All right. Sure."

As he left, I heard a burst of laughter from across the yard. Coop was walking toward my little corner of the party with Sherry holding so tight to his arm she looked like a third appendage. He caught my eye, then we both looked away. Sherry must have seen the glance, because she gave his arm a proprietary squeeze, then leaned her head on it for just a second. As they turned and changed direction toward the house, she cast a triumphant smile at me.

Dumbass. Coop could date all the bimbos he wanted. I wasn't interested in him as a boyfriend, but I sure did miss him as a friend. I stood up to stretch my legs and someone tapped my shoulder from behind.

"Karen! I haven't seen you in forever."

"I know. But I hear all about you from Carol," she said, leaning down from her 6-foot height to give me a hug.

"I bet. You look great. Your hair is super cute." I was used to seeing her silver-blonde hair in a no-nonsense short cut, but she'd grown it out to a layered bob that suited her narrow face.

She waved away my compliment, then hit me with what was on her mind.

"Leah, what's goin' on with you? Your mother is really worried. She told me," and here she leaned in a little and dropped her voice almost to a whisper, "she said you're convinced that Lacey was sexually abused, and you're risking your job and Max's business to prove you're right."

"Karen, don't you start on me. Despite what everyone seems to think, I didn't just dream this up." I gave her the shortest version I could of what I'd discovered, and to my surprise, instead of telling me I was crazy and irresponsible, she nodded her head.

"I see. That's not exactly how your mom explained it."

"No doubt. Look, I get she's concerned, but I've been doing investigative reporting for 10 years. I know when something is off. Yeah, yeah, so I'm emotionally involved in this. That doesn't mean I'm not on to something, does it?" I tried to keep my desire for her validation out of my voice.

"Kiddo, if you say there's something wrong with Lacey's death, then I have to take you seriously. But at this point, it looks to me like you know too much for your peace of mind, and not enough for a court of law. And Carol's right you're treading on dangerous ground.

"Miller is very powerful, and Georgia is very protective. She's not going to let a threat to his election go. And DeMoss Academy has influential friends. This priest you're after, the Catholic Church is going to protect him, too. You're out on your own on this one. Max has taken a clear step back. You could be sued for slander. And that could be a very expensive, career-destroying court case. Your professional and personal life, everything will be up for grabs."

"It doesn't matter. If it's true, it isn't slander. I just have to prove what I'm saying is true. And, Karen, I don't know all the answers, but I'm getting closer."

"Leah, are you getting enough sleep? You look so tired. You know, you're all your mother's got. You need to take care of yourself. She loves you like crazy. And so do I," she said, reaching out and putting a hand on my shoulder.

A warm glow infused me, and I thought, take that Coop, everybody else loves me. I had moved into a very mellow place in Margaritaville, and all things seemed possible. I reached up and pulled her down in a hug. "Karen, it's OK. I'm OK. And you're OK. And everything is A-OK. Don't worry."

"How much have you had to drink, Leah?"

"Oh, a couple. Small ones. I'm good," I assured her. I really was. I've heard that drinking brings out the side of your personality that you keep under wraps—that's why some people who are jovial, funny types turn into mean drunks. In my case, drinking turns me from a cynical smartass to an affectionate extrovert. With each sip, I become more enchanted with everyone.

At this point I found it hard to keep from giving Karen a pinch on the cheeks, because she looked so darn sweet with her face all scrunched up with worry lines, looking at me with big sad eyes.

"Look, give me a call tomorrow. I want to walk through this with you when you're fully functional. You need to understand what could happen if you're wrong. And maybe even more important, what could happen if you're right. Now, you settle down and eat something. I'll talk to you later."

As she started to move away, Ben came up with our drinks.

"Wait, Karen, this is my new friend Ben. He loves his grandma. Ben, this is Karen. She's really nice. Do you like her hair?"

They exchanged glances. "Nice to meet you, Ben. Take good care of your new friend."

"Don't worry. I've got it covered."

"Who was that?"

"My mom's boss. Karen. She's a good lawyer."

He nodded. "I'll keep that in mind if I need one."

He sat down next to me, and I drank freely from my replenished margarita while he started on a long story, which I vaguely remember had to do with a road trip with a friend in a 1982 Plymouth Reliant. I absolutely remember I found it hilarious. Toward the end I noticed I was getting cold. And I was hungry.

I stood up a little woozily and reached down to pull Ben up beside me.

"Whoa, steady there. You all right?"

"Yeah, yeah. Just hungry. Let's go in and get something to eat."

Inside I excused myself and headed for the bathroom. "Be right back." Of course, there was a line up. When I finally got through and headed for the kitchen, I saw Karen and Ben in conversation. Walking up to them, I said, "Hey, you guys. I really like you. Did you know that?"

Miguel came up just then, and I threw an arm up and pulled his head down and gave him a big kiss on the top of his head. "Miguel! Ben and Karen this is my Miguel." Which struck me suddenly as very funny, especially when I began to sing the Beatles "My Michelle," replacing it, of course, with "My Miguel."

In the middle of the chorus, I saw Coop in the doorway. I broke off mid-song. "Coop!" I shouted, so happy to see him. Then I remembered. "You're an asshat. This is my new friend, Ben. And this is my true friend, Miguel. And, Karen." I fixed him with a withering stare. Or at least what in my mind was a withering stare.

"Leah, don't you think it might be time to go home and get some rest?"

"Quit telling me what I think. I think you should just go call your best friend Miller Caldwell. I think you don't know who I think you aren't. Are. Thought you were. Think you know!" I finished incoherently, but with an unwarranted sense of triumph, as though I had scored a major verbal putdown. "I am going. I am going with my new true friend Ben."

From somewhere in the dark recesses of a childhood spent listening to my mother's *Best of the '70s* albums, I dredged up the Michael Jackson song "Ben." None of the words came to mind, but that was OK. I settled for humming and ad-libbing something along the lines of *"Ben, my new best friend. And I will not pretend. That you are not my friend. And I will never bend..."* And then, mercifully my lyric machine ran dry, and I sat down abruptly in the nearest chair. From there memory dims.

21

I woke up to the nauseating smell of bacon frying. I was in a bed I didn't recognize in a room I'd never seen before. Not a good feeling. I remembered the party. I remembered Ben and drinking margaritas and laughing and maybe singing and maybe, sort of, coming back here with Ben. But nothing was very clear.

I threw back the cover, saw that I was still wearing my jeans and oxford shirt. That seemed like a positive sign. I sat up. Then promptly lay back down and closed my eyes. My head was pounding. Was this Ben's house? I tried again to get myself upright, this time more slowly. I opened my eyes carefully and looked around.

The room was small and held only the bed I was in, a battered nightstand, and a threadbare rug. The wallpaper was a faded dark green festooned with big pink cabbage roses. The bed itself was the kind you see in old Westerns, a metal frame and springs topped by a blue ticking mattress. Well. No one could say I wasn't a cheap date.

OK, OK, pull yourself together. I swung my feet onto the floor and felt around for my shoes, which I located tucked under the bed. As I leaned over to put them on, a wave of nausea hit me, and I stopped mid-reach and took a deep breath. By employing this torturous start-stop-start method, I was able to get my shoes tied. I rose from the bed and grabbed my purse, which was sitting on the night table, and slowly made my way to the door.

The bacon smell now mingled with the scent of strong coffee. I made a stop in the bathroom across the hall, where I repeatedly splashed cold water on my face. I squeezed toothpaste on my finger and ran it across my teeth and tongue a few times. I studied myself in the mirror. There were huge bags under my eyes, and my hair was sticking out as though I was a cartoon character with a finger stuck in an electric socket. I dug around in my purse for a hairclip, yanked my hair back and clipped it up, searched within my soul for the few shreds of dignity I could muster, and followed the breakfast smells down the stairs.

I walked through a formal dining room and into a kitchen that looked like it came straight from the set of a 1950s sitcom. A big roundish refrigerator was set against one wall, next to a white stove with a solid door and chrome knobs. A dinette set with yellow Formica top and yellow-padded chrome chairs held center stage in the room. That's where Ben sat drinking a cup of coffee, as I trudged shamefacedly in.

"Hey, good morning, how're you feeling?" he asked in the hearty voice of someone who had not consumed way too many margaritas the night before. His eyes were clear, his smile bright. He was disgusting.

"OK," I whispered. "But could we talk in our indoor voices for a while?"

He grinned. "Here, a glass of water and a cup of coffee. That'll start you on the road to recovery. I've got some over-easy eggs, bacon—"

I shook my head rapidly, then dropped into the nearest chair to ride out a sudden wave of dizziness. "No, no thanks. Dry toast if you have it. That would be great."

I took a huge drink of water and ate a couple of bites of dry wheat toast before I said, "Look, about last night. I, uh. That is, I don't want you to think...uh, I don't usually...I didn't sleep with you last night, did I?"

"You don't remember?" he asked, a hurt look on his face.

Oh no. Oh hell. I took a deep breath, "Ben, I—"

Then I realized he was shaking with laughter. "I'm sorry. I couldn't resist. The expression on your face—" He lost control and started laughing again.

"You know, you're kind of an ass."

"Hey, now. Last night you told me I was your best friend. You even sang me a song about it."

I lowered my head into my hands and muttered, "Stop. Please. Just stop."

"C'mon Leah. Don't be embarrassed. No. We didn't sleep together. You were in no condition to drive. When we got in my car you couldn't give me your address. Said you didn't want your mom to see you. So, I brought you here, took your shoes off, tucked you into bed, and now here you are safe and sound."

"Thanks," I said. Then, anxious to change the subject, "So, this is your grandmother's house? It's pretty, uh, vintage."

"I know. Every time I come into the kitchen, I expect to see Lucy and Ethel having coffee. It's gonna take a while to update it."

"Well, it made a nice B&B for me. Thanks. But I should get going. Could you give me a ride to my car, and then I'll just head on home?"

"Nothing more to eat?"

"No, I'm good, thanks."

I've done the walk of shame a few times in my life, but this was the first time strolling into my mother's kitchen was part of it. As I pulled into the driveway, I noticed Miguel's bright red Toyota parked across the street. Yay.

I squared my shoulders and did my best to appear nonchalant and clear-eyed.

"Hey! Morning, Mom. Hi, Miguel. What are you doing here?"

"Miguel just brought me some *tamales* left over from the party last night. I could put a couple in the microwave for you," she said with an evil glint in her eye.

"No, no, that's OK," I said, as my stomach did a quick lurch.

"So, Miguel was telling me you had quite a good time last night, Leah. You don't look like you're having so much fun now." Her voice was filled with faux concern.

"Whatever, Mom. Let's just move on, OK? Got any coffee? I saw Karen last night."

"Oh?"

"Mom, if you're so worried about me asking questions, maybe you shouldn't be telling everyone what I'm doing."

"Karen isn't 'everyone,' and, besides, I already told you I talked to her. Don't get surly with me because you're hung over."

I held up my hand. "Sorry. Can we take it down a notch? My head is killing me."

"Serves you right," she said, but handed me a glass of water and some aspirin at the same time. "You're old enough to know better. Did Lacey's roommate reach you last night?

"Delite? She called here?"

"She said she lost your card, and she wanted to talk to you. I gave her your cell number. I thought about not doing it, but I knew that would only postpone the inevitable."

I unzipped my purse and started pulling things out and setting them on the table as I rooted around. Camera batteries, my wallet, a battered compact, a bottle of water, geez, my purse was way too big. "Damn!"

"You lost your cell again? Your *mamá* needs to make you one of those strings little kids use for mittens, only you can hook it to your phone," Miguel said.

"You know what's not funny? You. Help me think. I must have taken it out at your house?"

"Sorry, *chica*, I cleaned up everything this morning. If it was there, I would've found it. Maybe it's in your car?"

I dashed out and started ransacking my Focus. Not on the seats, not under the backseats, not in the door pocket, not in the glove compartment, not on the floor, not in the center console storage box.

"It's not there. Why am I so careless?"

My mother didn't say anything, but it was killing her.

"Maybe it's at Ben's. Do you have his number, Miguel?" He nodded and punched it in, then handed me his phone.

"Ben, Leah Nash. Hey, could you do me a favor and take a look around and see if I left my cell phone at your house, or maybe in your car?"

"Sure, I'll call you back in five."

As I waited anxiously, I grilled my mother.

"What exactly did Delite say?"

"I told you. She lost your card, and she wanted to get in touch with you."

"But did she say what about? Why?"

"She didn't say, and I didn't ask. You're going to do what you want to do, I know. But I don't have to be part of it."

"Don't you get it, Mom? Delite knows something, I'm sure of it. She as good as admitted that she lied about going with Lacey to a party that night. Maybe she's ready to tell me why."

"Now, Leah," she said in the tone she's used to correct me since I was two years old. "You need to settle down. You need to get some sleep. You need to take a step back. Honey, I'm worried about you."

"Don't be, Mom. I'm fine. I—"

Miguel's phone rang, and when he looked at the caller ID, he handed it over to me.

"Ben? Did you find it?"

"Sorry, Leah, no luck. I checked all the rooms you were in—bedroom, bathroom, kitchen. It's just not there."

"Well, thanks for looking. Talk to you later." I handed the phone back to Miguel.

"Hell to the max. It's got to be somewhere. I can't go without a cell phone. If I don't find it today, I'll have to get a new one tomorrow." Another roadblock loomed. "I don't have Delite's number!"

"Yes, you do, just look at the recent call list on Carol's phone," Miguel said.

My mother and I exchanged looks—hers slightly defiant, mine definitely I-told-you-so. "That would work, if Mom's phone was made in the 21st century. She's still got a 1994 Trimline phone—that one on the wall over by the bar. No tracking phone calls there, right, Mom?"

"It's a perfectly good phone. It does what I want it to do, and I don't leave it lying around all over town. I have an answering machine, isn't that enough? Don't get snarky."

At that moment, the phone in question rang. My mother answered it. "What? Yes. Of course. Yes, Max. She's on her way, I think. No, she's just running late. She lost her phone. All right. Tell Ellie good luck."

She hung up and glared at me.

"What?"

"Max is at the Fun Run at the county park with Ellie and Alex and half the town. He wants to know where you are. Leah Marie Nash, I lied for you, and I don't like it. I told him you were on your way. It's bad enough you get drunk and go home with a stranger last night, but I don't want Max to think you're so hell—"

I shot a glance at Miguel who was suddenly studying with rapt attention a recipe for curried chicken stuck to the refrigerator with a magnet.

"Sorry, Mom, sorry, sorry. I just forgot about it," I said, throwing things into my purse.

"It seems to me you 'just forgot' about everything except your current obsession. No one said you shouldn't be trying to find the truth about Lacey—"

"Oh, no. We're not going there are we? 'No one?' How about Max, Coop, you, Paul, everyone in this town except Miguel," I hissed back.

"Just a minute, missy—"

"Missy? Really, Mom? You haven't hauled that one out since I was 10 years old."

"Well, you're acting like a 10-year-old! A belligerent, willful—"

"OK, great as it's been talking to you, I've got to go. As you know, I'm late." As I banged the door shut, I heard her say, "Wait, Leah, please. I'm worried about you, I—"

But I didn't wait, I kept going.

22

The 5K Fun Run—which name seemed to me an oxymoron, fun and run being diametrically opposed activities as far as I was concerned—was an annual event to raise money for DeMoss Academy. The course skirted the county park, looped around a section of the Catherines' property, then came back by the river bluff where just weeks ago Sister Mattea had plunged to her death. Judging by the chattering crowd waiting for the race to start, and the runners joking and doing warm-ups, no one seemed to mind—or remember.

A bank of clouds advancing from the west suggested a storm in the offing, but if so, it was still miles away. Meanwhile, a few hundred yards from the finish line, volunteers fired up charcoal grills, set up serving tables with paper plates and plastic cups, and unloaded tubs of baked beans and coleslaw, mountains of hotdogs, buns and condiments. Farther over in the park, kids were playing on swing sets and slides. It was the first major event of the almost-summer, and the turnout was great.

As I got out of the car, Helen Sebanski, publicity chair for the event, spotted me and came bustling over with her characteristic half-walk, half-trot, a gait that left her perpetually breathless. She was resplendent in a purple track suit over a T-shirt imprinted with the MGM Grand logo. Her soft white hair was held back by a glittery gold headband.

"Leah, I'm so glad you're here. I was beginning to worry. I should have known we can always count on the *Times*," she said, panting discreetly and smiling as she took my hand in both of hers. I felt a stab of guilt that I tried to assuage with a hearty, "I'm happy to be here, Helen. Looks like a great event. Did you have fun on your senior excursion to Las Vegas?"

"Oh yes. I won $500 on the slot machines. It was just marvelous," she said, as she took my arm and fox-trotted me over to Sister Julianna and Reid Palmer.

"Sister Julianna, Mr. Palmer, this is Leah Nash with the *Himmel Times*."

"We're already acquainted, Helen," Reid said, smiling at her.

"Well, that's a small town for you, isn't it? But then it's a small world, too, I always say." She turned to me. "You won't believe this, but I ran into Sister Julianna when I was in Las Vegas. You brought me luck, Sister. I won $500 after I saw you."

"That's wonderful, Helen. Can I count on you to tithe 10 percent of that for the DeMoss development fund?" She winked to show she was kidding. Then she must have noticed the puzzled expression on my face. Las Vegas and Sister Julianna went together in my mind like the pope and McClain's Bar & Grill.

"I was attending a conference on adolescent dysfunctional behavior at the Bellagio," she said to me.

"Sister Julianna is being modest. She was the keynote speaker. She's a nationally recognized expert on adolescent behavior," Reid said.

"Well, we're just so proud of all the wonderful work you do," Helen said. "I—"

"Helen! We can't find the starting pistol!" someone shouted from the starting line.

"Oh dear, I have to go. But thank you both so much for all you do for the children. And, Leah, I'll look forward to seeing the write-up in the paper," she spoke from over her shoulder as she trotted off with a little wave.

"So, maybe I could do a feature about you and your work on the national level," I said to Sister Julianna. That might be an avenue for access to the Catherines that wouldn't upset Max.

She shook her head. "Reid is exaggerating. I just like to stay current and make a contribution. Actually, Leah, we were talking about you when you walked up with Helen."

"Oh?"

"I think you've mistaken my feelings about your inquiries. I understand that you need—we all need—to know the truth."

That was a 180. Had Reid engineered her change of heart? Mine not to reason why, mine but to step up and take advantage of it.

"I wonder then if you know why Delite lied to you about Lacey going to a party with her the night she disappeared?"

"You talked with Delite? She said she had lied?"

"Yes and no. Yes, I talked to her, but, no, she didn't admit she lied. She was clearly hiding something, though. Her story just doesn't fit when you factor in Danny Howard. When I pressed her on it, she got pretty belligerent. She also said Lacey couldn't stand Father Hegl. Do you know anything about that?"

"I don't think she can be right about that. They were both so interested in music and both such beautiful singers. And Father Hegl loves teaching, especially talented performers like Lacey. In fact, he's teaching a music class Wednesday nights at the technical college this semester, in addition to everything he does at DeMoss."

"Father Hegl is, as am I, a believer in the transformative power of music," Reid added.

It seemed to me that this sidebar on Hegl's devotion to music was a diversionary tactic to get away from the topic of Delite and her lie. "Why do you think Delite would have made up a story about going to a party with Lacey? Do you think it's possible she was trying to make you believe she was trying to be a better person by accepting responsibility for her behavior? So she wouldn't get shipped off to juvenile detention? Or, is it possible someone put her up to lying? Because—" My query was cut short.

"I'm sorry but I believe Helen is trying to get our attention, Reid. It looks like the race is about to start. Leah, you'll excuse us?" She started moving away before she even finished her sentence.

As Reid turned to go he said, "Please call me, Leah. I'm curious to hear more about your investigations." As they left, I saw Max striding toward me.

"Hey, Max. I saw Alex and Ellie headed to the starting line a few minutes ago. You're not running this year?" The last time Max ran anywhere was in 1989, when I accidentally hit a softball through his picture window. He ignored my attempt to keep things light.

"I hope you were talking to Reid Palmer and Sister Julianna about the race and nothing else."

"Don't worry, I've got it covered. It's all good." A lie by omission is still a lie, I know. It just doesn't feel quite as bad.

He fixed me with his fierce eyebrow stare. I stared right back, and then he surprised me. He put a hand on my shoulder.

"Leah, please don't make me do something I don't want to do."

Before I could ask him what he meant, the loudspeaker crackled and runners were ordered to the starting line. He dropped his hand. "I gotta go. I want Ellie to hear me cheering."

As the runners took to the course, I talked to committee members, got a tally on sponsorships and tickets sold, and how many runners had entered —the usual drill for an event like that. As I worked the crowd, I saw Miguel wandering around shooting photos. He must have taken pity on my unprepared state this morning, even though it wasn't his weekend to work. That was a good thing, because even with the foolproof idiot camera in my bag, I wasn't confident I could hold it steady enough to take any decent shots.

The first runners started coming in about 20 minutes after the race began. The last ones trailed in about half an hour after that. Ellie took first place in her group. Paul Karr finished 5th for the over-60s, and Miller's daughter Charlotte got a first. Helen Sebanski was in her glory on the dais, putting medals around the winners' necks, and Reid made a nice speech about the work DeMoss Academy did, and how grateful everyone on the board was for the community support.

People were still eating and talking as the sky got darker and darker. The more experienced committee members, used to the vicissitudes of Wisconsin weather, had begun packing up supplies when the wind started to pick up. By the time the first drops of rain fell, the tables were cleared and the vans loaded. After a few more tentative drops, the pace picked up and people scrambled to their cars.

Thunder rumbled to the west and I dove into my Focus just as a flash of lighting forked across the sky. I was blocked from leaving by an SUV filled with squabbling children and irritated parents who apparently elected to punish them—and me—by sitting in place until the kids stopped crying. By the time they left, the rain was pelting my little compact with such force that the windshield wipers couldn't keep up even on high speed.

I decided to stay where I was until the storm passed. A few other cars had the same idea, but I moved away from them toward the center of the lot to be out of range of any falling trees. Then I turned off the motor and tilted my seat back. The rain hit the roof and slapped at the windows with a hypnotic rhythm. I reached into the backseat, pulled out the raggedy blanket I keep there, and snuggled under it. I closed my eyes, safe from the storm in the warm cocoon of my car.

With no sound but the rain and my own breathing, my body relaxed and my mind quieted. I fell into a kind of trance. The tangled knot of regret, anger, and guilt that had been tightening around my heart since Sister Mattea's death, seemed to loosen. My failure to save Lacey, Max's problems, Coop's defection, Miller's involvement, Delite's stonewalling, Hegl's role, the mystery of what Sister Mattea knew—everything fell away, and I was just breathing in the semi-darkness of the storm.

At some point, I must have drifted off into sleep, because when I opened my eyes, the rain had stopped. I sat up with a start and looked around. It was still light but the shadows were long. I looked at my watch—eight o'clock. I'd slept for hours.

Stiff and groggy, I got out of the car to stretch and pull on my oversized hoodie. The area was deserted. A scattering of puddles in the parking lot and a few clouds overhead were the only evidence of the storm. I stood there in a post-sleep stupor, yawning, and staring blankly out across the river.

Gradually, a movement near the edge of the bluff caught my eye. Squinting in the dim light, I saw something that made my mouth go dry and my heart contract with quick thumping beats. At the spot where Sister Mattea had fallen something—or someone—was rising up over the ground.

I ran toward the edge of the cliff, my feet pounding the trail. I blinked my eyes to make the shape take form in the gloom as it moved slowly side-to-side. When I came within yards of the edge, I saw it clearly.

My heart slowed down considerably as I realized that the "ghost" of Sister Mattea was actually a Mylar balloon, one of those that had been on sale at the Fun Run. Some kid had probably let it go, but instead of soaring off into the stratosphere, its long string got tangled on one of the bushes that jutted out beneath the overhang of the bluff. It had just enough play to let the balloon rise up and float in the air, embodying in my fevered imagination the spirit of Sister Mattea.

I shook my head at my idiocy and then walked over to the edge myself. I looked down at the river running fast and deep more than 70 feet below and said a silent prayer for her. A light breeze tickled the back of my neck and carried the scent of spring with it, grassy and fresh. I inhaled deeply and closed my eyes. They flew open as a strong thump in the middle of my back threw me off balance and sent me hurtling over the edge.

23

I plummeted in a terrifying tumble down the sandstone bluff, flailing out to latch onto a jutting rock, a tree, a bush, anything to stop my relentless downward plunge. It happened in seconds that seemed to last hours. I was going to die just like Sister Mattea, and I didn't know why. Halfway down I felt a sharp yank on my neck and shoulders. My body swung out away from the bluff, then slammed back into the welcoming arms of a scraggly tree.

My baggy hoodie had snagged on a branch. That beautiful scratchy outgrowth was just tenacious enough to hold on and pull me into its rough embrace. I burrowed into the small tree, heedless of the nips and scratches inflicted by its bristly limbs. I stayed there motionless until my heart slowed, my ragged breathing returned to normal, and I could think clearly enough to assess my situation.

"Well, this is another fine mess you've gotten us into," I said out loud. I looked up and could see I had fallen maybe 30 or 40 feet. I didn't let myself look down. My only option was to try to climb back up, using whatever hand and footholds I could find.

It took everything I had to force myself to let go of the scrappy little limb I clung to. I put a tentative hand up, stretching my arm as far as it would extend. My fingers found a medium-sized handhold large enough for me to grab. I swung my body to the right to adjust my center of gravity, then pushed up and away from the security of my rescue tree. Thank you, ex-boyfriend Josh, for making me go to the climbing wall at the gym with you every Saturday for three months.

I found a toehold with my left foot and pulled up, then reached out again, fingers twitching and fumbling as they found a hold that let me insert them an inch or so. I moved methodically, feeling for the next outcropping or tiny crevice that would give me enough of a hold to move upward. It was a lot easier doing it on the climbing wall. With a safety harness. But I was making slow progress. I was almost up to another tree. I felt a surge of confidence.

I reached out and pushed off, but one leg slipped out from under me and scraped against something sharp. I scrambled to get my balance, throwing my body forward into the face of the bluff. All my weight rested on my right leg as my left foot kicked up and down, searching for something to land on. By the barest of inches, I found a tiny ledge under my foot and got my toes on it. I was splayed out on the side of the bluff, both arms outstretched, afraid to breathe let alone move. Involuntary tears sprang to my eyes, and I felt panic rising.

How could I possibly do this? A self-pitying sniffle snuck up on me. I snuffled it back and heard my mom saying, "Leah, you might not win by trying, but you'll always lose by giving up." Easy for her to say, she wasn't clinging like a bug 50 feet above rocks and a rushing river.

I leaned out more carefully this time, moving my leg, poking gently for another toehold, searching for any way to get purchase. Finally, when I extended my leg to the farthest reaches of my tendons, I found it. A shallow crevice I could wedge my foot against to give me leverage. I looked up, and in the faint light of the rising moon, I could see what I had to do. I shoved off with my leg and prayed for a sprinkling of fairy dust to fly me up to the swaying branch of a small tree. I stretched up, swung my body over and clung as the limb bent and creaked, but held. I twisted and wriggled and shinnied myself far enough up to reach the sturdier central trunk.

Once again, I found myself in a one-sided relationship with a tree. I gave a half-sob of relief and let out the breath I'd been unconsciously holding. I wrapped both arms around the tree and pressed my back into the crevice from which it sprung. My feet rested on a small outcropping. Then I felt something warm running down my leg. I looked and saw that my jeans had ripped and an ugly gash on my thigh was bleeding profusely. Now that the adrenalin jolt had departed, it hurt. The sweat I'd worked up was evaporating, leaving me chilled and shivering.

"Damn, damn, damn!" I yelled, just to hear a human voice. It rang out into the night, but what did it matter? There was no one to listen. I yelled it again even louder.

Then a voice called my name through the darkness.

"Leah? Leah? Leeeeaaaaahhhhh!!!"

Was it God? If so, He had a distinctive Latin lilt to his voice.

"Leah, *chica,* where are you?"

"Here, down here, Miguel, down here. Miguel! Miguel! Miguel!" I screamed as loud as I could, and the voice came closer.

"Leah!"

"Down here! Down the bluff!" The beam of a flashlight shone over my head, then on my face.

"Are you all right?"

The look on Miguel's face didn't make me feel any better than the involuntary "*ay, mierda*" he uttered when he took in my predicament.

"Yeah, sure, I'm fine. Well, no, actually. I can't get up any farther. And my leg hurts kind of bad."

"Hold on, *chica.* Hold on. I'm calling 911. Hold on, hold on." He swung the flashlight away, and I was surprised by how much I didn't want to be alone in the dark as I heard him give directions and urge the operator to hurry.

He hung up and focused the beam of light on me again. "What happened?"

"Somebody pushed me."

"What? Who? Why?"

"I don't know, I—Miguel—" An unwelcomed thought popped into my head. "Be careful up there. Whoever pushed me could still be around."

I was starting to feel a little woozy. The breeze that had been playing around the rocks was on its way to becoming a full-fledged wind. It was getting harder to maintain my balance with my bad leg, and I tried to press myself further back into the rock.

"Leah, hang on. I can hear the siren. Just a minute, *chica*. Just hang on. You can do it. Look at me, *chica*, just look up here. We can do this. You can do this."

I looked up again, and I could see Miguel had laid down on his belly so he could lean over the bluff. His face was directly above mine as he shone the flashlight for me. "You're like Cat Woman. Like Wonder Woman. Just another minute. You OK? You're OK."

"Great, I'm great," I croaked in a voice that sounded nothing like my own. The branch I was leaning on so heavily swayed. My bad leg slipped. My arms wrenched as my body dropped. I was treading air. Above me, Miguel shouted.

"*Chica*, listen, you just gotta swing to the left. Come on now. Just swing in, get back on the ledge. You can do it, I know you can."

"I—I'm so tired." My arms were burning, and I was hanging just like I did the instant before I fell from the hand-over-hands and broke my wrist —but that drop was only a few feet, not 50.

"You are not letting go, you are not letting go. You hold on. *Escuchame*. You hold on!" Miguel shouted. "*Mirame*! Look at me! I can hear the sirens. The rescue team, it's here. It's here. You will not let go," he said.

I looked up at him, and from that distance our eyes locked. And I held on. And I tried once more to swing to the left, and this time my toes landed, and I threw my weight forward and wriggled back into the tree and willed myself to stay there.

And then I heard a truck come roaring up, and the blackness lit up with headlights and floodlights, and someone barked orders and then hours later, or so it seemed, when I just couldn't hold on one minute longer, I felt arms wrap around me and a voice said, "There you go, sweetheart. Let go. It's all right. I've got you. You can let go now."

Only I couldn't. The fireman who had rappelled down in his harness had to pry my hands loose from the branch. When he did, I started to shake convulsively.

"Too much caffeine," I said weakly. He wasn't listening. He concentrated on getting us to the top. As soon as we were on firm ground, he got me on a gurney and under a warm blanket. An EMT did some preliminary poking and prodding, and then Miguel was beside me, his eyes suspiciously bright.

"Oh, *chica*, you scared me so bad."

"And you saved me so good," I said, reaching up weakly and ruffling his hair, perfect even in life and death circumstances.

"All right, sir, you have to step back," said the EMT, but then a familiar voice reached me.

"What the hell, Leah?" Coop came striding toward me, a mix of concern and exasperation on his face. Miguel stepped forward and started talking

"She was here alone up on the bluff and some—"

I interrupted before he could finish, giving him a look that I hoped said, *We speak not of this.*

"Coop! I'm OK, just had a little fall. Miguel found me and called 911. It's fine."

"What were you doing out here in the dark? Alone?"

"It's no big deal," I croaked, trying to sit up. It's hard to make your case lying down.

"What happened? Did you trip? Is the ground soft there? Damn it, there should be a guardrail." I tried to answer, but instead sank back down on the gurney.

"I was waiting for her at the paper so we could put together a story for the web edition on the Fun Run. When she didn't come, I thought maybe she had car trouble. I knew she didn't have her phone. I came looking for her. When I got here, I saw the car but no Leah. I started walking around, and then I heard someone shouting and swearing and I found her."

"Leah, you know how lucky you are, right? This is where Sister Mattea fell. You realize that?" The EMT who had stepped aside in deference to Coop asserted himself at that moment.

"Sorry, Lieutenant. We need to get her to the hospital."

"Wait a minute. I don't need to lie down. I don't need a stretcher. I don't want to go to the hospital. I just need to go home." I felt like I was talking really loud, but no one seemed to hear me. And it suddenly seemed like a really good idea to just be quiet. Before I knew it, we were on our way and the EMT—Phil, I read on his name tag—was expertly hooking me up to an IV.

"Phil, why?"

"Don't talk, Leah. You'll be fine. We just want to get some fluids in you, keep you warm, get that heart rate stabilized at a nice steady pace. It's a cold night for climbing, and you've got a nasty cut on your leg. Just lie quiet."

And I did. Just to be polite.

At the hospital, there were x-rays and blood work and stitches and a tetanus shot, which actually hurt more than anything else they did, before I was released to go home. In the waiting area, my mother gasped as they wheeled me in. I was surprised to see Miguel and Coop still there, and Karen had shown up as well.

"Mom! It's OK. Just protocol. See, I'm standing. I can take it from here. Thanks," I said to the aide who had pushed me out in a wheelchair. "Hospital rules are—" She saw the expression on my face, shrugged, and left me with my posse.

"You guys shouldn't have waited. Except for you, Mom. I think that falls under other duties as assigned in the mother job description. It's after midnight, Karen, geez, Mom shouldn't have called."

"She didn't. I was on my way home from dinner in Omico, and I saw the ambulance pulling away from the county park. Then I saw Coop's car. And then Miguel's. I stopped one of the deputies, and he told me what happened. Don't be so full of yourself. I'm here to take care of your mother, not you," she said, but with a smile.

"*Chica*, of course we stayed. We had to make sure you were OK. *Especialmente* with—"

He caught himself and stopped, but Coop had heard it.

"Especially with what?"

"Nothing, especially with a cut so deep, you know."

Coop looked about to pursue it, but Karen said, "All right, enough talking. Time to catch up tomorrow. Right now, I'm driving Carol and Leah home."

At home my mother fussed around making me tea and cinnamon toast, while Karen hovered over me as I changed from the scrubs the hospital had given me in place of my torn and bloody clothes. I pulled a long-sleeved T-shirt and a pair of sweats out of the closet and was surprised at how good their worn and soft fabric felt against my bruised body. I winced as I wiggled the top over my head and didn't object when Karen helped me with it as though I were a toddler.

Then she settled me on the couch with an afghan tucked round me and my comfort food and drink next to me on the end table. She and my mother both brought their cups of tea into the living room and watched as I devoured the toast, and then sipped slowly on my tea, letting the heat from the mug send a pleasant warmth through my hands.

My mother sat in the rocker across from me, and Karen occupied the wingback chair next to her. She drew her long legs up under her chin, wrapped her arms around them, and looked at me intently.

"All right. Now tell me. What happened tonight?"

"Like I said before, I was just out for a walk and—"

"OK, I'm cutting you some slack because you almost killed yourself tonight, but do not treat us like we're doddering idiots. Why were you teetering on the edge of a precipice alone in the dark?"

"It's not a precipice. It's just an overlook," I said crossly.

"Leah, stop it. Karen is right. There's something you're not telling."

I heaved a sigh. Then, my guard down from post-shock, the warmth of home, and a really effective painkiller that was kicking in, I went for broke.

"I fell asleep in the car during the storm. When I woke up, I thought I saw Sister Mattea. I ran over toward the bluff, and it turned out to be a stupid balloon. I was just standing there when someone pushed me off that bluff. I think it may have been Miller Caldwell."

"Leah! That's it. It's either the drugs talking, or you are certifiable."

Karen put a hand on my mother's arm to stem the flood. "Carol, let's let her talk."

I went through the evidence step by step—at least it seemed like I did. The pleasant haze I felt may have made me less cogent than I wanted to be, but my mom and Karen seemed to get the drift. I pointed out how much time Lacey spent with the Caldwells, then her abrupt cut-off of contact, Georgia's hostility and her insinuation that Lacey had seduced Miller.

I highlighted Delite's vague recollection that Lacey said "some big shot" had abused her, Miller's out-of-the-blue meeting with me, and his fishing expedition to discover what I knew. Then I told them about Mary Beth

Delaney's admission that Miller had funded Lacey's memorial site, and about the quotation that appeared every year on the site, the one that mirrored what Miller had said to me when we spoke. Finally, I pointed out Miller's lack of an alibi the night Lacey disappeared.

"It all adds up. He saw me at the park today. Maybe it was just chance that he came back and found me, or maybe he was waiting somewhere and watching. Either way, when I walked out by the bluff, it was the perfect opportunity. And I think he did the same thing to Sister Mattea." They were both quiet, but then it was Karen who spoke.

"Leah, I know how hard you've been working to find out what really happened to Lacey. And I have to give you credit. You've turned up a lot of things the sheriff's department overlooked or ignored."

I was liking how this was going. Karen was the first person other than Miguel to concede that I was on to something.

"But think for a minute. None of it is really evidence. It's circumstantial, it's speculation and, kiddo, it's not actionable. Leah, hon, you've got no proof that Lacey was abused, let alone that she was killed. No evidence that Sister Mattea knew anything about it, and no hard data that supports your theory that Miller was her abuser and possibly even her murderer."

"But what about her behavior changes? What about the money Lacey supposedly stole? What about the missing data on the phone? And Sister Julianna is hiding something. I could tell when I talked to her today. Maybe she's protecting Miller Caldwell. He's on the board, and he's got a lot of power. Maybe she even knows what really happened to Lacey." I heard a pleading note creep into my voice and willed it away.

Then my mother spoke.

"Leah, you've run yourself ragged since Sister Mattea died. You're not eating, you're not sleeping, you've put so much pressure on yourself. You carry the weight of the world on your shoulders—you always have. Look what happened today—you fell asleep for four hours in your car. That's how exhausted you are. No one can blame you if your judgment is skewed, but you can't, you just can't, accuse Miller of trying to kill you."

"Why would he risk killing you when he's not in any real danger? You don't have any evidence that he did anything to Lacey, and you haven't found any connection between Lacey and Sister Mattea. I'm sorry, hon, but there are alternate explanations for everything you've found," Karen said.

"But it wouldn't *be* risky for Miller. All he had to do was run up behind me, and give a quick push, and run away. And it worked, right? Because no one saw him and you don't believe me."

I didn't like the way my mother was looking at me, and the gentle way Karen said, "You need to take a step back. Think a minute, Leah. If a source came to you with this, there's no way you'd run with that story. You'd demand the facts, and the facts just aren't there."

"I didn't imagine that someone pushed me off that bluff. And I'm not imagining that Miller abused and then killed Lacey. I'm getting closer to proving it every day. You want facts? Wait and see. I'm going to make sure everyone knows what he did and that he pays for it. And then you can thank me for finding the truth. I'm going to bed."

My angry exit was marred somewhat by the fact that it hurt like mad to stand, and I wound up doing more of an old lady shuffle than a righteous reporter strut down the hall to my room. Out of the corner of my eye, I saw Karen put a hand on my mother's arm as she started to get up and come after me.

24

I came awake gradually the next day, until I tried to execute a slow stretch that quickly ended in a yelp of pain. Every part of my body ached and the cut on my leg both throbbed and itched. I realized that the sun was streaming through my windows. The windows on the west side of my bedroom. What time was it?

I sat up cautiously, but it didn't seem to have any impact on the pain level. About a 7 on a 10-point scale. I leaned slightly to reach my watch on the nightstand and was rewarded with a protest twinge from my rib area. I looked at the time. Squinted. Looked again. It was 2 p.m. I'd slept for 12 hours straight.

Inch by inch I managed to get up, maneuvered into a clean T-shirt and jeans, but didn't even try to bend over and put on a pair of shoes. Instead I slid my feet into some flip-flops and clopped my way to the bathroom. I brushed my teeth and then looked closely in the mirror.

My face was a mass of scrapes and beginning scabs. I had a dime-sized purple bruise on my right cheek. My hands were in worse shape—nails broken, fingertips cracked and split, knuckles abraded and my arms, though relatively unscathed, felt like someone was pulling them out of their sockets every time I forgot and extended them too far.

My thigh was covered with a bandage above my knee where the stitches were and judging by the generally oozy looking state of it, a dressing change was in my future. I just didn't have the stomach for it. On the counter was the Vicodin the doctor had prescribed, but I decided to tough it out. Instead, I grabbed a couple of ibuprofen and washed them down with a glass of water. Then I began the thousand-mile journey down the hall with a single step of my lime green flip flops.

I found my mother drinking a cup of tea at the bar.

"What are you doing here? Why aren't you at work?"

"Like I'm going to work without being able to check if you're still breathing. You get at least 24 hours special treatment. What can I fix you?"

"Mom, you don't—"

"I know I don't have to. How about eggs? Toast? A grilled cheese sandwich and tomato soup?"

"Grilled cheese and soup would be great. I can't believe I slept so long. Why didn't you wake me up?"

"Obviously, you needed it. You should still be in bed. Your poor face. You look like Rocky. The first movie. How does your leg feel?"

"It's OK. I'm all right. I look worse than I feel. The story of my life." I lied, because she looked so worried. "Oh boy, I better call Max."

"I already talked to him. In fact, you had a steady stream of visitors this morning. Max stopped by; Miguel came to see you; Karen ran in on her way to work; Coop called and said he'd be by later, oh, and he had one of his officers bring your car back. Even Ellie stopped after she took Alex to school to see how you were doing."

"Ellie came by? Wow, I must have been closer to dying than I thought if she came to check on me. She was pretty mad last time I talked to her. Of course, maybe she was hoping for bad news."

"That's not funny," she said, looking over her shoulder as she buttered two slices of bread. She placed one into a hot iron skillet, topped it with sliced cheddar and then the other piece of bread. The sizzle made me realize how hungry I was. She reached in the cupboard for a can of tomato soup before saying, "About last night. I need you to understand. It's not that I don't believe you—"

"It's just that you don't believe me," I said. "No, it's OK, Mom. I get it. You think I'm overwrought, and I've gone off the deep end about Miller.

Fine. I don't want to fight about it. I'll just prove to you how wrong you are."

She didn't answer, and it took me a minute to realize that she was crying.

My mother almost never cries. Carol Nash will yell, nag, rant, croon, cajole, but not cry. Not unless her heart is breaking.

I stared in horror, finally getting it. What I was putting her through, why she kept negating my findings, trying to get me to stop. She was really, seriously scared. I heaved myself up, wincing as my muscles cramped in protest, and lumbered over to her.

"Mom, it's all right. I'm all right. Nothing happened. Nothing is going to happen. I'll be careful."

"It already did happen, Leah. Something did happen. Someone pushed you off that bluff, and if it weren't for the fact that you're so damn stubborn, you'd be at the bottom of the river."

"You believe me?"

"Of course I do. Do you think I'm an idiot?" She snuffled and reached for a Kleenex.

Just then we both smelled something burning. "Damn!" She picked the pan handle up without a potholder and dropped it with a clatter. I grabbed a dish towel and lifted it from the burner, then turned off the stove.

"What are you going to do?"

Before I could answer, the front doorbell rang. The opening bars of "I Shot the Sheriff" were playing as I looked through the glass panel.

I opened the door and said, "Hello, Detective Ross."

He flashed his badge. "I got a few questions for you, Leah. Can I come in?"

"Actually, how about we sit on the porch?" I was mindful of my mother with her tear-stained face and burned grilled cheese.

He cocked his head, making little fat rolls ooze over the tight collar of his shirt. "You sure about that? You might feel more comfortable if we talk inside, private like."

"No, that's all right. It's a nice day, and I could use the fresh air." I pointed him to one of the chairs on the wide wooden porch. I leaned against the railing facing him. It seemed easier than the struggle to sit down and get back up again. I didn't want Ross to watch me wince. He didn't say anything about my bruises.

"All right then, let's get right to it. Leah, we got a complaint about you today from Mrs. Miller Caldwell."

"What, she didn't like a headline in last week's edition? She couldn't just write a letter to the editor?"

"It's a little more serious than that. Mrs. Caldwell says you been stalking her."

"What?"

"Two or more unsolicited contacts is stalking in Wisconsin. Mrs. Caldwell says you showed up at her house uninvited on Thursday. Says you accosted her daughter there, too. And she says you texted her 15 times on Sunday with threatening messages."

"That's ridiculous."

"You weren't at the Caldwell's on Thursday?"

"I was, but—"

"Did you accost Mrs. Caldwell in the driveway?"

"No! I—"

"You didn't tell her that she didn't have a very bright future?"

"I may have said something like that, but I—"

"You didn't send her threatening texts on Sunday?"

"Of course I didn't. What did they say?"

"Well, now, why don't you tell me?"

"How would I know? I didn't send them. I didn't even have my phone on Sunday. I lost it Saturday night. I still don't have it. Check with my mother, check with Miguel Santos."

"Lost your phone. Huh." He stared at me for a minute, his dull mustard-brown eyes narrowed. He wasn't wearing a hat, and there was a faint sheen of oily perspiration on his mostly bald head.

"Mrs. Caldwell says you were in her driveway where you proceeded to harass and threaten her on Thursday morning. She says you accused her husband of criminal sexual conduct. What do you say to that, Leah?"

"I say she's lying, or you are."

His fat cheeks burned bright with two red spots, but he didn't react otherwise.

"Are you denying you went to the Caldwell's on Thursday?"

"No, I'm denying I was uninvited. Miller Caldwell asked me to stop by and talk to him. So, I did."

"Let me get this straight now. It's your story that you weren't waiting for Mrs. Caldwell, and didn't approach her and threaten her?"

"How many times do I have to tell you? No!"

"Did you post a comment on the Miller Caldwell for Senator website suggestin' that he had sex with a minor?"

"No."

"Leah," he said, standing up as though finally realizing he'd lost his power position while he sat and I towered above him, "you know, and I know, your sister was a druggie who died because she was drunk and high. You can't change that by telling people all over town that I screwed up the investigation."

"Is that what this is really about, Detective Ross? Did I hurt your feelings? Are you trying to arrest me for slander? Because last time I looked, that's a civil offense not a criminal one, and you should know—it's not slander if it's true. And I'm doing nothing but telling the truth when I say you screwed up the investigation. Or, to give you credit, maybe you were persuaded to give it less than your best by Miller or his wife?"

His right fist clenched, and I watched him willing himself not to grab me and shake me—or smack me. I knew the feeling. He waited a minute, and as his hand relaxed he said, "Nash, we can clear this up quick and easy, or we can do it slow and painful. Are you willing to give me a look at your phone?"

I knew I'd gotten under his skin when he switched from calling me Leah to calling me Nash.

"I told you, I lost it. When did you say Georgia got those threatening texts?"

"Between 5 p.m. and 11 p.m. yesterday."

"Interesting. During a big chunk of that time I was hanging from a branch 50 feet over the Himmel River. Then I spent a couple of hours semi-conscious in the hospital, surrounded by medical personnel, then I was back home with my mother and a friend. You should do your homework, Detective Ross."

"I'm a good investigator, and I always do my homework, Nash. See, I know that you can get an app that sends out texts for you at a preset time."

"You can?" I asked, temporarily diverted.

"Yeah. So, you set up your little alibi, and then while your phone is 'missing,' it sends out the texts."

"You think I threw myself over a cliff, and almost died, to set up my alibi?"

"You're a smartass. That don't mean you're smart. What's your cell number, Nash?"

"I'm sure you know."

"As a matter of fact, I do," he said, pulling his own phone out of his pocket and punching in numbers.

In a second, the sound of "Rumor Has It" came tinnily from the direction of my car, parked next to us in the driveway.

"Aren't you going to answer that?"

A triumphant smile sat on his piggy little mouth.

Heaving myself off the railing and down the three steps to the sidewalk, I Frankenstein-walked over to my car and opened the door. There was nothing in the front seat, but the phone kept ringing. Louder now. With an effort, I opened the back door and at first glance didn't see it. Following the sound, I shifted the blanket I'd tossed in the back. There on the floor behind the passenger seat was my phone. Ross was looming behind me.

"It wasn't here. I looked all through my car. Ask my mother, ask Miguel."

"So how come it's there now?"

"Anyone could have put it back here. My car was in the parking lot at the county park all night. It's been in the driveway unlocked since this morning. Anyone could have had access to it."

"So, your story is someone stole your phone, sent threatening texts and emails to Georgia Caldwell, and then they just put it back in your car, all nice and neat. Why would anyone do that?"

"I don't know. To cause me problems, to distract me from finding out what happened to my sister."

"We know what happened to your sister. She got drunk, fell down and died. End of story. But now we got a new story. This ain't exactly your first rodeo is it, Nash?"

"What are you talking about?"

"It says here," he said, ostentatiously pulling a small notebook out of his jacket pocket, "it says right here that you don't play nice with others, Nash. A couple of your old bosses said you were," and here he paused to read from his notes "not a team player, impulsive, stubborn, unpredictable."

He shook his head in a parody of sad disapproval.

"The picture I got is that you're too bullheaded and full of yourself to hold a job for very long. Yeah, a few said you were good, but it seems like you're one of those types that are more trouble than they're worth. Pain-in-the-ass types. High maintenance. And, oh, let's see here." He made a minor production of flipping through the pages of his notepad. "It says you got fired from your last job for harassment." He gave me a little smirk.

"See, I told you I was good at homework. Seems your boss, Ms. Hilary McKay—your ex-boss that is—got some scary texts from you, after she started dating your ex-boyfriend. Some sick, angry stuff, Nash. You ever been in anger management?"

"Oh, come on, that's ridiculous. It was just a joke. It's not even what happened."

"No? Ms. McKay says it is. She says you were unstable, and she had to fire you, and she feared for her safety."

"Oh, really? Then how come she didn't press charges?"

"She felt sorry for you."

"That's not true. She didn't press charges, because the texts were sent anonymously and she couldn't prove they were from me. Which they weren't. She jumped to the conclusion it was me, and never really let go, not even when the guys that actually did it FOR A JOKE came forward when she came unhinged.

"I didn't know anything about it until she came unglued and freaked out at me in the office. I didn't do it. Maybe you should have had your mother check that homework you did. Didn't you learn anything after you botched Lacey's investigation?"

The angry red spots had spread so that his entire face was suffused with a dark maroon color. I started to walk back to the porch, but his bulk blocked my way. He was close enough for me to see a few drops of spit spray from his mouth when he said, "Button your lip, you wiseass."

The front door opened, and my mother stepped out onto the porch. "Everything all right out here?"

Ross turned and nodded to my mother, "Everything's just fine, Mrs. Nash. Just getting some information from your daughter."

"I wonder if you wouldn't want to come up here on the porch to wait, Detective."

"Wait ma'am?"

"Yes. I've called our lawyer. She should be here any minute."

As if on cue, Karen's SUV pulled into the driveway, and she was up and out beside us almost before the engine turned off.

"Detective. What are you doing here?"

"I'm investigating a complaint."

"Leah, you don't need to say anything."

"Detective Ross, are you arresting my client?"

"Not at the moment."

"Then I suggest you leave. She has nothing more to say to you."

"Wait a minute. Arrest me? You've got to be kidding."

"Leah, be quiet."

I shut up more out of surprise than compliance. Karen had never spoken that sharply to me before. I guessed that was the difference between friend Karen and attorney Karen.

"Don't think you can erase anything off your cell phone. We can get the records, you know. And, trust me, I'm gonna do a very thorough job investigating. Just like I did on your sister." Then he turned and left.

"Leah, inside."

Once we got into the living room, Karen said, "What did you tell him?"

"Nothing. He said Georgia Caldwell had accused me of stalking her, that I'd shown up at her house and threatened her, and that I sent her a bunch of threatening texts."

"Did you?"

"No! I wouldn't do something that stupid. Besides, my phone's been missing for two days. I just found it in the backseat of my car."

"But didn't you look there before?"

"You don't seriously think I did this?"

"You were very upset about Miller. This might have seemed like a good way to get under his skin."

"Oh, I'm so stupidly upset that I'd set myself up for a slam dunk conviction by using my own phone to stalk his wife? Come on, Karen."

"Take it easy, Leah. I had to ask. But if you didn't do it, who did?"

"Somebody had to have taken my phone. Probably Saturday night at Miguel's, and then put it in my car either last night at the park or today."

"Who would do that? Why?"

"To set me up, to damage my credibility, to get Max to turn against me, to prove I'm a mad, crazy troublemaker. In other words, Miller or Georgia would be perfect candidates."

"Who might know that you suspect Miller of being involved with Lacey?"

"Max, Ellie, Mom, you, Miguel, Miller, Georgia, Coop, Marilyn Karr, maybe Mary Beth Delaney, anyone she told in her family, anyone that overheard me talking to you at Miguel's—"

"Why didn't you just take out an ad that said, 'Miller Caldwell Killed My Sister'?" my mother asked.

"I thought about it."

"Who had the opportunity to take your phone—and get it back to you?" Karen asked.

"Dozens of people wandered in and out of Miguel's on Saturday, you know that. A lot of them were at the Fun Run the next day. Plus, I'm not one hundred percent that I lost it at the party, it just seems most likely. The last time I remember using it was mid-afternoon. I got a text from Miguel to make sure I was coming. Then I ran some errands, got my hair cut. I could've dropped it somewhere maybe, but that party seems like a place where I might have set it down."

She waved her hand impatiently. "How many people knew about your problem last year with your ex-boss?"

"I didn't think anyone but Mom knew, and I asked her not to say anything. I see she shared with you."

I raised an eyebrow at my mother. She had the grace to look abashed.

"Since she already told you about it, I hope she also said it wasn't a problem, Karen. Not like Ross made it sound. It was just a dumbass joke that got out of hand. My boss Hilary was a real piece of work. She didn't know a good lead from a lift quote. She had this bad-tempered, mouth-breathing little dog that she dressed up in a Dolphins cap and carried around the office in a baby harness for God's sake.

"Once she found out I used to date her fiancé, she wouldn't get off my case. She was almost as bad with the rest of the reporters. Nobody liked her, and a couple of them actually hated her. They got pretty wasted one night and decided it would be hilarious to make a fake ransom flyer for her dog Shadow—only she spelled it C-H-A-D-E-A-U-X—you can see what a pretentious idiot she was.

"They texted her a bunch of dumb things like 'I'll get you and your little dog, too.' One said, 'Who knows what evil lurks in the hearts of men? Your Chadeaux does.' With a picture of the hat her little dog used to wear."

I couldn't stop a little grin at the memory.

"Leah, are you laughing about this? Because it's potentially very serious."

"No, no, I know. I'm sorry. She thought the stuff came from me, and she freaked and she called me in and started screaming. That's when the guys who did it confessed, but Hilary didn't believe them. Thought they were covering for me. The police didn't pursue the complaint. They could see it was ridiculous. But she wouldn't let it go.

"We got into it. I was fed up. I threatened to quit. She said fine. So, I thought, all right then. I let her have it—verbally only. But it got pretty heated. After I left, she spun it like she had to fire me, because I was emotionally unstable. And I guess the scene I had with her in the office—but it was justified, I swear—I can see how some people might have thought she was right. And when your ex-boss tells every reference check that she fired you because you're crazy, well it's kind of hard to shake."

"Did you ask Ross how he found out?"

"He said he was a good investigator who does his homework. Ha."

"Would your ex-editor have talked to him?"

"Oh, yeah. But how would he know to check with her? You really think Ross has that much initiative?"

"Don't underestimate him, Leah. Or the initiative a push from the Caldwell family can give."

"Well, what do I do now?"

"Nothing. Don't speak to him again without me. I'll talk to a friend of mine in the DA's office, see how serious this is. I'll be in touch when I know something."

"Thanks, Karen."

"No problem."

As my mother walked out to the car with her, I hobbled over to the couch, thought better of the challenges of getting back up from its cushiony depths, and opted for the rocking chair. I opened my phone and looked for the text from Delite that should have come in on Saturday. Nothing. In fact, all my texts were gone—those I sent and those I received. I thought a minute, then decided to call the casino and see if I could get her supervisor to give me her home number.

25

"She doesn't work here."

"What? I just saw her there a few days ago."

"Well, she isn't here now."

"Did she quit?"

"I'm not allowed to say."

"You mean she got fired."

"I didn't say that."

"I'm an old friend. I've really got to get in touch with her. Could you please give me her number?"

"We don't give out personal information about employees. Or ex-employees."

"Please, it's about her sister. She's in a bad way, and I know Delite would want to know. It could be her last chance to talk to her. Ever."

"Her sister doesn't have her number?" she asked, suspicion replacing truculence.

"They had a falling out. It's been years since they've talked. If I don't reach Delite, she'll never have the chance."

"I don't know. I don't want to get in trouble—"

I heard the hesitancy and pushed. "Seriously, that's all I want to do. Just let her know about her sister. Brandee is hanging on by a thread. No one needs to know how I got the number. Please."

Sigh. "All right. It's 293-555-0124."

"Thank you, thank you. It will mean so much to Brandee."

I called the number immediately.

"This is Delite. You know what to do."

"Delite, this is Leah Nash. My mother said you tried to reach me Saturday. I lost my phone, so if you called or texted, I didn't get it. But it's back now, so please call me when you get this."

My leg was throbbing again. The effort not to let Ross see me sweat had taken a lot out of me. I caved then, and let my mother give me a Vicodin along with my grilled cheese and tomato soup. Soon I nodded in the chair, alternately dozing and floating in a Vicodin fog.

When I re-entered consciousness, I heard my mother talking to someone in the kitchen. I stretched without thinking, shooting a sharp pain through my shoulders and sending my phone clattering from my lap to the floor. I reached for it, but a large hand with a zigzag scar on the index finger beat me to it.

I looked up and smiled at Coop.

"Hey, you." He gave me the phone, then offered the plastic cup with straw he held in his other hand.

"Diet Coke, extra ice?"

"Absolutely. How you doin'?"

"Not so bad. A little stiff. And I'm gonna have a mark on my leg that'll put your wimpy old finger scar to shame. Otherwise, OK."

"So, how's your friend Ben? You want to sing me a verse or two?"

"Shut up. I don't know. He's OK, I guess. How's Sherry?"

"Fine."

"When did you guys become a thing?"

"We're not a thing. We just ran into each other at Miguel's."

"Huh. Looked more like she was welded to your arm."

"You know Sherry. She's affectionate," he said, giving me a half-smile. "Where did you and Ben meet? You two seemed to be getting on pretty well."

"You don't know the half of it," my mother said as she came into the room and rolled her eyes at Coop.

"Oh?"

I gave her a look that could freeze an open flame, and she shrugged.

"Nothing. Mom's being what she thinks is funny."

"What's his last name? He looked kinda familiar," Coop said.

"Kalek. He's not from Himmel. He's just here to fix up his grandmother's house for selling. She died a few months ago."

"Ah. How does Miguel know him?"

"How does Miguel know anybody? He met him at the gym and decided to take him home as a pet, I guess."

He laughed, and my mother excused herself and went down the hall to the laundry room.

"Are you going back to work tomorrow?"

"Yeah. Unless of course, Ross comes back and arrests me."

"What?"

I explained what had happened.

"Can't you just stay away from the Caldwells?"

"What? You think I'm some psycho stalker?"

"No, but I know how far you'll go to prove you're right."

"What's that supposed to mean?"

"You've been pretty pissed off, and I don't think your judgment is the best right now. I'm just thinking if you were a little out of it—like you were Saturday night—well, if you did anything stupid, maybe I can help get it straightened out."

"I didn't send those texts. Maybe Georgia sent them herself. Or maybe Miller did."

"Why would either of them do something like that?"

"To land me in a mess. Worst case scenario, I could wind up with a Class I felony, a fine, and maybe even jail time. Nothing like a stint in prison to enhance your resume. Best case scenario, charges are dismissed, but I'm remembered as the obsessed reporter who crossed the line and can't be trusted. It casts doubt on everything I do, and especially on anything I turn up related to Miller and Lacey."

"But wouldn't pressing charges just put attention on what you think they're trying to hide?"

"If Miller can make everyone think I'm a nut job, he won't have to worry about that. Nothing I find out will be taken seriously."

He tried a different approach.

"How would Miller or Georgia get your phone?"

"Maybe I dropped it somewhere?"

"Oh, and they were just trailing along after you, waiting for that lucky break?"

"At the party, then."

"They weren't at the party."

"Someone who was there gave it to them."

"Really?"

"They have money, they have influence. They could have someone working for them to get me."

"Leah, I'm gonna give you the benefit of the doubt and say it's the pain-killers talking. You sound like you should be in a steel bunker with a sliding panel, waiting for me to whisper the password to you."

"I am not paranoid."

"All right."

"Somebody pushed me. That's real."

"What are you talking about?"

My mother came in just then. "Oh, she finally told you."

"Not exactly, Carol. Why didn't you say anything before?"

"Who'd believe me? You don't."

"You could've at least told me."

"Why? So, you could dismiss it like you have everything I've told you for the past month?"

"Tell me now."

When I finished, he said, "You were lucky this time. If Miguel hadn't come—"

"I know. Like I know it was Miller who pushed me. Or maybe his crazy wife."

"Coop, talk to her. Tell her she needs to stop."

"She won't listen, Carol. She never has."

"Hello? She's right here. Listening."

"Good. Then you'll hear me when I tell you the push in the park isn't what you think. If you don't back away from Miller and Georgia, things could get ugly."

"What does that mean?"

"It means back off. It means trust that someone besides you knows how to do their job."

I stared at him, then all the tumblers clicked into place. "You've got something on Miller. All this time you've been jerking me around, telling me I'm way off base, practically telling me I'm mentally unstable and you were sitting on information."

He shook his head in frustration. "I'm not gonna get into this with you. Look, I'm asking you. Please leave it alone. You'll understand. I'll call you."

As he turned to leave, my mother grabbed his arm.

"Coop, just tell me. Is Leah safe? What if the person who pushed her last night decides to try again?"

"It's all right, Carol. I've got it covered."

"Mom, just let the great big man protect us. We women folk don't need to know about anything scary."

"Leah Marie, that's enough. Coop has had your back more times than I can count. Probably more times than I want to know."

I was still mad, but her words hit home.

"All right. Yeah. Fine." That's me, grace under fire.

"I'll see you later," he said, leaving by the kitchen door.

I was getting tired of apologizing every time I turned around. Of course, I guess if I didn't talk without thinking so often, I wouldn't be in that position. Still, Coop was holding out on me and I couldn't help feeling betrayed.

"Is your leg hurting you?"

"It's OK, not bad."

"Then there's no excuse for you to behave like such a little brat."

"OK, I'm sorry. I said I was sorry."

"Oh, really? That was your version of sorry, 'all right, fine, yeah'?" She shook her head in disgust.

"Okaayyy. I'll talk to him tomorrow. But you can see, can't you, that he's on Miller's tail? That he knows about him? He didn't have any right to keep that from me."

"In case you haven't noticed, you're not a member of the Himmel Police Department. You're really not even a member of the press on this. And the way you've steamrolled ahead, I can see why he didn't say anything."

"But—"

"No. We're not going to argue about this. You need to relax, eat a good dinner, and get a good night's sleep."

I sank back onto the chair without another word. I was ticked, but too tired to argue.

"Stay where you are, I'll bring you a tray."

"Mom, I'm not an invalid. I'm going to work tomorrow. I think I can walk two feet to the kitchen."

"Just stay there. Tomorrow is tomorrow; tonight, I'm taking care of you."

26

We ate off tray tables in the living room, neither one of us saying it, but both thinking how we used to do that every Friday night when Lacey was little. I guess current parenting theories say you should sit down around the dinner table to a nice meal, but we had some of our most fun times eating crock pot dinners on the couch and watching old movies on Friday nights. My mother loved classic films, so we learned to, too. My favorite was *Notorious* with Cary Grant and Ingrid Bergman. I loved how tough but vulnerable she was. And the closing scene, best ever.

Lacey and my mother liked the MGM musicals. The three of us would sometimes sing songs from the movies around the house—I know, corny, right? Can I help it if I got the music in me? Unfortunately, I don't have the voice in me, too. Lacey got her voice from Mom. I got mine from our father.

Sometimes when I joined them in a spontaneous song or bellowed out a solo in a particularly heartfelt off-key rendition, they would look at each other and Lacey would start to giggle, and eventually she'd laugh so hard she got the hiccups. I'd pretend to be insulted, and then she would feel bad.

Once in a fit of compassion, she said, "That's OK, Lee-Lee, you don't have to sing. Your talking voice is nice. Like caramel corn. Sweet and crackly. And everybody likes caramel corn." We laughed so hard.

And that night with Mom was fun, too, in a weird out-of-time-and-space kind of way. We watched *Notorious*. And repeated in unison the closing lines, "Alex, will you come in, please? I wish to talk to you," as a very wicked, but very scared, Claude Raines made the lonely walk to his doom.

———

Getting up the next morning was tough, but I'd set the alarm to give me enough time to stand in the hot shower for a while, and by the time I got out, I was feeling fairly loose. I lifted my arms to pull on my T-shirt without wincing and changed the bandage on my leg without grossing myself out. It had stopped seeping and actually didn't look too nasty, though it still gave me the willies.

When I got to the office, everyone was out except Courtnee.

"Wow. You look terrible, Leah. If you want, I could try to cover up those scrapes and maybe that bruise on your chin," she said, pulling out her drawer and grabbing a bag presumably filled with make-up cures. "I don't really have anything for that puffy spot over your eye though."

"No, that's OK, Courtnee, I'll just stay *au naturel* today. Where is everybody?"

"I don't know. Nobody ever tells me where they're going."

Max was old school, and even though everyone had cell phones and was accessible day and night, he still insisted we use the sign-in sheet at the front desk so Courtnee could keep track of us. As if that were going to happen.

I swung the clipboard over and scanned it. Max was at a Chamber meeting, Miguel was at the Middle School Awards Assembly, Duff, an advertising sales rep, was at a Rotary breakfast.

"Courtnee, it says right here where everyone is."

She rolled her eyes. "If you already know, Leah, why did you ask? I'm too busy to play your games," she said, turning back to the Facebook page that was up on her computer.

"You're right. Sorry."

Back in the newsroom, I lowered myself gingerly onto my chair and went through my messages, then pulled up the copy for the week's paper and started editing. I dimly heard Max come in, but he didn't stop by the newsroom. It was close to noon when I heard the excited voices of Miguel and Courtnee in the front.

Then Max yelled for me from the back. He didn't sound happy. Apparently, I wasn't going to get even a one-day get-out-of-trouble-free card, despite my battered body. His door was open, and I gave a slight knock. He turned from his computer screen. His face was as red and angry as I'd ever seen it.

"What the hell is wrong with you?"

"I—"

He turned up the volume on his computer and moved so I could see a blonde anchor staring into the camera and speaking with local news gravitas. An unflattering photograph of me loomed in the background over her left shoulder.

This just in. Local reporter Leah Nash of the *Himmel Times Weekly* is the subject of a Himmel County Sheriff's Department investigation. Ms. Nash, 32, has been accused of stalking by Georgia Caldwell, wife of prominent businessman and state senate candidate Miller Caldwell. Nash allegedly sent multiple texts and email of a threatening nature to Mrs. Caldwell and showed up uninvited at the couple's residence. No arrest has been made. Police are refusing comment on what they say is an ongoing investigation.

However, WTRS News has learned that Nash left a position at the *Miami Star-Register*, a Florida daily newspaper, following similar accusations. Nash did not respond to attempts to contact her. We'll keep you posted on this developing story.

"How did they get that story?"

"How did they get it? How could you do it? Christ, Leah, this is your idea of taking it down a notch? You just tanked your career. I hope you haven't taken the *Times* down with you."

"But, Max, I didn't do it. Somebody set me up."

The little vein above his right eye was pulsing again. His hands pressed down so hard, he had to be leaving indentations on the top of his wooden desk.

"Enough. I've had enough. Clean out your desk. You're done."

"What? But, Max, please, listen, I—"

"No! No more talk, no more chances. I don't want your excuses. I don't want your side of things. I don't want anything from you. You've got the writing chops and the smarts, but it's a waste, because you've got no judgment and no self-control. And no loyalty either."

"Max, I'm sorry. You have to believe me. I didn't do this. But listen, Miller is the person who abused Lacey. I think he's the one who pushed me off the bluff. Probably Sister Mattea, too, I just don't have—"

"You don't have anything, Leah. Most of all, you don't have a job here. You're done." He turned his chair around to face his computer as though I'd already left, his solid back a bulwark against any attempt to explain.

I turned and went to my desk. Courtnee and Miguel were there, their eyes wide with sympathy and shock. I didn't say a word, just walked to the copy machine, dumped a ream of paper out of the box sitting next to it, and carried the empty container to my desk.

"*Chica*, what happened? What was Max talking about?"

I shook my head. I didn't trust my voice not to shake as well, so I said nothing as I pulled open drawers and threw their contents into the box.

"When my boyfriend Jace broke up with me, I sent his new skank girlfriend some texts like that. Didn't you know you can buy a phone at Target for, like, really cheap for stuff like that?" Courtnee gave me what I guessed was her version of comfort and solidarity.

"I know you didn't do that. You wouldn't do anything so crazy?"

The slight uptick on the end of his declaration made me feel as bad as anything Max had said. He wasn't sure I hadn't.

"No. I didn't do it. Someone set me up."

"Ohhh." Courtnee nodded with sudden comprehension. "I've seen that on *Pretty Little Liars*. You know, where somebody wants like Hannah or Aria or somebody to get blamed, so they make it look like she did something only she didn't. Only sometimes she did, so it's not really fake, but—"

"Who would do that?"

"You know who. The same person who pushed me off the bluff."

Courtnee's eyes got even bigger. "Somebody pushed you? Who?"

I didn't answer, just swiped my arm across the top of my desk and swept everything into the box. Then I slung my purse over my shoulder, picked up my belongings, and awkwardly tottered out. Before I got down the hall, the box was lifted from my hands, and Miguel was beside me.

"I know you didn't send those texts. I know you didn't stalk the Caldwells. But *chica*, I don't think Miller abused Lacey."

"*Et tu*, Miguel?"

I took the box from him and tossed it in the backseat. I got in the car and drove away.

27

My cell phone rang. I let it go to voicemail. Then it rang again, and again, and again all the way home. I ignored them all. I pulled into the driveway, then trudged in the house with my box of stuff and set it down on the counter. Thank God, my mother was out of town, delivering some legal papers in Appleton. She wouldn't be back until late, and I wouldn't have to go over this with her—as long as she didn't catch the news or hear it on her car radio.

I pulled out my phone and saw the missed calls were from Miguel, from Coop, from Courtnee, one from Rich Givens, a WTRS reporter, even one from Ben. Great. He probably wanted to tell me what a nice photo that was of me on the noon news.

Nothing from Karen. That was weird. She should've called by now to tell me what was going on with Georgia's complaint. I punched in her number, but it went straight to voicemail. I tried the office line, then realized it was lunch time and they were closed.

How had WTRS gotten the story? It had to be Ross. That jerk. He had to know it wasn't true by now. He also knew that once it was out there, no matter what retractions and corrections were made, all people would remember was that Leah Nash was some kind of stalker, wasn't she?

I sat down on the rocker and closed my eyes. I woke when my phone rang an hour later. Before I could say hello, the caller started talking.

"Leah, I promised Ben I wouldn't forget to tell you, but then I did, but it's not really my fault, because it was kind of crazy with you getting fired and all. And I called before, but you didn't answer."

"Who is this?" I shook my head to clear the grogginess, then immediately regretted it.

"It's me. Courtnee. Are you having a concussion? I'm talking about Ben. Ben Kalek. You know, Miller Caldwell's nephew. He came to see you, but it was kinda awkward, 'cause we could hear Max yelling at you. I mean, everyone in the building could hear Max yelling, right? So, he said he'd come back later, but I said you might not be here later, right? And—"

"Wait. Ben Kalek is Miller Caldwell's nephew?"

"Well, duh, yeah—"

"How do you know that?"

"Well, his grandma lives next door to my grandma, doesn't she? Of course, his grandma is dead, so she doesn't live there anymore. I mean, he's not blood nephew, just marriage nephew. His mom is Georgia Caldwell's sister. His grandma is their mom. Or she used to be—"

Courtnee droned on, while I tried to grab just one of the dozen thoughts flashing through my befuddled brain. Ben was Georgia Caldwell's nephew. Ben had easy access to my phone. Ben just happened to meet me at Miguel's. It made sense that Miller or Georgia would use him.

Ben was an IT guy. Who knew what kind of damage he could do? Even if the stalking set-up fizzled out once Karen dealt with the DA, the Caldwells could keep making major trouble for me. With access to my phone, Ben could screw up my whole life—identity theft, ruined credit scores, bad recommendations, huge debt. The worst-case scenarios of the wired world danced through my head as Courtnee yammered on.

"So, like, I promised Ben I'd tell you he stopped and wants you to call him. He's a hottie, Leah, and you should know you don't get that many chances at your age—"

"What's his number, Courtnee?"

"987-555-0136."

I hung up without saying goodbye.

I just sat there for a minute, thinking about what to do. I should call Karen, but she'd just try to talk me out of what I wanted to do. Which was confront Ben. Though I could see where that might not be a good idea just yet. Maybe I should call Karen and tell her that I wanted her to come with me to talk to Ben. She could be a witness and—my internal debate was cut short by the ringing of my cell phone.

It probably isn't the smartest thing I've ever done. I'm sorry to say it's not the dumbest either. But once my caller asked for a meeting, I had no choice.

The EAT diner is one of the worst restaurants in Himmel, but one of the best places for a quiet meeting, because it's almost always empty. As I pushed open the door, I spotted my quarry and headed to the last booth on the left. There was no one else in the diner.

"Leah, thanks for coming. I got you a coffee," he said, pushing it toward my side of the table before blurting out, "My God, what happened to your face?"

I lowered myself into place, ignoring the screams of all my major muscle groups as I tried to make it look natural and easy. No way did I want him to know how bad I was hurting from the other night.

"I'm sorry, that was rude."

"Not as rude as shoving someone over the river bluff though, is it? Why did you call me, Miller? Should I be expecting Ross and his minions to jump out from the kitchen and arrest me for stalking you?"

"Leah, that's what I want to talk to you about. Or part of it—"

"Really. Actually, there's one or two things I want to talk to you about. But you go first." Under the table I hit record on my phone.

"I don't know quite how to start."

"How about with what you did to my sister?"

"Leah, I know what you think, but you have to believe me, I never touched Lacey, never thought of her that way, I never would. I couldn't."

"Oh, really? Then why did you pay for her online memorial? Why did you post on it anonymously every year since her death, thanking her for making your life less difficult? Did you meet her that night, Miller? Was it planned, or did you just run into her on your way back to the dinner?

"Did she tell you that she was going to expose you? Is that why you killed her? Or was it not you at all, Miller? Was it Georgia? Did she find out about you, and decide to take care of the Lacey problem, so nothing would ever come out that would affect your political career or her social position?"

"No, Leah, no. Just hear me out, then I'll answer anything you ask."

He started speaking in a low monotone, looking down as his hands turned his coffee cup in half circles to the left, then to the right.

"It was the last weekend in June. Lacey was supposed to take Charlotte and Sebastian to a movie, and they were very excited. At the last minute Georgia decided to take the children with her to her mother's for a few days. I didn't know she'd forgotten to call Lacey and cancel. I thought I was alone for the weekend."

He paused, looked at me, cleared his throat then looked back down and continued.

"A friend stopped to see me. We were together, and I didn't hear Lacey when she knocked on the front door. She came in. She saw us in the study. We were in a ... compromising position. For a minute, our eyes met. Then she turned and ran out. I went after her, but she'd ridden her bicycle over, and she was already too far down the path for me to catch her.

"I panicked. I could see my whole life crumbling, everything I worked for, everything I loved. All in the power of a 14-year-old girl. I didn't know what to do, what to say, how to fix it. Every time the phone rang, I expected it to be Georgia saying Lacey had called her. By evening I was a wreck.

"Finally, I called Lacey. As soon as she came on the line, I said, 'I want you to know. Whatever you saw this afternoon, it isn't what you think. It was just a mistake. I don't want you to—' I don't even know what excuse I was going to make, but she cut me off. I'll never forget what she said.

" 'Mr. Caldwell, I'm sorry. I was going to call you to apologize. I forgot all about babysitting this afternoon. My mom says I have too many things on my plate. I guess she's right. I don't think I'll have time to babysit for you anymore.'

"I knew she was there. I saw her. Yet it sounded like she wasn't going to say anything about it. I had to be sure. 'Lacey, I just want to say that sometimes things are very different from the way they look. And if anyone were to misinterpret things, well, they might not mean to but they could hurt innocent people. And I'm trying to say—'

"She wouldn't let me finish. She just said that her mother said she needed to set priorities, and she was really sorry she forgot to come over. That was it. And there I was, my entire future resting in the hands of an adolescent. But she never said a word to me about it again, or, I presume, to anyone else.

"I heard about her problems later, of course, but then when she died so shockingly, I was stunned. I wanted to do something to mark the passing of your truly remarkable sister, so I funded the online remembrance. I asked Mary Beth to have your mother think it was just part of the services she'd paid for.

"When I talked with you last week, and it became clear you suspected me and that you weren't going to stop asking questions, I spoke to Georgia. I told her you were investigating and that you had mistaken ideas, but that there was something I did need to tell her. She wouldn't let me. She got hysterical and I—I backed away. Then she got the texts from you and she went to the police.

"I'm sorry. I understand how angry you are. I know you were just trying to force the issue, but you don't need to do that anymore. I've decided to come out with the truth. And I'll see the investigation into your texts is dropped."

"Uh-huh. I suppose this girlfriend can give you an alibi for the night Lacey was killed? She'll say you were meeting her, not Lacey, the night you walked out on the fundraiser?"

"Leah, you don't understand."

"Sure I do. You may get burned a little for having an affair, but you confess, say a few *mea culpas* with Georgia by your side, and you're good to go. It works for politicians all the time, doesn't it? And look what a great guy you are, taking pity on crazy stalker Leah Nash and forgiving her for sending those nasty texts to your wife."

"You're not listening. I wasn't having an affair with a woman. I was with a man. My lover is a man. I'm gay."

I was shocked into silence.

"I'm gay. And I'm coming out. I'm ending my marriage, hurting and possibly alienating my children, ruining my political career, and breaking my father's heart. But I've spent every day of my life since I was 13 years old fearing exposure, humiliation, and exile from my family and my faith because of who I am. I can't do it anymore."

I was having trouble reconciling what I thought I knew with what he was telling me.

"But Miller, all these years—you supported the anti-gay marriage amendment. Georgia chairs the Mothers Against Same Sex Marriage coalition. How—"

"How could I be such a fraud? Please, Leah, you have no trouble accusing me of heinous sexual crimes, and even murder, but you can't bring yourself to think I'm a hypocrite?"

"You're saying that you wouldn't have abused Lacey, because you're sexually attracted to men."

"No, I'm saying I'm not sexually attracted to children. That I have been unfaithful emotionally and physically to my wife many times, but always with adult men. I'm saying that the night I left Paul Karr's office, I was going to meet my lover. If necessary, he has agreed to make a statement, but I hope I don't need to invade his privacy as mine is stripped bare."

He spoke with such weary resignation that it was hard to hold onto my conviction that he was guilty. I wondered how his children would cope with the news, and I even felt a twinge of sympathy for Georgia.

"All right, say it's true. You didn't have anything to do with Lacey's abuse or her death. But, Miller, I didn't send those texts to Georgia. In fact, up until a minute ago, I was convinced that you or Georgia got your nephew Ben to steal my phone and set me up."

"Ben? I don't understand. What does he have to do with anything?"

"I'm not sure now, but I met him at a party Saturday night. The next day my phone was missing. I searched everywhere, and Ben had plenty of opportunity to take it."

"But, why would he? And why would he send messages to Georgia, suggesting that if I didn't get out of the race, I'd be sorry, that she was married to a fraud, that both of us were going to be sorry?"

"I thought you two had asked him to do it, so you could get me off your back. I'd get arrested, or at the very least, fired and have my credibility destroyed. Good plan, by the way. Whoever designed it. Max canned me today, and I made the noon news as crazy stalker."

"I'm sorry, Leah."

"Yeah, well, just don't take it out on Max. I know he's got a loan application at the bank, and he's been taking heat for me."

"Leah, you said earlier that someone pushed you off the river bluff? Is that true?"

"Yeah. Sunday night."

"Who? Was it to do with Lacey's death?"

"Well, I don't think it was someone unhappy with my coverage of the Elks Pancake Breakfast. I thought it was you. Or Georgia. If it wasn't, I don't know who. Or why. Just for the record, where were you Sunday night?"

"I was at St. Stephen's rectory, talking with Father Lindstrom, from around 8:30 to midnight."

"Pretty good alibi. How about Georgia?"

"You can't seriously think—" but looking at my face, it was clear I did seriously think. So he added, "She was with my campaign manager, going over a speech she gave yesterday at the Omico Women's Club."

"That can be verified?"

He nodded.

"Miller, I'm sorry that my investigation into Lacey's death has pushed you to the brink like this. I only want to find the truth."

"And that will set us free, Leah? I'm not so sure."

28

I felt sick. Confused. And mad as hell. Coop must have warned me off Miller because he knew who really molested Lacey. He knew, and he didn't tell me. Did that mean he knew who killed Lacey? Did he even believe Lacey was murdered? Or that I was pushed? Or that Sister Mattea was?

How could he stand by and let me waste so much time on the wrong man? I reached for my phone to call him, then put it back down. To hell with him. If he didn't trust me enough to tell me what was going on with my own sister's case, I wasn't going to beg him for information. If he figured it out, I could too.

Who else had means, motive, and opportunity? There was still Paul Karr, but really? I had nothing but Marilyn's assertion that he wasn't home when he said he was. And she was a bitter, vindictive woman who hated my mother. It was Marilyn's word against Paul's, and I just didn't think it was Paul.

But Hegl now, that was entirely different. He lied about knowing Lacey before she went to DeMoss. He had plenty of opportunity there to try and start up with her again, or to try to ensure she kept their secret, or both. If Lacey said no, if she threatened to tell, or even if her daily presence was just too threatening to him, he could have decided he had to get rid of her. And there was his history with Olivia Pérez Morgan. But if he was involved, did Sister Julianna and Reid Palmer fit in the picture, too?

It was so frustrating. What did Coop know that he wasn't telling me? I tried to think of inadvertent hints he might have dropped. What about Cole Granger? Coop had warned me the first time I talked to him about Lacey's abuse that Cole was a con man.

What if Cole had told me just enough of the truth to sound plausible, but he was actually covering up his own involvement? What if he met Lacey, like he admitted, and they got into a fight, like he said. But there wasn't any kid with her. And she didn't kick him in the balls, he knocked her in the head, hard enough to kill her. Then he panicked and took her body into the woods and dumped her. He could've told me about the sexual abuse both to distract my attention from him and to point me in the direction of the abuser as the killer.

I had driven all the way back home, and still I didn't know which way to go now that Miller was out of the picture. I sat in the driveway staring blankly. It took a minute to realize my phone was vibrating. I looked at the caller ID. Delite Wilson.

"Hello."

"I seen you on the news. Looks like you're screwed."

"Yeah. Delite what did you call me for on Saturday?"

"I had some bad luck. Your fault."

"My fault?"

"Yeah. My boss saw me talkin' to you that night. She fired me."

"She fired you for talking to me?" I asked, not hiding my skepticism.

"Maybe not exactly that. I missed my shift a coupla times, and she was pretty mad about that. Anyway, she fired me and I'm sorta short of funds."

"What's that got to do with me?"

"Well, I was thinkin' you're lookin' for information and I figure maybe it's worth somethin' to you."

"You picked the wrong door, Delite. I don't have any money."

She snorted. "I thought you wanted to know the real story about the night your sister disappeared. Isn't that worth somethin'? Like maybe $5,000?"

"$5,000? I don't have that kind of money. But if you know something about Lacey's death—"

"I'm not sayin' anything unless I see the money. I'm not tellin' for free. I'm tired of everyone takin' advantage of me."

"Who's taking advantage of you?"

"Never mind. Just bring me the money."

"I can't get that much. It's not possible. I might be able to scrounge up $1,000?"

"$1,000? For what I got to tell you? No way."

"Look, maybe I can get $1,500 bucks together, and that's it, take it or leave it."

She went quiet, but I thought I heard another voice in the background.

"Hello? Delite? Are you there?"

"Yeah. Meet me at 6 tonight at 229 Elm."

"You're here, in town?"

"I'm stayin' with a friend. I gotta go. Bring the money if you want the information."

I drove straight to an ATM. I pulled out everything I had and still I was $600 short. I didn't want to ask my mother—she'd only try to stop me, or call in Karen or Coop, and if Delite really had information, the fewer that knew about it, the better. Miguel.

"*Chica*, I've been so worried. You didn't call me back."

"I'm fine. I'm OK. Can I borrow $600?"

"To take out a hit on Detective Ross? I don't know if I'm down with that."

"I'm not kidding, and I hate to ask, but I really need it."

"Sure, of course. But only if you tell me what's going on."

"I don't want you involved."

"Then I guess you don't want my money."

I hesitated, and he stepped into the pause.

"I'm going to the ATM, I'll be right over. And then you're gonna tell me everything."

Which is why, two hours later, there were two of us in the car as I pulled into the drive of 229 Elm Street, a rundown house with a cobbled together appearance. A sagging screened-in front porch, a patchy lawn strewn with bits of broken things—a cracked clay pot, a bicycle wheel, a rake with most of its tines missing. A drooping maple, more dead than alive, bent toward the gravel driveway where a rusty purple Camaro was parked.

"I'm going in with you."

"No. You're not. I don't want to spook her. I shouldn't have let you come."

"You had to. I'm a shareholder."

"Whatever. I'll be fine. Just wait here for me."

I reached for the doorbell until I noticed it was only loosely connected to the doorframe by a frayed wire and opted instead to rap loudly on the peeling front door. It opened, and a figure stepped out from the shadows.

"Well, well, well. If it ain't big sis."

"Cole. Is Delite here?"

"Welcome to my humble home," he said, ushering me in with a mock bow and a wave of his arm.

Inside was even more depressing than outside. A stained and scarred wooden floor, bare light bulbs in the ceiling, a sagging, threadbare blue couch patterned with big pink and white flowers sitting in the middle of the room. The air smelled faintly of burning weed though none was in evidence. Delite looked at me and sat up from her semi-reclining position.

"Delite, look who come to visit. Sit down now, won't you, Leah?" he said, pointing to a metal folding chair and pulling up another for himself.

"I didn't come to talk to you."

"But I'm what you might call Delite's personal representative. Like her lawyer, kind of, just to make sure her interests are safe."

I turned away from him and looked at Delite. "OK, so what's the information?"

"Now hold on there. Let's just see some evidence of your part of the deal," Cole said.

I reached in my purse and pulled an envelope out, opening it slightly so he could see the bills within. He nodded.

"All right then. Delite, you go ahead now, darlin.'"

"I wasn't with Lacey that night. We didn't go to a party. I never saw her after lunch."

"Where were you that night?"

"With Hegl. He got a car from the carpool and sneaked me out under a blanket. We went and saw *Knocked Up* and got a pizza, like a date. Then we hadda go back to DumbAss Academy. I did his bj in the car. If we'da got caught, they woulda bounced him, and Queenie prob'ly woulda killed him herself. Me, well straight to juvie for sure. But he liked to do stuff like that. He wanted to do it twice. The second time in Queenie's office."

"You had sex with Father Hegl in Sister Julianna's office?"

"Not sex," she said in an annoyed voice. "Just a bj." She shrugged. "I got pizza, didn't I? And I liked that movie. He sat in Queenie's chair. He wanted me to crawl under the desk. So, I did. He finished, then we heard like a door openin.' I ran out Queenie's side door while he was zippin' his pants. I don't know what happened after that."

Lacey. Lacey had gone to the administration building to get a car after Cole refused to take her with him.

"What time was this?"

"We got there a little after 10:30. I could see Queenie's clock from under the desk. I hadda get down there, he hadda get in the chair; I was there maybe 10 minutes or so. Hegl wasn't exactly pre-jack but he never lasted very long. Queenie's clock chimed when I was leavin' just like Cinderella leavin' the ball." She gave a scornful laugh.

I turned to Cole. "What time did you leave Lacey?"

"Hold on a minute. My information ain't part of this deal. If I'm gonna give you anything, I got to get somethin', too, don't I?"

"Tell me, or I'll call your parole officer and we'll see how a drug test comes out. I'm pretty sure smoking weed will get you kicked right back to jail."

"Don't be such a high and mighty bitch."

"Just tell me."

"I got a speedin' ticket, right? When I was on Dunphy Road. That was 10:50 p.m. according to Officer Asshole who wrote the ticket. So, I musta left there about five minutes before that."

"The files say you told Ross you were with your girlfriend Amber all night. They don't say anything about you getting a ticket that night just a few miles away from DeMoss."

"I guess he didn't check with the state po-lice, did he? Cause that's who give me the ticket. And that ain't my problem. I told you I didn't need to get mixed up in any of that shit."

I turned back to Delite. "You're sure you didn't see who came into the reception area? You didn't hear anyone speak?"

"Nope."

"Why did you come forward with that story about Lacey and you being at a party?"

"After they found her body, Hegl said with all the pokin' around they were doin', they could find out he took a car and took me out that night. Maybe even that we hooked up in Queenie's office. He said I should say Lacey went to a party with me and got wasted. That'd quiet things down, and he promised to make sure I got to stay outa juvie."

"Didn't you realize that by lying you altered the whole course of the investigation? If you hadn't made up that story, then they might have actually tried to find out what happened, and Lacey's murderer wouldn't be walking around."

"She's dead either way, right?"

"Delite here was just protectin' her own interests. Now, as I see it, you got what you wanted, and if you hand over what we want, this deal is concluded."

"No. Not yet."

"You're not tryin' to back out on us, are you? 'Cause I gotta tell you, I don't see that you have a real strong negotiatin' position here." He moved in closer, his body odor strong enough to make my nostrils flare, and his fists clenched with latent menace.

I ignored him. "Delite, what do you know about Danny Howard?"

"Ralphie. That's what your sister called him. 'Cause he looked like that loser kid in the Christmas movie. Used to follow her around. Little wussy kid."

"Do you know what happened to him? Do you know where he is now?"

"I seen him once."

"Where? When did you see him?"

"Me and Cole seen him at a truck stop at the Dells a coupla months ago."

"Did you get his number?"

"Yeah. We're gonna get together next week and plan the DumbAss Academy reunion. No, I didn't get his number. I said I seen him. I didn't talk to him. He was kinda busy."

"Do you know how to reach him?"

"Look, he was workin,' and it's not like we was big buddies. That was him and your sister."

"He was working at the truck stop? Is he a bus boy? A server?"

"I s'pose you could call it that," she said with a smirk. At my confused expression she said, "He was hustlin', OK?"

"You mean he's a male prostitute?"

She made a sound between a laugh and a snort.

"Yeah, he's a 'male prostitute'," she said, mocking me with a simpering, prissy tone.

"Do you know how I can reach him?"

"What do I look like? 411? I told ya, we didn't trade phone numbers."

"I think that about wraps up our business, Leah. Me and Delite got plans. Now, if you'll just hand over the cash."

"Delite, what did you mean when you said you were tired of 'all of them' taking advantage of you. Who is all of them?"

"After you came sniffin' around, I figured there might be somethin' in it for me. I reached out to Hegl for a loan, like. He treated me like dirt. Told me if I tried to spread lies about him, I'd regret it. Said he could make more trouble for me than I ever could for him. Nobody would believe a liar like me. Asshole. I don't have to take that anymore. Then Cole said maybe I should call you. Now, I'm thinkin' maybe I even got a bonus for you," she gave me a sly grin.

Cole cut her off.

"Shut it, Delite. Nothin' is free. Now, if Leah comes up with a little more cash—" I had no scruples about paying for information, obviously, but I was tapped out.

"I haven't got anything more. This is it. But—"

"Then our business is done here." He reached out and snatched the envelope from my hand. "And don't think any of this is on the record, cause it ain't. And we definitely ain't standin' behind it. You're on your own."

29

I had refused to talk on the ride back home, waiting until we were seated at the breakfast bar, each with a bottle of Supper Club lager in front of us. I had barely ended with Delite's hint that there could be "bonus" information if I came up with the cash, when Miguel started peppering me with questions.

"Hegl is the *pendejo* who molested Lacey? But how could she go to DeMoss and see him and know what he did? Wouldn't that be *muy* hard for her?"

"Yeah, I'm sure it was really hard for her. But Lacey was a strong kid. Stronger than we knew. By the time she got to DeMoss, seeing Hegl every day maybe made her more angry than afraid. So angry, she decided she had to come out with the truth no matter how he threatened her."

"So, what do you think happened the night Lacey disappeared?"

"I think she wanted to get away before she outed him, and she thought Cole could take her into town, to our house. Then when Cole wouldn't go along with it because of Danny, she had to come up with a new plan."

"But what could she do?"

"Steal a car. That was her fallback position. She took Mom's car a few times, and her last hurrah before she got sent to DeMoss was trying to get to Chicago with it. I'm guessing that after Cole let her down, she figured her last option was to get the car keys from the administration building and take one of the pool cars. The keys are just hanging there on a board behind the reception desk. She left Danny to wait for her while she got the car."

"Only Hegl was there with Delite."

"Exactly. Maybe Hegl left the front door unlocked, on purpose, to heighten the 'danger,' or maybe Lacey just busted in. Either way, she got in, made a beeline for the keys, and Hegl heard her and came out to reception. He confronted her, asked her what she was doing there.

"She snapped. Told him she was going to go forward, tell everyone the truth, and she didn't care whether anyone believed her or not. Maybe he stepped in too close, maybe he taunted her—maybe she slapped him. He was backed into a corner and he was furious."

I could see the scene in my mind's eye. Lacey, small, defiant, lashing out verbally and physically. Hegl, enraged and motivated by self-preservation, hitting right back.

"Oh, wait a minute—"

I jumped up, and ran down the hall to my room, searching through my desk for the case folder, then flipped quickly through the papers. There it was, the medical examiner's signature: Donald Straube, M.D.

I went back to the kitchen and grabbed my phone to look up Dr. Straube's number. "What? What is it, *chica*?"

I waved my hand to shush Miguel as the call rang through.

"May I speak to Dr. Donald Straube?"

"Speaking. Who is this?"

"Leah Nash, Dr. Straube. You were the medical examiner on the case for my sister, Lacey Nash, five years ago. I just want to ask you a couple of questions. It won't take a minute."

"Young lady, I'm retired. Have been for four years. I can't remember details at this date. You should be able to get a copy of the autopsy from the sheriff's department."

"No, no, that's OK. I have a copy. I just wanted to ask you, in your report you say the cause of death was head trauma from a blunt object, probably from her head hitting a rock or a tree stump when she fell down the ravine."

"Yes, yes. I do remember now that you specify. Sad case, very young girl."

"Dr. Straube, is it possible that my sister didn't die from the fall? Could she have been struck in the head, and her body transported to the location where it was found?"

He got a little ouchy then. "Miss Nash, I am a qualified medical doctor who met every standard of the state of Wisconsin for medical examiner. A licensed pathologist conducted the autopsy. Are you suggesting our findings were not correct?"

"No, please, not at all. I'm just wondering if there was specific evidence that proved she died at the site where the body was found."

"The site was trampled by the unfortunate woman who found the body, as well as by some of the more inexperienced members of the sheriff's department. Furthermore, your sister's body was badly decomposed."

"I understand. I'm not criticizing your findings. I just want to know if it's possible that she could have received a blow to the head, and afterward her body was dumped at the location where it was discovered. Is there anything in the findings that would say that wasn't possible?"

He sighed. "No, nothing I recall from the autopsy or the crime scene investigation that would preclude that. But given the findings of the investigators and the location, the most likely cause of the head injury seemed to be her head striking a rock or tree stump as she fell. Perhaps you should be talking to the detective in charge of the case. He would have managed the crime scene and would be able to help you better than I."

"No, you've helped me a lot. Thank you, doctor. I'm sorry for disturbing you."

I hung up and turned to Miguel, who was bursting with the effort of not talking.

"I know. I know how Hegl did it." I looked back down at my phone and clicked on photos. Nothing. "No!" I had forgotten that everything on my phone had been deleted.

"What? What? *Dígame*."

"Miguel, do you still have that text with the picture I sent you? The one I took at Father Hegl's?"

"I don't know."

"Look, look, look!"

"OK, OK, chill." He pulled out his phone and started scrolling back through texts, and then handed it to me. The wall of religious statues at Hegl's popped up crisp and clear. On the second shelf from the bottom, in the corner, there it was. I zoomed in on the photo, then showed it to Miguel.

"The murder weapon. Taken from Sister Margaret's desk the night Lacey was killed. The Virgin Mary, with a long white scratch on the base."

"*Ay, Dios mío!* Are you sure? But why would he keep the murder weapon?"

"Haven't you ever heard of hiding in plain sight? Think about it. He kills Lacey and then he's in a panic. He's got to get rid of a body, a phone—he doesn't know what she might have on it—and a murder weapon. He can reset the phone to factory settings, no problem. He can take one of the 4-wheelers and dump her body in an out-of-the-way place on the property and plant some pills and bottles with her.

"If he's lucky, the weather and animals will take care of things. If he's not lucky, and she's found right away, well, there are the pills, the empty bottle. And running away fits her pattern. She's just another kid who couldn't turn her life around.

"But what can he do about this big, old statue? He can't throw it with the body. That would raise way too many questions if it was found. He can't throw it in the trash; he knows Sister Margaret will be having a fit when it's missing, and someone is sure to look there. He makes a bold move. He puts it right on the shelf with a hundred other statues."

"That takes *cojones*, *chica*. What if Sister Margaret or one of the other nuns saw it?"

"Unlikely. The nuns don't drop in on Hegl. And even if they did, he could say that one of the students must have put it there as a joke, and he has so many statues he didn't notice. Anyone else who might visit—they wouldn't see it among all the other statues. I didn't. And even if they picked it out, it wouldn't mean anything to them."

"What are you going to do now? Call Coop?"

"No. I botched things with Miller. I don't think Coop has much faith in my crime theories just now, and I think he's working on one of his own. Maybe it involves Hegl, maybe not. He's not telling me anything. Once I get the statue, though, he'll have to believe me. Then he can work it with Ross. I sure as hell am not going to that nimrod."

"How you going to get the statue? 'Please, Father Hegl, give me the statue you used to kill my sister?' " His teasing grin turned to dismay when he saw the look in my eyes. "No, no, no. Don't even think about it."

"I'm not thinking it. I'm doing it. I'm going out to Hegl's, and I'm coming back with that statue."

"No," he repeated.

"Yes. He teaches a music class at the community college tonight. He shouldn't get back home until 10:30 at the earliest. It's only 7:30 now. Plenty of time for me to get in and get out. I know right where the statue is," I said, walking over to the kitchen drawer to pull out a flashlight. It was still daylight, but it would be dark before I was done.

Miguel followed me out to the garage, still protesting while I rummaged through a disorganized workbench before finding the canvas Piggly Wiggly bag and plastic gloves I was looking for. He continued arguing as I headed toward my car, but as I reached to open the door, he grabbed my arm. "No, let's take my car. I'm behind you."

30

We drove into the county park and left the car at the far end of the lot, then took the path that wound along the edge of the Catherines' property. About a quarter of a mile in, we cut across a field that rose gently to a modest hill. When I got to the top, Miguel was trailing behind, stopping to wipe something off his very expensive shoes.

"If you're coming, come on!"

"You know how to show a boy a good time. If I knew we were going mud bogging on foot, I wouldn't have worn my new boots," he grumbled.

"You don't have to be here, you know, but if you are here, I need you to not be whining." It was a little sharp, but I was more nervous than I was letting Miguel know.

"I'm in, I'm in," he said, giving up on his shoes with a shrug and a half-grin.

Spread below us, the campus of DeMoss Academy looked idyllic.

"There's Father Hegl's, that cottage to the right, see it?"

"Yes. But how we gonna get there without anyone seeing us?"

"Geez, Miguel. I didn't know you were such an old lady. Just follow me. It's half-dark now. Do you see anyone out there? All the little children are tucked in their dorms. The cottage is dark; Father Hegl won't be home until 10:30. It's 8:30 now, so it's all good."

We were quiet then as we hurried down the hill and cut across the bumpy, muddy ground. It wasn't until we reached the back door of Hegl's small house that either of us spoke.

"Oh-oh." In my haste to get there, get in and get out, I forgot about the possibility that Hegl's door might be locked. The knob turned, but when I pushed, it didn't open.

"OK, then I guess we better *vámanos*. Try again another day." He turned and was already moving across the backyard.

"Wait a second, wait." I turned and pushed, putting some force into it. "Sometimes these old locks don't really click into place and with a good— oof!—shove. There we go! See, the door is open. I'll just give a shout."

"Father Hegl? Anybody home? Your door was open." When there was no answer, I motioned for Miguel to follow me in. I turned on the flashlight and led the way down the short hall to Hegl's small living room. There, tucked away in a corner near the bottom of his shelf, was the statue of Mary. I pulled on the gloves I'd taken from home and reached out to pick it up, but Miguel said, "Wait, *chica*, wait."

He turned on a lamp, looked around, and grabbed a copy of *USA Today* lying on the coffee table in front of the sofa, and handed it to me. "Go there by the statue. No, don't pick it up, just kneel down off to the side. Hold the paper so I can see the date. *Bueno*, now point to the statue."

He snapped two pictures, then switched to video. "Stay there a sec. I want to get the room in the video, so you can see it's really the padre's house." He panned around the room and for good measure zoomed in on the newspaper again with me holding it, and then the statue, which I had picked up to show that it did indeed have a long scratch down the side, as Sister Margaret had described it.

"OK, I think we've got enough." I had turned to put the statue into my canvas bag when we heard it. The sound of tires on gravel. A millisecond later headlights flashed on the wall. We both froze. Then the slamming of a car door threw us into frenzied action. I snapped off the lamp, handed the bag to Miguel, and shoved him toward the kitchen, whispering, "Go, you've got to go."

"Aren't you coming?"

"You're way faster than me, and we've got to get the statue out of here. I can handle Hegl. I'll catch up." The front door opened, and there was movement in the living room. I gave him a push out the door, and he took off. I stepped out right behind him, pulled the back door shut and immediately began knocking loudly—or maybe that was my heart pounding. Either way, it brought a surprised Hegl to the door.

I had positioned myself to block his view of Miguel's retreating figure in the gathering dusk.

"What are you doing here?"

"I need to talk to you."

"Not a good idea." He started to pull the door shut.

"No, wait, please. Just for a minute, that's all." I wanted to turn and see how far Miguel had gotten, but I didn't dare. If I could just keep Hegl talking for another minute or two, I could be sure Miguel had gotten away.

"Where's your car? How did you get here?"

"I came in the back across the fields. Please, it's been a really bad day. I'm just asking for a minute to talk to you."

Bizarrely, he smirked.

"Yeah. Saw you on the news." I noticed then his words were slightly slurred. As he turned his head, I got a whiff of JD. I realized then that he was drunk, but one of those drunks practiced in the art of appearing sober.

"Do you have just a minute? I wanted to ask you about Olivia Morgan."

That got his attention.

He opened the door wider and grabbed my arm. "You better come in."

I tried to pull back, but his grip was firm and his lean frame was deceptive. He was very strong. Up close his eyes were red-veined and bleary. I opted for feigned nonchalance. "All right, thanks."

In a painful imitation of gentlemanly behavior, he force-walked me toward the living room with a vise-like grip on my elbow, then deposited me roughly in a chair. He bumped the edge of his desk as he tried to navigate around it on his way to the sideboard holding several bottles of whiskey. He poured himself a generous shot, then tipped the bottle toward me.

I shook my head. But I was happy to see he was still thirsty. The more he drank, the better chance I had around his befuddled wits and out the door. He pulled up a chair and took a long gulp. He was facing me, directly across from his wall of statues. If I didn't keep him distracted, he'd see the gaping hole where I removed Sister Margaret's Virgin Mary from his collection. I needed him to focus on me, fast.

"Carla Pérez says you were having an affair with her sister Olivia. She thinks you were with Olivia the night she died."

"She's lying." He stared into his glass.

"Why would she lie?"

"To make trouble."

"Like her sister Olivia? Did Olivia try to make trouble for you?"

He had dropped his head down and was silent so long I thought he might have fallen asleep. When he raised his glass to take another swallow, a little bit of the dark amber liquid spilled on his shirt. "Wasn't my fault. An accident." He had a defiant look on his face.

"What happened the night Olivia died?"

"It wasn't my fault," he repeated. "She shouldn't. She should. She." He stopped to gather his fuzzy thoughts.

"What happened?" I prodded.

"She, she—" He paused again and took another drink. "She grabbed the wheel. Not me. It wasn't me. She did it. It was raining so hard. She."

His voice had dropped to a whisper, so I had to lean in to hear. Staring into his glass, he said, "I tried to stop. We rolled. We rolled and I —I—I—"

I couldn't see the expression on his face.

"What about Olivia? What happened to Olivia?"

His head jerked up, and his voice was anguished now. "There was blood. So much blood. I couldn't. I couldn't." He started to cry, reaching out his hand and grabbing my wrist. Tears were running down his face.

"I couldn't help her."

I wasn't moved. "So, you left her, lying on the road. Olivia was still alive when the ambulance got there. You left her to die alone."

"No, no, no. I had to go. I had to go. My rib. I broke my rib," he said pitifully, as though by his injury he could absolve himself of his culpability. "I called the ambulance. I called."

"You called? But you didn't use your cell phone, did you? You waited until you got to a pay phone. A mile away. You waited, what? A half an hour? All the while Olivia's life was bleeding out because you didn't want to get caught."

His mouth quivered, and he wiped the thin line of mucous running from his nose to his upper lip with the back of his hand. "I couldn't help it."

"You keep telling yourself that, Hegl. It's a first-degree felony in Florida to leave the scene of an accident when someone dies. And you were driving. You could go to prison for 30 years."

The tears stopped. He stared at me sullenly. When he spoke, his voice was harsh.

"Prove it. Nobody can prove it."

"Yeah? Then why have you been hiding out here for years? Something's got you scared."

He was suddenly cautious, a sly expression on his face. "God. God protects drunks. Drunks and fools, don't you know that?" He started to laugh then went into a coughing jag. When he finished, I tried again.

"Why did you come to DeMoss?"

" 'Can't afford a scandal, Sean.' " He had lowered his voice and was attempting to look out from under his eyebrows in what I assumed was an imitation of someone. His uncle?

"Who knows about the accident? Your uncle the bishop? Who else?"

He didn't answer. Instead, he stood abruptly and staggered toward the hall. For half a second I considered waiting on the chance I could talk to him about Lacey, get more out of him, but my reptile brain was saying "Run! Run! Run!" It won. As soon as I heard the bathroom door close, I ran.

Miguel was waiting at the top of the hill.

"*Chica*, what took you so long?"

I huffed for a few minutes, then panted out an answer. "Hegl was drunk. And talkative. He admitted he was driving the night Olivia died. He was drunk, and he left her there. He left the scene of the accident. His uncle got him out of it."

"But why would his uncle send him here?"

"I don't know. Maybe Uncle Bishop didn't want to deal with **Drunken Priest Kills Lover in Car Crash** headlines. If his uncle wanted him stashed away in a backwater, he couldn't find a much better place. And Hegl would have a good reason to settle down and play nice up here. Maybe his uncle has something else on him, something even worse, who knows? But if the bishop's buddy ever rescinds his alibi, Hegl's in big trouble."

"I get that. But why here? What's the connection?"

"I don't know. Sister Julianna? Reid Palmer?" I bent over and tried to catch my breath.

"You didn't ask him about Lacey?"

"No, I just tried to keep him distracted, so he wouldn't notice the statue was gone."

"Look—your *amigo* is looking for you." He pointed in the direction of the cottage. From our vantage point we could see Hegl, silhouetted in the light flooding out his open back door.

"*Ádale!* Let's go. Maybe he noticed his statue is missing." We took off.

31

My mother was sitting up at the bar drinking a cup of tea when I tried to sneak in the house without waking her. I hadn't returned her calls after my surprise appearance on the noon news, just texted to say I was all right, it was a mistake, and I'd talk to her.

"How was your day?"

"I would guess a lot better than yours. At least I didn't lose my job."

"Who told you?"

"Courtnee. When I called the paper."

"I'm sorry, Mom. I just needed a while before I could talk about it, can you understand that?"

"Frankly, Leah, there's very little I understand about you these days." She sighed, then said, "All right, yes, I guess. But I want to hear about it now."

I stood uncertainly for a minute. She hadn't asked about the canvas bag I was carrying, so I pulled out the stool next to her and casually set it down, pushing it off to the side. I gave her a scaled down version of the day's events leading up to my trip to Father Hegl's.

"I had to get proof, Mom."

"Proof of what?"

"Proof that Father Hegl is the one who abused Lacey—and the one who killed her."

She just sat there.

"Did you hear me, Mom? I said Father Hegl—"

"Yes. I heard you. I heard you when you said it about Paul. And about Miller Caldwell. Leah! You've been thrown off a cliff, investigated by the police, nearly arrested, publicly humiliated, fired from your job, and now you seem determined to get yourself killed. I am so angry at you right now, I can barely speak."

"Why are you so mad?"

"You broke into Father Hegl's house! What if you're right, what if he did kill Lacey? Why wouldn't he kill you too? Do you realize the chance you took? Don't you care about anything but what you want to do?"

"Mom! Of course I do. Miguel was with me. Weren't you listening? I didn't break in; the door was open ... pretty much. We had to get the statue out. And we did." I lifted the bag and opened it slightly.

"First thing tomorrow I'm taking it down to the police station. I'm giving it to Coop, along with proof that it came from Hegl's, and then he can get it to Ross and the DA—I don't think I'd get far with either of them until this Caldwell thing is straightened out."

"So, you're saying that once you give the statue to Coop, you're done? No more questions, no more investigating?"

"Well, no, not exactly. I still need to—"

She shook her head, and put up a hand for me to stop talking. "You do what you want, Leah. You always do."

Then it was my turn to get angry. "Oh yeah, that's me, Leah livin' large, back in my old bedroom, roomies with my mother, working at the crappy weekly where I started. Or I was 'til I got fired. That's me, doing what I want. You think I want to go over and over this in my head every night? You think I want to face the fact that I let Lacey down, that I was too busy to take her call, and maybe if I had, she'd still be alive?"

"Lacey called you?"

"Yes, Mom, she did. And I didn't pick up, and by the time I listened to her message, she was already gone. I didn't tell you because I didn't want you to know what I'd done—or hadn't done. I didn't want you looking at me the way you are right now."

"What did she say? What was the message?"

"She kept breaking up, there was lots of static. I thought she said something about legal—like maybe she was in trouble again. That's why I thought she was drinking and had run away again."

I paused to take a breath. My mother continued to stare at me.

"I can't bring her back. But I can make sure the person who did it pays. And I'm sorry if that upsets you, or worries you, or pisses you off. I'm not feelin' so happy myself right now." And I grabbed the statue and went to my room, slamming the door behind me. There had been more door slamming in that house in the last month than in all of my teen years and Lacey's combined.

Once in my room, I checked my Facebook account. It was blowing up with people asking me about the stalking charges. I was hearing from classmates I hadn't talked to in years. As I scrolled through the commiserations and questions, I suddenly realized that this might be a way to reach Danny Howard. I tried a search and didn't find him under his own name, but I didn't really expect to. I hit it though, when I typed in a search for RalphieP. The kid from *A Christmas Story*.

He didn't have any identifying information I could look at beyond the fact he was from Wisconsin. But I felt pretty confident. I made a friend request, and I hoped the name Leah Nash would pique his interest. And then I had to wait.

The next morning Melanie was at the front desk when I walked into the police station. She gave me an odd look. Maybe it was the Blessed Virgin poking her head out of the Piggly Wiggly bag under my arm that caught her eye. I shifted it discreetly toward my back and said, "Is Coop in? I need to talk to him."

"He's in, but he's busy right now."

"How long will he be?"

"Not sure."

"Well, I guess I'm gonna wait."

"Suit yourself."

She turned back to her computer screen, and I settled in on one of the hard plastic chairs.

But I noticed that instead of returning to her own dimension, where only she and her computer screen existed, Melanie kept sneaking glances at me. What was up with that?

I sat for a while, replaying the scene with my mother, and wishing I'd just kept my mouth shut. Thinking about what I could have said, and should have said, and what actually came out of my mouth. Why did I tell her about Lacey's phone call? She was never going to forget—or forgive me. How could she? I couldn't forgive myself.

Finally, I got up and paced the small waiting area, then walked up and leaned on the counter to talk to Melanie.

"Hey, Melanie, what's taking Coop so long?"

She shrugged. "He's interviewing a suspect."

"What's going on?"

"I couldn't say. But what's goin' on with you, Leah? You're gettin' pretty famous. I saw you on the news yesterday."

"Yeah. That. Well, it wasn't true, I didn't send those texts and stuff to Georgia Caldwell."

"I figured. So, now you're writing the news and in the news this week, eh?"

"No. I won't be writing the news this week. I don't work at the *Times* anymore."

Before she could ask the question so clearly on her face, her phone rang.

"Right. OK. Oh, Leah's here to see you. Yeah. Sure." She hung up and came over to lift the counter for me to walk through. "Coop's in his office. He wants to talk to you."

"Not as bad as I want to talk to him."

"Don't be so sure of that."

I hustled down the corridor, mentally counseling myself to stay calm, to lay out the facts clearly, not to lose my cool if Coop didn't get on the same page with me right away. I could convince him, I knew I could, if I didn't push too hard.

"Leah, I was just goin' over to the paper to see you."

"Don't bother. You won't be able to catch me there. I got fired yesterday."

"What?"

"Yeah. When WTRS got hold of the story that the sheriff's department was questioning me about stalking Georgia Caldwell, Max lost it. He fired me on the spot."

"Ah, geez." He ran his hand through his hair. "I'm sorry. C'mon in."

I pulled up the chair across from his desk and set my evidence bag on the floor.

"Coop—"

"Leah—"

We both spoke at the same time, then both gave the polite, slightly nervous laugh of strangers caught in an awkward two-step while trying to pass each other on a sidewalk.

"Let me go first, please. I know I was wrong about Miller. I've been wrong about a lot of things, but this time I have it right. If you'll just listen, you'll see."

"All right." He sat back and waited, but the look he gave me was so sad, it threw me off stride.

"OK. OK then." I was surprised that my hands were sweating. I wiped them nervously on my jeans. "Do you have some water?"

"Sure." He reached around to the small refrigerator behind his desk, pulled out a bottle, opened it and handed it across to me.

I took a big swig and then started in. I laid out everything I knew about Hegl, including ground we'd covered before to try to make him see the big picture—starting with his involvement with Olivia Morgan, the fatal car crash, his sudden departure from the parish, his bishop uncle, and the role he played in getting him out of a felony charge.

I reminded him about Hegl's opportunity to connect with Lacey during the production of *The Wizard of Oz*, Lacey's subsequent downward spiral, her animosity toward Hegl at DeMoss, his involvement with Delite, his lie about where he was that night. I told him Delite's story about someone interrupting them in the administration building the night Lacey disappeared. Her admission that she'd lied about the party.

"And finally this, Coop." I reached into my Piggly Wiggly bag and pulled out the statue.

"What is it?"

"It's what he killed Lacey with. Sister Margaret's marble statue—the one that went missing the night Lacey disappeared. The one I found on a bookshelf in his cottage." I set it on his desk.

"You found—Leah, tell me you didn't break into Hegl's house."

"I didn't break in, not technically. We knocked, the door was open. Stuck maybe, but definitely open."

"I assume 'we' means you and Miguel. Was Hegl there?"

"Not at first. He came home before we expected him though."

The look on his face told me I'd better talk faster if I didn't want to get another—probably deserved—lecture on using commonsense, and not jumping in feet first without thinking.

"I got Miguel out with the statue before Hegl showed up. And I didn't accuse him of anything, if that's what you're worried about. But, Coop, he has the motive. And look! This is the murder weapon. I'm sure of it. I thought if you could get it tested, there might still be some DNA on it. It's been cleaned, no doubt, but see this crack here? If blood got in there—"

He had stopped listening to me. He pushed the heels of his hands into his eyes and rubbed for a minute, his long fingers resting on his scalp. Then he brought them down, took a deep breath and heaved it out so forcefully, the papers on his desk fluttered.

"Leah, we've arrested the person who sexually abused Lacey—and at least two other girls."

"What? When did you make the arrest?" How could he have let me go on and on when he already had Hegl in custody?

"Early this morning." He stopped, came around his desk and sat on the edge so that he could reach out and touch my shoulder. His voice was gentle as he spoke, but the sound echoed in my head as though he'd shouted through a megaphone.

"Leah, it's not Hegl. It's Karen. Karen McDaid was Lacey's abuser."

32

"What?" I heard what he said, I just couldn't process it.

"I'm sorry, Leah. A senior at the high school came forward a few weeks ago and told us Karen had a sexual relationship with her for over a year when she was a freshman. We've turned up two more since then."

A wave of nausea so powerful surged through me so fast I couldn't do anything but grab the waste basket and heave. Tears came to my eyes as I gagged and coughed, and I felt the pressure of Coop's warm hand on my back.

"Sorry," I choked out, my head still half in his wastebasket.

"Take a breath and hold it a second. That's right, hold it, now let it out slow and easy. That's right. That's good." I focused on the sound of Coop's voice, and my breathing came under control. I sat up and took a small sip of water.

"Are you sure? Are you sure someone's not setting her up? I mean, who's saying this? Who's corroborating it?"

"It's a solid case—we've been building it for weeks. Leah, there are pictures on her computer. They—well, it's very clear the girls are telling the truth."

"Pictures? Is—are there pictures of Lacey?"

He nodded.

"Did Karen—did she kill Lacey?"

He shook his head. "She couldn't have. Karen was in Arizona for the whole month of November that year. That's when her mother died."

I remembered then. Karen had called every day to ask if there was word on Lacey. She was so kind, so helpful, such a rock for my mother.

There was a knock on the door, and one of the detectives I knew slightly stepped in without waiting for an answer. He looked at me, then quickly looked away.

"Not now, Randy," Coop growled.

"Sorry, Lieutenant, but it's Ms. McDaid. Darmody told her Leah was here when he brought her coffee. She says she'll sign whatever we want, if we let her talk to Leah. She says she doesn't want a lawyer, she just wants to talk to Leah."

"This isn't a hostage negotiation, she's not getting anything—"

I knew he wasn't just taking a stand on proper police procedure with a suspect; he was trying to protect me, too. I appreciated it, but I actually needed just the opposite. I had to see Karen.

"Coop, wait. I want to. Let me talk to her."

"That's not a good idea."

"Please."

Something in my eyes must have told him that I had to do this. That I wouldn't be able to eat, or sleep, or breathe until I could confront Karen and stop this rising tide of fury that was building up inside me.

"I've got to talk to the DA first. Wait here, Leah." Then he leaned down and pulled the liner from his trash, knotted it and handed it to Randy, whose face had shown a growing awareness that something unpleasant had happened here. He took it and left the room behind Coop, holding it at arm's length.

When I walked through the door, Karen was sitting on one side of a metal table, an empty chair across from her. Devoid of make-up, her skin was ashen and seemed to have collapsed in on itself. There were hollows and wrinkles on her cheeks, little lines around her mouth and chin. Her eyes, those slightly uptilted blue topaz eyes that had always sparkled with intelligence and humor, were dull and sunken. Her shiny silver-blonde hair was flat and lifeless. Her hands holding a coffee cup looked corded and old.

Her eyes met mine as I sat down.

"Leah, you came. I was afraid you wouldn't."

"I had to, Karen. I had to look at the person who destroyed my sister."

Her head recoiled. "Leah, don't say that. I loved Lacey."

"You loved her?" Under the table my hands clenched into fists and I held them on my knees by force of will. "You ruined her life!"

"No, no, no." She started shaking, and tears ran down her cheeks. "Don't say that. Just listen, please, please, please just listen a minute."

I pressed my lips together to keep more invective from spilling out, and then I nodded.

"Lacey was such a beautiful child, so bright. She reminded me of a little butterfly. She used to make me laugh, and I loved to hear her sing. I always enjoyed it so much when she stopped to see your mother after school." Karen's eyes had a faraway look.

"Of course, I always loved you, too, Leah," she added, as though I might be jealous that I hadn't made the Pedophiles Pick of the Week list.

"But Lacey was special. I remember that day we became more than friends. Your mother had a weekend retreat, and you were away with that boyfriend nobody liked. What was his name? Zach? Carol asked if Lacey could stay with me for the weekend. We had such a wonderful time. She was so sweet, so unsure, so...." Again, she seemed awash in memories that I didn't want her reliving.

"She was 14 years old, Karen, and she trusted you. She looked up to you. She was 14. Don't try to make this some special, loving thing. You molested her, and you kept on doing it, and you are a sick, hypocritical monster!"

"But I told you, I loved her. I would never harm Lacey. We both wanted it. I didn't force her. I never forced her. But later, she got very upset. Said she was going to tell people. I begged her not to, I knew no one else would understand. So, I had to help her see what could happen to her, to me, to your family if she did."

"What did you do, Karen? Did you threaten her? Did you tell her it was her fault? Did you say no one would believe her? Did you kill her to keep her quiet?"

"No, no!" she said sharply, a horrified expression on her face. "I would never harm Lacey. But I had to convince her to keep quiet."

"How did you do that?"

"I told her we didn't need to hurt each other. Someday, she'd realize how special our relationship was, but some people wouldn't. You and your mother for instance. That you would be disappointed in her, angry. Like you are right now. And I could lose my law practice. Then your mother wouldn't have a job.

"And then I told her I would publish the photos I'd taken of her online, if she wasn't sensible. But she was." Her voice was barely a whisper now, and I had to bend forward because her head was hanging down, and she was staring at her hands folded in front of her on top of the table.

"You put all that on a 14-year-old kid? How could you do that? And how could you work with my mother every day? How could you pretend to be her friend, her best friend?"

"But I am her best friend. I knew Carol wouldn't understand. I didn't want to hurt her. I didn't want to hurt you. What Lacey and I had was beautiful, but it was just for us. What harm did it do?"

"What harm? Are you really that insane?" An idea came to me. "You sent those texts to Georgia Caldwell, didn't you? And you gave Ross an anonymous tip about me getting fired in Florida. It was you, trying to frame me."

"You wouldn't leave it alone. You kept asking and asking about Lacey, and I knew when you realized it wasn't Miller, you'd keep asking. I had to do something to make you stop. I took your phone when you set it down at the party that night. Then I put it back in your car on Monday morning, when I stopped by your house."

"You pushed me off the bluff that night. You almost killed me!"

She shook her head, "Leah, no! I wouldn't do that to you. I couldn't. I love you."

"Yeah? Like you loved Lacey, like you love my mother? You make me sick. And whatever feeling is festering in that garbage dump you call a heart, it sure as hell isn't love."

"No! No! I love you, Leah. And I love Carol. You have to believe me."

I stared at her, trying to reconcile the self-deluding, twisted predator that sat before me with the kind, generous woman I had loved and respected. What was it that Father Lindstrom had said? Something about all of us wearing habits to hide our secret selves. Karen's habit of warmth and humor had been the perfect disguise to hide the twisted ugliness within.

"Actually, no. I don't. And I don't have to listen to another self-justifying word you say. Goodbye, Karen."

I could still hear her calling my name as I slammed the door and walked down the corridor.

I went back to Coop's office, collapsed in a chair and put my head in my hands. Karen with Lacey. Karen taking advantage of Lacey's trust, her enormous respect and love for Karen. Then the confusion and the shame she felt. Trying to break free, longing to turn to Mom, or to me, but thinking she couldn't because of Karen's threats. She must have felt so helpless. So hopeless. And me too busy and too blind to see. No wonder Lacey lashed out against the people who should have protected her. Me and my mother.

"How could I not have seen that?" I must have spoken out loud, because walking into the room just then, Coop answered.

"Stop, Leah. Lacey didn't want you to see it, she worked damn hard to protect you and your mother. When you did suspect, you acted on it right away. You wouldn't let go."

"But I had it all wrong. Even when it was staring me in the face. Delite told me it was 'a big shot,' and I knew it had to be someone who spent a lot of time with Lacey. No other adult was with her more than Karen. But I never even considered her. This is going to kill my mother."

"Don't underestimate Carol. You two are a lot alike."

"How long did you know? And why didn't you say anything? Why did you let me think you thought I was crazy?"

"You thought that up all on your own. I admit I did try to steer you away from the investigation. And I felt bad, real bad, when you thought I didn't have your back. But it wasn't true. Not for a second."

"Then why didn't you tell me?" The shock was wearing off, and I was starting to feel both stupid and ill-used. "Didn't you trust me?"

"Leah, come on. It was an open investigation, and you were very personally involved. You couldn't be objective. I barely could. We had to be very careful. You were so determined to get justice for Lacey. Karen was a close friend of yours. I couldn't take the risk."

I leaned forward and opened my mouth to yell at him, tell him he had no right to keep that from me, tell him that he should have trusted me, should have known I wouldn't do anything to jeopardize his investigation. And then I slumped back in my chair and didn't say anything, because I knew he was right. I'd been crazed since I suspected Lacey was abused, and I doubted I would have been able to stay away from Karen, or keep from telling my mother. He was right. It hurt to admit it.

"Who else knew about it?"

"Just me, my team and the DA."

"Not Ross?"

"Not at first, not until we realized there was more than the original victim involved and we started putting it all together. Lacey was his case, the county's case. We had to put him in the picture."

"How many girls did she hurt?"

"Don't know yet. She's writing a statement now. So far, we have the three, counting Lacey."

"What do you think will happen?"

"You know her better than I do. Do you think she'll recant her confession and contest the charges?"

"I thought I knew her. Clearly, I didn't. I have no idea what she'll do." I stood up to get a cup of coffee. My foot bumped against my forgotten bag. In the immediate aftermath of the Karen revelation, I'd forgotten all about my original mission.

"Coop—what about Hegl? You're going to check out this statue, aren't you? Get it tested? I understand Lacey wasn't killed because she was abused. But she was killed. I know it. And that statue is going to help prove it."

"I can't, Leah."

"Hegl lied about knowing Lacey; he lied about where he was the night she died; he got Delite to lie; he warned her against talking to me; he admitted he was driving the night Olivia Morgan died—and even if I don't have proof, it has to be investigated. And what was this statue—Sister Margaret's missing statue, the statue that disappeared the same night Lacey died—doing in his house? He's in it up to his neck."

"I'm not arguing with you. I'm saying this is Ross's case. He's gotta take the lead. I already called him. He should be here any minute."

"I'm not talking to that asshat."

"You're going to have to. I'm not playing your middleman here. You're a big girl, and you can handle it. Just know that Ross is already royally pissed off at you. He's going to give you a hard time about illegal search and seizure. Hold firm. The door was open; you went in to ask Father Hegl about the statue. He wasn't there; you saw it and seized it as possible evidence of a crime. You're a civilian, you don't have to follow the same rules we do."

He gave me a warning look.

"If there's anything there, the DA will be able to get it into evidence. For God's sake, Leah, don't snatch defeat from the jaws of victory. Just stay away from Hegl and the rest of them, and let Ross do his job."

33

An hour and too much caffeine later, I sat in the conference room, the Virgin Mary on the chair by my side, both of us waiting for Coop to bring Ross back.

He came truculently into the room, running his finger around his too tight collar in a vain effort to give his neck roll some breathing space.

"Nash, why is it every time something smells bad, there you are in the middle of the stink? All of a sudden, Mrs. Caldwell drops her stalking complaint—even though we could nail you on that. Now, Coop tells me you got some kinda statue supposedly used to kill your sister. I ain't buyin' it."

"I'm not selling, Ross. If you'd done your job, you wouldn't have wasted time on that stupid stalking complaint at all. And if you had half the brains of an amoeba, you wouldn't have done such a half-assed job investigating my sister's death when it happened. Maybe the smell is the crap I have to shovel to clean up after you."

"That's it, that does it."

"Both of you, knock it off. Charlie, Leah's got some information for you. Leah, just give him a statement without editorializing." Coop turned on the tape recorder.

I gave Ross the story.

"Miguel can corroborate. And he has the photos that prove the statue was at Hegl's the first time I visited back in May, and still there where we found it last night. I wore gloves when I picked it up, and it hasn't left this bag except to show it to Coop."

"Let me get this straight. You broke into the priest's house—"

"I didn't break in. The back door was open. I thought he'd be there. I wanted to talk to him." I lied without guilt or hesitation.

"And you just walked in and stole property from his shelf," he continued as though I hadn't said anything.

"We went in, and when I saw the statue, I seized it as evidence of a crime. I didn't steal it. I knew it had been taken from Sister Margaret, and I had reason to think it had been used to kill my sister. I'm just a private citizen. I don't need to have a warrant. Look it up. Now are you going to take the statue and have it tested, or do I have to do everything on this case myself?"

"I don't need to tell you what I'm going to do. I was solving crimes when you were still watching *Scooby Doo*. I'm warning you, Nash, stay out of this case and away from Father Hegl, or you'll regret it. You got lucky on the criminal sexual conduct thing, but that's a long way from a murder investigation.

"You still haven't convinced me there's anything but an accident involved in your sister's death. It's the DA's call if we go to the expense of testing this statue, and right now, Nash, your track record ain't so good."

"Only an insensitive jerk like you could call it 'lucky' that I was right about my sister's sexual abuse. Just do your damn job this time, Ross, and don't worry about what I'm doing."

"Which should be sendin' out your resume from what I hear, Nash."

I left without saying anything else. But I wanted to.

My mother's car was in the driveway when I got home. She jumped me as soon as I walked in the door.

"Something strange is going on. When I got to work this morning, Karen wasn't there. I tried to reach her, but she isn't answering her cell. I drove by her house and her car is there, but she isn't. The house was locked. I knocked, but no one answered. She had two client meetings this morning, and she didn't show up. She never misses a meeting! I cancelled the rest of her appointments, but I'm getting really worried about her. I think we should go back over and try to get in through a window. Maybe she—"

"Mom, Karen's been arrested." She kept on talking as though she hadn't heard me.

"She could have fallen in the shower or—wait, what did you say? Arrested? Is that supposed to be funny? I'm seriously concerned, Leah." I grabbed her by her shoulders and looked straight into her eyes.

"Karen was arrested this morning on criminal sexual conduct charges involving two high school students. She's confessed. And she—she," I struggled to get it out. "She told me she had a sexual relationship with Lacey, too. Karen is the one, Mom, the one who abused Lacey."

At first, she didn't react, just tilted her head and drew her eyebrows together in a frown, as though I'd said something she didn't quite catch. Then she grabbed my arm and pulled me over to the couch and sat us both down. "I don't understand. It just doesn't make any sense."

"The police found pictures on her computer—some of them were Lacey. I was at the police station this morning, and when Karen heard I was there, she wanted to talk to me. She said if she could talk to me, she'd sign a statement."

Again, there was that look of confusion, as though I were speaking in a language she was familiar with, but not quite fluent in. "But that can't be right. Karen loved Lacey. Loves you. Remember how strong she was for us when Lacey died?" She paused, and I could almost read her thoughts from the growing horror on her face.

"She didn't kill Lacey, Mom. At least not directly. She was away the whole month of November that year, with her mother in Arizona."

I told her what Karen had said, her self-serving explanation, her feeble attempt to justify what she'd done, and how she'd kept Lacey quiet with guilt and threats. The longer I talked, the tighter my mother gripped her hands together, until her knuckles were white with effort.

"Oh, God," she moaned when I finished. "How could I have been so stupid? I thought it was wonderful that Karen took so much time with

Lacey. I thought it was so good for Lacey to have a strong, professional woman as a role model. Why did she do this? How could she do this?

"How could she look me in the face every day? How could she pretend to care when Lacey started getting into trouble, or when she ran away, or when she went to DeMoss? She always acted so concerned, so kind, so...." Her voice trailed off as she tried to make sense of the betrayal.

"She's sick, I guess, and she couldn't stop herself—or wouldn't stop herself. I don't understand how she could compartmentalize her life that way, but that's what she did. She believes she loves you and me and Lacey too, but it's a crazy kind of love. She couldn't admit, especially to herself, that what she rationalized as beautiful was toxic. But another part of her knew—that's why she begged and finally threatened Lacey to keep it quiet."

"It makes me sick, physically ill. And it makes me want to kill her." She jumped up and went to the cupboard, pulled down the Jameson and poured it in a glass and drank it straight down in one gulp. Then she got some ice and poured another.

The phone rang. I answered and handed it to her.

"Mom, it's Paul."

I got up, went into the kitchen and banged around in the freezer for a while getting ice out. Then I got a glass and some Jameson. By the time I went back to the living room, she was off the phone.

"Paul's coming over to get me. He said you should come, too. He wants to fix us dinner."

"That's nice of him, but no, I don't think so."

Things were still pretty awkward between me and Paul, and the thought of going over and over things with my mother and him was more than I could bear. I knew that for Mom, talking was the only way to vanquish the falling-to-the-bottom-of-a-mine-shaft feeling. But I wasn't ready to hear all the guilt and recriminations and what ifs and whys—I had my own battle. Paul was much better equipped to be her listener, and they didn't need me there.

As we finished our drinks, his car pulled in. My mom ran out to the driveway with me trailing behind. He opened his arms wide, and she collapsed against his chest and started to cry. I realized then how much he cared about her, and how hard my suspicions had been on both of them. He stroked her hair and looked at me over the top of her head.

"Leah, I'm so sorry."

"No, I'm sorry, Paul. I—"

"No. You were right. I didn't believe you when you started out, and then when you came after me—or it felt like you came after me—well, I lashed out. I understand you had to ask, Leah. I still wish you hadn't, but—well—I get it, and I'm not mad anymore."

I gave my best attempt at a smile.

"Thanks, I appreciate it. And I'm glad Mom will be with you tonight."

"Are you sure you don't want to go with us, Leah?" Her voice was thick with tears yet to come.

"I'm sure, I'm fine. Yeah. I'll be all right."

"Try to eat, don't just drink Jameson all night."

"I'll make a sandwich or something. Don't worry."

After several more attempts to get me to join them, they got into Paul's car and drove off. I went back inside to think about the question my mother hadn't asked, but which had been on my mind since I left the PD. If Hegl wasn't Lacey's abuser, what was his motive for killing her? And if he didn't do it, what was he doing with the statue?

34

I sat down in the rocking chair and moved slowly back and forth, talking out loud to myself.

"OK, Hegl is a ladies' man who likes them young—Delite was 17, Olivia was 19, who knows how many others? He's having fun with Olivia, but he wants out when she wants to get serious. When the car crash happens, he cuts and runs and that makes things get a whole lot more serious. He could go to jail on this one. With his position of supposed moral authority and his chickenhearted behavior, chances are good he will. So, he runs to Uncle Bishop, who provides an alibi and a witness to corroborate it."

I got my laptop out and googled the Most Reverend Joseph Ramsey.

Twenty minutes later, I had it. A website set up for the St. Lucian School alumni. Lots of old photos and reminiscing, and in the middle of all that upper-class male bonhomie there they were, their arms jauntily slung over each other's shoulders. The pride of the Class of 1978, the most Reverend Joseph Ramsey and Reid Palmer, then known as Joe and Reeder.

The class update noted that Joe was now the Most Reverend, and Reeder was now Reid Palmer, attorney-at-law, retired hedge fund manager and benefactor of too many charities to mention. It also contained a quote from the Bishop: "The older I get, the more I value the days I spent at St. Lucian's. *Fratres in vitam*. Brothers for life."

And so, when his nephew got into some bad trouble with a girl, a drunk girl, who wound up dead, Joe turned to his old friend Reeder.

What if Reid Palmer supplied an alibi and a refuge for Hegl, and maybe even some money to persuade Vince Morgan that a slow boat to Key West was the best way to get over his dead wife? Carla could be right about everyone ignoring things. With a little nudge from the bishop, the sheriff could have fast-walked his investigation right into an accidental death finding, no one involved but the drunk girl herself.

Much the conclusion that Ross reached just as speedily up here. But even though Hegl walked away from a felony, he was now and forever under the thumb of his alibi provider, Reid Palmer. If he ever recanted, Hegl was in a world of hurt.

But what was in it for Reid Palmer, beyond the joy of doing a helpful turn for an old friend? And how did Sister Julianna fit in? Did she? If Palmer suddenly thrust a choir director priest on her, wouldn't he have had to offer some explanation? And what had Delite been about to tell me when Cole cut her off?

I got up and did some nervous eating—a peanut butter and honey sandwich, a chocolate cupcake with about an inch of frosting. Then I stretched out on the couch as my sugar buzz bottomed out. My eyelids started to droop, and I was sound asleep for the next hour. When I woke up it was 8:30, but my mind was clear and I knew my next step. I pulled up the recent call list on my phone and selected Delite's number.

"Yeah?"

"Delite, this is Leah Nash."

"I know who it is."

"Is Cole with you?" I was going to try to persuade her to give me the "bonus" information she had hinted at before. It would be easier if Cole wasn't around.

"No. He ain't. That asshole took my money and took off. Left me with nothin'. Not even enough for bus fare. My brother in Minneapolis said I could crash with him, but I don't even have enough for a ticket."

"I might be able to help with that," I said cautiously, trying not to sound too eager. She needed cash pretty bad and didn't have much of a negotiating position. "If you tell me what you meant by 'bonus' information that night I met with you and Cole."

"That'll be 500 bucks."

"Come on, Delite, get real." As we were talking, I pulled up bus fare from Himmel to Minneapolis. $52. "I can give you $75. That's it." Which it was. I had an emergency $50 tucked in my wallet. My other source of bribery funds would have to be the $25 or so my mother kept in a miscellaneous cash cookie jar.

She sighed, but she must have been really desperate, because she didn't try to bargain.

"Meet me at the bus stop. I can catch the 10:30 if you move your ass."

When I pulled up, she was leaning against the brick wall of the all-night diner that served as Himmel's bus stop. She looked small and tired as she smoked a cigarette with quick, impatient puffs.

She saw me and straightened, throwing aside her cigarette and assuming her usual aggressive stance.

"What happened?"

"I told you. Cole took the money and cleared out. Left me with nothin'. I'm goin' to my brother's. He said he can get me a job at the factory where he works. You got the money?"

I reached in my purse, and she put out her hand. "No. Wait a minute. First I want to hear the information."

"Fine. I seen Queenie up at the casino. More than once."

"What was she doing there?"

"Do I gotta draw you a picture? She was at the casino. Playin' the slots."

"Sister Julianna was gambling?" I was dumbfounded. "Are you sure it was her? Did you talk to her?"

"Yeah, I'm sure. I spent enough time in her office starin' at her while I was gettin' yelled at, didn't I? She didn't see me, and I didn't talk to her. She never had anything to say I wanted to hear."

"Why would she drive all the way to Mixley to gamble? There are closer places."

"Duh! So nobody would see her, whadya think?"

"That doesn't make sense. A nun in a habit playing the slot machines would attract a lot of attention no matter where she was."

"Are you retarded or what? She wasn't wearin' her nun clothes. Now, are you gonna give me the money or what?"

I thrust it into her outstretched hand.

"It still goes, ya know. This ain't on the record. I'm not gettin' mixed up with any of that crowd again."

"I'd stay away from Cole Granger, too."

"Don't worry. I can take care of myself." Then she turned and walked into the restaurant/bus stop to buy her ticket. She didn't say goodbye, and she didn't look back.

At home, I typed Sister Julianna Bennett into Google. She popped up in conjunction with multiple professional associations and conferences. I pulled up the program for her recent Las Vegas conference, the one where she had run into Helen Sebanski at the slot machines. There was her bio with highlights from her vita. As Sister Margaret had said, Sister Julianna did a lot of professional traveling.

Funny thing, almost all the papers she presented and the keynote speaking listed took place in cities that also boasted casinos with conference facilities. Well-known gambling meccas like Las Vegas, Detroit, Reno, Albuquerque, as well as a number of smaller towns like Mt. Pleasant, Michigan, and Black Hawk, Colorado featured heavily in Sister Julianna's professional life.

I thought for a minute, then typed in gambling nuns. Soon I'd read several stories about Catholic nuns and priests who had embezzled money —big money, like millions of dollars in some cases—from their order, their parish, their school. They used it to buy vacations, purchase condos, give lavish gifts to friends and family, and to cover gambling sprees. The fraud went on for years, in many cases, before it was discovered.

Clickety-click went my little brain as I recalled Sister Margaret telling me how precarious the school's finances used to be. Clickety-clack it picked up speed, thinking of her recounting the arrival of Reid Palmer and the subsequent stabilizing of funds. And then clickety-clackety-click-clack-click, we rolled into the station. I heard Sister Margaret saying that Sister Julianna did everything herself. That Sister Mattea's surprise revamping of the accounting system would take such a burden off her.

Sister Mattea's brother. I had to get ahold of him.

Scott Riordan hadn't called me back, but maybe his snotty receptionist hadn't given him the message. I looked at my watch. 10:00 p.m. It would be 7:00 p.m. in California. Miss Moneypenny would be gone for the day, and maybe I'd be able to leave a message directly on Scott's voicemail. I crossed my fingers and called.

After three rings, I was readying a coherent message to leave when an actual male person answered. "Riordan Software."

"Oh! hello. My name is Leah Nash. May I speak to Scott Riordan please? It's very important."

"Hello, Leah. This is Scott. What can I do for you?"

"Scott—I didn't expect to connect directly to the boss. Last time I called, I couldn't make it past your receptionist."

"Miss Adams takes her job seriously. I've been out of the country actually, just stopped in on my way home from the airport to see what my desk looked like. You're lucky. I can't stand to let a phone go unanswered. What is it you need?"

"It's sort of complicated, so I'm going to skip a lot that I can fill in later. I know you were donating a new online accounting system to DeMoss Academy."

"Yes. I still plan to. What about it?" His tone of voice had gone from friendly to curious.

"And Sister Mattea, your sister, that is, did she provide you with financial records to be entered into the new system, so you could get it operational and ready to go when she presented the system as a surprise to Sister Julianna?"

"Yes."

"Did you find anything unexpected?"

"Leah, I can't really talk about this to you. The financial data is confidential."

"I understand. I'm not asking for particulars. I just wondered if there was anything that concerned you at all. Please. It's important."

"I guess I can say that there is some information I plan to bring to the board's attention."

"Don't! Not yet, please!" I blurted out.

"Excuse me?"

"Your sister trusted me. I need you to trust me too."

"What do you mean?"

I told him about Sister Mattea's note, and that I'd been working for weeks to figure out why she reached out to me and what she wanted to say. "I think part of what she wanted me to know was personal to me. But part of it might have had to do with financial problems at DeMoss. Have you found anything that indicates there could be fraud or embezzlement going on at the school?"

"You're putting me in a tough position."

I held my breath. Finally, he spoke again.

"The proprietary software my company developed is very sophisticated. I asked my sister to give me records going five years back in order to demonstrate all the program could do for the school."

"The software detects fraud?"

"Yes, but it's not that simple. It uses data mining and algorithms to classify and segment information, find associations and determine patterns and deviations in behavior. When a dissimilar behavior is identified in a pattern of transactions that should be similar, for example, it can signal a problem."

"Like fraud or embezzlement, right?"

"I want to be clear here. These pattern anomalies are not proof of fraud, Leah. They are indicators. Further analysis and additional information is always required."

"Has your software ever identified real-life fraud, for other companies, I mean?"

"Oh yes. Absolutely. We had a situation last year where a vice president for finance at a nonprofit had embezzled more than $3 million dollars over a 10-year period. He wrote checks to himself, forged signatures, destroyed cancelled checks the bank provided. He covered losses by inflating the number of unfulfilled pledges, and he was able to get away with it because there were no checks and balances.

"He reconciled the books and handled everything. Then, while he was seriously ill for an extended period, the organization brought in an acting manager who was familiar with our software and convinced the board to purchase it. The system revealed the indicators of fraud and within months the man was caught."

"So, you think that could be happening at DeMoss?"

"I didn't say that."

"OK, but it could be right?"

"I'm comfortable saying that nonprofits and religious organizations have among the highest rates of fraud. They rely on trust rather than verification, and they invest too much authority in one person."

"But Sister Mattea never said anything to you about it? You didn't talk to her?"

"No. I didn't pinpoint any problems until after she died. And truly, I'm not comfortable talking to you about it, Leah. As I said, I intend to talk to Reid Palmer and suggest some areas for additional data gathering and alert him to potential problems."

"Scott, please don't, not yet. Just give me a few days before you do."

"I really don't understand."

"And I can't explain. Yet. But if you give me just a week or so, I will."

"I don't know...."

"No one but Sister Margaret knows you're working on this, right? It's not like anyone's waiting to hear from you. I promise you what I'm doing is exactly what your sister would have wanted me to do. I know it is. Just give me a week. Whatever is or isn't wrong with the DeMoss accounts—a few days isn't going to make any difference, right?

"I suppose not, but I—"

"Thanks, Scott. I'll be in touch as soon as I can. I promise."

Sister Julianna was stealing money. Had Reid Palmer found out? Was he covering for her like he was for Hegl? But why would he do that? And what did any of that have to do with Hegl, Lacey, and the statue?

"Damn." The more I found out, the less I knew.

Discouraged, I slumped back in my seat.

There was a light tap on the kitchen door, and when I looked up I saw Miguel peering through the window. I waved him in.

"*Chica, que va?* What did Coop say about the statue? And what about Hegl? And Karen! Did she—Lacey, was she the one who—"

"Coop turned the statue over to Ross, who gave me grief about breaking into Hegl's, which remember we absolutely did not do. And he'll give me nothing about the investigation. If he even does one. Karen swore she didn't kill Lacey—and she was out of town, so that's probably true. But she did admit she was the one who sent the texts to Georgia."

I got up and went to the refrigerator and got us each a beer. We both sat down at the bar, drank, and didn't say anything for a few minutes.

"You knew it wasn't Miller all this time, didn't you?"

"I didn't know it was Karen. I never thought—"

"No, but you *knew* it wasn't him. Not just you didn't think, you actually knew."

He shifted on the stool and looked down, staring at his Supper Club.

"It's all right. I know he's gay. He told me. And he told me he's coming out. But why didn't you tell me? You let me go after him, and all the time you knew he was gay?"

"I tried to push you in a different direction. It's hard to turn your boat around, *chica*. But I couldn't tell you about Miller. *Lo siento.* I'm sorry. It wasn't my secret."

I waved away his apology. "I probably wouldn't have listened to you anyway. I've pretty much had my head up my ass for the last month or so, I think we can all agree."

"So, what's next?"

I was a little hurt that he didn't fight me on the head up my ass thing.

"Well, I've just spent the last hour backing myself into a corner of this godforsaken maze, and I can't seem to think my way out of it."

"*Dígame.*"

I explained my attempts to link Hegl, Palmer, Sister Julianna, and Sister Mattea together. I told him about my phone conversation with Scott, and my belief that Sister Julianna was an embezzler with a gambling problem. Miguel was as excited as I was at first, and then his face fell. Just like mine.

"So—what does Lacey have to do with all that? And the statue? You still think Lacey was killed, right? That it wasn't an accident?"

"Yes. But I don't know why."

"Maybe she found out about the embezzling?"

I shook my head. "I don't see how she'd even stumble across something like that. And if by some wild chance she did, I doubt she'd get the significance. She was just a kid."

"What are you gonna do?"

"I don't know. Think some more, I guess. It's not like I have a job taking up all my time anymore."

"That could be good." The encouraging note he tried to inject in his voice was sweet, but kind of comical at the same time.

"Hey, it's gettin' late. You don't need to babysit me, I'm OK. In fact, I think I'm going to put all this stuff away for now and listen to some music and try to get some sleep. Maybe something will come to me in my dreams."

"OK, *chica*, if you're sure."

"I am."

35

After Miguel left, I fussed around in the kitchen for a while, putting stuff away, doing the dishes, wiping down the counter. I'd told him I wanted to get some sleep, but I was too restless. On the other hand, my brain felt too fried to figure out anything coherent. I walked down to the hall closet and reached way back on the top shelf and pulled out a sturdy banker's box marked *Lacey*.

I carried it into my bedroom, set it on the bed, and sat down next to it. Sometimes, Mom would get the box down and look at the things inside, but I rarely did. It was just too hard. But that night I wanted to remember.

I took the top off and started sifting through the contents. Cards she'd gotten from me and Mom, a wall poster of *Wicked*. A small notebook filled with quick drawings of things that caught her fancy. I flipped through a few pages—a tree with bare branches, her cat Zoey, Mom sleeping on the couch, a bird, the swing on our front porch.

I put it aside to look at later, with the half-formed idea of pulling out some of the pictures to mat and frame for my mother's birthday, then resumed my digging. A book of word puzzles. She loved crosswords, word search, anagrams, all that stuff. Some old report cards. The next thing I pulled out was a half-bald, one-eyed, matted, stuffed dog she called Fluffy

Pete that I gave her when she was three. For years, she wouldn't go to sleep without it.

That's when I started to cry. Once I began, I couldn't stop. It went from tears running down my face to shoulder-shaking sobs. I cried for Lacey and the life that was stolen from her, for my mother and the pain she had endured, and for myself and my inability to save her. I cried until my nose was stuffy, and my eyes were swollen, and my throat hurt. And then I cried some more.

When I finally stopped, I reached in the box for one more thing. Lacey's MP3 player. If I could listen to what she loved, maybe I'd feel connected to her again. Maybe somewhere, somehow, she'd know how sorry I was. I fumbled to turn it on, but, of course, it wasn't charged after all this time. I plugged it in the charger, and put the rest of the stuff away except for the sketch pad and Fluffy Pete. Then I layed down on my bed with the tattered stuffed animal beside me and fell asleep.

The next thing I knew my iPhone pinged. I leaned over and looked at the time: 7 a.m. When I saw that RalphieP had accepted my friend request, I shook off my sleepiness. He was still online. I started typing.

Danny—I'm Lacey's sister.

I know who you are.

Can we meet or can I get your number and call you?

Not a good idea.

Why were you with Lacey the night she disappeared?

I hated DeMoss. She said I could go with her.

Why didn't you?

You tell me.

What do you mean?

She left me. Went to get a car. Never came back.

She didn't leave you. Lacey was killed that night.

He didn't respond for so long I wondered if he left his computer. Then the cursor started moving.

I got outplaced. Off the grid. No TV, no Internet. Home schooled. No one told me.

How long were you there?

Two years. Ran away.

What happened after Lacey's friend Cole took off?

Lacey went to get the car. She didn't come back.

What did Lacey know that would make someone want to kill her?

I don't know. I have to go.

And that was that. He went offline. But I learned three things from our chat: he was scared, he knew something, and I was right, Lacey *was* in the administration building the same night Hegl and Delite were there. But why would Hegl have had to kill her? All he'd need to do was call security and report her. If he wasn't her abuser, what was the motive?

But what if it wasn't Lacey coming in at 10:45? Maybe Hegl and Delite heard someone else enter the building, not Lacey. Not yet. If Sister Julianna or Reid Palmer—or both—were on the scene, Lacey could have walked right into the middle of something when she got there. And never walked back out.

***

I got out a pencil and paper and made a timeline. Delite and Hegl get to Sister Julianna's office just after 10:30. They have round two of their romantic tryst, and as they finish up, they hear a noise in the outer office. Delite runs out the back door at 10:45, leaving Hegl with his pants down. Literally.

According to Cole, he got his ticket on Dunphy Road, a five-minute drive from Simon's Rock, at 10:50. If that was true, then he must have left Lacey at 10:45. It would take her at least 10 minutes to get to the administration building from the Baylor Road entrance, especially in the dark. And Delite was very sure it was 10:45 when they heard the noise. If it wasn't Lacey coming in, who was it?

Everyone else was at the dinner, which didn't end until after 11. Including Sister Julianna and Reid Palmer, except maybe not. I recalled the bitter words of Marilyn Karr. How he had sabotaged her. How he had offered to retrieve the drawing he'd forgotten in his office. How he didn't get back until it was too late for her. Had his unexpected arrival at the administration building ensured that it was too late for Lacey, too? But why?

"Damn it!" I shouted out loud, then immediately shut up so I didn't wake my mother. I sighed and pulled Lacey's MP-3 player out of the charger, inserted my ear buds and hit play. I picked up the notepad of drawings I'd set aside the night before, intending to leaf through it while I ate my breakfast. My mother's door was still closed as I passed down the hall. I set the sketchpad on the bar and went into the kitchen.

The songs on Lacey's player moved from Avril Lavigne to Justin Timberlake and on to the Black Eyed Peas. I had to smile when Simon and Garfunkel showed up. We are our mother's daughters, I thought, as I put bread in the toaster, poured a glass of orange juice, cracked an egg into the frying pan. Then a song came on that made me stop in my tracks.

Except it wasn't a song at all. It was two people talking. And what they said turned my stomach.

Danny, what are you doing in here all by yourself? The unmistakable soft Southern drawl of Reid Palmer.

Listening to my player. A young boy, nervous and high-pitched.

Well that's fine, Danny. I know that's a favorite pastime of boys your age. But wouldn't a nice soak in the hot tub after all our exercise today feel good?

That's OK. I want to stay here.

Danny, what's wrong? Didn't you have fun today? Didn't you like the horses? Didn't we have a grand time?

I guess.

Danny. Let's go now. Everyone is waiting.

Silence. Then Danny's voice came in a rapid-fire burst.

I don't want to. Just take me home. I just want to go home, Mr. Reid.

Home, Danny? You mean back to DeMoss? Well, of course, you can go, anytime you want. But I would have to tell Sister Julianna that I think you are having some adjustment problems. And that could mean you need to be outplaced. Then you wouldn't be able to stay in touch with your little brother. What is his name now? Justin?

You can't do that!

Of course I can. Not that I want to. I hope you'll realize that my friends are your friends, too. They all like you very much. Is it the camera, Danny? Does that worry you? Don't even think about it. We all like to remember special times, don't we, Danny?

I just don't want to do it. Please, Mr. Reid.

It's up to you, of course. I can take you back to DeMoss. And you can abandon Justin. Like your mother abandoned you.

The small voice of a frightened and defeated 12-year-old whispered, *Fine. I'll stay.*

That's wonderful. Why don't you put away your music now?

That's why Danny wanted to run away. That's what Lacey knew. And that's why she died, to stop Danny from suffering the same way she had.

I went to my laptop and Facebooked Danny with my phone number and a message: I know what Palmer did to you. I have the recording. Call me.

Then I waited. Within 10 minutes my phone rang.

"It's Danny."

"I know about Reid Palmer. Why didn't you tell me?"

"My little brother is only 10. He thinks I'm in technical college. He can't know about what happened. What I did. What I am."

"Danny, I need your help. We can stop this. Stop Palmer."

"No. You can't. Lacey thought she could, and she's dead."

"Is it just Palmer, Danny? Do Sister Julianna and Father Hegl know what he did to you? Are there others?"

"They know. Sister Julianna picks out the kids. The ones like me, with nobody who gives a crap about them. If you go along, you get special privileges. If you don't, you get outplaced. And if you tell, nobody believes you. And they have pictures, video, stuff that shows what you—that you—everybody can see what you did. Anyway, you're just a lying screw up. That's why you're at DeMoss, right? After Lacey left—died—Hegl said, if I kept my mouth shut, they'd take me off the website. And they'd let me stay in touch with Justin."

"What website?"

"Where they post the videos. For the SLB."

"The SLB?"

"His club. His friends. The St. Lucian Boys—that's what they call themselves. The ones he brought us for."

I almost dropped the phone. "These friends, Danny, they were people Palmer went to school with?"

"I guess."

"How many are there? Did you know any of their names? Was there a Joseph?"

"There were different ones. Mr. Joe. He was the worst."

"If I showed you a picture, would you recognize him?"

"Yeah."

"Just a sec." I pulled the diocesan website up on my phone, did a screen capture and texted it to him. "Have you got it?"

"That's him. Mr. Joe." Danny had just identified the Most Reverend Joseph Ramsey.

"Did you tell Lacey about the website?"

"She said if we could find it, prove there was a website, we could go to the cops. They'd have to believe us. They'd shut the SLB down. I'd be safe. But we didn't know how to get to it. So, she gave me her MP3 player to record Palmer. I was supposed to get him to say something about the website, but I was too scared, I couldn't."

"You were really brave just to record him, Danny."

"I wasn't brave like Lacey. The night we tried to run, I started to cry when her friend left us. She put her arm around me and she gave me this big smile. She said, 'Don't worry, Ralphie. The eagle has landed. I've got what we need.' Then she went to get a car, but she never came back. It started to snow. I waited two hours, and she never came."

"I don't understand. Did she mean she found the website?"

"I don't know. Look, all I have left is my little brother. And the only way I can keep him is to lie to him. I can't help you. Please, leave me alone."

"But, Danny—"

It was too late. He was gone.

I called him back but he didn't pick up. I texted. "Danny. Please. I need you."

I got one back almost immediately. "This ain't Danny."

I called again, and a woman answered.

"I'm trying to reach Danny Howard?"

"Well, I'm not him. Quit callin' my phone and textin' me, will ya? I let him borrow it for 10 minutes. I wasn't plannin' on startin' a dating service." The call ended.

I tried Facebook, but he was gone. Not just not online, gone. He'd unfriended me or deactivated his account. Either way, he wasn't interested in talking to me again.

36

So that was it. Reid Palmer had some kind of freaky pornography site that he shared for fun—and maybe profit—with his friends from prep school. Their housemother was Sister Julianna, strewing throwaway kids in the path of the St. Lucian's Boys in exchange for Palmer helping cover up her own crimes. And Lacey had died because she found out and tried to rescue Danny.

Palmer probably uncovered the embezzling when he joined the DeMoss Academy Board, and "set things right," as Sister Margaret had said. But he set them right in exchange for Sister Julianna's help in securing suitable boys for himself and his SLB friends. Palmer and Sister Julianna knew about Hegl's felony. Sister Julianna and Hegl knew about Palmer's sexual crimes. The three of them were an unholy trinity of mutually assured destruction.

It was 8 a.m. Mom was still sleeping. I couldn't stand to sit at the kitchen table a minute longer, my mind running in circles. I cleared away my dishes, went to my room and threw on jeans, a T-shirt, and pulled my hair into a ponytail. Then I put on a Badgers cap, wrote her a note, and let myself quietly out the kitchen door.

The streets were full of traffic. People who hadn't lost their jobs all had somewhere to go. I wondered if Miller Caldwell would be making his big

announcement today. Odds were he'd be losing his job then, too, and probably a whole lot more. I tried to stop thinking and focus on just moving
ahead, one step at a time. I walked through familiar neighborhoods, past
my old elementary school, the park, JT's Party Store.

I walked until the sidewalk narrowed and the concrete squares were
heaved up at crazy angles by erupting tree roots. In some places, there was
more dirt than cement showing, and, finally, at the edge of town, the sidewalk stopped altogether. The street petered out, ending with a broken-
down wooden barricade topped by a Dead End sign.

I sat on a downed tree that lay half across the road, facing the fields
beyond the barricade. As soon as I paused my forward motion, the peaceful
non-thinkingness I'd cultivated on my walk disappeared. I had to find that
website. And, somehow, I had to get Hegl to tell me what really happened
the night Lacey died. I considered my options.

I could talk to Coop and tell him what Danny had said and what I'd
figured out. But could I trust him not to go to Ross? Probably not. It was
Ross's case, Ross's jurisdiction, and Coop would have no choice. And Ross
would just screw things up.

I could boldly go out to the Catherines' and run a bluff on Hegl. Tell
him I knew everything. Tell him Delite was coming forward, and Danny
was going to testify. Tell him he couldn't trust Palmer, that he'd already
tried to throw him under the bus. Tell him he needed to get ahead of the
curve, or he'd be saddled with Lacey's death. But he was up to his neck in
everything, and I couldn't be sure he wouldn't turn on me like a cornered
rat.

Then there was the X factor. Was Sister Mattea's death an accident? Or,
was she killed not because she knew about Lacey's sexual abuse, but
because she had figured out something about the financial fraud even
before her brother had used his super-duper software?

And there was also me. Who pushed me off that river bluff? It had to be
Hegl, Palmer, or Sister Julianna, and I sure wasn't going to let any of them
get away with it.

And what did Lacey mean *the eagle has landed?* What kind of word game
was that? Why couldn't she just say, "It's all good, Danny. I have the address,
and here it is."

I was so intent on trying to untangle the threads and formulate a plan that I didn't hear the approaching sound of bike tires behind me. But the little hairs on the back of my neck began to prickle and I whipped my head around. There was Vesta straddling her bike, flowered grandma dress riding high on nonexistent hips, decorum preserved by the pair of rolled up men's khakis she wore underneath it. Her little dog was asleep in the basket attached to her handlebars, snoring gently.

"Vesta! Hi. I didn't hear you," I said, in the overly loud and cheery voice I sometimes use with very small children and the elderly. "How are you?"

"Lord, dost thou not care that my sister hath left me to serve alone? Bid her therefore that she help me."

I blinked. That was a little too apropos to be entirely comfortable. She got off her bike and put down the kickstand. I stood up from my tree seat as she walked the few steps toward me. She kept coming until she was well within my personal space comfort zone. Her hair was damp with sweat, and she had a pungent, garlicky smell. I took a half-step backward, but the branch at my back didn't give me much room.

"Your sister is gone."

"I know, Vesta. I know you found her. That was a long time ago."

"For nothing is hidden except to be made manifest; nor is anything secret except to come to light." She was getting that agitated look again, the way she had when I dropped the box off at her house. I took care to speak in a low, almost crooning voice.

"OK. Right, that's true, I know. You're right about that. It's good to see you, but I'll let you get back to your riding. I've got to get home myself. If I could just scoot around you here?"

I tried to move past her, but as I did she clutched my arm. Her dog woke with a start and emitted a sharp little bark. I tried to ease out of her grasp, but she was stronger than she looked.

"For the prophet and the priest are defiled: and in my house I have found their wickedness, saith the Lord."

Her faded blue eyes were big and almost beseeching. Vesta spent long hours—both day and night—rambling the county roads. Fences and property lines meant nothing to her. She was such a common sight, and had been for so long, that people didn't even see her anymore. But that didn't mean Vesta didn't see them.

"Vesta, did you see something the night Lacey died?" I asked with an urgency that seemed to scare her.

She released my arm and started to shake her head and back away. Her little dog Barnacle began softly growling.

"Vesta! Vesta! Is it Father Hegl? Are you talking about Father Hegl? What did you see?" This time it was my turn to grab her. I held her twitching fingers in my hand. I shook her, and she jumped and pulled away. She looked at me, eyes wide with fear.

"I'm sorry! I'm so sorry!" I said.

She began to scuttle backward as I repeated, "I'm sorry, please. I didn't mean to frighten you." Tears were streaming down her face, and I felt horrible. "I'm so sorry, don't cry, please." I took a step toward her and she moved with surprising agility and speed. She jumped on her bike and turned it so rapidly Barnacle, who had begun barking frantically, almost fell out. She pedaled down the road, leaving me calling after her.

When I got home, a note on the table said my mother had gone into work to try and organize things, and let clients know that the office would be closing. It hadn't occurred to me until that moment that my mother, like me, was now out of a job. I sighed as I put the kettle on for tea.

What had Vesta tried to tell me? Had she been there that night? Had she seen Lacey being carried through the dark woods, to be dumped like an old mattress or a sack of trash at the bottom of the ravine? Did her tangled thoughts and her fear prevent her from describing it? But she hadn't abandoned Lacey. She'd gone back until Lacey was found.

I heard my mother's car pull in the driveway. When she came in, I said, "You better sit down, Mom. I know why Lacey was killed, and I know what's going on at DeMoss Academy, and it's really, really bad."

37

I told her everything—Sister Julianna's embezzlement, Hegl's complicity, Palmer's perversion, Danny's recording, the website, my encounter with Vesta. She listened without saying a word. Then she went to the cupboard, got out the Jameson and two glasses, and poured it for us straight over ice. By the time I finished this investigation, we'd both be candidates for detox.

"Mom. It's only one o'clock." But I took a sip anyway.

We carried our glasses into the living room. She took the couch, and I took the rocker. In the back of both our minds was the image of Karen sitting on the now empty wingback chair. Neither of us wanted to go there.

"What are you going to do?"

"I don't know what to do. I've got the recording, but I'm not sure we'd be able to prove it's Palmer. And without Danny's cooperation, I won't even be able to prove he's the boy talking. If I could get to that website, I'd have something solid. Without something tangible like that, Ross is not going to listen or do anything. He hates me, and I hate that everything I have is circumstantial, and I'm going to be up against a nun, a priest, and a rich guy. And I'm already not the most credible source in the world, thanks to Karen's texting on my behalf."

I stood up and started pacing around the room. When I got by the bar, I stopped and pounded the top three times shouting, "Damn it, damn it, damn it!" As I did, the force of my blows sent Lacey's sketch book flying off the bar, and it fell to the floor with pages fluttering.

"Well. That was productive," my mother said, getting out of her chair and stooping to pick it up.

"Sorry. It's one of Lacey's old sketchbooks. I found it in the box of her things."

She started leafing through it and smiling. I stood looking over her shoulder as she paused to study a page. It was the drawing of a bird, only now that I was paying closer attention, I saw it wasn't a random bird. It was an eagle. I stared at it. Hard. *The eagle has landed.*

"Mom, what's the legend about Zeus and Ganymede?"

"The god Zeus fell in love with a mortal boy, Ganymede, and took him to live with him in Mt. Olympus. Zeus is sometimes shown as an eagle or a swan." She waited for me to explain my out of left field query.

"So, basically Zeus was a pedophile and Ganymede was his boy toy?"

"That's one way of putting it. But the ancient Greeks thought that a relationship between an older man and an adolescent boy was a good thing. Leah, what—"

"I'm sure that's what Palmer and his St. Lucian Boys tell themselves. They're not sick predators. No, they're wise mentors to young boys, like the ancient Greeks. This eagle Lacey drew. It's rougher, not as detailed, but still it looks a lot like the one in a pencil sketch of Zeus and Ganymede that Palmer has in his office. He has the same statue at his summer home."

"But why did Lacey sketch the eagle? And how would she know Palmer had the drawing in his office?"

"She was in there for almost half an hour when Palmer "rescued" her from the scene with the kid who flipped out the morning she was waiting to see Sister Julianna. Palmer's sketch is very good. It would have caught her eye. It did mine."

I paused lost in thought. Lacey loved the hand-drawn Christmas cards my mom's friend Adrienne sent every year. Adrienne always cleverly concealed her name somewhere in the picture—in the mane of a horse, the bark of a tree, the curl of a wisp of smoke—the feathers of a bird.

"Remember how Lacey loved to find the hidden letters in Adrienne's cards? You and I missed them half the time, but Lacey could always see them."

"Yes, but—"

I took the sketch pad from her hand and stared at it, willing my eyes to see what had to be there. After a few seconds letters and numbers began to disentangle themselves from the shadows and hatch marks that made up the eagle's feathers. I grabbed a pen and frantically wrote them down.

"Leah, what are you doing? What do you see?"

I shook my head, intent on my task, searching carefully to make sure I had found them all. Then I looked at what I had written and groaned in frustration.

"What's the matter?"

I shoved the paper over to my mother. She read it out loud.

"4PzsLBe?.onion. What is this, Leah?"

"I thought it was going to be the URL for Palmer's pornography site, but it doesn't make any sense. The domain should be ".com," or ".net," or ".org," or something like that. I've never heard of ".onion" as a domain. This can't be right. We're back to nowhere." I slumped down on the bar stool.

"Just try it, see what happens," my mother said.

"It's not going to work, Mom. There's no kind of address like this, or else it's some kind of code. And Lacey was the word game code breaker, not me." I sat mired in frustration and self-pity for a minute before my mother spoke. When she did, it shook me up.

"Leah, think about Lacey sitting there alone in Palmer's office. Wondering if Sister Julianna was on to her plan to get Danny out, probably scared out of her mind. She notices Palmer's sketch. Goes over to look at it to distract herself. Then she sees it, the numbers, recognizes it's a web address. She starts a quick sketch, not knowing when he'll be coming back, roughing out the bird, inserting the letters and numbers, maybe finishing it just before she hears him coming down the hall.

"It's the key to everything, Leah, it has to be. It's what she was saying when she called you that night. Not 'legal,' she was saying 'eagle.' She trusted you, and I trust you, Leah. You can figure this out. You've come all this way on your own, but Lacey's with you now, you know that, don't you?" She had gripped my arm and was holding so tightly it hurt.

I don't share my mother's faith in the belief that our dead continue as benevolent presences in our lives, watching or encouraging us from afar—or at least I didn't used to—but I knew she was at least partly right. Lacey had trusted me. And the answer was here somewhere for me to find.

I got my laptop, and I typed the URL in my browser. Nothing. "Cannot find." I tried a browser with a different search engine. This one brought up a list of sites for *The Onion* a satirical newspaper, and recipes for onion rings, and nothing remotely related to perverted sex sites. I tried inserting http// in front of the string of letters. Still nothing.

"Nothing. I am so sick of this!"

My cell phone rang. My mother picked it up and glanced at the caller ID.

"It's your friend Ben."

Ben. I'd forgotten all about him. He called when? Was it really only two days ago?

"Hi, Ben."

"Leah. I've been trying to get hold of you." His voice was tight and clipped.

"I meant to call, but a lot's been happening. Look, I have to call you back I—"

"I wasn't sure you got my message. But after talking to Miller this morning, I'm pretty sure you did. Leah, you seriously thought I stole your phone and tried to set you up? What the hell?"

I didn't have time for this.

"Listen, Ben, I'm trying to find out who killed my sister. Someone pushed me off a cliff the other day, I got fired from my job, and the one thing I was counting on to give me the answers turned out to be a bust. I can't deal with your hurt feelings right now. I'm sorry I suspected you. Truly. I was misinformed. Now, I've got to—"

"Wait, wait, hold on! Don't hang up. Is that for real? Someone tried to kill you?"

"It's not the next freaking installment of *Scandal*. Yes, it's real."

"What were you counting on to give you answers?"

"A URL. Really, Ben, I have to go."

"Wait, maybe I can help."

"How?"

"What do you mean the URL doesn't work?"

"I typed it in, and it goes nowhere. I've never seen one like it before. It ends in .onion. I think it might be some kind of code."

"Did you try the dark web?"

"Dark web? That sounds like something Harry Potter would get caught in."

"No, I'm serious. If your URL ends in .onion, Google won't get you there. You need to download the Tor browser."

"I don't have any idea what you're talking about, but I need your help. Now."

To his credit, he didn't ask for any more explanation than that.

"What's your address?"

I gave it to him, hung up, and turned to my mother.

"Ben said the URL is part of some, I don't know, underground web or something that you can't get to just Googling. He's going to come over and show me what to do."

When his car pulled in the drive, I was waiting with my laptop open on the bar. If he was startled to hear "Puttin' On the Ritz" as he rang the doorbell, he didn't show it.

"Ben. Hi, c'mon in."

I took him into the kitchen.

"Mom, this is Ben. Ben, this my mother, Carol Nash. Here's the address."

"Good to meet you, Ben. You can see we're a little anxious to get started."

"No problem. I'm glad to help if I can."

"What about the URL?"

He glanced quickly at the paper I'd thrust under his nose. "All right, yeah, that's part of the Tor network, I'm sure. The first thing to do is download the Tor browser on your laptop."

"What does that even mean?"

"Like I started to tell you on the phone, the web most people use every day only accounts for a small percentage of what's out there on the Internet. The dark web or deep web—some people call it the invisible web—is a huge storehouse of information that's not accessible to regular search engines."

"Why not?"

He had pulled up a stool next to me and was already tapping on the keyboard, checking security configurations and my computer's RAM and storage capacity while he talked. My mother hovered on the other side of the bar.

"Search engines send out spiders—essentially roving algorithms—that constantly scan the web, indexing pages. When you type in a query, the engine matches your query with its indexed pages on the topic and gives you a list of sites to choose from. But any password-protected sites, or private networks, or paywalled content, or pages without hyperlinks— anything like that won't show up when you do a search, because the spiders can't index them.

"That's where the dark web content lives. Most of it's benign and boring. Academic databases, scholarly research, directories, raw data, stuff like that. But some of it isn't. There's criminal activity going on there too—like selling drugs and guns and pornography, and it can all be done anony-mously using the Tor network."

"How?"

"When you use the Tor browser, basically, you're assigned a false iden-tity. Your search is routed through dozens of computers in sites all over the world. Your real identity is buried under so many layers, it becomes impos-sible to find you. That's where the .onion domain came from—Tor hides you behind layers, like the layers of an onion."

He had continued typing and now he turned the computer to face me and said, "There. I downloaded Tor, that should let you find this address. Go ahead."

I looked at the paper, typed it in and waited expectantly.

"Damn it!"

"What's the matter?"

I turned the laptop around so my mother could see the screen. A little box blinked politely, asking me to please enter the password.

I flipped it over to Ben.

"You don't have any idea what the password could be?" he said.

"None. I don't suppose you're a code breaker as well as an IT consultant, are you?"

"Sorry."

"Me, too."

Ben's face was crestfallen, and I realized I hadn't been as gracious as I could have been, given that he'd dropped everything and come over to help, no questions asked.

"It's OK, Ben, I'll just have to come at it from another direction. But thanks for your help. And for the dark web lesson."

"I could stick around, see if we could play with it a bit. Maybe we'd come up with that new direction for you."

"No, thanks anyway. I need some time to think this out."

"But you haven't told me what's really going on."

"I can't." I stood up. "Thanks again, Ben."

"Well, OK," he said, standing finally and moving toward the door as I all but pushed him there. He seemed surprised, but then a guy who looked like him probably didn't get shoved aside very often.

"Ben, thanks so much for your help," my mother said, adding her own polite verbal nudge.

"Yeah. Sure. Call me if I can do anything."

38

"OK, OK, Mom," I said when he left. "Help me think. What do people use for passwords? Birthdays, anniversaries, their mother's maiden name ... none of which we know for Palmer."

"What about a pet?"

"As far as I know he doesn't have one."

I sat staring morosely at the blank screen on my computer. And then I turned to her.

"Mom, maybe it has something to do with the eagle. That's why Lacey didn't just write the URL down, she replicated the eagle sketch because both things were part of it—the URL was hidden, and the eagle is the password!"

I opened the Tor browser and typed in the dark web URL again. When I reached the password box I typed Eagle. Nothing. OK, just a setback. I started on a round of variations. EagleGanymede, EagleZeus, ZeusEagle, GanymedeEagle. Nothing. ZeusGanymede. GanymedeZeus. All caps. All lower case. Alternating upper and lower case. Nothing. Nothing. Nothing. It had to work. But it didn't. My brilliant idea was a bust.

I started to exit the site in defeat. Then, though I never told my mother this, I heard a password in my head as clearly as if Lacey were whispering it in my ear. I typed SLBeagleganymede1978.

Bingo. I was in. And immediately wished I was out. The screen was filled with thumbnail images of boys and men in various states of arousal, engaged in a variety of sexual positions. A click on any one led to video footage. Most of the boys looked to be between 10 and 14. Their faces were clearly visible. However, the men, who seemed to be mostly middle-aged, judging by the flabby muscles and sagging posteriors, had their backs to the camera, or their faces blocked, or were so far out of the center of the frame that it was impossible to identify them.

My mother came up behind me, and I heard her gasp. I kept checking video, hoping for something that would connect with Palmer. I half-heard her cell phone ring, and after a few minutes she came back over and touched my shoulder.

"That was Paul. I forgot he offered to help me pack up more of the files. I just want to get done and out of that office. We were going to grab a late pizza when we finished. I told him to skip it tonight."

"What? No, Mom, seriously. The sooner you're done with everything to do with Karen, the better. Go ahead. I'm fine, there's nothing for you to do here, really. Call Paul back. Have him come and get you. There's no reason both of us have to make ourselves sick looking at this garbage."

"You'll be all right? You'll call Detective Ross, and tell him what you found? Or at least Coop?"

"Yes, absolutely. As soon as I really have a handle on this."

"I'll call Paul." I didn't hear any of her conversation, but a few minutes later she tapped me on the shoulder again.

"Paul's coming by to pick me up. Will you meet us later? Say around 10 at McClain's?"

"Mmmm, maybe. Depends on how long this takes me. Maybe I can grab something with Coop, when I fill him in. Who knows, I might still be going over files when you get back."

"Leah, you are going to turn this information over? You're not going to pursue this yourself?"

"Of course. I just—"

"I know. You just can't let go."

"It's not that, really."

"Yes. It is. Really. I've half a mind to call Coop myself."

"No! Mom, I'll call him. I will, all right? When I'm ready."

A horn tapped lightly in the driveway. She sighed. "I have to go. But if you don't call him, I will. This is too big and too dangerous for you to be playing around with on your own."

I nodded, but didn't look up as the door closed behind her. I turned back to the videos. After a few more minutes of viewing the sad, sick variations on a theme, I admitted the truth. Palmer was way too smart. I was not going to find anything on that site that would remotely link to him. I shut it down.

I had gone as far as I could. I had to turn over everything, I knew. I felt a pang about Danny—once Ross got onto him, there was scant hope he'd be able to hide his current life from his brother. But he was key to bringing down Palmer and the rest, maybe some of the St. Lucian's Boys as well.

I picked up my phone and hit Coop's speed dial number, but I got his voice mail. I didn't leave a message, instead I called Melanie to see where he was.

"He's over to a meeting with the prosecutor, then he's got a Law Enforcement banquet in Omico. He's not coming back in the office this afternoon. Did you try his cell?"

"Yeah, it went to voicemail. I'll just text him later."

"Hey, after Miller's press conference this morning, it looks like you're not the big story anymore. Think you'll get your job back?"

"I don't know, Melanie. I really don't know." In truth, I hadn't thought about it at all. The stalking fiasco was the last straw for Max, but he'd been building up a steady list of my offenses for a while. Maybe the fact that I wasn't guilty wouldn't matter that much to him. "Well, I gotta go. I'll catch you later."

I tried to imagine what Coop would say when I told him about the site. I tried to address all of Ross's potential objections. The voices on the MP3 player could be anybody. My star witness was, by my own admission, a teenage hustler.

The dark website was real. They might even be able to identify DeMoss boys on it, but there was no other connection to Palmer or Sister Julianna.

If I was right, and Lacey picked the address out of the sketch in Palmer's office, that would be a direct connection, provided I could get the original.

And really, why couldn't I?

39

OK, I probably shouldn't steal the sketch. Palmer would notice that immediately. But I could get a good photo of it, sitting on the shelf in his office. Good enough so a person could pick out the numbers and letters. If they were there. They had to be there. An idea took shape. I made a quick phone call and got the information I needed. Then I paced back and forth down the hall between the kitchen and my room, waiting for darkness to fall.

Finally, a little after 9, I left a note for my mother telling her that after viewing all that filth, I needed to get out in the open air. I was going for a drive to think and clear my head. And not to worry. I might stop by Coop's before I came home. That way, by the time she started to worry, I'd be back. I had to take her car, though, because she'd blocked me in.

I grabbed the lanyard with her car key from the hook by the door and put it around my neck, then hopped in her Prius and took off. My plan was simple, and if I was lucky, easy. I would enter the Catherines' property at the Baylor Road entrance and park at the Rock, the same spot where Lacey had met Cole. Then I'd walk down the road, which was little more than a track, to the administration building. As long as Sister Margaret hadn't been busted yet for leaving her window open "for a bit of fresh air," I should be able to slide into the building that way.

I cut the lights as I left the main road. I pulled in next to Simon's Rock and turned off the car. The night was cloudy and cool and it was lightly sprinkling. I looked at my watch as I started out. I thought about Danny, shivering there as the night turned cold, and the snow fell along with his hopes, as he slowly came to believe that Lacey had abandoned him. I pictured Lacey hurrying along the trail, black hair flying behind her, determined to get Danny out, not realizing she was running toward the last few minutes of her life.

I felt a fresh surge of anger. Anger that my smart, brave sister and a scared little boy were crushed by that triad of ruthless hypocrites. The fury powered me forward so that I practically flew down the unfamiliar terrain. The bony fingers of slender branches caught in my hair and snapped on my cheeks. I flung them away impatiently. Something small and furry darted in front of me and I jerked, my heart thumping. I flashed my light, and it scurried into the bushes.

When I reached the building, I checked my watch again. Twelve minutes—and I was really hustling. It would have taken Lacey at least that long. I surveyed the scene. Security lights in the drive lit the front of the building, and in the rear more illuminated a small parking lot for staff. Darmody's brother, Delbert, a security guard at DeMoss, had happily divulged his entire nightly routine when I called him earlier.

Guards walked the perimeter of the campus, checked doors of the main buildings—academic, counseling center, library—every two hours, starting at 9. By 9:30, they were back in the maintenance building watching video feed from the newly installed security cameras and eating junk from the vending machine. He didn't question why I was asking. He even volunteered the location of the security cameras.

It was just ten o'clock, so I had over an hour before a guard was due. And I knew just where to go. The security camera in the back of the building was mounted on a light pole and aimed at the back entrance. I wasn't planning on using the back door, and as long as I didn't cross in front of it on my way to Sister Margaret's secret window, I should be golden.

I slipped around the back, staying close to the wall. Sister Margaret's window, cracked just a few inches, was well away from the security cameras. Keeping my body pressed along the side of the building, wary of motion sensor lights Delbert may have neglected to mention, I crept to the opening. The sash lifted easily and silently, no doubt from regular illicit use by Sister Margaret.

I tossed my flashlight through but getting in myself took a little more effort. Even opened as far as it would go, the window was small and required some origami-like body folding and flattening. For a few minutes, it looked like I might be found lodged half-in and half-out during the next security guard rounds. I gave a final desperate push with the leg I'd managed to get onto the floor, and that popped me through like a cork shooting out of a bottle. I landed in a heap and added yoga classes to my mental list of future fitness activities.

I picked up my flashlight and paused in the doorway. My breathing and the thumping of my heart were the only sounds. I moved forward out of the small copy room and patted Sister Margaret's chair for luck as I passed it on my way to Palmer's office.

I'd come prepared to jimmy his office lock with a credit card trick that a source once taught me. No need. Not only was Palmer's door not locked, it wasn't even shut. Arrogant bastard. As though no one would dare violate his sacred space. No ambient light from the parking lot or plugged in electronics relieved the cave-like blackness of his office.

I took a couple of steps inside and shined the beam of my flashlight on the far end of the room. There it was. The eagle sketch sitting on its easel. I hurried over, grabbed it and focused the flashlight on it. I stared at it with single-minded concentration, until gradually the distractions of the dozens of fine lines, cross-hatching and shadows fell away, and the numbers and letters of the deep website came into clear view.

I dug my phone out of my pocket. Took a second to double check that the ringer was off. Then I set my flashlight on the shelf and angled it toward the picture. I zoomed in and took a shot. Not great, but I could make out the letters. I zoomed out and took another shot that showed the sketch sitting on the shelf with the rest of Palmer's tchotchkes to put it firmly in context. For good measure, I emailed the pictures to myself and copied in Miguel.

I turned to leave the office. My eyes were hit with a blinding flash as the overhead light flicked on. I was still blinking and squinting when Sister

Julianna said, "Hello, Leah. I'm surprised to see you. Especially since Reid is in no condition to visit."

She nodded her head to the left, and I turned in the direction of what had been the darkest corner of the office when I entered. Sitting at his desk was Reid Palmer. And he was very, very dead.

I couldn't take my eyes away from the gaping hole in his head, out of which oozed blood and brain matter, or from the spattered wall behind him. I swallowed back a sudden urge to throw up.

"Leah, do you feel faint? Help her, Sean." I turned and saw that Hegl was standing in the doorway as well.

I waved him away, and shook my head. "I'm all right. What happened?"

"Isn't it obvious? Reid has committed suicide. After leaving a note confessing to heinous crimes. Including killing your sister and engaging in pedophilia with some of our most troubled students. It's truly shocking."

I wasn't firing on all cylinders. "Palmer confessed? How? Why?"

"Well, I think you have to take some of the credit, Leah. Your relentless pursuit of your sister's death really put a great deal of pressure on him. He was extremely depressed and despondent and apparently—at least according to his note—he had a great deal to answer for."

"Wait a minute, wait a minute. You're saying that Palmer was responsible for everything?"

"Who else?" It was then I saw the glint of mockery in her eyes and realized just how much trouble I was in. Did she know I'd pieced together everything—including her embezzlement?

"I know I shouldn't be here—"

"No, but you seem to make a habit of being places where you shouldn't be. I wonder, what were you looking for in Reid's office?"

When there's no other option, the truth will sometimes work. "I was trying to find something incriminating on Palmer."

"And did you?"

"No."

"I see."

"Aren't you going to call the police?"

"Yes, certainly. Just not this very moment." She inclined her head slightly, as though making up her mind about something, then said, "Sean, let's take Leah to the reception area. We all need to get away from this office."

I had no choice but to move down the hall with them. When we got to reception, Sister Julianna stopped and turned to face both of us. "Leah, where is your car?"

"I parked by Simon's Rock and walked from there."

"I see. Sean, walk Leah back to her car, would you? Then I think you should drive her home. She's had a very upsetting evening. I'll follow and bring you back."

I didn't care for the look that passed between them at all. Sister Julianna seemed perfectly normal, clear-eyed and calm. Hegl was another matter. He'd had at least a fortifying shot of whiskey not too long ago, judging from his breath. The sour odor that wafted from him spoke of recent heavy drinking, as his red-rimmed eyes did of sleepless nights. He was wearing jeans and a Henley t-shirt that looked and smelled as though it had been pulled from the bottom of a laundry basket.

"That's OK, I'm fine. I don't need a ride."

"Nonsense. It's very late, and you've had a shock. I insist."

"No. Really. I don't." I made a fast break for the front door. I thought if I could reach it, I might be able to set off the alarm. But hung over or not, Hegl was fast on his feet. He grabbed me roughly by the arm and yanked me back.

"Leah, don't make it so hard for us to help you."

"Sister, I'm not the only one who knows what's been going on here. I've talked to other people."

"I'm well aware, Leah. I told you Reid was driven to his death by your hounding. Not that he didn't have a great deal to answer for. The confessions in his suicide note are horrifying."

I tried to keep her talking, playing for time until I could think of some way out of this.

"Sister Margaret was right. You really did set up the appointment to ask Lacey to sing, but she got spooked after being in Palmer's office and took off. Later, after Palmer killed her, you made up the story about her using drugs again, and the missing money, to make it seem more plausible that she ran away."

"Really, Leah. You should try your hand at fiction. Mysteries or suspense thrillers perhaps. But I'm intrigued. Do go on."

"At first I thought that Sister Mattea was killed because she knew who killed Lacey. But that wasn't it at all. She was killed because she found out about your embezzling. Palmer knew too, didn't he? And about your gambling. And you knew about his young boys. He covered for you, and you found boys for him, isn't that right?"

"Absolutely not."

"You killed Sister Mattea. You pushed her off the bluff."

"I didn't kill Sister Mattea. You should harness that imagination of yours. It's going to get you into trouble someday. We need to go, Sean."

She reached behind Sister Margaret's desk and hit a few buttons on a keypad, presumably disarming the front door. Hegl had my arm pinned up against my side, and he marched me roughly out the door.

"Sean, I'll wait for you at the Baylor Road entrance. We'll be taking River Road."

"That's not the way to town," I said, though I already knew they had no intention of taking me home. "The police are reinvestigating. They've got the statue. You won't get away with this."

She looked at me then and smiled. "It's a long shot, I agree, Leah. But as the saying goes, you'll always miss 100% of the shots you don't take. Good-bye." She stepped up into her black SUV and was off on the road leading out of the campus.

40

A car accident on River Road may not have been the original plan for getting me out of the way, but it wasn't bad improvising. The lanes are narrow, the curves are poorly marked, and the puny wooden guard rails wouldn't stop a bicycle, let alone a car. Accidents happen fairly often. And everyone knew how stressed I was, how tired, how bad my judgment had been. And I had so thoughtfully laid the groundwork by lying to my mother about going for a long drive to clear my head. Another tragic accident in the making.

Hegl yanked me along the trail, and I struggled to keep up with his long strides. Why had Sister Julianna allied with him? He seemed more logical as the fall guy than Palmer. Maybe she was tired of Palmer running the show. Maybe she wanted someone she'd have under her thumb. So, she persuaded Hegl to turn on Palmer. His death and the fake suicide note would save them.

But maybe not. Because in choosing Hegl, Sister Julianna disregarded one of the hard truths of life: you can't manage stupid. And Hegl's inability to control his appetites rendered him stupid.

The rain was coming down steadily as Hegl and I reached Simon's Rock. He pushed me up to the car, staying close behind me, then released my arm so I could open the door.

I brought both elbows down hard and back and jabbed him in the stomach. He wasn't prepared, and it knocked the wind out of him. I turned and ran toward the woods, thinking I had a better chance there than on the main road, where by now Sister Julianna would be waiting.

I only got 20 yards or so before my legs were jerked out from under me. I landed on the muddy ground face first and felt the pressure of something hard and cold in my back. I lifted my head and turned my neck. Hegl was leaning over me, pushing something into the small of my back. He had a gun.

"Get up!"

I moved slowly onto my hands and knees, then lifted my hand to rub my throbbing jaw. "Get up!" he yelled a second time.

"Get the damn gun out of my back so I can stand up."

He took a step back, but the gun was still pointed at me as I struggled to my feet. He waved me toward the car.

I used to wonder why victims ever obeyed their killer's orders to get in the car, or walk to the edge of the cliff, or kneel and raise their hands, when clearly, they were going to be murdered no matter what they did. Why make it easier?

But walking at gunpoint to the driver's side of my car, I finally got it. Because every fraction of time I bought with my compliance was a minute, or a second, or a millisecond when I wasn't dead. And if I wasn't dead, I still had a chance to figure out how to stay alive.

So, I did as Hegl said, and I got behind the wheel.

"Start the car."

I pushed on the starter button, and then turned on the lights and wipers. The rain was coming down so hard it looked like someone was throwing buckets of water at the windshield. His cell phone rang, and he dug it out with difficulty while keeping the gun trained on me. Sister Julianna gave him specifics on our ride in the country.

"Where are we going?" I asked.

"Drive out to Baylor. Keep going until you get to River Road."

I backed up, did a three-point turn, and drove the short distance to the Baylor Road entrance. Sister Julianna's black SUV was waiting on the shoulder. I braked and hesitated, then felt the nudge of the gun in my ribs.

"Go on. And don't try anything."

"I wasn't. I just didn't know if she wanted me to go first or follow her," I said in a small voice to convey that I'd given up, and I was putty in his shaky hands. We pulled out, and Sister Julianna followed. Baylor Road was fairly straight, but once we turned onto River, things were going to get interesting.

The question was, where did they plan to do it? My guess was the overlook. It would be easy enough to have me park the car with the engine running. A knock on the back of the head to put me out, a good push and it would be too bad, so sad, Leah must have driven off the road and drowned.

I stole a glance at Hegl. He was on the ragged edge. The gun was in his lap, his trembling hand still clutching it.

"How far are we going?"

"Until I tell you to stop."

"All right, I was just wondering." I was silent for a few seconds, then I gambled on the one thing I was sure of. Hegl was the weak link. This was my only chance to break it.

"You know, Father Hegl, I realize now, everything that's happened, none of it was your fault." It almost gagged me to give him the honorific 'Father,' but I wanted to convey a respect and sympathy I didn't feel and remind him just a little of what he was *supposed* to be. He didn't say anything, so I continued.

"I know you didn't want Olivia to die. And I know you didn't mean to hurt Lacey either. I understand that now." I waited.

"I didn't want anyone to get hurt. I didn't."

"But you haven't done anything, not really. Palmer made you hurt Lacey. He found you there, didn't he, the night you were with Delite? Then Lacey came in and she...." I trailed off, hoping he'd fill in the blank space. He did, talking fast as though the words had been damned up inside for a long time.

"She was stealing the car keys. Reid said he'd call the police. She said she knew about Danny, and she had proof. Then she kicked him hard, trying to get away. He went crazy. It wasn't me. He went crazy." He was still pointing the gun, but his hand was shaking so much I was afraid it might go off by accident.

"What happened then? What did Palmer do?"

"He took the statue, and he smashed her. He hit her so hard, she fell and she didn't get up."

My eyes filled with tears, but I had to keep going. I had to try and turn him. "Father Hegl, who took Lacey to the woods? Was it you?"

"Reid erased her phone. Sister Julianna brought the Vicodin to put in her purse and the empty liquor bottle, so it would look like she was drunk and fell. She said we should say money was missing, so the police would think Lacey stole it to run away. They made me take the four-wheeler to dump her body. It wasn't me. I didn't want to do it. But Reid said he'd recant his story about me having dinner with him and my uncle the night Olivia died. It wasn't my fault. None of this is my fault."

"What about the statue?"

"Reid told me to hide it in my collection for a while, then later get rid of it."

"Why didn't you?"

"I forgot about it."

I almost lost it then. That narcissist could sit in his living room across from the piece of marble that had crushed my sister's skull, and not have one moment's discomfort because he "forgot about it."

"Why did you have Delite lie for you?"

"To give us more protection when they found the body. I thought if she came forward the police wouldn't look any farther. And they didn't. Reid and Sister Julianna weren't happy. They didn't trust her. But it was fine until you started poking around."

His hand steadied a little. So did his voice. This wasn't going like I hoped. He wasn't swinging to my side. He was focusing his anger on me.

"Did Sister Julianna make you kill Palmer?"

"Quit asking questions."

"She did, didn't she? She told you he could be the fall guy. But don't you get it, Father? You're going to be the fall guy."

His brain, dulled by anxiety, alcohol and fear, was slow to process what I was saying. I glanced in the rearview mirror. Sister Julianna was a good fifty yards behind us. We had reached River Road. I had no choice. I turned.

"We'll be at the overlook soon. That's where she told you to do it, isn't it?

What's the plan? Have me park the car? Hit me in the head like Palmer did Lacey? You going to shove my car over and watch me drown?"

He shook his head slowly and raised one hand, swatting at the air as though trying to still the buzz of my angry questions like a bear trying to rid himself of angry bees. I pressed on, but changed my tone.

"Father, don't let yourself get dragged any further into this mess. You can still get out of this. It's all on Palmer and Sister Julianna. And now she's going to put it on you. Don't you see? She's not going to let you go. She can't afford to."

The rain had lessened to a light patter, but I could see thin wisps of fog starting to curl around the edges of bushes and trees.

He tightened his grip on the gun, and I knew I had lost him. He was too cowed by her, too befuddled by fear and guilt. He couldn't do anything but what she planned for him. My hands were sweating on the wheel. I was running out of time. We were nearly at the overlook.

"Slow down. Pull over here."

As I started to brake, I looked in the mirror again. Coming very fast toward us was Sister Julianna's SUV. She was rolling the dice again, betting on taking us both out at once. She wasn't going to give Hegl time to make trouble. She was sending him over the edge with me. The big heavy vehicle banged into the back of my mother's car and sent us hurtling through the guard rail and out into space like Thelma and Louise.

For an instant, we were suspended in midair. Then we dropped, hitting the water with a huge splash. The airbag deployed and I took a solid punch in the face. It deflated immediately. We were still floating when I hit the button to lower the window. The car started filling with water. I lifted the latch on my belt, but instead of retracting, the thick nylon restraint refused to budge. I tugged, and as I struggled, Hegl slipped out the window and into the river.

The water was up to my waist, but instead of seeing my life pass before me, I saw my mother standing in the kitchen, extolling the virtues of her lanyard. I grabbed at my neck for the mini Swiss Army knife. I tugged so hard it came right off the cord.

My fingers fumbled as I tried to pull out the blade. My breath came in short gasps. Cold water rose to my armpits, and the car rocked in the current. With a last urgent tug, I got the blade free, but the knife flew out of my hand.

Frantic, I flailed with my arms underwater, on the seat, between my legs; it wasn't there. The hood of the car began to tilt forward. *Where the hell was that knife?* I took a last gulp of air before the water rushed past my head, and the car began to nosedive. I felt something bump against my hand. The downward motion had dislodged the knife from whatever cranny it had settled in. My fingers reflexively curled around it, and I grabbed it blade first into my palm. I turned it over. With two desperate strokes, I cut the strap and pulled it free.

I thrust my arm out to the side. My hand felt the window frame. With fear-fueled strength, I pushed myself through and started furiously kicking my legs and clawing through the water. My lungs were screaming to exhale. I broke the surface wild for oxygen. I blew out the pent-up air in my lungs and took a big breath.

Treading water, I fought the current as I tried to orient myself and regulate my breath. Hegl was nowhere in sight. I was alone, and not getting any warmer or stronger in the fifty-degree water.

Then I saw a flash of lights, white at first, then red and blue. It had to be cars on the River Road. Police too. Someone had called in the "accident."

I struck out for shore with a shaky crawl. The Himmel River is deep, but not very wide at that point. I kept repeating my survival mantra—it's less then 100 yards, it's less than 70 yards, it's less than 50...

With each stroke, my arms got weaker. My legs were barely kicking, and the urge to keep going was fading. I felt so weak. And so cold. If I could just rest. From a distance, I heard voices.

Was that in my head, or was it real? It was just too hard to lift my face out of the water. I took in a gulp of river instead of air.

I started to choke. I wanted to shout for help, but my throat was seizing up. I couldn't breathe.

My body bobbed straight up and down for a second. I began to sink as a bright white light washed over me.

41

When I came to, puking and coughing, I was on the shore, sharp rocks cutting into my back. My eyes flew open as someone rolled me on my side. My head was lifted. Fingers rammed into my mouth and did a sweep. That started a gag reflex, a fresh round of coughing, a little more puking. Either the white light I'd seen had been an emergency police floodlight, or heaven was not living up to its advance PR. I tried to talk, started choking again, and sank back down and out.

When I woke, I was in a dimly lit hospital room hooked up to a monitor and an IV. The equipment emitted soft, periodic beeps, and the blood pressure cuff on my arm inflated and deflated at regular intervals. For some reason, my hand was wrapped in a big white bandage. I thought I saw my mother, but I wasn't sure, and I was floating too high to ask. My eyelids fluttered back down.

The next time I opened them, sun was streaming through the window. My mother was seated beside the bed, her head down, her hand touching mine.

"Hey, what does a girl have to do to get some breakfast around here?" I croaked.

She squeezed my hand, and her eyes were bright with tears. "How about a late lunch instead? It's two o'clock."

"A drink of water would be great." She held a Styrofoam cup with a straw up to my lips. The cool water washing over my parched throat felt so good, I began gulping on the straw, until my mother moved it away. "Easy there, the nurse said a few sips when you woke up. You'll make yourself sick if you drink too fast."

"Mom," I began, "I'm sorry. I didn't—"

The door opened wide, and Miguel came bursting in, followed by Coop at a more measured pace.

"*Chica*! What am I gonna do with you! What were you thinking? Why did you go out there alone? What happened? You know Palmer is dead, right? You feel better now, yes?" He was fairly oscillating with pent-up anxiety as he stood next to my mother.

"How did anyone know where I was?"

Coop, who had come to stand by the other side of my bed, nodded in Miguel's direction. "You can thank your partner in crime."

I looked back at Miguel, who was smiling broadly. "I told you—there's no Frodo without Sam, no Lilo without Stitch –"

"OK, OK. Seriously. How did you know I was out there?"

"Your email. The eagle sketch. I called to ask *que démonios*! You know, what the heck is this? But you didn't answer. I knew you were awake, because you just emailed me. I called your *mamá's* landline and no one answered. So, I tracked your iPhone."

"You have a tracker on my phone?"

"No! Well, yes, a little. I activated the Find My iPhone app for you. After you got yours back."

"You can follow me with that? What are you, the NSA?"

He was unrepentant. "Are you going somewhere you shouldn't be, *chica*?"

"I think we know the answer to that is a big fat yes," my mother said.

"All right. We're losin' the thread here," Coop said. "The point is, Miguel got worried when he saw your phone was at the Catherines' at 10:30, then on River Road. He called me, and I called central dispatch and asked them to send a car over to that end of the county.

"A deputy got there just in time for Sister Julianna to pass him like a bat outa hell. He radioed in and kept going in the direction she'd just come from to see what was chasing her. He found the busted guardrail, and then saw your mom's car in the river, sinking fast."

"Yeah, about that, Mom – "

She shook her head. "We'll talk about that later. What I want to know is what were you thinking? Why did you go out there? How did you wind up in the river?"

I explained that I wanted to get the sketch as a tangible piece of evidence that linked Reid Palmer to the dark website, and how I stumbled onto Palmer's staged suicide.

"Hegl was supposed to drive me to the overlook—he thought he was going to push me over, but Sister Julianna double-crossed him and tried to take us both out. Did you get them both, Hegl and Julianna?"

"The deputy caught up with Sister Julianna as she was pulling into the Catherines' property. She's a cool one. She asked him to come with her, said she was worried about Reid Palmer. She was afraid that he might be planning to harm himself. She led him to Palmer's office. He was dead, complete with a suicide note admitting that he'd killed Lacey, was abusing boys from DeMoss, even that he'd been embezzling money."

"Go big or go home, I guess. She let it all ride on Palmer's number."

"She might have gotten away with it. If Hegl had died like he was supposed to, she could have made a case for him being in with Palmer and said that he'd abducted you at gunpoint. But her luck ran out. Hegl has the survival instincts of a ship rat. And you—" He stopped and shook his head.

"You know what they say. Weebles wobble but they don't fall down. How did you get Hegl?"

"He was stumbling around about a mile from where your car went in. Tried to get a ride from a car full of teenage girls. They called 911. When the deputies picked him up, he was pretty talkative."

"Did he confess? Did he tell you what they did to Lacey? Did he admit to killing Palmer? Who pushed me and Sister Mattea, him or Sister Julianna?"

"Hegl waived his right to an attorney. He admitted what happened the night Lacey died, but he wouldn't cop to pushing you or Sister Mattea off the bluff. Sister Julianna lawyered up right away, and so far, she's not talking. But I think her luck has pretty much run out. A player from one of the big casinos in Vegas saw her on the news. He had some interesting things to say about her gambling losses."

"I think *she's* the one that pushed me off the cliff. Then she tried it again at the overlook with her SUV. You know, if at first you don't succeed, try, try again. She probably pushed Sister Mattea, too. That asshat Hegl left me to drown. I couldn't get that stupid seatbelt off. I hate to admit it Mom, but your lanyard saved my life. And the Grantland County EMTs."

"It wasn't an EMT who pulled you out of the water, Leah, it was Coop."

I didn't know what to say. To any of them.

"You know. I just. All of you. Well, thanks." I stumbled over the words. Why was it so easy for me to be a smartass and so hard to be real?

"Forget it," Coop said.

"No, *chica*, I want you to remember it. And don't go running off without me next time."

There was a light tap on the door. Ellie, Max, and Alex walked in.

"Hey you guys!" I felt a bubble of happiness rise at the sight of them. Max looked embarrassed, and Ellie was uncomfortable as she thrust a bouquet of flowers at me, but Alex ran right up and put a small packet on the bed.

"Leah! You're on TV! I saw you on Channel 9! Oh, wow!" He paused and examined me closely. "You look like a cage fighter. You got a black eye! And what happened to your hand?"

I looked down in surprise. I'd forgotten about the bandage, and with the pain killers I was on and the high of not being dead, my hand really didn't hurt. But I flashed on the water over my head, the frantic search for the knife. I shivered, but before I could answer, Ellie stepped up.

"Leah, I'm glad you're all right. And I'm sorry about Lacey, and that I was so hard on you. I know you were just doing what you had to for your family."

I felt awkward and ill at ease. Apologies usually affect me that way. "Never mind, Ellie. It's OK. It wasn't anything."

"Yeah, it was," Max interrupted, his voice gruff. "I'm sorry, too, Leah. I was just so uptight about the business and the bank. I didn't act much like a newsman. Or a friend."

This was getting excruciating. "No, it's OK. Forget it. We're good." I had to make it stop. "So, Alex, what's this you brought me?"

"It's a book I made. I thought you'd like to read it. It has stories about my family. Ancestors and stuff in it. We did them for school. The cover's awesome, isn't it?"

The hand-drawn cover featured a red-haired man with a superhero physique brandishing a sword, inscribed with the name McAllister, over his head. Next to him was an equally buff warrior woman wearing a crown emblazoned with the name Cameron.

"See, they're Scottish because my mom and my birth dad's families come from Scotland. That's their names. But look on the back." He flipped it over, and there was a picture of a sturdy looking man in short sleeves sitting at a computer.

"And that's my dad Max. He's a writer and that's what Schreiber means in German. Awesome, huh? So, there's some German stuff in there, too. It's pretty great."

"Alex! Don't brag."

"But, Mom, it is pretty great."

"That's right, *hombrecito*. Own your excellence!" said Miguel.

Alex started giggling and chanting, "Own your excellence." As Ellie tried to settle him down, I remembered something.

"Coop have you talked to Scott Riordan yet? He's been doing some accounting voodoo on the DeMoss books, and I think he's got proof that money was being embezzled. I asked him not to tip off Reid Palmer. He's not going to believe it when I call and tell him why."

"It's not my case, Leah. All that stuff is going to Ross. For the moment, anyway."

I latched on to the bone of hope he threw me.

"For the moment?"

"A joint investigation is in the works. And the Internet Crimes Against Children task force is in the picture now. The higher-ups have been fielding calls from the bishop—the local, not your guy in Florida. The media are going crazy. No way the sheriff's department is going to ride herd on this one. So be nice. Let Ross get his statement. He won't be the only one you'll be talking to, I'm sure. I'm kinda surprised he hasn't been here already."

And as if on cue the door opened, and we all looked up expectantly. But it wasn't Ross who walked into the room. Instead a slight young woman wearing blue hospital scrubs hesitated in the doorway, holding a tray which immediately held my attention.

"I'm sorry to interrupt. I'm just delivering some lunch?"

"I'm starving! Come in, please."

"We should get out of here and let you eat," Ellie said.

"Yeah, we should go, let you get some rest. I'll call you later, kid," Max said, patting me on the leg.

"Don't forget to read my book. You'll love it!" said Alex.

Coop and Miguel pulled up stakes as well, and I sent my mother down to the cafeteria. As the aide set up my tray, she introduced herself as Angela and got me fresh water.

"Your nurse will be in soon to change your dressing and check your vitals. Do you need anything else? Are you in pain?"

"Nope, I'm good, thanks, just hungry." I found it a little awkward to eat with my left hand, particularly since my meal consisted mainly of spoon-reliant foods—tomato soup and jello. She hung around waiting to make sure I could manage. Then, as she was leaving, Ross walked in.

"Nash."

"Ross."

"Hey, Angela!" I called to her retreating back. "Tell the nurse I need some pain medication, please."

42

They released me from the hospital the next morning with strong admonitions to stay home and take it easy for a few days. I wasn't inclined to argue. I was physically and mentally beat, my hand ached, and I was sporting some pretty spectacular bruising, not just the shiner that impressed Alex.

I tried to reach Scott Riordan the first day I was home, but he was out of town, and I had no more luck with Miss Adams than I had the first time I called. I kicked myself for not getting his cell phone number the last time we talked. But not too hard, in light of all my bruising.

What hurt worse than my injuries was having to sit back and see the story I'd uncovered reported on by other journalists. It irritated me that the 24/7 cable "news" channels spent more time on speculation and hype than on the facts. Though maybe I didn't have much room to complain. Reporters had called begging for interviews, but I didn't answer, and I didn't call them back, even though I itched to set the record straight. I knew it wasn't wise to start feeding the sharks.

On Friday, I assured my mother I would be fine, and after much protesting, she agreed to go with Paul to a Brewers game in Milwaukee. As they pulled out of the driveway, I got a call from Clinton Barnes.

Clinton was the one agent out of about a million I'd sent my book proposal to who had agreed to represent me. I hadn't heard anything from him for a while. But his last email had made me think he was just about to cut me loose, after a very tepid response from publishers to my proposal. But the DeMoss story reawakened his interest.

"You have the inside track, Leah—the journalist out to avenge her sister's death. You've got some really great stuff to work with—depraved millionaire, gambling nun, homicidal priest! Great stuff. And that dark web thing is a really on-fleek angle. It puts a new spin on the whole Catholic altar boy thing, which is getting a little tired, right? Anyway, I know I could sell your story. Do you think you could work up an outline, maybe a few chapters? There could be some serious money involved."

"What about my book on the Mandy Cleveland murder?"

"Oh, well, that's still out there, sweetheart. But this is the one that could really be epic. It's your story, your sister. You should be the one to tell it. What do you say?"

"I don't know, Clinton. I'll think about it."

"Don't wait too long. Somebody is going to write this book. It should be you!"

"I'll get back to you."

When I started out, I had no intention of writing a story, getting a scoop. I just wanted to find out what happened to Lacey. If I turned around and did it now, was I as much of an exploitative jerk as the hungry reporters that were driving me crazy? Or was I even worse, because she was my sister?

On the other hand, if I wrote the book, I could tell Lacey's real story. How smart she was, how brave. How because of her no more kids from DeMoss would be exploited by Palmer and his friends. Besides, if I didn't try to write it, what was my alternative? Callie Preston, the reporter I was filling in for, would be back from maternity leave in another few weeks, and then where would I be? It wasn't like I'd been fielding job offers.

I went to the kitchen and made a sandwich. On my way back to the living room, my eye fell on Alex's history of his family sitting on an end table. I knew I'd better read it while I was thinking about it, because there was no way he wasn't going to ask me for a reaction the next time I saw him.

It was typical Alex—research and writing skill beyond his years coupled with young-kid imagination and enthusiasm. His stories wove his ancestors into historical events in Scotland. Mixed in among actual family photos were Photoshopped pictures of Alex next to a fierce spear-wielding Scotsman in a kilt, and swimming with the Loch Ness monster.

A standard family tree showed no aunts, uncles or cousins. I hadn't realized both his parents were only children. I paused at a photo of his "real" dad, Ian McAllister. He had fiery red hair and bright blue eyes the same as Ellie had. His cocky grin reminded me of Alex.

My eyes began to droop. My need for sleep seemed to go up in inverse proportion to the amount of work I did. But what else did I have to do? I lay down on the couch and surrendered. I woke up when my phone rang. Finally, a return call from Scott Riordan.

"I just got back from Singapore. I've been reading some of the stories online. Is it true?"

"Most of it. Pedophilia, pornography, priests, gambling nuns—it's the stuff cable news dreams are made of."

"No wonder you didn't want me to contact Reid Palmer about the accounts."

"Scott, I asked before, but now that everything's come out, can you think of anything Sister Mattea—that is, your sister Teresa—said that might have been a hint about embezzling at DeMoss?"

"I've gone over it and over it since we talked, but honestly, Leah, I can't think of anything. All Teresa said was she wanted to bring the order into the 21st century. If she suspected anything, she didn't tell me. But then maybe she wouldn't have."

"Why's that?"

"Her membership in the Catherines was the one big thing in life we didn't agree on. If she was worried something wasn't on the up and up, maybe she thought I'd give her an I-told-you-so."

"You don't like the Catherines?"

"It's not the order in particular. I just don't have much use for organized religion in general. An order of nuns dressed up like something out of the Middle Ages it just seems, well, ridiculous to me."

"Obviously, your sister didn't feel that way."

"She used to. Neither of us grew up religious, but then 10 years or so ago she changed."

"Why was that?"

"I always thought it had something to do with a friend of hers. Elise."

"She was a nun?"

"No, no. It was, well, I guess it doesn't matter if I tell you the story now."

I waited for him to go on.

"Teresa had an abortion when she was 18. Our mother insisted. It was tough on her, but I thought she was OK with it. She never talked about it until years later when this nurse at the hospital where she worked had a baby that died.

"Then it was all Teresa could talk about—how unfair it was. How Elise had lost her husband in Iraq, and then her baby died, too. I mean, I was sympathetic. It was a sad story. But Teresa went off the deep end. All this guilt I didn't even know she had, shame, regret about her abortion—she just couldn't shake it. Even when Elise moved to Ohio, Teresa couldn't let it go."

"So, what happened?"

"She hooked up with the Catherines somehow, I don't remember exactly. Went to a retreat, and the next thing I knew she was signing up. She gave up her whole life—a great job at Regent Hospital in LA, friends, a nice guy she was dating. She just threw it all away to join some outdated cult."

"That's a little harsh."

"I know. You're right. She needed answers I didn't have. I guess she found them at the Catherines. As time went by, we sort of agreed to disagree. We just didn't talk about it when she came out to visit. Numbers make sense to me. Religion doesn't. But I had to accept that was her choice. That's why I agreed to donate the software, really. I wanted to show her that I respected her right to decide, even if I didn't agree."

"If it's any consolation, she seemed happy to me."

"Yeah, I think she was. And that's good." He was quiet for a second, then said, "There were just the two of us you know. Now there's just me. You'll let me know if you find out anything else?"

"Yes, sure, of course I will, but I'm pretty much out of it now. There's a big deal task force investigating everything to do with the Catherines, DeMoss, Reid Palmer. I'm sure someone will be talking to you soon."

Then he asked me the question I didn't have an answer for.

"Leah, if Teresa did know about the fraud and she mentioned it to someone there, is it possible that her death wasn't an accident?"

"I don't know, Scott. Any more than I know why she left me a note and an old newspaper clipping about my sister's death. And maybe we have to accept we'll never know."

———————

I didn't feel near as Zen about things as I'd pretended to Scott. In truth, I couldn't stop thinking about the why. Everything else had fallen into place except that. Why, why, why had Sister Mattea left that note and that clipping for me? I hadn't turned up anything that linked her to Lacey or even to Palmer or Hegl.

I got up and vacuumed. I dusted. I loaded the dishwasher, and still I couldn't sit still. Something was nagging at me like an itch you can't reach, or a TV actor you can't place, or the words of a song you can't quite remember. I just couldn't settle down.

I went to my room and started cleaning up my files. My desk was a mess. I tend to favor a horizontal filing system—everything I'm working on spread across the top of my desk in little piles. But after a while, when the piles start to slide and the whole thing is in danger of landing on the floor, I have to do some re-ordering.

I picked up a fat folder, but it slipped out of my hand, scattering its contents on the rug. The clip Sister Mattea had given me was on top. It had landed with the grinning picture of Alex, Max and Ellie face up. They all looked so happy. I gazed at it for a long time. Then I put it down and got out my laptop.

An hour later the itch had been scratched, the actor recalled, the song lyric identified, but I didn't feel any better. I felt much, much worse.

43

I was still struggling with what to do when the doorbell rang.

"Max! What are you doing here?"

"Hey, aren't you glad to see me, kid? I brought you something." He held up a bottle of Jameson and one of ginger ale.

"What's the occasion?"

"A celebration. Because you're coming back to the *Times* Monday morning, I hope."

"Let me get a couple of glasses."

"I'll do it. I know where they are. You go take a load off. You've still got a coupla days special treatment comin.' "

A minute later he came into the living room carrying two drinks and handed me one before sitting on the couch opposite me. I took a sip even though I prefer my Jameson straight. Between the fizziness of the ginger ale and the strength of the drink, I started to cough.

"This is pretty stiff. How much whiskey did you put in here?"

"Just enough. You can handle it. Besides, I know you're not driving. I saw Carol and Paul leaving town for the Brewers game in your car."

I took another sip. It went down smoother this time.

"It'll be good having you on the job again, Leah. I talked to Callie today, now she wants to stay off the job until September. So, if you're willing? And for the record, I want to say again that Ellie and I, we both feel bad we gave you such a hard time...."

I couldn't stand it. I couldn't sit there and pretend I didn't know what I knew. Not to Max, not to one of my oldest friends.

"Max, there's something I need to ask you. I talked to Scott Riordan tonight. Then I did some research online and made a few phone calls."

The color drained from his ruddy cheeks. He leaned forward and rubbed the cold glass in his hand across his forehead for a second before he said anything.

"Ah Christ, Leah. You know, don't you?"

I nodded.

"I was worried the other day, when you said you were going to talk to Riordan again. I was afraid you might turn up something. How did you figure it out?"

"I've had most of the pieces all along, but I didn't realize it until tonight. How could you think no one would find out?"

"No one did. For almost 10 years."

"But then Sister Mattea saw the picture of the three of you."

He nodded. "She recognized Ellie. Only she knew her as Elise. She knew her baby had died. And she knew a baby Alex's age had been taken outside a neighborhood bar in LA the same time that Ellie left town."

"Did you always know about Alex?"

His big, heavy featured face crumpled.

"No. Not 'til a couple months ago. I came home for lunch one day and caught Ellie packing. She broke down, told me everything. How her baby died after Ian was killed. How she went numb. For days, she couldn't eat. Couldn't sleep. Couldn't get rid of the baby's stuff. Couldn't do anything but drive and drive and drive all over Los Angeles. Didn't matter where, she just had to be drivin.'

"One afternoon she stops for gas in this little neighborhood. Sees a woman pull up and park across the street. Ellie goes into the convenience store to buy some water, and when she comes out she hears a baby crying. The sound is coming from the woman's car. Nobody else is on the street. She walks over to check.

"The rear window is open, but it's so hot that day the door almost burns her hand when she touches it. This little guy is wet and dirty and cryin.' his lungs out. She reaches in and picks him up, and he just grabs on her finger and looks right at her and stops crying. She can't let go. She takes him. Goes back to her apartment, packs everything up and leaves that night."

"But how did she explain having the baby when hers had died?"

"She didn't tell her aunt when her baby died. She couldn't bring herself to talk about it. Then when she gets Alex she calls and says she's on her way, that her baby had a few problems but he was ready to travel. She got to Ohio, and Alex was her baby. He still is. He's our son, our Alex. You get that, don't you, Leah? Nobody could love that boy like we do. That woman Ellie rescued him from, she didn't deserve to have a baby. You see, you understand, don't you?"

The anxious plea in his voice cut me to the heart.

"But, Max, Ellie stole another mother's baby."

"That woman left him in a hot car in the middle of the summer while she went into a bar. He could have died if Ellie hadn't saved him."

"What happened when Sister Mattea contacted Ellie?"

"She said she knew that she was really Elise, that Alex wasn't her son. Ellie panicked, but then she asked to meet with Sister Mattea to explain and talk things through. Sister Mattea agreed, but Ellie wasn't going to meet with her. She was just going to run.

"That's when I walked in on her packing to leave. I convinced her to stay. I told her that she and Alex were the world to me, and I'd walk away from everything else in a heartbeat, if we had to. But I thought I could explain things to Sister Mattea, so she'd understand. I convinced Ellie to wait. That day Sister Mattea came into the paper to see you, I set up a meeting with her early at the Point where no one would see us."

I knew what was coming next.

"When we met, I tried every way I could think of to get her to back off. I told her if there is a God, he gave Ellie and Alex to each other. They saved each other. I told her how happy he was, what a great job Ellie had done as his mother, how much better his life was. But she said it didn't matter. It wasn't right for Ellie to take Alex away from his real mother. And nothing good could come from it."

He stopped and took a drink from his glass, then looked at me steadily. "She was wrong, Leah. Everything good in my life came from that."

I thought about the other mother, the one who had come out to her car and found her baby gone. But I didn't say anything, just let Max keep talking.

"I told her it would kill Ellie to lose him. It would be even worse than when her baby died. She said she was sorry. That she'd help us in any way she could. Help? She was the one destroying our lives.

"We were out at the edge of the bluff. No one else was around. I put my hand on her arm just to make a point. She stumbled and lost her balance. It was muddy there, and she slid. She grabbed onto a bush at the edge. I reached for her, but she slipped again and I missed. She was hanging over the side, kicking with her legs. I stretched out to take her hand. But then I stopped. I didn't push her. But I watched her fall."

The words were devastating to hear. I imagined Sister Mattea, begging for help, struggling, terrified, then falling, falling, falling.

I said in a flat tone, "I thought it was Ellie. That night on the bluff, I smelled her cologne. Like grass and spring. But Alex made it for both of you. It was you, Max. You pushed me that night after the race, didn't you?"

"I asked you not to make me do something I didn't want to do. I warned you over and over, but you just kept pushing with Lacey and what did Sister Mattea want to tell you. I knew you wouldn't ever let go. You were getting too close. I couldn't let you find out."

"Does Ellie know what you did?"

He shook his head. "I told her that Sister Mattea agreed not to tell. That she must have fallen after I left. She doesn't know about your accident either. No one has to know, Leah. It's done."

I took a long drink. Maybe it was the Jameson, or maybe it was the surreal quality of the conversation, but my head was starting to feel fuzzy.

"I knew, but I didn't know, Max. There were all these shiny little pieces, like a kaleidoscope. You lied about your tire. You said you were late that morning Sister Mattea died because you were changing a flat. But you couldn't have changed it because you didn't have a spare. Cole told me it was at Jorgenson's for months."

I paused. I knew the words I wanted to say, but I was having trouble getting them out.

"Leah?" he prodded, his voice coming from a distance.

"Ian had O negative blood. Mom said she and Ellie were at the blood drive, because they were both O negative. Alex's blood is B positive. Two O negative parents can't have a B positive child. In Alex's book. The picture of Ian. He has red hair and blue eyes. Ellie has red hair and blue eyes. Alex has brown hair and brown eyes."

"But how did you connect that to Sister Mattea?"

"When I talked to Scott, he said a friend of his sister's had a baby that died. Her name was Elise. She was a nurse from LA. Ellie is a nurse from LA. Ellie's husband died in Iraq. Elise's husband was killed in Iraq. Ellie's son is 10 years old. Elise's baby died 10 years ago. Elise went to Ohio. You met Ellie in Ohio.

"Then I went online. Read the stories about a baby who disappeared from a parked car while his mother was inside at the bar. He was never found. I turned up an old online picture of Elise McAllister in a Regent Hospital newsletter. Different hair, younger, but it was Ellie."

"You've always been a damn good reporter. Too damn good," he sighed. "What are you going to do?"

"What am I going to do? Max! Ellie stole a baby. You let Sister Mattea die. You tried to kill me! What do you think I'm going to do?"

"Who else knows? Coop, Miguel?"

"Nobody. Max, how could you do that to me? I thought you cared about me?" My words were angry but I felt oddly as though I were floating above the scene.

His eyes were bleak. "I have to protect Ellie and Alex. I don't want to do this."

"Do what Max?" but I knew. Knew why I was feeling so detached and lethargic. Why Max had mixed Jameson with the sweet tasting ginger ale. To mask the Ambien or Vicodin or whatever he'd put in my drink to slow my reactions.

He wanted to find out if I was ready to let things rest, just assume Palmer, Hegl and Sister Julianna were behind Sister Mattea's death and the attempt on my life. If I was, I'd just have an extra-long sleep that night. If I wasn't, then—my mind couldn't hold onto the thought.

"Max, don't. Please. It won't work. Please." I tried to get up.

"I'm sorry, Leah. I'm sorry." Tears welled in his eyes as he leaned over me with a pillow.

I thrashed around as it pressed down on my face. I couldn't breathe. I twisted my head and tried to kick out my legs, but I was going down. No bright white light this time.

And then the pressure stopped and there was a thud. I pushed and the pillow lifted easily from my face. I struggled to a sitting position. Max was lying on the floor, gripping his left arm, his face twisted in a grimace of pain.

"Max? Max?" I forced myself to focus. I picked my phone up from the table and called 911.

"Heart attack. My friend is having a heart attack. 607 Fletcher Street." The operator was talking, but I dropped the phone. I knelt beside him. His breathing was shallow and tight.

"Leah."

I leaned in. I could barely hear him. I put my ear next to his lips.

"Don't tell. About Alex. Don't. Please."

When the EMTs arrived, I moved to the kitchen chair while they worked. Coop had heard the scanner call and got there as they were loading Max into the ambulance. He offered to take me to the hospital to wait for news, but I said no. I told him that Max and I had been drinking a Jameson, and I'd forgotten I'd taken a sleeping pill earlier. That I was having a hard time functioning. That I wouldn't be any good until it wore off. He stayed with me until my mother got home.

44

Max's funeral was three days later.

At the wake, I was sitting in a corner by myself when Courtnee came up to me. Her pretty face was streaked with tears.

"I'm gonna miss him, too, Leah. I can't believe he was, like, in the office Friday and now, I'll never see him again."

"Yeah, it's hard to take in."

"You know, Leah, I'm not saying this is for real. And I'm not blaming you or anything, but a lot of bad stuff sure happened after you didn't help Sister Mattea. Maybe it's not so good not to help a nun when she asks."

"What are you talking about?"

"You know, how she left that note asking you to help her write that history for the nuns, and you didn't do it. So, like, if someone, you know, *holy* wants your help, maybe you should just do it?"

"Courtnee, could you put the brakes on the stupid train just for today?" I snapped. "Sister Mattea didn't ask me to write a history of the nuns. That's not what her note was about."

"Well, she told *me* that she wanted you to help her write a history or something for the nuns' anniversary, and she left you a note. Don't you remember how you yelled at me because you lost the envelope?"

"She wanted to talk to me about my sister Lacey. That's why she put that page from the *Times* in the book she lent me."

"I know you're probably being so snotty because you're sad about Max, but you don't have to be such a biatch. Anyway, Sister Mattea didn't put that newspaper page in the book. I did."

"What?"

"After she left, I saw she dropped the copy of the *Times* page I made for her when she was in the week before. I put it in the book inside the envelope so you could give it to her."

"Why didn't you tell me that?"

"I tried, but you wouldn't let me finish. Remember? I told you I was trying to give you context, but you were so grouchy that day. Just like now."

I stared at her. Then I started to laugh.

"Leah, are you OK? Are you hysterical? Should I slap you?"

"I'm all right. It's just...I thought Sister Mattea was giving me a message about Lacey. It's why everything started. And now you're telling me it was all completely random."

"Oh. Sorry. I guess.

Ellie and Alex left town a week after the service. I saw her once before they went. She was angry. She said that I'd let Max down. That if I hadn't been drinking, I could have saved him. Maybe she was right.

I didn't tell her I knew about Alex. I didn't tell her what Max had done for her. I didn't tell anyone. I did find out that Alex's birth mother had died of a drug overdose eight years earlier. Sister Mattea was trying to reunite Alex with a ghost.

So, it was all good, right? Ellie had saved Alex from a sad and dangerous life. He had a mother who loved him and the memory of a great dad in Max. If I told the truth now, Ellie would go to prison and Alex would go into foster care.

Ellie's decision to take Alex had set off a series of events that resulted in the death of Sister Mattea, Max, and, indirectly, Palmer. Would my decision not to tell the truth set off another chain of unintended consequences?

I didn't know. But I couldn't do it. *Finding the truth isn't always the same as finding the answers.* I didn't understand what Father Lindstrom meant when he had said that to me weeks ago. But I was beginning to.

My mother thought I was mourning the loss of Max and should talk to a grief counselor. Coop thought I had PTSD and wanted me to see a doctor. Miguel thought I was depressed and should go for a makeover and a new wardrobe. They were all a little bit right. But I knew there was only one place I might find what I needed.

One night late I walked up the steps of a small brown house with an arched front door. The porch light was on as if I was expected. When I rang the bell, the door swung inward and a little man with fluffy white hair stood on the threshold. He was holding an *X Files* mug from which rose a wisp of steam.

"Come in, Leah. I've been waiting for you." Father Lindstrom smiled, and I stepped inside.

DANGEROUS MISTAKES: Leah Nash #2

**A Small Town Death Looks Like Suicide—
to Everyone but Reporter Leah Nash.**

Leah Nash is trying to keep her head down under the icy glare of her new
boss at the *Himmel Times Weekly*. Then a local surgeon commits suicide,
but his daughter insists he was murdered. Hard-headed Leah has a soft
spot for lost causes. She steps in, and is soon hunting a cunning killer who
has no intention of stopping. Neither does Leah.

Dangerous Mistakes is the second standalone book in the Leah Nash series
of complex, fast-paced murder mysteries featuring quick-witted dialogue,
daring female characters, and plots with lots of twists and turns.

**Get your copy today at
severnriverbooks.com/series/leah-nash-mysteries**

ACKNOWLEDGMENTS

It took a lot of family, friends and encouragement to launch the Leah Nash Mysteries series with this first book, *Dangerous Habits*. I owe thanks to all, but especially to my husband Gary, who patiently endured the many ups and downs of the writing and production process.

I also want to single out another person for special acknowledgement, my dear friend, Irene Pavlik. If not for her, Leah might have remained a ghost of an idea, flitting in and out of my imagination at irregular intervals, never to be given shape and structure. Irene died unexpectedly and tragically before this book was written. I'm sorry that she didn't live to see the fruits of her belief and encouragement.

ABOUT THE AUTHOR

Susan Hunter is a charter member of Introverts International (which meets the 12th of Never at an undisclosed location). She has worked as a reporter and managing editor, during which time she received a first place UPI award for investigative reporting and a Michigan Press Association first place award for enterprise/feature reporting.

Susan has also taught composition at the college level, written advertising copy, newsletters, press releases, speeches, web copy, academic papers and memos. Lots and lots of memos. She lives in rural Michigan with her husband Gary, who is a man of action, not words.

During certain times of the day, she can also be found wandering the mean streets of small-town Himmel, Wisconsin, looking for clues, stopping for a meal at the Elite Cafe, dropping off a story lead at the *Himmel Times Weekly*, or meeting friends for a drink at McClain's Bar and Grill.

DISCUSSION QUESTIONS

1. The setting of *Dangerous Habits* is a small town in Wisconsin. Is that important to the story? Why or why not?

2. The book is written in the first person, so the reader sees everything though Leah's eyes. Does Leah's view of other characters affect the way you feel about them?

3. Leah is "equal parts smart and smartass." How do these character traits motivate Leah through the story? Is she motivated by one more than the other?

4. What aspects of a mystery—setting, dialogue, characters, conflict, point of view, plot twists—are most important to you? Which aspects did you like most in *Dangerous Habits*?

5. Which plot twists were most unexpected? How did they change your suspicions of who was guilty?

6. Did you learn something from the book that you didn't know before? What?

7. Leah is quick to pass judgment, yet she seems to have no trouble forgiving Max, and keeping his secret. Why?

8. If it's true that we're known by the company we keep, what does Leah's choice of friends say about her? Who is she drawn to and why? What does this say about Leah's values?